STARTING OVER

Rachael pushed the heart cookie cutter into the dough. She loved Caleb, and no other man would measure up to him. She had prayed enough to know God was telling her to trust Caleb. God had pricked her conscience and shown her through the Scriptures in the Bible that she had been wrong.

Magdelena gave her a mischievous grin. "You have a visitor. I'll leave you two alone to talk."

"*Danki*, Magdelena." Caleb came to her side and passed her the flowers. "These are for you."

She was impressed he'd put them in a Mason jar with water. "I'll set them on the counter, where I can look at them while I work. They're beautiful. *Danki*. I should wait until I'm not up to my elbows in flour and dough, but I have waited long enough. Caleb, I'm sorry for all I've put you through. Will you forgive me?"

"Yes. Rachael, I've never stopped loving you, and I mean what I said. You are the bride for me . . ."

Books by Molly Jebber

The Keepsake Pocket Quilt series

CHANGE OF HEART

GRACE'S FORGIVENESS

TWO SUITORS FOR ANNA

The Amish Charm Bakery series

LIZA'S SECOND CHANCE

ELLIE'S REDEMPTION

HANNAH'S COURAGE

MARYANN'S HOPE

MAGDELENA'S CHOICE

RACHAEL'S DECISION

Collections

THE AMISH CHRISTMAS SLEIGH
(with Kelly Long and Amy Lillard)

AMISH BRIDES
(with Jennifer Beckstrand and Amy Lillard)

Published by Kensington Publishing Corporation

Rachael's Decision

MOLLY JEBBER

ZEBRA BOOKS
Kensington Publishing Corp.
www.kensingtonbooks.com

ZEBRA BOOKS are published by

Kensington Publishing Corp.
119 West 40th Street
New York, NY 10018

All Kensington titles, imprints, and distributed lines are available at special quantity discounts for bulk purchases for sales promotion, premiums, fund-raising, and educational or institutional use.

Special book excerpts or customized printings can also be created to fit specific needs. For details, write or phone the office of the Kensington Sales Manager: Kensington Publishing Corp., 119 West 40th Street, New York, NY 10018. Attn. Sales Department. Phone: 1-800-221-2647.

ZEBRA BOOKS and the Z logo Reg. U.S. Pat. & TM Off.
BOUQUET Reg. U.S. Pat. & TM Off.

First Printing: February 2023
ISBN-13: 978-1-4201-5071-1
ISBN-13: 978-1-4201-5072-8 (eBook)

10 9 8 7 6 5 4 3 2 1

Printed in the United States of America

Misty and Kevin Campbell
The best daughter and son-in-law I could ask for.

Thank you to:

Ed, my wonderful husband and soul mate, for your encouragement.

Dawn Dowdle, agent, and John Scognamiglio, editor-in-chief, for their support, kindness, and guidance. I'm grateful for you both.

Mitch Morris, the best brother, friend, encourager, and someone I admire.

Sue Morris, my mother, a beautiful, elegant, and amazing woman.

To Mary Byrnes, Lee Granza, Elaine Saltzgaver, Debbie Bugezia, Nancy Wimsatt, Connie Melaik, Barbara Visco, Mary Salan, Doris Kerr, Debbie Casto, Donna Snyder, Melanie Fogel, Peggy Barton, Kelly Hildreth, Linda Schultz, Lynn Smith, Debra Bledsoe, Beverly Hancock, Marcia Appel, Cyndee Perkins, Peggy Barton, Sigrid Davies, Shirley Madden, Darla Landren, and my other Southbridge, quilt group, and church friends. You know who you are and how much you mean to me.

Bob and Margie Saenz—Thank you for your friendship, encouragement, and support.

Aunt Sharon Sanders, Beth Sanders, and Aunt Sheila Walters for their support, love, and memories.

Patricia Campbell—My very wise writing mentor and close friend I love and admire.

Marie Coutu and Southwest Florida Romance Writers' group for your advice, love, and friendship.

To Connie Lynch, you are such a blessing in my life. I appreciate your friendship so much.

To Marilyn Ridgway and Carolyn Ridgway—I treasure your friendship and you've lifted me up more times than I can count! You're such a blessing!

To Sandra Barela, Celebratelit.com—Thank you for your friendship, advice, and encouragement!

To my readers—I couldn't do this without your encouragement and support. Thank you so much.

Chapter 1

April 1, 1915
Charm, Ohio

Rachael Schlabach served vanilla cake with white frosting to Nathan Wagler and his two *kinner*. She cut a slice for herself and sat at the Waglers' round kitchen table on Thursday evening.

"I love this cake, Mamm." Joy giggled and scooped icing onto her finger and licked it.

Rachael froze. She was used to the six-year-old saying whatever came to mind, but this was the first time she'd called her *mamm*. She'd helped with Nathan's late *fraa* Katherine's funeral eight months ago. She'd gone to the Waglers' home and washed clothes, cooked evening meals, and cared for Joy and Thad after work most nights since then. Their *daed* still mourned Katherine's death, and he spoke about her often. She considered Nathan a close friend, but would their friendship ever grow into something more?

Nathan cleared his throat. "Rachael is our special friend. You should call her by her given name. Your *mamm* is in Heaven."

Thad, at eight, was wise beyond his age. He crossed his

skinny arms. "Peter calls Liza Mamm and his real *mamm* is in Heaven. Mamm wouldn't mind. She would have liked Rachael."

Rachael didn't want this awkwardness to linger. It had been two weeks since he'd asked her to give Katherine's clothes and things to the Amish who could use them. She'd kept handkerchiefs, a bonnet, and a brush and comb for Joy when she was older. She would try to help them understand. "Liza married Jacob and they adopted Peter. Liza is his step*mamm*, but they've agreed he can call her Mamm. I'm your neighbor and friend who loves you both. I'm here to lend a helping hand for a while. You should call me Rachael. I love you no matter what."

Nathan stood and carried dirty plates to the sink. "I'll wash."

"Don't worry about the dishes. Go to your sitting room. The *kinner* and I will clean up, like always."

Thad dragged Joy's wooden stool covered in crayon marks to the sink for her to stand on.

Rachael waved Nathan out of the large kitchen, with twice as many cabinets as she and Mamm had at home. "You go relax. We'll be fine." She was relieved when he headed to his sitting room and put an end to the conversation. She would like him to ask for a private conversation to discuss if and when he would court her. But she was patient. Did she really want him to ask? It would be a risk. Their friendship wasn't guaranteed to blossom into love. But she loved the *kinner*. She could envision herself being their *mamm*, and they would be worth maybe never falling in love with Nathan.

She limped to the sink and washed and dried the china dishes with a red apple in the center of each one. She admired the unique design. She allowed the *kinner* to help her and then worked a puzzle with Joy and Thad in the sitting room while Nathan read his Bible. A half hour later, she bid them all a good night. She drove the short distance to her farm next door and went inside. Mamm had already gone to bed. What would she do if Nathan pursued her? Maybe she didn't need to ponder it. He might not find her attractive. Should she back away from the Wagler family? It was too late. Her heart would break not being around the *kinner*. She prayed to God for guidance.

Rachael overslept Friday morning. She dressed and kissed Mamm's cheek. "I don't have time for breakfast."

Mamm passed her a wrapped fried egg biscuit sandwich. "Take this. You need something in your stomach."

She accepted the sandwich. "*Danki.*" Then she ran outside, harnessed her mare to the buggy, and drove to the livery. She crossed the wide road, waved to other shop owners unlocking their doors, and entered the bakery. "Good morning, Magdelena. I'm sorry I'm late." She loved her best friend and *schweschder*-in-law. Magdelena was perfect for her *bruder*, Toby. She slipped her apron over her head and tied the strings behind her back. She stood at the big, hardwood, waist-high worktable centered in the room, where they had enough space to create their delicious desserts.

Magdelena grabbed the rolling pin and pushed it back and forth over her dough. "You're only a couple of minutes late. Don't apologize. I've been late a time or two. Anything new with the Wagler family?"

"Joy called me Mamm." She told Magdelena what Thad had said.

"How did you feel about it? Do you want to be their step*mamm* someday?" Magdelena stopped rolling her pin and stared at Rachael.

Rachael recounted to Magdelena what she and Nathan

told the *kinner* and how Joy and Thad reacted. "I don't know where Nathan stands. I may love him, but I'm not in love with him. Not to say I couldn't fall in love with him, but who knows? It's not like I'm overrun with suitors knocking on my door. I love the *kinner*. Any advice?"

"I'm not sure what to tell you. Let's pray about it together." Magdelena offered a prayer to God to intervene on Rachael and Nathan's behalf. To close the door or open it for a courtship.

"*Danki*, Magdelena."

For the next two hours, Rachael and Magdelena discussed the Waglers, recipes, and gardening as they baked bread, pies, and cookies to sell.

"I should've unlocked the door for customers ten minutes ago." Magdelena hurried to the front room, where a display case showed their desserts for sale and white metal "ice cream" parlor chairs and tables were available to customers to enjoy their purchases inside the bakery. She unlocked the door.

Rachael slid a tray of molasses cookies onto the glass shelf in the display case. She stood and caught her breath.

A handsome Amish gentleman walked into the bakery. He met her gaze with his big, sky-blue eyes. He was tall, with broad shoulders. She guessed his age close to hers. He didn't have a beard. He must be unmarried. "Good morning."

He smiled, and his teeth were white as snow. He tipped his hat, and he had a head full of thick blond hair. He'd probably never go bald. "Good morning, ladies. I'm Caleb Yutzy and I'm new in town. I hope you have cinnamon bread."

Rachael pressed a hand to her heart. She couldn't wrench her gaze from his. "I'm Rachael Schlabach. We have a fresh loaf right out of the oven."

Magdelena waited on the two customers who came in behind Caleb.

"I'd love a loaf and a slice of it right now, if you don't mind." Caleb chose a middle table among the other five "ice cream" white-metal chairs and tables in the café area decorated with red tablecloths.

"Would you like coffee or hot chocolate?" Rachael cut a thick slice of bread from the loaf and packaged the rest. Then she limped over to him and served him the warm cinnamon bread with butter and a cup of coffee. What was happening to her? She couldn't quit staring at this tall, lean-framed man.

He pulled out the other chair at the table. "Will you take a break and join me? I promise to not keep you long."

Rachael's heart fluttered, and she hesitated. He was bold, but she didn't mind.

Magdelena approached them. "She'll be glad to. I'm Magdelena Schlabach, Rachael's *schweschder*-in-law. I overheard you say your name is Caleb Yutzy and you're new to Charm. Where are you from?"

"Nappanee, Indiana. I moved here with my *bruder*, Stephen, and his *fraa*, Frannie, and their *boppli*, Lily."

Two women entered the bakery.

"Excuse me. I should take care of these customers. Rachael, take your time." Magdelena greeted the women and returned to the display case.

Rachael sat at the table with Caleb. She could gaze into those blue eyes all day. "What brought you and your family to Charm?" She wanted to know everything about this man.

"Stephen and his family lived with Frannie's *mamm*. When her *mamm* died, she found it difficult to live with the memories attached to the *haus* she grew up in. Stephen suggested they sell the *haus* and move here. He'd passed through Charm a time or two and he was made to feel *wilkom*. The town made a lasting impression, and he mentioned it to Frannie, and she was in favor of moving here. I sold our parents' place and came with them." Caleb sipped his coffee. "Do you have a suitor or husband?"

Rachael's cheeks warmed. "No. I live with my *mamm*. Daed died last year. Magdelena married my *bruder*, Toby, in September, and they live not too far from us. Forgive me. I'm rambling."

"Please continue. I want to know everything about you." He winced. "Stephen says I'm too direct sometimes." He covered his mouth with his hand, then dropped it. "I hope I haven't offended you."

She smiled and shook her head. "I'm not offended." She wanted to encourage him, but she didn't want to be too forward.

He finished the last of his bread. "Would you like to *kumme* to supper tomorrow night at my family's *haus*? I'd like for you to meet them, and we could get to know each other better. Give me directions to your *haus* and I'll pick you up."

"Yes. I'd love to meet them." She gave him directions. "I should get back to baking, but I'm pleased to have met you, and *danki* for the invitation." She couldn't wait to spend more time with him.

"The pleasure is all mine." He stood and made an exaggerated bow. "I'll be at your *haus* at six tomorrow evening." He bid her good day and left.

Magdelena served a patron coffee and then pulled Rachael aside. "What a handsome fellow, and his interest in you is apparent. Caleb didn't waste any time finding out if you are unmarried."

Rachael waggled her forefinger at Magdelena. "Were you listening to our conversation?"

"Of course. The connection between you and him was

immediate. You and Caleb couldn't quit smiling from the time your gazes met. His high cheekbones and square chin with those blue eyes give him a striking face, and he must be a little over six feet tall. If he wasn't Amish, he could've been an actor. He does need some meat on those bones. He needs you to invite him to supper." She chuckled. "I'm proud of you. You didn't hesitate to meet his family."

"I don't know what came over me. One look at him and I was smitten. I didn't flinch when he asked me to supper, having just met him. My limp didn't seem to bother him. I haven't had any Amish men show interest in me like this for quite a while. With Nathan, I invited myself and pitched in to care for him and the *kinner*. But our situation is different. He's lost and mourning his *fraa*. I didn't have any expectations where he and I are concerned."

"You're giddy about Caleb."

Rachael grinned. "I'm excited to meet Caleb's family and talk with him tomorrow night." She picked up a towel on the counter and gripped it. Joy and Thad might be upset when she told them she had plans and wouldn't be joining them for supper. This would be a definite break in their routine. Would her plans with Caleb matter to Nathan? She'd break the news to them this evening.

Magdelena beamed. "I'm happy for you, my friend. This could be the beginning of something wonderful for you and Caleb."

"I hope so." Rachael's heart soared.

Magdelena's dark eyes and coal-black hair, plus her slender frame, usually captured everyone's attention first. But Caleb had been different. He'd set his gaze on her. She had questions to ask him. What were his likes and dislikes? Had he been in love before? Did he plan on staying in Charm?

At the end of the workday, she drove to Nathan's *haus*.

He had a wraparound porch in front and a swing she and the *kinner* liked to sit in. He had cows grazing in the field, and his smoke*haus* and barn were on one side of the property and the garden was on the other side of the *haus*. He had a small pond beyond the garden. She liked the layout.

Joy ran to her, holding a picture. "I've been waiting for you."

Rachael tied her mare to the hitching post and then held her arms open wide. Joy's bonnet fell off her head, showing her white-blond curls as she ran into her arms. She was a beauty. She'd have a line of suitors at her door when she was ready to court.

Rachael hugged the child. "What did you draw?"

Joy held her picture high for Rachael. "You, Daed, me, and Thad. Oh, and my barn cats."

Rachael's heart sank. She didn't want to disappoint or hurt Joy, but this picture portrayed them as a family. Joy had drawn her and Nathan holding hands. "This is a wonderful picture. Did you show this to your *daed*?"

Joy nodded. "He liked it. Thad did too. I'm keeping it on my dresser. Is Eleanor *kumming* for supper?"

Rachael had invited Mamm often to the Waglers' for supper, but she'd accepted the invitation only a couple of times. Mamm had friends who kept her busy. She worked hard, and she suspected Mamm would like for Nathan to take an interest in Rachael as more than a friend. Rachael stopped asking her to join them each time and told her she was always *wilkom*. Her *mamm* went to Magdelena and Toby's a couple of times a week for supper.

"Not tonight. How was your day at school?"

"Thad and I played hide-and-seek with Peter and Charity at dinnertime. I slipped and fell in the mud chasing the yellow cat, and I had to change clothes when I came home."

"We'll wash your dress after supper. Accidents happen."

Joy stained her clothes with dirt or food more than Thad. Her favorite thing to do was make mud pies. Joy pumped water from the pump in anything she could find and then poured the water over the dirt to make mud to play in.

"Where are your *daed* and Thad?"

"Daed has a chicken plucked and ready to cook. He wanted to surprise you, so don't tell him I gave away his secret." She giggled and held her forefinger to her lips. "Thad and he plucked the feathers off the chicken together."

"What should we have with our chicken?"

Joy often stayed by her side in the kitchen, waiting for tasks to do. "Mashed potatoes."

Rachael tweaked Joy's cheek. "You'd have mashed potatoes every day if you could."

Joy laughed. "Yes, I would. They're my favorite. You let me mash them when we cook, but Daed insists on doing it himself."

They entered the house and went to the kitchen.

Thad grinned and pointed to the table. "I set the table and filled the water glasses."

"The chicken is ready to *kumme* out of the oven, the potatoes are ready, and there's brown bread sliced in the basket." Nathan pulled out her chair. "We'll serve you."

She hadn't expected this. He'd not made supper before this evening and he'd gone to a lot of trouble.

"I appreciate this. *Danki*." Rachael sat, unfolded her napkin, and spread it out on her lap.

Nathan had readied a chicken for her to bake or fry in the past, but he'd not prepared the entire supper. He'd even changed the plain yellow tablecloth to a red one edged with lace. He had cloth napkins to match. Was this a *danki* or something more?

Nathan and the *kinner* took their seats. Nathan bowed his head and said a prayer to God for the food. "Enjoy.

We'll have enough food left over to have the same thing tomorrow evening. You won't have to work as hard." Nathan removed the chicken from the oven, cut and put the pieces on a platter, stirred the drippings into the gravy, and carried it to the table. He had the mashed potatoes warming on top of the stove, and he put the bowl next to the meat.

Thad placed the bread basket beside the butter, and raspberry jelly was already on the table. "Would you like bread?" He passed the basket to her.

Thad's chocolate-brown eyes gazed at her. With his lanky build and wavy, light brown hair, he was a handsome boy. She loved his kind and wise demeanor.

"I want one." Joy reached in and took a slice as Rachael accepted the basket. She wouldn't call Joy bashful. The six-year-old always let you know what was on her mind.

"Will you bring home some iced sugar cookies for dessert tomorrow night?" Joy held a scoop of potatoes on her spoon.

Rachael traced the rim of her glass. She hoped they wouldn't get upset. "I have plans tomorrow evening with a friend, so I won't be joining you. You can have the leftover chicken and make sandwiches."

Joy grinned. "We'll *kumme* with you. Bring the cookies to your friend's *haus*. We'll all have dessert together."

Thad shrugged. "Yes. Where does your friend live? What's your friend's name?"

"Caleb Yutzy. He's new in town." Rachael's cheeks heated.

Nathan avoided eye contact with her. "Enough with the questions. You're being rude. Rachael doesn't expect to go with you when you go to a friend's *haus*. It's not proper to invite yourselves to tag along with Rachael and her friend."

Joy pouted. "You want us to *kumme*, don't you, Rachael?"

"I'm sorry. Your *daed* is right. It's not appropriate for me to bring you. We'll talk at church on Sunday." She avoided eye contact with them.

Nathan and the *kinner* frowned and the room went silent.

She had to bring smiles to their sad faces. "Would you like to mix a batch of sugar cookies before we do the dishes? It wouldn't take us long."

Joy's head bobbed. "Yes!"

Thad grinned. "I'll stir the batter."

Nathan put his napkin on the table. He'd left half the food on his plate. "I'll be in the barn if you need me." He left the room.

She pressed a hand to her nervous stomach. Nathan and she had no romantic relationship. They hadn't flirted or hinted at even the possibility of courtship. Why had he acted hurt? She understood the *kinner* might get upset, but why Nathan? Or had he gotten used to their routine and didn't want it interrupted? She wouldn't confront him about his abruptness. She'd wait until he was ready to discuss it.

She instructed Joy on what and how much of each ingredient to put in the bowl.

"This is fun." Joy followed her directions.

"Thad, you can stir."

He waited for Joy to step aside, and he stirred the batter. Joy stood close and watched his every move.

Rachael let them each scoop small amounts of batter onto the cookie sheet. She slid the cookies in the oven and put the ingredients away.

Joy slid her finger around the bowl and licked the batter from her finger. "I like the batter more than the baked cookies." She giggled.

Thad took the bowl from her. "Leave me some." He swiped out the rest of the batter with a wooden spoon and licked it. "So good."

Rachael washed and let Joy and Thad dry the dishes.

Joy handed a plate to Thad to put in the cabinet. "I'll miss you when you go to your friend's *haus*." She pouted.

Thad stayed quiet.

"I'll miss you too." She didn't know if she'd resume their routine. She didn't want to say too much. She wasn't sure what the future held. She took the cookies out of the oven. "We'll let the cookies cool while we wash Joy's dress."

She and Joy washed the muddy dress. Thad hung it up to dry.

Thad entered the kitchen and grabbed a container for the cookies. "I'll put the cookies away and leave out four for us so we can each have one."

"*Danki*, Thad." Rachael waited for him to empty the baking pan and then washed and dried it. She put it away.

Joy reached for a plate on the counter and placed four cookies on it. "I'll carry the cookies to the sitting room and choose a board game for us to play."

Rachael and Thad followed her to the sitting room. Joy carried the plate of cookies to each of them, and they took one.

Joy sat on the floor next to Rachael. They finished their cookies, laughed, and had a good time.

Nathan came inside. His tone was stern. "*Kinner*, time for bed. Change into your nightshirts, and I'll be in to say prayers and good night in a minute."

"Daed, we saved you a cookie." Joy pointed to the plate. "Do we have to go to bed now?" she begged.

"Yes, and don't whine." Nathan pointed to her room. "Go now."

The *kinner* hugged her goodbye.

Rachael went to the door. "Sleep tight."

"Rachael, *danki* for taking care of the dishes. You don't need to wait if you'd like to go home."

"*Danki* for the delicious food. Good night."

"Good night." Nathan headed to Joy's bedroom.

Rachael drove home. Nathan wasn't himself tonight. His mood changed from jovial to serious after she said she had plans tomorrow evening. Should she have asked him why he was upset? His extra effort with supper could've been a *danki* for taking such good care of them. She wasn't sure what to make of it. Why would he avoid her and not talk about it? She went inside the *haus* and Mamm was reading her Bible.

"How was your evening?"

"Nathan cooked supper. He did a marvelous job. He's never expressed interest in me. The supper could've been to show he wanted to reciprocate and not expect me to do all the cooking. I'm not sure. When I told him I have plans tomorrow, he became quieter than usual. I didn't press him about it. Tomorrow evening, I'm having supper with a new family who moved to Charm. I'll tell you more about them and introduce you to Caleb when he picks me up."

"Who is Caleb? What's his last name?" Mamm put her Bible on the end table. "I need more information."

"Yutzy. Caleb lives with his *bruder*'s family. He came to the bakery and asked me to join them."

"You've talked to him once and you agreed to go to his *haus*? Isn't this too soon? If he's new in town, no one knows much about him." Mamm worried her brows.

Rachael shook her head. "We'll be with his family. I can't explain it, but I was drawn to him on sight. I haven't gotten giddy over a man since John died. It's been four years. I'm curious about Caleb."

"Since his family will be present, I suppose it's all right. When you told Nathan and the *kinner* you wouldn't be with them tomorrow night, it was probably hard for them. They are used to you having supper with them. Nathan may have cooked to show interest in you. I'm uncertain, but it would explain why he was upset. What about the *kinner*?"

"Nathan should've said something instead of sulking. Joy and Thad were disappointed. I'm not sure Nathan and I will ever be more than friends. I love the *kinner*, and I'll always be there for them if they need me. I'm taking this change one day at a time. Who knows what will happen with Caleb. This might be my first and last supper with him."

"You're right about everything you've said. There's no reason not to get acquainted with Caleb and his family." Mamm reached for her Bible and opened it. The binding was loose and she handled it with care.

"Mamm, do you have plans tomorrow?"

"Yes. I'll already be at the Yoders for supper before you get home from work. I'm going early to help them cook and bake. Have a good time. I'll look forward to meeting Caleb when you *kumme* home." Mamm kissed her *dochder*'s cheek.

Rachael hoped it would be the first of many times she and Caleb would spend time together.

Caleb dried and put away the last dish from supper Friday evening. Rachael had occupied his mind since he met her today. She had beautiful emerald eyes and a pleasant voice. She had pretty, light brown hair where her *kapp* was set farther back on her hair. She didn't seem put off by his questions or his interest in her. She had a positive attitude and a genuine smile. She had a limp. Was she born with it? He'd find out soon enough. He went to the porch and sat in the white-painted rocker near his *bruder*, Stephen, and his *schweschder*-in-law, Frannie, holding Lily on her lap. "What a beautiful evening. I'm glad we could switch from coats to light sweaters. I'm ready for summer."

Frannie cocked her head to Caleb. "*Danki* for taking care of the dishes."

"You're *wilkom*." Caleb hadn't told them about Rachael. Supper had been more chaotic than usual. Lily had been fussy, and Stephen had knocked over his water glass. He'd sent them to the porch to relax, hoping they'd be in a better frame of mind when he told them he'd invited company for tomorrow night. He prayed it would be calmer when Rachael was with them.

He braced himself. "I met Rachael Schlabach at the bakery in town today. I invited her here to meet you and have supper with us tomorrow evening." He was on pins and needles waiting for Frannie's reaction.

No surprise. Frannie raised her brows. "I'm not ready for guests. The *haus* is a mess most of the time with Lily's toys, unfolded laundry, and dirty dishes in the sink. I can't keep up with inside chores and take care of Lily too. The last thing we need is company. Take her to a restaurant."

"Now, Frannie, don't fret." Stephen patted her hand. "Caleb and I will help you. We need to make friends in Charm. Be happy a girl has caught Caleb's eye."

"I'll make potato soup and ham sandwiches. Easy to make and clean up." Caleb bit his tongue. He didn't want to say something he'd regret.

Frannie was a burden for Stephen. His *bruder* pushed himself hard to meet her demands and take care of the farm. Stephen had tired eyes and slumped shoulders most of the time. He stayed up late and got up early to straighten the *haus* or cook food for them. Frannie got plenty of rest. She was spoiled. Not the kind of woman Caleb wanted for a *fraa*.

Frannie waggled her forefinger. "I'm counting on you both to keep your word."

* * *

Caleb woke early Saturday morning and hurried to do his chores throughout the day. Later, he made the potato soup as promised, and left it on the stovetop to keep warm. He was ready to fetch Rachael.

Frannie placed Lily in the playpen in the living room. "Did you set the table? Is the soup finished? When will you make the sandwiches?"

His stomach clenched. She was the most demanding woman he'd ever met. "The table is set and the soup is done. I'll warm it when we're ready for supper, and then I'll make the sandwiches."

"Did you slice the ham or do I have to?" Frannie sighed.

"The ham is sliced and in a container on the counter. I'll be back soon." He would've told her she was being unreasonable to not help prepare the food, but he didn't want to start an argument. He wanted Rachael to feel *wilkom* when she met them.

Frannie pursed her lips and nodded.

He'd make it to Rachael's *haus* right at six if he hurried. She lived about a mile from him. When he arrived, he found her waiting on the porch with a beautiful smile on her face, holding a white tin cake carrier.

"Good evening."

She got inside the buggy and placed the cake carrier on her lap. "*Danki* for the invitation to meet your family. I brought a white double-layer cake from the bakery. It has vanilla frosting with pink roses on top."

"I should've invited your *mamm*. It's not too late to ask her. We have plenty of food." Caleb shouldn't invite Mrs. Schlabach without warning Stephen and Frannie, but he would take his chances Frannie wouldn't be rude.

"You're thoughtful to invite her. Mamm's at a friend's *haus*, having supper with them. I would like you to *kumme* in and meet her when you bring me home."

"It will be my pleasure." He flicked the reins and headed home. "I'm pleased and surprised you accepted my invitation. I should've spoken with you at the bakery and church a couple of times before I asked you to supper. But the minute I met you, I wanted to become better acquainted. At the bakery there are too many customers around, and at church you're surrounded by friends. After supper, we'll take a walk or buggy ride, if you're all right with this suggestion."

She chuckled. "I appreciate your forthrightness. I'd enjoy a buggy ride with you this evening."

"I'm relieved. The last thing I want to do is offend you." He halted the buggy near the *haus* and tied the mare to the hitching post. He patted the horse with affection.

Rachael stepped out of the buggy, holding her cake carrier, and joined him. "The wraparound porch on the *haus* must be a wonderful place to relax on the swing or rocking chairs."

"It's what drew all of us to this *haus*. The farm is about one thousand acres, and the barn and smoke*haus* mirror many of the structures of our Amish neighbors. The porch and layout of the *haus* is what sold Frannie on this place." He didn't want to warn her about Frannie. He hoped his *schweschder*-in-law would behave and *wilkom* Rachael as a new friend.

They walked to the *haus* and went inside. Caleb introduced Rachael to his family.

Frannie narrowed her eyes and balanced Lily on her hip. "Please take a seat."

Stephen stood next to Frannie. "We're glad you could join us this evening, Rachael."

"*Danki* for having me." She reached for Lily's chubby hand. "What a pretty little girl with her light brown hair and big brown eyes. How old is she?"

"She's two and full of energy. She wears me out," Frannie harrumphed.

Caleb kissed Lily's forehead. "She's a cheerful little girl." He addressed Rachael. "I'll make the sandwiches and heat the soup. You stay and visit."

Rachael shook her head. "I brought dessert. I'll take it to the kitchen since Frannie has her hands full. I'd like to help." She followed him to the kitchen and gestured to a container. "Is this the ham? May I use the bread in the bread box?"

He pointed to a covered plate on the counter. "You'll find the ham on the counter, and the bread in the bread box next to it. You can make the sandwiches and pour water in the glasses, if you don't mind. The pitcher is behind you on the other counter." Caleb was relieved Frannie had kept the fire going in the stove. His soup was warm.

"I'd be happy to." Rachael prepared the sandwiches and poured water into the glasses.

Caleb called out to Stephen and Frannie through the open archway from the kitchen to the living room, "Supper's ready." He poured the soup into a white porcelain tureen and added a ladle.

Frannie lowered Lily into her high chair, and the rest of them took their seats.

Caleb offered a prayer to God for the food. He stood. "Pass me your bowls and I'll fill them for you." Each of them did as requested.

Rachael's eyes widened. "Caleb, you've outdone yourself with this soup. The parsley was a nice touch."

He beamed. "*Danki.*"

Frannie mashed the potatoes in the soup and fed Lily. She then buttered a biscuit and tore it in pieces for her. "This should keep you busy while the adults chat."

Lily used her fingers to put a small piece in her mouth.

"Stephen, would you pour a small cup of water for Lily?" Frannie bit into her sandwich.

Stephen left the table and returned with a small tin cup of water for Lily.

Frannie stared across the table at Rachael. "How do you work in the bakery and manage to do your chores at home?"

"Our farm and garden are modest compared to most in this area. Toby, my *bruder*, helps us, and so do some of the Amish men who live near our place. Mamm is in good health, and she enjoys taking care of the garden and inside chores. We have a small *haus*, so it's easy to clean. We work well together. The bakery brings in extra money, and I love working there."

Frannie shrugged. "I could never work outside the home. Chores inside and outside this *haus* and caring for Lily are more than I can handle. I still don't know how you do it." She cocked her head. "I'm surprised you haven't married."

Rachael's cheeks reddened. "I had plans to marry a wonderful Amish man, but he was killed over three years ago."

Frannie sat ramrod straight. "What happened?"

Stephen covered his *fraa*'s hand. "Rachael doesn't know us. This may be too personal a question for her to answer." He nodded to Rachael. "You don't have to explain."

Caleb nodded. "Yes. Rachael, you don't have to answer."

Rachael smiled. "I don't mind. Daed wasn't comfortable keeping his money at home. He knocked over a kerosene lantern once, and we put out the small fire before any real damage occurred. From that day forward, he was worried about it happening again and causing a destructive fire. He kept his money in the bank. On one occasion, Daed asked John and me to take money to the bank to deposit for him. On the way to town, hooligans circled our buggy and tipped it over. John was killed, and I was injured and left with a permanent limp."

Frannie's mouth gaped open. "How tragic."

Caleb was embarrassed Frannie had asked such a personal question. Rachael might never accept an invitation to his *haus* again, and he wouldn't blame her. "I'm sorry that happened to you."

"*Danki*. God has given me the peace and strength to overcome my grief. The bakery has been a fun place to work with friends and create yummy desserts our customers enjoy. I taught myself how to make pretty flowers on cakes. And we're always experimenting with new recipes. It's fun."

Stephen licked his lips. "You're making my mouth water talking about cakes. I can't get enough of sweets."

Lily grinned and finished the last of her biscuit. She wore soup and butter on her face and bib.

Frannie pouted. "Look at the mess our *dochder*'s made for me to clean up."

Stephen said, "Don't worry about it right now, sweetheart."

Caleb didn't want to listen to Frannie whine. He had to listen to her complain about how tired she was most of the time. She'd *kumme* from a home where she'd been spoiled, and Stephen continued to pamper her. "Do you decorate all the wedding cakes?"

"Yes. You met Magdelena at the bakery. She's my *schweschder*-in-law. She and my *bruder*, Toby, married last October. They requested a large cake with lots of roses. I enjoyed making it for them."

Frannie yawned. "Stephen, can you wash your *dochder*'s face and hands? She has food all over her."

Stephen finished the last of his sandwich, rose, and poured water from the pitcher to wet a cloth. He washed Lily's face and hands.

Lily pushed the cloth away and whimpered, "No. No."

Stephen got the worst of the food off of her, the high chair, the table, and her bib. He gave her a butter cookie and took his seat.

"Stephen, you didn't ask me if she could have a cookie." Frannie rolled her eyes.

"She needs something to occupy her while we visit with Rachael. She's fine." Stephen smiled at Rachael. "Tomorrow will be our first time attending the Sunday service. We're looking forward to it. I'm anxious to meet more of the Amish here."

Rachael gave them directions to the Yoders' place. "The service begins at nine. The ladies bring cold cuts, meat spread, salads, and desserts for the after-service dinner. I'd be happy to introduce you and Caleb to my bruder, *Toby*, and he'll introduce you to the other men."

"I'd appreciate it." Stephen pushed his plate away to make room for his elbows.

Caleb said, "I'm anxious to make new friends here too. *Danki*, Rachael."

"Frannie, Liza has a *boppli*, Lorianne. She's about two and a half. Liza owns the bakery, and she's a close friend. Ellie has a *dochder*, Emma, ten months old, and Maryann has Betsy, who is about two and a half. Hannah doesn't have a child yet. They are my closest friends. You'll meet them all tomorrow. We also have socials at the bakery or someone's *haus* now and then. You'll have to *kumme*."

Frannie waved a dismissive hand. "I don't have time for friends."

Caleb stood abruptly. He couldn't take another minute of Frannie being rude and insensitive. "I'm ready for dessert." He removed the lid of the white tin cake carrier. "Rachael, this cake is lovely. The roses are amazing." He brought the cake to the table.

Stephen's eyes widened. "You are talented. The roses look hard to make."

Frannie glanced at the cake. "They're pretty."

"*Danki*." Rachael rose. "Where are the plates? I'll serve dessert."

Caleb pointed to the middle oak cabinet above the sink. He then put a pot already filled with water on the stove to heat for washing the dishes while they had dessert. He stifled his reproach to Frannie. Her nonchalant attitude set his teeth on edge.

Rachael removed the plates and waited while he put a slice of cake on each one. She served Stephen and Frannie and carried over her and Caleb's desserts.

Lily clapped her hands. "Me." She pointed at the cake.

"Is it all right if I give her a little piece?" Rachael addressed Frannie.

"Sure, but make her piece very small. I wouldn't let her have cake if she had finished her cookie." Frannie snatched the rest of the cookie off Lily's high-chair table.

Rachael cut a small piece for Lily and gave it to her. "I'm sorry, little one. I didn't mean to leave you out. Enjoy."

Lily grinned and clapped her hands together and then took handfuls and put them in her mouth.

"Someone likes the cake." Caleb chuckled. He was ready for time alone with Rachael.

Frannie had been better than he'd anticipated, but she'd asked inappropriate questions and hadn't attempted to help in the kitchen.

Stephen closed his eyes. "This cake is delicious. And I don't understand how you make these delicate and beautiful roses."

"It takes a lot of practice and patience, but I enjoy creating them. *Danki*." Rachael finished her small piece.

Caleb devoured his cake. "Rachael, let's take a buggy ride around town, and then I'll take you home."

Frannie frowned. "What about these dishes?"

Stephen went to the sink. "I'll do them."

"No. Wait until I return. We'll do them together, *bruder*." Caleb swallowed his frustration.

Frannie was lazy and selfish.

Stephen rubbed his eyes and yawned. "I don't mind."

Rachael nudged Caleb. "Let's wash and dry the dishes together. We can have this kitchen clean in no time. I'll clear the table and you fetch the water."

He didn't want to waste time with this, but he didn't want to leave Stephen with the task. He doubted Frannie would lend him a hand. He picked up the dishpan. "Stephen, go relax. You need some rest."

"Yes, Stephen. *Kumme* with me. I'll put Lily to bed, and you and I will sit together in the sitting room." Frannie picked up Lily.

"You go ahead, Frannie. I'll carry the dirty dishes to the sink." Stephen gathered dirty utensils.

Frannie left with Lily without another word to anyone.

Rachael finished the last two bites of her cake and then stacked dirty dishes. "Take advantage of this time to relax. Stephen, Caleb and I can do this. Go enjoy your time with Frannie and Lily."

"You're thoughtful, Rachael. *Danki*." He dropped the utensils in the dish tub and patted Caleb on the back. "You should hang on to this girl." He winked at him and departed.

"I plan to." Caleb grinned and enjoyed Rachael's blush. He added hot water in the pot on the stove to the washtub in the sink.

Rachael smiled at him. She washed, and Caleb dried the dishes. "It was sweet of you to provide us with the cake. I'm sorry to make you work for your supper. First, you help prepare it, and now, you're cleaning up. This isn't very hospitable of us."

"It gives us a chance to become better acquainted and help your family at the same time." Rachael washed the last dish and handed it to him.

He dried it and then stacked it on top of the clean plates in the cabinet. He poured potato soup into a container and set it on the counter. "This is for your *mamm*."

"*Danki*. She'll appreciate it." Rachael dried her hands.

"I like to cook, but it's a necessity around here if you don't want to waste away to nothing. Frannie does everything she can to avoid preparing food for us." He stared at the floor. "I'm sorry. I shouldn't disparage her. We've just met."

"You and Stephen do most of the cooking?" Rachael hung the damp dish towel on the hook by the sink.

"Yes. We'd rather prepare the meals than listen to her grumble and complain all day. My poor *bruder* can't get a minute's peace. He runs himself ragged to keep up with the farm, and then she expects him to also take care of the *haus* chores and Lily. I wish she wasn't lazy and didn't take such advantage of Stephen. Enough about Frannie. Let's go on our buggy ride and talk more about you. We'll tell my family we're leaving and then we'll be on our way."

Caleb and Rachael went to the sitting room, where Stephen was fast asleep and snoring in the chair and Frannie was knitting.

Frannie rose, set her yarn and needles in the chair, opened the door, and then they all stepped outside onto the porch. "I don't want to wake Stephen. He has a difficult time getting back to sleep when he goes from the chair to the bed. Are you leaving, Rachael?"

"Yes. *Danki* for a lovely evening. Is Lily asleep?"

"Yes."

"Give her a kiss for me. You have an adorable *dochder*. I'm glad we had a chance to talk and get acquainted." Rachael smiled.

"Caleb didn't leave me much choice." Frannie smirked at him.

"We should go." Caleb cupped his hand at Rachael's elbow. "Wait here a moment." He went back inside the *haus* to the kitchen, retrieved the soup he'd put in a container for Rachael's *mamm*, and returned. "Are you sure you don't want to take your *mamm* a piece of cake?"

Rachael nodded. "No. We've got desserts at home. *Danki* again, Frannie."

Frannie gave her a curt nod.

Rachael and Caleb went to the buggy.

Caleb waited for her to get in, and then took his seat. He put the soup container between them on the bench. He grasped the reins. "When are you free to meet again?" He passed her a lap blanket he kept in the back of the buggy. "You may want this."

Rachael covered herself with it. "*Danki*. We can talk after the church service tomorrow. I have plenty of food to bring tomorrow. Don't worry about cooking anything."

"You're generous and a big help. I appreciate it. Next time, I'll make sure I have a dish to bring." He reached for her hand and gently squeezed it. "You're a bright ray of sunshine in my life, Rachael."

He drove them for a short time around town and then on the country roads going past a couple of Amish farms on the way to her *haus*. "Are you warm enough?"

She patted the blanket on her lap. "I'll keep the blanket over my lap for now and then take it off if I need to. It's not too cool outside."

"I'm sorry Frannie asked you such personal questions."

He had been surprised she'd shared information about her accident and the loss of her beau. He hoped she'd volunteer more, but he didn't want to push her.

"I'm not offended. My limp draws attention, and I've gotten used to strangers asking how I acquired it. I'm not as self-conscious about it as I was when it first happened," Rachael said.

"I can't imagine the agony you suffered in losing the man you loved. Are you open to marrying?" He didn't know what the future held for them, but he prayed they'd grow a close friendship as they got better acquainted. He was captivated by her.

"Yes." She stared at her hands above the blanket. "It's my turn to ask you questions. Have you been in love?"

Caleb glanced at her and then back at the road. "Two years ago, I proposed to Cora Troyer. We'd been neighbors and friends since childhood."

"What kept you from having a future with her?"

He hesitated. "She had a tragic accident."

"What!" Rachael covered her open mouth. "How did it happen?"

Caleb's sadness tore at his chest. "She worked at the general store. A week before our wedding, she climbed a ladder in the store's supply room. When she didn't return, the store owner went to check on her, and he found her dead on the floor in a pool of blood with the ladder on its side. She must've lost her balance, fell, and hit her head hard."

Rachael winced. "How sad. I'm so sorry."

"I was stunned when the store owner and doctor told me. The store owner felt terrible. He had the supply room jam-packed with supplies on the shelves and floor. It wasn't safe for anyone." He hadn't been interested in another woman since Cora's passing until he met Rachael. They didn't look anything alike.

"Tell me about her."

"Cora was short with bright red hair and freckles dotting her cheeks and nose." She'd had a fuller frame than Rachael. "She loved to tease me, and it was a rare occasion if she was sad or frustrated."

"She must've been a joy to be around."

Caleb nodded. "She had a jolly laugh, and she was quick-witted. I came here with Stephen and his family to help him, and also to get away from the memories of her. I was ready to move on with my life, and I'm glad we've met." He grinned.

She grinned too. "Me too. Do you plan to stay in Charm?"

"Yes. Have you ever considered moving?" He had good reason to stay in Charm now he'd met her, but it would be good to know her plans.

"No, I love living here. My *daed* died last year. My family is close, but I'd say we've become even closer since his death. I wouldn't want to leave Mamm, Toby, my friends, or my job at the bakery. I hope to never part from them."

"What was your *daed*'s name?" Caleb wanted to know details about her family.

"Vernon. He was the sweetest and kindest man. None of us minded caring for him when he was ill. He kept a good attitude from the time he became ill until he passed away. Tell me more about you."

"I kept my parents' *haus* after they died, and Stephen and Frannie had a home next to me. I miss having privacy, as I'm sure they do. I'd like to buy a place. What can you tell me about any properties for sale?" Caleb would grow roots in Charm and concentrate on his friendship with Rachael. She was thoughtful, sweet, easy to talk to, and a good listener. He was like a schoolboy around her.

"I don't know of any for sale right now, but stop by and

check the postings at the general store and post office. They'll have the farms for sale listed there," Rachael said.

"*Danki*. I'll stop by one day this week and read the postings." He pulled into her lane and stopped the buggy. "I would like to officially court you. We've just met, but the purpose of a courtship is to learn more about each other and find out if there's a future for us. Do you agree?" He gave her an impish grin. "I can't run the risk of another man asking you."

"Yes. I'm happy you asked."

He kept his hand over hers. "I'm intrigued by you."

"I'm excited about our courtship for the same reason." Rachael gazed at his hand on hers.

"I've kept you longer than I intended. You must be tired from a long day at work."

Rachael grinned. "I've enjoyed our evening together." She folded the blanket and handed it back to him. "Would you like to meet Mamm before you go?"

He nodded and opened the door. Her *mamm* sat on the settee, stitching a hole in an apron.

Rachael gestured to Caleb. "Mamm, I'd like you to meet Caleb Yutzy."

Caleb removed his hat. "Nice to meet you, Mrs. Schlabach."

"Please call me Eleanor. We're not formal. Did you have a pleasant evening?"

Rachael grinned. "Yes. I met Frannie, Stephen, and Lily, Caleb's *bruder*, *schweschder*-in-law, and *dochder,* who is two. She's a cutie, with light brown hair and pretty brown eyes."

Caleb offered Eleanor the container of potato soup he'd brought for her. "I doubt the soup's as good as your recipe, but I hope you'll enjoy it."

"*Danki*. How considerate of you." Eleanor accepted the container.

He cleared his throat and traced the brim of his hat. "I've asked Rachael if I may court her. She said yes. It will give us both time to get better acquainted, and we'll discover if we want a future together. I promise to honor and respect your *dochder*. I realize this is sudden, but we'd like your blessing."

"A courtship this soon after you have just met is sudden." She smiled. "But I trust Rachael's judgment. You both need to discover if you're compatible. Yes, you have my blessing."

"*Danki*. I should say good night. You ladies enjoy the rest of the evening. I'll see you tomorrow at the service." He pushed his hat on his head.

Rachael and her *mamm* wished him well.

He left their *haus*, got into his buggy, lit the lantern attached to it as the night was growing dark, and whistled on his way home. He liked this time of evening. Quiet, except for the clippity-clop of the horse's hooves against the dirt road, frogs, and katydids chirping. The days were warmer and the nights had been cool. Eleanor had the same kind and calm demeanor as her *dochder*. He looked forward to talking with her more as he and Rachael proceeded with their courtship.

He was relieved Rachael hadn't been upset with Frannie's direct questions or laziness. She hadn't hesitated to help in the kitchen or to answer Frannie's nosy questions. He wouldn't have blamed her if she'd changed the subject or refused to answer. Her bakery job was impressive because she and her *mamm* were alone to take care of their place. She must be a hard worker to bake at the bakery and assist with chores at home. He liked her a lot and would enjoy her company again tomorrow.

Chapter 2

Rachael sipped her coffee at the kitchen table nestled against the window on Sunday morning with Mamm. "I had a wonderful time with Caleb and his family last night. I'm glad you were still awake to meet him. I realize his asking to court me came as a surprise, but there's something about him I can't explain. Our connection was instant. I like him a lot, even though we've just met."

Mamm grinned. "Your *daed* captured my interest at our first meeting. Our friendship grew into a serious relationship fast. We were married three months from the day we met. It was one of the best decisions I ever made. I pray Caleb turns out to be the man for you. Protect your heart and learn all you can about him."

"I will." She beamed.

Mamm cocked her head. "How did you like his family?"

"His *bruder*, Stephen, is a soft-spoken and easygoing man. He's of average height and build. He doesn't resemble Caleb. Lily is precious, with wisps of brown hair and chubby cheeks. Frannie is outspoken. She has a small frame, dark brown hair, and a round face. She'd be prettier if she smiled more. Her dark brown eyes are serious most of the time. She was curious why I'd never married. I told her about John, the accident, and my limp. I'm relieved to have told them this part of my life and to have it out of the way. Caleb later told me of the girl he loved, who also died in an accident."

Eleanor pressed a hand to her heart. "How awful. What kind of accident did she have?"

Rachael traced the rim of her coffee mug. "It's a shocking story. Her death was sudden. She worked at the general store in Nappanee, Indiana. She went to the supply room to get something, climbed the ladder, fell, and hit her head. He explained the room was overcrowded with things and not organized. The store owner felt horrible about it."

"Dreadful." Mamm frowned. "I'm sorry you and he have lost the ones you thought you'd marry. You're both young to have experienced such tragedies." She cocked her head. "On another matter, you sit with Nathan and his *kinner* most Sundays at dinner. If Caleb and his family are there, who will you choose?"

"I'll invite Caleb to sit with Nathan, Joy, Thad, and me. His *bruder*'s family is *wilkom* to sit with us too. They need to make friends in Charm." Rachael checked the clock. "We'd better finish getting ready or we'll be late." She wasn't sure how Nathan would receive Caleb. He hadn't been happy about their change in routine, but the men should meet sometime. This was a tight-knit community.

"You're right. The time got away from me." Mamm hurried to her bedroom.

Thirty minutes later they left home and arrived at the Yoders'. Rachael tied the horse to the hitching post next to a row of other buggies.

Mamm stepped onto the ground, lifted her basket full of food dishes off the bench, and carried it. "I'll take this to the table to add with the other food. You can find us a seat together."

"All right." Rachael headed inside. She found enough

room for her and Mamm on a bench, then she scanned the crowd for her friends. She found Hannah, Ellie, and Maryann sitting together with their families. Caleb and Nathan and their families weren't at the service yet as far as she could tell.

Mamm entered and sat next to her.

Bishop Fisher stood in front of the congregation. He *wilkomed* the Yutzy family and asked everyone to introduce themselves to the family after the service. She turned her head and saw they were taking their seats on the back row bench. Caleb had Lily on his lap. He met her gaze and winked. Nathan and his *kinner* were sitting two rows ahead of them. Joy and Thad waved to her, and Nathan smiled and nodded.

The bishop prayed to God to give him the right words to speak to the congregation. He led them in several hymns from the Ausbund and then gave a message on humility. The bishop reminded them not to be prideful or boastful. He admonished them to be thankful for all things. And not to take their health or possessions for granted. She and Caleb had thought they had a lifetime ahead with John for her and Cora for him. Since then, she had learned to make time for loved ones and friends.

The bishop asked the congregation to stand, and then he offered a prayer to God to bless the food, and then he dismissed them.

A crowd encircled Caleb and his family.

Joy pushed through the sea of Amish and wrapped her arms around Rachael. "*Kumme* sit with us. Thad and Daed are saving us places. Daed said for you and me to fill our plates first, and then they'll get in line."

"Mamm, do you want to sit with us?" Rachael patted Joy's back.

"You go ahead. I'll sit at the widows' table with my friends. Joy, you're growing like a weed."

Joy beamed. "*Danki.*" She clasped Rachael's hand and dragged her to the food table. They filled their plates and sat with Nathan and Thad.

"We'll keep your places while you get your food."

Nathan smiled at her. "We missed you last night."

Thad nodded in agreement. "Supper was boring without you. *Kumme* on, Daed. I'm hungry. Let's go."

Nathan chuckled. "We'll be right back." He ducked in and out of the crowd of families and joined the food line with Thad.

Joy held her cheese and meat spread sandwich. "How was your dinner last night?"

Rachael's cheeks heated. She didn't owe the child any information about Caleb, but she wanted to be honest and open with her. "The Yutzy family were enjoyable, and the dinner was good."

Nathan and Thad returned to the table.

Joy pouted. "Rachael had supper with the new family in town last night. Now you met them, you don't need to go to their *haus* anymore. I didn't like not having you with us."

Caleb came to the table. "Is there room for one more?"

Rachael stiffened. Had he overheard Joy's comment? "Yes, please join us. This is Nathan Wagler and his *kinner*, Thad and Joy. And this is Caleb Yutzy."

Nathan didn't smile but shook Caleb's hand.

Caleb greeted Thad and Joy and sat across from Rachael. He grinned at her, but his eyes stayed serious. This wasn't going well. Nathan had been dismissive of Caleb, and he wasn't trying to make conversation. She'd help them along. "Nathan, are there any properties for sale in Charm? Caleb would like to purchase a place."

"If there are, I'm not aware of any." Nathan avoided eye contact with Caleb.

Caleb didn't react to Nathan's curtness but turned to the *kinner*. "Joy and Thad, what do you like to do?"

Joy gulped half her water and set the glass on the table. "I like to make mud pies, play with the barn cats, and toss a ball."

Thad puffed out his chest. "I like to play tag, any board game, and baseball."

"Those all sound like fun things to do." Caleb grinned at them.

Joy narrowed her eyes at Caleb. "Rachael won't be *kumming* to your *haus* anymore. She belongs to us."

Rachael's eyes widened. She darted her eyes from Nathan to Caleb. The two men stared at her. Nathan wasn't giving her any indication he would *kumme* to her defense. She returned her gaze to Joy. "Caleb is my new friend. I need to make time for him too."

"Caleb, you can *kumme* to our *haus*. Then Rachael won't have to leave us," Thad said.

"I appreciate the invitation, young man." Caleb cleared his throat. "Rachael, let's get dessert."

Joy beamed. "I'll go with you."

Rachael kissed Joy's cheek. "I'll bring a plate of cookies to the table for you, Thad, and your *daed*."

Nathan avoided looking into her eyes. "Joy, stay here."

Joy harrumphed.

Rachael and Caleb stepped away from the table. She fetched a plate and filled it with an assortment of cookies she knew Nathan and the *kinner* liked.

Caleb motioned to a bench under the willow tree. "I'd like for us to have dessert apart from Nathan and the *kinner*. I have some serious questions for you. I'll wait for you there."

She nodded and carried the plate of cookies to Nathan, Joy, and Thad. "Here you go. I'll be back later."

Joy tugged on her sleeve. "Will you toss a ball with me?"

"You play with the other *kinner* and Thad. I need to talk with Caleb in private." Rachael waited for Joy and Thad to take their cookies and join their friends. She moved to Nathan. "Is everything all right?"

"Are you *kumming* over tomorrow evening? I'd like to have a private conversation." Nathan's tone was more serious than usual.

"Sure. I'll *kumme* after work. We'll have time to talk then." Rachael left them and sat by Caleb. She didn't want dessert. Her stomach was doing flip-flops. "Would you like to meet some more of my friends?"

"No." He set his plate on the ground with half of his apple pie still on it. "Rachael, is Nathan courting you? Why would you accept my invitation if you are already committed to another man?"

"Nathan is a friend. His *fraa*, Katherine, died about eight months ago. They were newcomers to Charm, and he needed help with Joy and Thad. They live next door to me. I'm helping them adjust to a life without her. I've grown close to Joy and Thad, so I can understand why they might be protective about me. With regard to Nathan, we're not courting." She didn't understand why Nathan had ignored Caleb. They had no understanding of anything more than friendship between them. They had gotten used to her being at their beck and call.

"Nathan doesn't agree with you, from what I observed today. He doesn't want anything to do with me, and he didn't like my showing interest in you. The *kinner*, I understand where they might be confused. But you're wrong about Nathan. He's interested in you for more than a friend."

She glanced around them, relieved they were far enough away from Amish in clusters, enjoying their friends and food, and the *kinner* playing tag and horseshoes. She didn't want anyone within earshot of them. Her heart thudded fast against her chest. Nathan had acted like a jealous school-boy. She was confused about Nathan's intentions toward her. "I'll speak with him. But he has never asked to court me. As far as I know, he's still not over his *fraa*'s death. We haven't tried to find time alone. We're always with the *kinner*."

Caleb narrowed his eyes. "Do you have romantic feelings toward him?"

"No. I would never have accepted your invitation to supper if I did. His reaction to you today is new for me. I wouldn't have asked you to sit with them if I had known he'd be opposed."

"He may be a poor communicator. His reaction is the reason I'm sure he would like something more serious with you than friendship." Caleb crossed his arms.

Rachael fidgeted her hands. "I apologize for making you feel uncomfortable."

He shook his head. "I shouldn't have been so hard on you. I can tell you're as surprised as I am about Nathan's reaction. Let's put this behind us. I'll take you to the restaurant in town for supper tomorrow night."

"Nathan requested I *kumme* to his place tomorrow evening for a private conversation. I should go and clear up any misunderstanding between us. I assure you I'll tell him we're courting." She wasn't sure what to do about the *kinner*. She loved them, and they might still need her.

"He needs to know where you stand, and it's no longer appropriate for you to go to their *haus* so often, now we're courting. Do you agree?" Caleb tilted his head.

"Yes, with the exception of tomorrow night. He asked for a private conversation, and I've agreed to listen. I don't want any ill will between Nathan and me."

Caleb nodded.

Joy and Thad approached them.

Joy hugged her. "Daed said we have to leave. I wanted to tell you goodbye first."

"Will you be at our *haus* tomorrow after work?" Thad darted his gaze to Caleb and back to Rachael.

"Yes. I'll bring maple sugar cookies for dessert. Say goodbye to Caleb."

"Goodbye, Caleb." Joy waved her little hand.

"Nice to meet you," Thad said.

"I'm blessed to have met you both. *Danki* for letting me sit with you at dinner today. Enjoy the rest of your afternoon." Caleb smiled.

Joy and Thad nodded and then went to their buggy, where Nathan waited.

"Nathan didn't *kumme* to say farewell. There's no question he's upset." Caleb watched Nathan drive away.

"I'll know more when I speak to him tomorrow evening." She didn't want to discuss Nathan anymore. She wanted to concentrate on Caleb. "Spring is upon us, and summer will be here soon. I'm ready for hot weather. Mamm wants to add brussels sprouts to our garden. I didn't like them as a child, but I love them as an adult."

"I have always liked them. I love any kind of potato dish, so I'm making sure I plant plenty of those." He gestured to the parking area. "Most of the buggies are gone. I suppose we should go."

Stephen, carrying a picnic basket, waved to them. "Caleb, are you ready to go?"

"I'll meet you at the buggy," Caleb yelled back to him. "Who is the man your *mamm* is talking to? They're both holding their stomachs and laughing."

Rachael looked where he pointed. "Joseph Ramer. He's

been a widower for six months." She couldn't picture her with anyone but Daed.

Caleb glanced at her *mamm* and back at Rachael. "How long has it been since your *daed* died?"

"About ten months. I'm sure they're friends having a chat." But she wasn't convinced of that.

They seemed too familiar, and Mamm acted like a smitten schoolgirl around him. Joseph acted captivated by her. She'd ask Mamm about Joseph later. She was surprised Mamm might be interested in another man.

"You're right. I didn't mean to insinuate anything." He escorted her to her buggy and faced her *mamm* and Mr. Ramer. "Good afternoon."

Mr. Ramer extended his hand. "Joseph Ramer. Pleasure to meet you."

Caleb shook his hand. "Caleb Yutzy. Pleased to make your acquaintance."

Mamm blushed. "Rachael, you know Joseph."

"Yes. Good to see you, Mr. Ramer." Rachael smiled.

"And please, all of you, call me Joseph. Eleanor, I'll bring over the shirt I need mended tomorrow, and *danki* again. Have a pleasant day." Joseph smiled, tipped his hat, and left them.

Caleb waited until Rachael and Mamm were in the buggy. "I'll stop in at the bakery tomorrow, Rachael." He bid them farewell and went to join his family.

Rachael elbowed her *mamm*. "You're mending clothes for Joseph?"

Mamm avoided looking directly at her. "Yes. Why not?"

"You are an excellent seamstress, but you've turned down mending for anyone but family. You always said sewing wasn't enjoyable for you, like it is for some of your friends. It's last on your list of things to do." Rachael stared at her.

"He doesn't have a *fraa* to mend his shirt. He said he was going to have to turn his favorite shirt into rags. I offered to stitch the hole in it for him. Why are you asking so many questions?" Mamm bristled.

"Are you interested in Joseph as more than a friend?" Rachael held her breath. She wasn't sure she was ready for Mamm's answer.

"I'm not sure. It's too early to tell. He's a delightful man. Can we please talk about something else?" Mamm focused on the road ahead.

"I'm shocked you'd consider another man. You and Daed had such a close bond and strong marriage. I can't imagine you with anyone but Daed." She shouldn't be opposed.

Joseph had a stellar reputation in their community, and Mamm deserved happiness. It would take time for her to get used to the idea that her *mamm* might want to marry again someday. Joseph was handsome, with his steel-gray hair, lean, tall frame, and coffee-brown eyes.

"Rachael, I will always love your *daed*. Joseph took me by surprise, seeking me out at after-church meals and finding reasons to visit me. He's brought me dinner, and I find him charming. He's not pushy but pleasant. I look forward to our dinners, suppers, and conversations. I'm not opposed to marrying again because of the loving marriage I had with your *daed*. Right now, Joseph and I are enjoying our time together. He's taken me to dinner in town a number of times. It's been fun."

She would've been at work when Joseph and Mamm went to dinner, as opposed to supper. She was surprised Mamm hadn't mentioned him before now. Mamm didn't owe her an explanation or account for her days. Rachael's stomach churned at this change. She wasn't happy about Joseph showing interest in her *mamm*, but she'd work on it. Mamm had been supportive of her and Caleb's courtship.

She'd change the subject. "I'm in trouble with Nathan, but I'm not sure why. He didn't have much to say to me or Caleb. I shouldn't have brought the two men together at dinner."

Mamm glanced at her. "Nathan may have taken for granted you'd always be there for him and the *kinner*. If he wanted a courtship, he should have asked you. Who would you choose if Nathan asks to court you?"

"Caleb. I don't want to upset Nathan or sever ties with the *kinner*. I could care for the *kinner* at our house after work sometimes, if Nathan needs to have a nanny for the evening. I'm not sure if he will ask after I tell him Caleb and I are courting." Rachael's stomach clenched. "He's asked to speak with me in private tomorrow, and I'm not looking forward to going there."

Mamm pulled into their lane and parked the buggy. "Before we take another step, let's pray about this." She clasped Rachael's hand. "Dear Heavenly Father, please give Rachael guidance and the words to say when she speaks with Nathan. We pray for your will in each of our lives. Bless Joy and Thad and guide Rachael to accept what she should do or not do for them. Help them accept and adjust to Rachael's absence from them as she courts Caleb. *Danki* for all you're already doing for us. We love you. Amen."

"*Danki*." She hugged Mamm and got out of the buggy. She reached for the picnic basket on the bench. "I'll carry this in and be back to assist unharnessing the mare."

"I'll take care of her if you'll put the empty dishes we took today in the dishpan. We'll let them soak, and I'll wash, dry, and put them away tomorrow morning."

"All right." Rachael strolled to the *haus*, enjoying the sunshine on her cheeks. She went inside to the kitchen and set the picnic basket on the counter. Then she went outside and filled the dishpan with water. She returned and placed the dishes in the dishpan. She dreaded having to talk to Nathan after the way he'd behaved around her and Caleb. Nathan had been frustrated with her today. What would she do if he severed their friendship when she told him about Caleb?

Caleb lowered a sleeping Lily into her bed, tiptoed out of the room, and closed the door. He'd love being a *daed* someday, and he hoped God would bless him and his *fraa* with many *kinner*. He prayed his *fraa* would be Rachael, if their friendship and courtship blossomed into a marriage in the future. He went to the porch, where Stephen and Frannie were enjoying the sunshine. "Soon, the temperature will be hot and not a perfect cool like today. Summer will be here before we know it."

Stephen rocked in the high-backed chair. "I'm anxious for warmer weather in the evenings too. During the day, our temperatures are warm. I like Charm. The Amish at church today flocked to us after the service. They *wilkomed* us, and several of the men offered to lend a hand whenever I need it."

Frannie moved to the swing. "I met Rachael's *bruder*, Toby, and his *fraa*, Magdelena. They've been married less than a year. She works with Rachael at the bakery, and she praised her. I also met Hannah. She worked at the bakery before she was married. I like them. They said the bakery socials are fun and I should go whenever they have one again."

Caleb grinned. "I covet any time I can be with Rachael, so I didn't mingle. Since we had a hectic morning with Lily being fussy and you both were in your room when I got home last night, I haven't told you my news. I asked Rachael if I can court her. She said yes, and her *mamm* gave us her blessing."

Frannie quirked her brow. "What? You should've waited

until you'd had more conversations with this girl. You couldn't have spoken to her enough to make such a commitment. You should slow down. I'm surprised her *mamm* would agree to this."

Stephen shook his head. "I don't agree, Frannie. They're grown adults. Courtship is for discovering more about each other. Rachael's *mamm* must trust her *dochder*. Congratulations, Caleb. Rachael's a nice girl. She's *wilkom* here any time."

"*Danki, bruder.*" Caleb could count on his *bruder* to support him. Frannie's negative comments irked him, but they weren't worth an argument. He'd keep his mouth shut.

Frannie huffed. "What's done is done. As long as she doesn't have any expectations when she *kummes*, it's fine by me if she visits. I'm not going to worry about the *haus* being tidy, the laundry overflowing, or the dishes piled in the sink. She seems nice enough. Who was the man sitting with you and Rachael at dinner?"

Caleb frowned. Frannie had given him another reason to move from here and find his own place. She didn't make much of an effort to make friends or care to make a good impression on others.

"Nathan Wagler. He's a widower. His *fraa* died about eight months ago, and Rachael has been caring for the *kinner* and fixing meals for them after work most days. Rachael insisted they're only friends, but he was cold toward me. I suspect he was jealous of the attention Rachael gave me. He asked her to *kumme* to his *haus* after work tomorrow for a discussion. He may not be too happy when she tells him we're courting." Caleb didn't want to lose Rachael. Would she be torn over who to court if Nathan wanted more than friendship with her?

Stephen waved a dismissive hand. "Rachael couldn't take her eyes off you when she was here. I doubt she'll have any trouble telling him where she stands. He should've asked to court her before this if he was interested in her. Sounds to me like he took her for granted and wasn't in any hurry to make a commitment."

Frannie waggled a forefinger at Stephen. "I wouldn't be too sure. Since she's spent more time with him than with Caleb, she may be swayed to give him a chance. She knows little about Caleb."

Caleb pinched his lips. Frannie could be exasperating. And she liked to stir up trouble. He hoped she was wrong.

Monday morning, Caleb waited until the bakery opened and then went to town to visit Rachael. He had woken several times throughout the night, curious as to what the outcome of her meeting with Nathan would be this evening. He wanted to show her he was serious about their courtship by his visit. "Good morning."

Rachael beamed. "Hot chocolate?"

"I would like hot chocolate rather than coffee this morning. You have good instincts." He grinned.

Magdelena came from the kitchen to the counter. "Caleb, *wilkom* and congratulations. I'm happy about your courtship. My friends and I will be watching. You'll have to treat her well." She smiled.

Caleb chuckled. "Your request is an easy one to fulfill. I assure you, my intention is to make her happy."

Dr. Harrison and Sheriff Williams took the same seats they took every morning the bakery was open. Dr. Harrison sat next to Caleb.

Rachael introduced the men to Caleb. She served Caleb hot chocolate and coffee to the other men and then gave them each a slice of cinnamon bread.

They all thanked her.

Magdelena grinned. "What Rachael and Caleb didn't say is, they're courting."

Sheriff Williams cocked his head. "Rachael is special to us. You'd better treat her well or you'll have to answer to us. She and Magdelena are friends of ours."

"Yes, sir." Caleb watched the men split the newspaper while he answered their questions about where he'd moved from and where he lived in Charm.

Dr. Harrison shook his head. "This morning's news is troubling. Germany protests to the United States, claiming we must insist Britain lift its blockade and declare American neutrality."

Sherriff Williams harrumphed and straightened his broad shoulders. "This war is getting ugly. Germany doesn't have any right to tell us what to do. You mark my words. I predict within two years the United States will have to enter this war against Germany."

"I'm afraid you may be right. It doesn't look like there's any end in sight. I hope we're both wrong." Dr. Harrison sighed.

Caleb had picked up bits and pieces of what was happening in the war from conversations he'd overheard from Englischers sitting outside the general store and post office. The war sounded complicated and scared him. He wasn't sure what the United States was in for or how it would affect them. He didn't agree Amish should stay out of it, as the bishop had told them, to avoid outside world news and influences.

He couldn't let this opportunity to speak to Dr. Harrison go by, even if it might not be appropriate. "Dr. Harrison, I'm worried about my *bruder*. He's tired all the time, and he has trouble catching his breath sometimes. It's not natural for someone his age. I'm twenty-five, and he's twenty-eight. Do you have any idea what might be causing these symptoms?"

"I'd need to examine him before I can answer your

question. Bring him to me anytime." Dr. Harrison went back to reading his paper.

"*Danki*, Doctor." Caleb wasn't sure Stephen would listen to him. He'd do his best to coax him to go to Dr. Harrison's office. Frannie had suggested he go to the doctor, but Stephen had made excuses and refused to go. He prayed his *bruder* would listen to him.

Caleb didn't want to be a nuisance to Rachael. She had work to do. "I should go. Pleasure meeting you both, Dr. Harrison and Sheriff Williams. I'll be in again tomorrow, Rachael. Take care, Magdelena."

Rachael and Magdelena bid him farewell.

The men also bid the girls farewell and went ahead of Caleb and left. Caleb lagged behind and held Rachael's gaze, tipped his hat, and departed.

He drove home, where he found Stephen sitting in a chair with his head in his hands.

"Do you have a headache?" Caleb walked over to him.

His *bruder* had lost weight, and his gray face concerned him. He was too young not to have more stamina.

"No. I'm tired most of the time. I don't have the energy I used to."

"Frannie expects too much of you. Why do you coddle her? She's capable of doing far more than she does of the household chores and taking care of Lily. Tell her it's too much for you and ask her to handle more of the inside work."

"Her parents spoiled her, and I've done the same. I knew what I was getting into when I married her. I love her, and I enjoy making her happy. If anything happens to me, please take care of her and Lily."

Caleb's stomach clenched. "You're young. We have a long time before either of us needs to worry about departing this earth. What prompted you to say such a thing? And of course I'd take care of your girls, but I won't coddle her."

"Since we're not promised tomorrow, I needed assurance you will take care of Frannie and Lily if something happens to me, which would mean you settling in Charm." He grinned. "After meeting Rachael, you'd be a fool not to plant roots here. She's easygoing and delightful."

"I wasn't sure how long I would stay in Charm when I moved here with you, but now I've met Rachael, I plan to stay. I may inquire about a farm for sale. You and Frannie need more privacy."

Stephen cleared his throat. "Are you uncomfortable living with us? We're fine. You don't bother us. Please stay. You make life easier for me by pitching in on chores and caring for Lily. I must be tired from relocating and having a young child. I'll adjust eventually. Until you get to know Rachael and find out if you and she will plan a future, you don't need to buy a place."

"Is there anything you're not telling me? Are you sick? Do you have pain? I met Dr. Harrison this morning at the bakery. He's a congenial man. You'd like him. Let's hop in the wagon and visit him. Let him examine you. Something's not right, and we need to find out what it is and what we can do about it. Your weakened condition concerns me."

Stephen waved a dismissive hand. "It's nothing. Don't worry about me. But please stay. You make life easier for me and I like having you around."

"I'll stay and help you." Caleb didn't miss the relief that came over his *bruder*'s face. He wouldn't pursue buying property until his and Rachael's courtship grew more serious. He would keep a closer eye on Stephen. Stephen wasn't being honest with him. He was sick and refused to face it.

Chapter 3

Rachael drove to the Waglers' home Monday evening. She'd loved getting to speak with Caleb today. She wished she was with him this evening, but she wanted to honor Nathan's request to speak with her. She pulled into Nathan's lane. He kept his property in excellent shape, with his porch always swept, kept his garden free of weeds, and had the straightest rows of vegetables in his garden. The sun was warm and the sky was clear.

Joy greeted her outside. "Yay! You're here. Daed made me a swing and tied it to the big oak tree. I love it. Do you want me to push you on the swing?"

She hugged Joy. "Maybe later. I'm hungry, aren't you?"

Joy rubbed her stomach. "I am too."

Rachael clasped Joy's hand. "What should we put together for supper?"

"You're not cooking. Daed made beef stew and biscuits." Joy led her into the *haus*.

She inhaled the beef aroma. This was the second time Nathan had cooked for them.

Thad pulled out her chair from the rectangular maple table. "You're here at the right time. Supper is almost finished. You sit."

Joy giggled as she sat across from Rachael. "We made butter cookies for dessert."

"How was your day?" Nathan put the pot of stew on the already set table.

"There was an auction in town. Many of those attending stopped into the bakery after it was over, so we had a steady stream of customers later in the morning. It was a busy and successful day for us." Rachael reached for Nathan's bowl. "I'll serve the stew for us."

"No. Please stay seated. Let us spoil you this evening for a change." He stood, gazed into her eyes, and smiled, then filled each bowl.

"I poured water in the glasses." Thad grinned, sitting ramrod straight.

She suspected Nathan's pampering was to show his interest in her. Why the change? She hadn't known what to expect from Nathan this evening after the way he seemed tense on Sunday. She found all this awkward, but she didn't want to appear ungrateful. "You've all done an outstanding job. Nathan, the food is delicious. How did you have time to cook and bake today?"

"I got up earlier than usual, and the *kinner* pitched in to help me after school. Tonight is special." He reached for her hand.

She gave him a weak smile. "*Danki.*" She moved her hand away.

Nathan was being attentive and he had gone out of his way to make this evening special for her. Had he overcome his grief for Katherine?

Joy drank half her water. "I like Peter, but Charity told me they're getting married when they're sixteen."

"Was she angry with you?" Rachael raised her brows.

Magdelena's little *schweschder* had planned to marry Peter for a while. Those two were inseparable.

Joy shook her head. "No. I like Charity, so I said she could have him."

Thad rolled his eyes. "You're too young to have a beau."

Joy huffed. "I am not. I'll have a beau if I want to."

"Don't argue." Nathan shook his head. "Thad's right. You don't need to worry about having a suitor. Enjoy your friends."

"Daed has a new friend. Her name's Ava. She brought a custard pie. She was here when I came home from school." Joy shrugged her shoulders. "She wanted to stay and make supper for us, but Daed told her we had plans. You wouldn't have cared if she stayed, would you?"

"No. Not at all. Ava is a superb cook, and she's a jolly girl to be around." She liked Ava Raber for Nathan and the *kinner*. She'd been a widow for a year. She was pretty, with her reddish-brown hair and freckles sprinkled across her nose. Ava didn't have *kinner*, and she was sure Ava would love Joy and Thad. She hoped Nathan wouldn't discount Ava. It would make her friendship with Nathan easier as she and Caleb courted.

Nathan carried his plate to the sink. "Who wants pie?"

"I do." Thad raised his hand.

"Cookie for me." Joy handed her plate to Thad to take to the sink with his.

"Pie for me." Rachael rose. "I'll help you."

"No. Relax. Let me serve you." Nathan cut the pie and served it. He passed Joy two sugar cookies and grabbed two more for himself.

"Ava sure can bake. This pie is scrumptious." Rachael forked another bite. "You don't care for custard pie, Nathan?"

"I like it, but not better than sugar cookies." He broke his cookie in half and enjoyed a corner of it.

"Will you work a puzzle with Thad and me before you

go home?" Joy swiped crumbs from her mouth with the back of her hand.

"Use your napkin, Joy." Nathan lowered his chin and scowled at her.

"Sorry." Joy picked up her napkin and wiped her lips.

"Rachael and I need some grown-up time. You and Thad can work the puzzle." Nathan stacked the dessert plates and forks. "*Kinner*, you both are excused."

Joy pouted and followed Thad to the living room.

"The water on the stove should be the right temperature for doing dishes. We can let them soak and I can wash them later. Let's go to the sitting room, away from the *kinner*."

Rachael grabbed a dish towel hanging on a metal hook by the sink. "I insist we wash and dry these dishes. With the two of us, we can have them back in the cabinets where they belong in no time."

"You drive a hard bargain." Nathan washed, and she dried the dishes. "Rachael, I've gotten used to our routine. The nights you weren't here, I missed you."

"We've become close friends. I enjoy my time with you and the *kinner*. I was glad to help out with chores and the *kinner* after Katherine's passing."

He took the dish towel from her hands and set it on the counter and then clasped her hand and led her to the sitting room. He faced her and put his hands on her shoulders. "I don't want to lose you to another man. Rachael, I'd like to court you."

Rachael tensed. She didn't want to hurt his feelings, but he was too late. She had her sights set on Caleb. Before Caleb, she might have considered him with the hope she'd fall in love with him over time. But she wanted to fall in love again, like she had with John, her fiancé, before he died. With Caleb, she was already headed in that direction. "Nathan, I care for you and the *kinner*. You, Joy, and Thad filled a void in my life after Katherine passed. But why now?"

"It took you breaking our routine to make me *kumme* to my senses. I have taken you for granted. I cooked supper to show you I care for you, and I'm ready to take you to a restaurant, on buggy rides, on long walks, and wherever else you would like to go while we court. I'll always love Katherine, but it's time for me to consider the future. Please, Rachael, will you allow me to court you?"

She wrenched her gaze from his. His sincerity was without question, but she had to be true to herself. "You're a wonderful *daed* and a man I admire. I didn't allow myself to fall for you, because you were grieving your *fraa*'s death. I wasn't sure you'd ever be ready to consider courting again or even if you and I would fall in love. Caleb and I are interested in each other. I've accepted his invitation to court. I'm sorry, Nathan."

He dropped his hands to his sides. "Caleb's new in town. It's too soon."

"It's not too soon. We have a connection, a spark I can't explain." She'd said too much. She didn't need to defend her courtship with Caleb to him. She took a deep breath. She didn't want to leave tonight with Nathan upset with her. She cared about him as a friend.

Nathan looked at the ceiling and back at her. "I'm frustrated with myself for waiting to have this conversation. I assumed you'd always be here. How arrogant of me. It's early in your courtship with Caleb to know what the future will bring. I'll wait for you. Until you agree to marry him, I have a chance."

Rachael clasped her hands tight in front of her. "Please don't wait on me. You and the *kinner* would benefit from having a wonderful woman like Ava in your lives. She loves *kinner*, and she didn't have a chance to have her own. She and her husband were only married for a short time."

His sad eyes gazed into hers. "There is no one else but you for me. I care about you and I'm comfortable around you. It will be worth it. I'm patient."

She cared for him and didn't want him to remain a widower. She had to distance herself from them to be fair to Caleb. But she could still watch Joy and Thad for him if the need arose. "If you need someone to care for Joy and Thad, Mamm or I will be happy to oblige."

"*Danki*. We should tell the *kinner* together why our routine is changing."

She nodded and headed with him to the living room, where the *kinner* were working their puzzle. She dreaded telling Joy and Thad she wouldn't be there for them. She sat on the floor with them. "You're doing a great job fitting the puzzle pieces together. Can you give me your full attention for a couple of minutes?"

Joy and Thad nodded as they gazed at her.

"I love you both very much, and I enjoy my time with you. I told your *daed* Mamm or I will care for you at our *haus* when you need us."

"I don't understand. You *kumme* here after you're off work to play with us. Are you still *kumming* to our *haus* as usual?" Joy wrinkled her nose.

"No. I have a new beau, Caleb. He and I are courting and getting better acquainted. You met him at yesterday's service. He's asked me to spend more time with him." She fidgeted her hands. This was as difficult as she'd expected. "We'll talk at Sunday services, and you can *kumme* visit me."

Thad crossed his arms. "Why don't you like our *daed*? I asked him if he liked you and he said yes. He made supper for you. Tell Caleb you don't have time for him."

Nathan put his hand on Thad's shoulder. "No, son. This

is my fault. I didn't tell Rachael of my interest in her earlier. We have to accept this. Rachael has a right to court whoever she chooses. It doesn't mean she doesn't love you and Joy."

Joy stood with her hands on her hips. "I'll tell Caleb to leave you alone. I told him you belong to us. Why won't he listen?"

"She's right. Caleb should find another girl to court." Thad glared at her.

Rachael's throat dried. "This isn't Caleb's fault. I like him, and I agreed to court him. It's my decision too. Please be kind to him. You can visit me anytime I'm home. Please don't be angry with me." She held out her arms.

Thad stomped past her. "I'm going to my room."

Joy followed him. "Me too."

"*Kinner*, you're being rude. Return at once and hug Rachael." Nathan scowled.

They ran to their rooms and shut their doors.

Nathan took steps to the hallway.

Rachael grasped his arm. "Don't force them to say goodbye. This is a big change for them, and they need time to adjust. I dislike making them or you sad." She would miss their regular routine. They'd been her chance to be a *mamm*. She hadn't told Caleb her secret. She didn't like talking about it with anyone, and she wouldn't tell Caleb until she had to. It was a big risk, and she wanted to have as much time as possible with him. She was afraid her secret would be reason enough for him to end their courtship. She couldn't face it right now.

Caleb worked alongside Stephen to sow oats and seed all day. He wondered how this evening went with Nathan and Rachael. He should concentrate on Stephen right now. He'd find out what happened at Nathan's tomorrow. He followed his *bruder* to the water pump, where they took turns washing their hands. They should've had supper two hours ago, but neither one had wanted to stop what they were doing.

"I'm hungry. How about you?"

Stephen's shoulders slumped, and he dragged his feet to the front door. "I'm bushed and famished. I hope Frannie has something prepared. I don't have the energy to cook."

Caleb patted him on the back. "If she doesn't have something ready for us, I'll rustle up some sandwiches."

"You boys are late." Frannie sat in her favorite maple chair with her feet propped up on a cushioned, four-legged stool. "You'll have to fetch yourselves supper. We've got sliced ham and some potato soup left over from Saturday. I craved oatmeal cookies, so I made some. You can each have two."

"Is Lily asleep?" Stephen faced her.

"Yes. Please keep your voices down. I'm comfortable and relishing my peace and quiet." She directed her gaze from him to the knitting needles in her hands, as if to dismiss him.

Caleb bit his tongue. She made cookies and then always told them how many they could have, so she'd have plenty for herself to snack on as she wished. He wouldn't cause an argument, but he came close to telling her how tired he was of her selfishness and laziness. She could've made time to fix them supper. He and Stephen weren't *kinner*. They didn't need her to tell them how many cookies they were allowed. She was ridiculous. "Stephen, follow me to the kitchen and take a seat."

Stephen went ahead of him to the kitchen and opened a cabinet to remove plates. "I'll set the table."

Caleb grasped his arm. "Please rest. Pull out a chair and put your feet up." He put the soup on to warm.

His *bruder*'s eyes had dark circles under them, and he was pale. He was afraid Stephen would faint. His *bruder* had to stop every few minutes while they were working today. Caleb slathered peach jam on ham sandwiches and sliced them in half, and then he poured the warmed potato soup into two bowls.

"*Danki*. I'll pray a blessing to God for the food." Stephen recited the prayer, then raised his head. "*Danki* for not scolding Frannie. Your pinched lips told me you were ready to tell her what was on your mind, and it didn't appear it would be polite."

Caleb lowered his voice. "I won't lie. I don't have the patience you have with her. She's arrogant and thinks only of herself. How do you put up with her? Aren't you frustrated with her bossy and lazy attitude?" He didn't understand how Frannie could ignore her husband's obvious weakness and shortness of breath. She didn't express any concern or show of support.

"We've had this conversation many times. She's not the ideal *fraa*, but I love her. I don't care if the laundry or dishes pile up. She or I will get these chores done eventually. You have made sure that doesn't happen by pitching in and helping to get those things done. I appreciate all the work you've done inside and outside, including caring for Lily often. My gratitude is more than I can put into words."

"I'm not asking for your praise. You should express to her that you want her to cook, clean, and assist with chores outside." Caleb snapped his fingers. "I forgot the water." He rose and poured them each a glass of water. "I've held my tongue long enough. I will discuss my concerns with her."

"No. Please. Let it go. She made cookies and took care of Lily." He drank half his water. "Anything new with you and Rachael?"

Caleb wouldn't badger him anymore tonight about Frannie. He didn't want to upset his *bruder*. "She's been helping Nathan Wagler and his *kinner* since his *fraa* died. Nathan asked her to have supper, saying he needed to talk to her."

"Do you suppose he's interested in courting her?" Nathan dipped his spoon in his soup.

"I hope not, but I wouldn't be surprised if he asked to court her. He was cordial, but he wouldn't engage in conversation with me. His two *kinner*, Joy and Thad, are adorable. I'm afraid Rachael may be swayed to reconsider our courtship due to being close to them. We haven't known each other long, and she's been with them for the past eight months." He loved his niece, Lily. After having lived with his *bruder*, he had gotten close to the *boppli*. Joy and Thad loved Rachael, and she loved them. They could have a strong hold on her heart.

"Nathan has waited too long. You came along and upset the applecart, and he must've realized he cared for her. She can have the *kinner* over to her place once in a while, and she'll speak with them at Sunday services. I doubt they'll have any influence on her decision to court you."

Caleb prayed he was right. She did say she would tell Nathan about their courtship. He should trust her and push any doubt out of his mind. "*Danki* for your encouragement. On another subject, please let me take you to Dr. Harrison. Stephen, please, do it for me and my peace of mind."

Frannie entered the room. "Don't overreact, Caleb. Stephen doesn't have the stamina you do. It doesn't mean he's sick."

"How would you know? You're not with him working in the garden, barn, or fields. Although it's hard to miss how exhausted he is when we sit down for meals or for a break in the day. But you're too busy with what you want to do to notice. Furthermore, it's appalling you don't cook for us after all we do to manage the inside and outside chores." He avoided looking at Stephen and centered his gaze on Frannie.

"How dare you! I have a *boppli* who demands my attention. I haven't asked you to wash or fold laundry or wash and dry dishes or any of the other chores you've taken upon yourself." She glowered at him.

"We couldn't walk through this *haus* or sit on the furniture if I didn't take care of those things. Lily takes naps, and you have ample time while she's playing in the playpen or sleeping to take care of the inside chores and cook. Furthermore, the limitations you put on desserts for Stephen and me is outlandish." He wouldn't cease telling her what he thought until he'd listed it all. He'd held in his frustration long enough. He couldn't let it go, not even for Stephen.

"Stephen, say something. I shouldn't have to take this scolding from your *bruder*. It's rude. He's in *our haus*." Frannie put her hand on her husband's shoulder.

"Frannie, this *haus* is as much Caleb's as ours." He shifted to Caleb. "*Bruder*, please, calm down. Don't say anymore, for my sake." Stephen looked at him with pleading eyes.

He held up his palms. "I'm done." He picked up the dishes from the table.

Frannie took them from him. "I'll wash and dry the dishes. There aren't many. You and Stephen can go to the living room."

Had he gotten through to her? She must've felt a little guilt. It would, no doubt, be short-lived, like the other times he'd made subtle remarks to her, but he'd take it.

Frannie kept her focus on the dishes and remained quiet. She usually had something to say, but he supposed she kept silent now for fear he'd cease doing inside chores, and she'd didn't want him to stop helping her. He followed Stephen to the living room. "She needed to hear what I had to say."

"I understand." Stephen devoured the cookies, then rested his head against the high back of his chair. He soon fell asleep.

Caleb listened to his *bruder*'s rhythmic, low snore. Stephen cleaned his plate at most meals, but he didn't appear to gain weight. Maybe it was the way his body worked, but he doubted it. Short of dragging his *bruder* by force to the doctor, there was nothing more he could do. He'd have to wait until Stephen was ready to face his problem.

His mind drifted to Rachael. She had stolen his heart in a short time. His attraction to her kept growing. She had a jovial laugh, and he missed her when they weren't together. He was anxious to speak with her about what had happened at the Waglers' when he visited the bakery and made plans with her. He woke Stephen and helped him to bed, and then he went to his room.

That night, he tossed and turned as rain pelted the rooftop. Lightning flashed near the *haus* and lit up his room while several loud booms shook the building.

It matched the worry consuming him about his *bruder*, Frannie, and his future with Rachael.

Tuesday morning, Caleb fixed biscuits and fried eggs. Bacon sizzled in the skillet. He had changed Lily's nappy and set her in her high chair.

"Unkie." She held out a corner of her egg to him.

"No. *Danki.* You put the egg in your mouth." Caleb was happy Lily was generous, unlike her *mamm* and more like her *daed*.

Frannie came in the kitchen, rubbing her eyes. She kissed

Lily's forehead. "You're up early, Caleb. I'm surprised to find Lily in her high chair."

"I woke earlier than usual, and she was playing with her rattle in bed. She grinned and raised her arms to me, and I couldn't resist her. She's keeping me company. Breakfast is ready." Caleb was glad she didn't mention their argument last night. He wanted to put it behind them. He'd had guilt over his outburst after Stephen had asked him not to confront Frannie. He should've spoken to her in private. But maybe she'd listened to him and would do her share of the work around the *haus*.

"You already have the coffee made and table set. You didn't have to do all this." Frannie forked a pancake and put it on a plate for Lily. She buttered it and poured syrup on it. She then cut it in pieces for her *dochder*. She fixed herself a pancake the same way she'd prepared Lily's. "These are delicious, Caleb."

Stephen padded into the kitchen, yawned, and took a seat. "I love waking up to the aroma of bacon. Pancakes and eggs too. What a treat."

Frannie prepared a plate for Stephen and poured him a mug of coffee. "How are you feeling?"

"I slept well. I'm at my best in the mornings. As the day moves forward is when I lose my energy faster than I should. But no worries. I'm fine." Stephen sipped his coffee.

Caleb poured milk in Lily's tin cup. She grasped it with her chubby fingers and drank it all. She grinned with a white mustache above her lip. "More."

He poured her another half cup and chuckled. "She finished her pancake and I haven't started on mine. She must've been hungry."

"Uncle Caleb's pancakes are the best. Right, Lily?" Frannie tore another pancake into pieces for her *dochder*.

Stephen finished half of his three stacked pancakes and pushed the plate aside. "I've had all I can handle of the pancakes. *Danki*, Caleb. You're a good cook."

"My pleasure." Caleb didn't know how Stephen could keep such an even temperament. His *bruder* had always been the more patient of the two. But Stephen was being too tolerant of Frannie's bad behavior. He wouldn't apologize for what he'd said to her. "I'm going to town."

Stephen nodded.

"I'll take care of the kitchen." Frannie smiled at him.

Caleb nodded. It was the least she could do. He bit the inside of his cheek. He wouldn't ruin the goodwill he had made this morning with her. "I'll not be long." Caleb kissed Lily's forehead and left. He planned to speak with Rachael before the bakery opened to customers. He should wait until after work, but he couldn't bear the anxiety. He parked the buggy in front of the bakeshop and went inside to the kitchen. "You left the door open, so I let myself in."

"I always forget to lock it." Magdelena smiled. "I'm glad I forgot this morning, since you came to visit us."

"What brings you here so early?" Rachael pinched the piecrust she'd set in her pan.

"Can I have a couple of minutes of your time in private?" Caleb gazed into her beautiful emerald eyes.

"Sure. I won't be long, Magdelena."

"Take your time." Magdelena slid a tray of molasses cookie dough balls into the oven.

Rachael led him to the baked goods display case in the café part of the bakery. "Would you like anything?"

"I had a big breakfast and too much coffee. *Danki*. I'm curious as to how your evening went with Nathan." Caleb's stomach tightened.

She frowned, and then her gaze met his. "He asked me to court with him, and I told him in a polite way I wasn't interested. He's cooked the last two meals we've had together, and I thought he made them to show his appreciation of what I'd done for them the last eight months. I didn't realize he wanted to make a change from friendship to courtship."

"How did he take your rejection?" Caleb wanted to know everything about her evening with Nathan and his *kinner*. He hoped Nathan wouldn't pursue her to try to change her mind.

"Not well. He blames himself for not making his wishes known before now. I have an inkling you entering my life was what prompted him to ask me to court. I'm not sure how much longer we would've kept our routine, with my helping out at his *haus*, before he would've suggested anything more serious than friendship."

"How did the *kinner* take the news?" Caleb was afraid she'd have a harder time parting from them on a regular basis than she would Nathan.

"They were upset. I will miss them the most. I offered to care for them if Nathan needs me to watch them after work sometimes. I'm unsure whether it would be a good idea. Ava Raber is a widow who came to their *haus* with a pie. The *kinner* mentioned her. I turned twenty-five about a month ago, and she and I share the same birthdate, March twentieth. I suggested he get to know her, and he said he'd rather wait for me."

"Wait for what? We're courting with the hope we'll plan a wedding sometime in the future. Why would he wait? I don't understand what he means." Caleb didn't want Nathan to keep fighting for Rachael's heart.

"He doesn't want to show interest in another woman until we marry. I told him not to wait. My prayer is Ava will win him over with her desserts and finding excuses to talk to him. They would make a perfect match."

"I'll pray Ava wins Nathan over too. I'm happy you chose me." He reached for her hand.

"Of course, I chose you. Why don't you *kumme* over tonight after work?" Rachael kept her hand under his.

"Let me make sure Stephen has supper and then I'll be over by six." Caleb rose. "I shouldn't keep you too long from your baking."

"Isn't Frannie cooking supper?" Rachael quirked her brow.

"We never know from one night to the next. She cooks breakfast and dinner, but not always supper. I scolded her last night when she didn't have something prepared for us. We'd worked later than usual and we were exhausted. She told us what food was available and left us to fend for ourselves. I fixed sandwiches and warmed soup. I told her what I thought until she whined to Stephen to take up for her. She did wash, dry, and put away the dishes. I was sick and tired of her bossy, selfish, and lazy attitude."

"Even if you don't agree with Frannie's ways, don't argue with her. Stephen is in the middle and it's an awkward place for him. As long as he's accepted her ways, go along with it. I'm not saying I agree with her, but it's Stephen who matters."

"It's easier said than done when I'm right there. Stephen would've gone to bed hungry if I hadn't made sandwiches. I worry about his health. He refuses to go to the doctor and insists he's fine. However, you're right. I have to let go of my frustration with her. It does upset him when she and I argue." Caleb respected and *wilkomed* her advice. "*Danki* for letting me bend your ear about Frannie. I should get to work." He smiled. "I'm looking forward to our time together this evening."

Rachael walked with him to the door. "I am too."

He brushed his hand against hers and let his gaze linger

on her eyes, and then he left. When he arrived home, he found Stephen seeding hay. He was relieved Stephen had the energy. It gave him a glimmer of hope Stephen was feeling better.

Caleb took care of his horse and gave the barn a good and thorough cleaning. He scraped manure and put fresh bedding in the stalls and tightened the latches on each one. He liked keeping the barn as clean as possible to eliminate flies and prevent animal diseases.

At five, Stephen joined him in the barn and plopped down on an old, weathered chair. "You left early this morning."

Caleb studied Stephen. His *bruder* had color in his cheeks and he appeared more energetic. "I had something to ask Rachael before the bakery opened."

"I'm surprised you wouldn't wait until this evening, when she's at home." Stephen cocked his head. "Must have been important."

"You wouldn't call me patient. I was anxious to find out what happened last evening when Rachael went to Nathan's. We haven't known each other long, and I was afraid their history and her fondness for his *kinner* might have enticed her to change her mind about me. She told me Nathan did ask to court her and then said he'll wait until we are married to give up on her. She declined and told him not to wait on her."

"You're in love with her, aren't you? Don't rush this relationship. Marriage is forever."

Caleb didn't miss the split-second, rueful expression on his *bruder*'s face.

"It sounds foolish, but I'd marry her tomorrow. I can't imagine anything will ever change my mind. I realize she may need time to get to know me." Caleb couldn't explain the deep connection he felt for her.

She occupied his mind most of the time. He realized

most of their friends and family might have doubts, thinking they were rushing things, but he was sure about her. He couldn't explain it, but he knew she was the one for him.

"Yes. Enjoy the courtship." Stephen rose. "Let's go inside the *haus* and have supper. I'm hungry."

Caleb hoped Frannie had prepared food. He didn't want Stephen to snack and not have a healthy meal. As they walked to the porch, Stephen's breathing was heavy. "Do you want to stop for a minute?"

Stephen nodded and put his hand against the oak tree to brace himself. "I must've overdone it in the field today."

Caleb stood beside his *bruder* and waited for him to catch his breath.

"I'm all right." Stephen began walking again.

They went inside the *haus* and to the kitchen.

Frannie had her cooking apron on, the table was set, and ham and beans and corn bread were on the table. "You're right on time. I was about to call out to you to *kumme* in and have supper."

Caleb smiled. He didn't know what to expect from her from day to day. Some days she was chipper and cooked and cleaned. Other days, she didn't lift a finger except to take care of Lily. He was thankful she'd cooked. His *bruder* loved ham and beans. "Frannie, I'm sorry to miss this wonderful food, but Rachael invited me to her *haus* this evening."

Frannie pinched her lips and turned her back on him.

Stephen kissed Lily on the back of her hand. "Give her our best wishes and have a great time."

He tousled Lily's soft, dark brown hair. "I will."

Frannie poured water into Stephen's glass. "Be quiet when you return. I wouldn't want you to wake Lily."

"Will do." Caleb struggled not to lash out at her again. He put Frannie out of his mind, left, and drove the short distance to Rachael's *haus*. He parked next to another buggy as Joseph Ramer climbed out. He must be here for supper too. "Greetings."

"Here for supper?" Joseph waited while Caleb tied his mare to the hitching post.

"I am." He walked with Joseph to the front door.

Eleanor greeted them and led them to the living room. "Make yourselves comfortable. Rachael's in the kitchen and we're almost ready to put the chicken and rice casserole on the table."

"Sounds wonderful. Here's a little gift for you." Joseph handed Eleanor a small package.

She grinned at Joseph. "How sweet of you. *Danki*. Should I open it now?"

"You're busy. You can open it later." Joseph chose a chair across from Caleb.

"I'm glad you're both here. Caleb, I'll tell Rachael you're here. She's slicing bread at the moment. I'm going to help her set the food on the table and then we'll be ready." She left the room.

Caleb was curious about what Joseph gave Eleanor. Maybe he should've brought Rachael something. "Do you live far from here?"

Joseph shook his head. "About five minutes, I'd guess. How about you?"

"Not far at all. I'm living with my *bruder*, Stephen, and his family. Do you have *kinner*?" He didn't remember Rachael mentioning anything about Joseph having family here.

"I had a son, David. He died about five years ago in his sleep. The doctor was puzzled as to why. My *fraa*, Edwina, was never the same after we lost him. I believe she died of a broken heart. We missed him terribly. I still do." Joseph cleared his throat.

Caleb's stomach clenched at Joseph's story. "I'm sorry. I didn't mean to bring up sad memories for you. I can't imagine how difficult your *fraa* and son's deaths must've been." Caleb felt sorry for the man.

"Eleanor has brought a lot of joy into my life. She's bringing me much happiness just being around her." Joseph grinned. His happy expression put Caleb at ease.

Eleanor entered the living room. "Gentlemen, you may take chairs at the table."

Rachael followed her and smiled at Caleb. "I'm sorry I didn't greet you before now. I had too many things going on at once to leave the kitchen."

"I understand." He took a deep breath. "The scent of warm bread is the best."

They all sat down at the table.

"And we have apple butter." Rachael put a small dish of it near him.

"Perfect." Caleb put a spoonful on his plate and passed the dish to Joseph.

"I can't resist apple butter." Joseph accepted the dish. "Rachael and Eleanor, you've outdone yourselves."

"*Danki*." Rachael's cheeks reddened. "How are you, Joseph? I apologize for not greeting you earlier."

"No need. I'm happy since your *mamm* and I have been getting better acquainted." He exchanged an endearing look with Eleanor. "I appreciate being here and sharing this delicious food with all of you. Shall we bow our heads for prayer?"

Caleb nodded.

Joseph offered a prayer to God for the food, and then they passed the dishes around until their plates were filled. "How is everything at the bakery, Rachael?"

"Magdelena and I have kept up with the baking and

waiting on customers since Maryann quit. I love working there. It's more of a hobby than a job."

Caleb observed Rachael. She didn't look at Joseph and she wasn't her bubbly self. She must still not be comfortable with her *mamm*'s interest in Joseph. He'd ask her later.

Eleanor addressed Caleb. "Rachael said you're concerned about your *bruder*'s health. How is he?"

"*Danki* for asking. He had a better day than most today. He planted hayseed and had the cows out to graze in the pasture. He seemed to have more energy, but around five, he had trouble catching his breath. He's stubborn and won't go to the doctor. He insists he's fine, but I don't believe him. I worry about him."

Frannie was no help. She didn't seem concerned. It was easier for her to ignore problems. He had to keep those thoughts to himself. He shouldn't complain about her here.

"I'll keep your *bruder* in my prayers," Eleanor said.

"I will too." Joseph gave Caleb an empathetic smile. "Rachael and Caleb, please join Eleanor and me for a stroll through the market Friday evening. They'll have picnic tables available, and we can buy food after we've shopped."

"I haven't been to the event. What do the vendors have for sale?" Caleb had read an advertisement for the event, but he had forgotten about it. He was glad Joseph mentioned it. What a fun thing to do with their ladies.

Joseph grinned. "They're locals who have farms or other businesses. Most have hobbies on the side, and this gives them an opportunity to sell anything they don't use or things they've made. There are dry goods, cooking utensils, pots, pans, tools, yarn, fabric, clothes, toys, potato boxes, hope chests, and more for reasonable prices. I don't always buy something, but it's fun to browse."

Caleb glanced at Rachael. She hadn't said a word. "Rachael, would you like to go?"

She focused on buttering her bread. "I'm not sure how long I'll be at the bakery on Friday. It's usually our busiest day. May we discuss it later?"

Something was troubling her. "Sure." Caleb wouldn't press her in front of her *mamm* and Joseph.

Eleanor stood and took her plate to the sink. "Ready for dessert? Rachael brought home lemon bars."

"I'd love two." Caleb gave Eleanor an impish grin. "They're one of my favorites."

"One for me. *Danki*." Joseph patted his stomach. "It's all I have room for."

Rachael carried the rest of the dirty dishes to the sink, her limp more pronounced. "I'm going to pass on dessert." She checked the water on the stove she'd had heating for the dishes.

Caleb frowned. Was she tired? Was she ill? It wasn't like her to be unsociable.

Eleanor served dessert and ignored Rachael. "Enjoy."

Caleb hurried to clean his plate. He joined Rachael, washing the dishes, and grabbed a dish towel from the counter. "I'll dry. Eleanor and Joseph, we'll take care of the kitchen if you'd like to enjoy the sunset happening soon."

"*Danki*, Caleb. We'll take you up on the suggestion." Eleanor lifted her plate. "Let's take our lemon bars to the back porch. We'll finish our dessert, and then I'll open your present. I left it on the end table by my chair in the living room."

"*Danki* to you both. I've enjoyed our time together." Joseph smiled at them.

Rachael gave him a weak smile and nodded.

"I have too." Caleb patted Joseph on the back.

Eleanor and Joseph left them alone.

"Are you all right?" Caleb accepted a platter she'd washed.

"Yes. Why?" Rachael didn't meet his gaze.

"You're quiet and your limp is more noticeable tonight. Are you in pain?" He didn't want to mention her limp, but he'd noticed it was better some days than others. He was worried about her.

"I'm tired, but my leg isn't the problem. I'm shocked Mamm is interested in Joseph. It's difficult to see her with a man other than Daed." Rachael scrubbed a plate she'd already washed.

Caleb reached for the plate, set it aside, and held her wet hands. "No one will replace your *daed*. But he's gone. Your *mamm* deserves happiness with Joseph, if she chooses. Why are you not happy for them?"

"I should be delighted for them. He brings her gifts, and she's got a lilt to her step and has been giddy ever since they've been spending time together. She beams when she mentions his name, which is much better than her mourning Daed for the rest of her life. It's been difficult for me, but I shouldn't stand in her way."

Caleb understood Rachael's hesitation because this was new and different for her. He had no doubt she'd put her desires aside and support the couple. "It's a blessing she and Joseph are courting. We should support her in her newfound happiness."

She nodded. "It helps to have discussed them with you. I'm ashamed for not showing her more support. I should trust Mamm's judgment and be nicer to Joseph."

Eleanor and Joseph joined them in the kitchen. Eleanor held out a carved box with a heart on top. "Isn't this lovely? Joseph made it for me. I can keep my dress pins inside it."

"It's beautiful, Mamm." Rachael accepted the box from

her and examined it. She passed it back to Mamm. "Joseph, you do nice work." She met Joseph's gaze. "And Caleb and I will go to the market with you and Mamm Friday evening."

"I'm so pleased. *Danki*, Rachael." Mamm squeezed her arm.

"I am as well. Do you want us to meet you at the bakery or do you want to *kumme* home first?" Joseph grinned.

"I'll meet you in front of the bakery at five. Is this all right with you, Caleb?"

"Yes. It suits me fine." Caleb was proud of Rachael.

She had made the effort to show her *mamm* her support. He stayed and visited with Rachael, Joseph, and Eleanor for a half hour and then he bid them farewell. He hoped they'd spend more time with Rachael's *mamm* and Joseph. Caleb was protective of Rachael and Eleanor. He hoped Joseph would prove worthy of these two important women in his life.

Chapter 4

Rachael added a teaspoon of cinnamon to her cookie batter Wednesday morning. "Magdelena, what are your thoughts about Joseph Ramer?"

"I don't know him well. He and his *fraa* moved to Charm two years ago. It's sad his *fraa* died this past year. I noticed him and your *mamm* sitting together after Sunday services. Are they courting?"

"Yes. Mamm told me he visits often and brings her gifts." Rachael sighed. "He hasn't given me any reason to distrust him, but what do we really know about him?"

"His *fraa*, Edwina, was a shy and frail woman. I spoke with her a couple of times." Magdelena scraped warm oatmeal cookies from a tray onto a plate for the display case. She frowned. "I'm not sure how I would feel if Mamm died and Daed courted another woman. But everyone wants to be loved. Mr. Ramer is a soft-spoken gentleman who has kept to himself since she died. I've never heard a negative comment about him. Your *mamm* is wise. Trust her." Magdelena glanced at the clock. "It's time to unlock the front door for customers. I'll be back."

Rachael carried a tray of raspberry jam pastries from the kitchen to the café and slid them into the display case. Caleb and Magdelena had given her advice. She should be thankful Joseph came into Mamm's life, and she'd be more encouraging. She should get to know Joseph better, rather than depend on what others said about him.

An attractive woman stepped into the bakery, holding Joy's hand. She had the prettiest honey-blond hair tied back with a white ribbon. She had a beautiful smile and kind brown eyes.

"Rachael!" Joy hurried to her and hugged her legs.

She didn't understand why Joy was with this Englischer. Where was Nathan? She bent to meet Joy's eyes. "What's wrong?"

The young woman came behind Joy and addressed Rachael and Magdelena. "I'm Holly Maxwell. I'm visiting my aunt for a couple of days. I found this little one on the main road and thought she was too young to be walking alone. I offered her a ride and suggested I take her home. She insisted I bring her to the bakery to speak with Rachael. I assume you're Rachael."

Rachael kept her hand on Joy's shoulder as she stood. "Yes. I'm Rachael Schlabach, and I'm close to Joy and her *bruder*, Thad." She nodded to Magdelena. "This is my *schweschder*-in-law and coworker, Magdelena Schlabach." She faced Joy. Nathan wouldn't have allowed Joy to take a walk alone. "You didn't tell your *daed* you were leaving home, did you?"

Joy frowned. "No."

"He'll be worried sick about you." Rachael would need to take her home.

Magdelena lifted the glass dome on top of the display counter and removed six sugar cookies. She put them in a bag and held it out for Holly. "Please accept these as a gift. It was kind of you to bring Joy to us."

"Thank you. The warm bread and sugary scents are

delightful. I'd like to purchase the vanilla cake. My aunt will love it."

Magdelena accepted her money and handed her the wrapped cake. "Thanks again."

Holly squeezed Joy's hand. "It was nice meeting you. I should be on my way. You take care, Joy."

Joy beamed at her. "*Danki* for the ride."

They bid Holly farewell, and then Rachael faced Joy. "You know better than to leave without telling your *daed* where you're going. Holly could've been a kidnapper. We're fortunate she is a sweet Englischer. You should not accept rides from strangers. Why didn't you tell him you wanted to talk to me?"

Joy shook her head. "I asked him to take me to your *haus* or the bakery and he refused." She shrugged. "I'm a big girl, and I thought I could walk to town. I didn't realize it was so far. I chose the bakery, hoping you'd give me a cookie. I'm glad Holly offered me a ride. My legs were tired."

Why had Nathan refused to bring Joy to visit her? She understood his feelings might be hurt, but that was no reason to keep her from the *kinner*. Was she being naïve? Maybe he thought it best to create distance between them. He had to move on with his life.

"I have missed you. I'm happy you're here, but I'll take you home now. Your *daed* won't be happy you left home without telling him where you were going."

Joy pouted. "No. I want to live with you."

Magdelena waited on two customers.

Rachael guided Joy to the kitchen. "Has something happened to make you unhappy at home?"

"Daed isn't gentle like you when he brushes my hair, and he doesn't play with me. He's sad all the time. I'm sure he misses you too. Why won't you marry my *daed*? We need you."

Rachael's heart ached. Joy's plea and worried eyes filled her with guilt. She'd missed Joy and Thad, and she had made herself stay away from them to allow Nathan to seek Ava or another woman. She should've known it wouldn't be easy for this little one to accept she wouldn't be there for them as she had been before Caleb entered her life. "I never meant to upset you. I'm sorry, Joy."

Caleb cleared his throat. "Good morning."

Rachael startled. She hadn't noticed him entering the kitchen. "Good morning." She couldn't think of a worse time for him to appear. "Joy, greet Caleb."

Joy crossed her arms and pouted. "No. It's all his fault. He took you away from us."

Caleb squatted in front of her. "I'd like us to be friends. Will you give me a chance?"

"No. I want you to go far away from here. We want Rachael back." She scowled at him.

"Treat Caleb with respect. You don't talk to adults that way. Now apologize." Rachael's head hurt. She didn't want to scold Joy. This little girl needed love and attention.

She acted as if Rachael had abandoned her. After losing her *mamm* and now Rachael, she could understand why Joy was frustrated. What was the solution?

"Joy left home on foot to visit me. An Englischer offered her a ride, and she insisted the woman bring her to me here."

"Would you allow me to take you home? Rachael has to work. Does your *daed* know you're here?" Caleb kept his distance from her.

"No." Joy harrumphed. "I want Rachael to take me home."

This was going from bad to worse. "I'll take her home. Magdelena won't mind."

Caleb nodded. "I'll leave the two of you. I came to tell you I'll pick you up at your *haus* Friday evening after work instead of you staying in town and both of us driving home separately. We can also follow your *mamm* and Joseph to the market event in case they want to leave earlier than we do."

"*Danki*." She gave him a warm smile. She looked forward to spending time with him.

He tipped his hat to them and left.

She held Joy's hand and walked to the main café part of the bakery. "Magdelena, I'll take Joy home and be right back." Rachael's fingers hurt from Joy squeezing them. But she wouldn't complain.

Magdelena stooped to Joy. "You should tell your *daed* where you are at all times, and you should be careful not to trust everyone. Again, it's not safe to accept rides from strangers."

Joy sucked in her bottom lip and avoided Magdelena's gaze. "She was pretty and nice. She wouldn't hurt me."

"You cannot tell if a stranger has good intentions or not. I mean it, Joy. This is an important rule to follow." Rachael hoped she was getting through to Joy. The child was too trusting.

Joy shrugged. "I won't accept a ride from a stranger again."

"I should hope not. Give Magdelena a hug." Rachael didn't want to face Nathan with having caused his little girl such heartache and confusion.

This time, Joy obeyed.

"Goodbye." Magdelena hurried to greet the customer *kumming* in as they left.

Rachael needed to run her errand as quickly as possible.

She didn't want to leave Magdelena alone any longer than necessary.

Rachael retrieved her buggy from the livery. She was glad Nathan's *haus* wasn't far.

"Remember Ava?" Joy toyed with her *kapp* ribbon.

"Yes. She's a kind and caring woman. Why do you ask?"

Joy crossed her arms. "She's visited us, but she pays more attention to Daed than me."

"She would be a good friend for you, Thad, and your *daed*." Rachael was a tinge jealous that Ava might be taking her place with the *kinner*. Caring for them had been one of the happiest times in her life. She'd promote Ava to Joy. It wasn't fair of her to be jealous. She'd chosen Caleb.

"She can be my friend, but she can't marry Daed. I told her so, and she hasn't been back since then." Joy gave Rachael a naughty grin.

"You cannot make decisions for your *daed*, and he would be upset if he knew you were unkind to Ava. You should apologize to her. You are to respect her." Rachael was concerned Joy was too outspoken.

She reminded her of her friend, Ellie, who was now married and had a *boppli*. Ellie was bold and protective of her friends. She spoke what was on her mind and didn't hold back. She'd mellowed a little since marrying her other friend, Maryann's *bruder*, Joel. This wasn't a trait she wanted Joy to keep.

Joy folded her hands in her lap. "Next time we have Sunday service or if she *kummes* to our *haus* again, I'll apologize."

"Good girl." She parked the buggy in front of the barn.

Nathan met them. "Joy, where have you been? I've been trying to find you. Thad and I searched the property, went to the school, knowing it would be too early for anyone to be there, and I asked our neighbors. I was ready to go into town. Rachael, how did she end up with you?"

Thad's eyes widened. "Rachael, I'm glad you're here. Joy, you've been bad. How could you worry us like this? We thought someone kidnapped you."

Joy huffed. "You wouldn't have let me go to the bakery, so I didn't ask. I met a new friend. A real pretty lady named Holly. She offered me a ride and my legs were tired, so I said yes. And I brought Rachael to our *haus*, where she belongs. I did it all by myself." She jumped out of the buggy, wearing a satisfied grin.

Nathan glared at her. "You're in big trouble, young lady. Go into the *haus*, sit in your room, and think about what you've done. You disobeyed me, put yourself in danger, and kept Rachael from work."

Rachael stepped out of the buggy, and Joy hugged her. "Please don't stay away from us this long again."

"Get in the *haus*, Joy." Nathan pointed to the front door.

Joy dragged her feet to the *haus* and went inside.

"I apologize for Joy's behavior. We shouldn't keep you any longer." Nathan's sad eyes bore into hers.

Thad waved her inside the barn. "Before you go, I'd like to show you the baby goat. We named him Scruffy."

Rachael and Nathan followed him.

"He's cute, with his scruffy white coat and larger ears than most goats." She should head back to the bakery right away, but she didn't have the heart to say no to Thad. Her heart pounded in her chest and her headache hadn't subsided. She had no idea what to say to Nathan or Thad. She'd been hit with a dose of reality from Joy. She had kidded herself if she thought this transition in their routine and her courtship with Caleb would be easy. She'd ignored the tickling thoughts to check on them when she missed them.

She wanted them to grow accustomed to their separation and her spending time with Caleb.

Nathan opened the small stall door, and they stooped to pet Scruffy. Scruffy rose to his feet and tried to lick Rachael's cheek.

She reached out and scratched his ear. "You're a loving little pet."

Thad rubbed the goat's back. "He's been fun. I feed and take care of him. Joy liked him at first, but she prefers playing with the barn cats."

Nathan grabbed the empty bowl in the stall. "I'll fetch some water."

"I'm happy you're here, Rachael. I've missed you. Daed explained we needed to leave you alone while you and Caleb court. He said you chose him and we should respect your decision. Is it hard for you not to visit us?" Thad held his mouth in a grim line.

Thad was a wise little boy. "Yes. You and Joy are on my mind often. But in order for your *daed* to consider another woman and for me to accept Caleb's offer to court, we have to let each other go. It's hard on you and Joy, but I don't know how else to handle it." Her stomach rolled with guilt.

"Daed said he would've married you, but he was too late. We need you more than Caleb does. He doesn't have *kinner*. We need a *mamm*, and Daed needs a *fraa*. Can't you forgive him for waiting too long?" His pleading eyes tore at her soul.

"I care about your *daed* as a friend. He's a wonderful man. But Caleb has my heart, and I'm sorry this has caused you unhappiness. In time, your *daed* will court a woman he deems appropriate for him and for you and Joy." This was too much adult talk for Thad, but she didn't want to shrug off his concerns or be dishonest with him.

Nathan returned with a full water bowl for Scruffy. He

set it near the pet. "Rachael, I would like to have a private talk with you before you leave. Can you spare the time? I'll understand if not. I realize you need to return to the bakery."

Thad hugged her neck. "I'll see you at Sunday service."

She nodded. "It was good to speak with you today, and it was fun to meet Scruffy. Take care."

Nathan and she strolled along the pond's edge. The purple, white, and yellow wildflowers added to the beauty of the blue water and sunshine. "Joy has become a challenge to raise. She's smarter, braver, more stubborn, and more determined than your average six-year-old."

"Don't let her manipulate you." She gazed at him. "I would be happy to keep them for you from time to time, and so would Mamm, to give you a break."

"It's best we don't give them hope we'll have a future together. They would read too much into it. Don't get me wrong—I would marry you tomorrow if you'd let me."

Her cheeks warmed. "I care for you, Nathan. I really do. But your heart wasn't free when Caleb came into my life. His heart was ready. It would've been convenient for us to marry, but I chose not to settle where love is concerned a long time ago. The *kinner* are resilient, and they'll accept things as they are over time. May I ask where you stand with Ava?"

"She has brought desserts and full meals to us. I didn't invite her in the first couple of times she came to our *haus*, but she kept bringing food dishes and desserts. I finally did relent and she spent time with us a couple of evenings. She's not you, and you're the only one for me. I'll wait until you marry Caleb, then I'll be resigned to make an effort with another woman."

She opened her mouth.

He held up his finger to her lips. "You said not to wait.

I'm also determined and stubborn, like Joy. Although I'm more patient." He shrugged with his hands out and grinned.

Caleb sat at the supper table with his *bruder* and family. He'd combined all the vegetable leftovers and added ham bits to create a stew. He wondered if Rachael had stayed long at Nathan's when she returned Joy today. Nathan was a good catch for any woman. He didn't discount him as a threat to his relationship with Rachael. He trusted her, not Nathan. She would no doubt end things with him before she would take up with Nathan if she chose to make a change. Those were words he hoped never to hear.

Stephen, pale and short of breath, managed to grin. "I'll pray." He offered a prayer to God for the food.

Frannie raised her chin and wore a sly grin. "I picked up *boppli* clothes from Liza that her *dochder*, Lorianne, has outgrown for Lily today. I noticed Rachael and Nathan together taking a stroll. They looked like a couple in love."

Caleb's brows furrowed. "Frannie, stop with this. You want to rile me and you're a gossip. You have no idea what was said between Nathan and Rachael." Why did she provoke him?

Her sly grin said she took satisfaction in it. It annoyed him.

Stephen held up his palm. "I agree with Caleb. Don't make something out of nothing."

Frannie smirked. "Don't say I didn't warn you." Again, she seemed to take satisfaction in provoking him. She frustrated him.

Stephen glowered at her. "Frannie, enough. Don't say another word."

Frannie shrugged.

Caleb kept to himself the rest of the evening. He went to the barn to avoid Frannie. He trusted Rachael. Frannie was a troublemaker. Why wouldn't the woman want him to be happy? Was she afraid of losing her cook, nanny, and cleaner?

Friday evening, Caleb changed into a fresh shirt and pants and drove to Rachael's *haus* to pick her up for their outing. He'd been too busy in the garden yesterday to visit her. Stephen's stamina wasn't holding out for an entire day, and he'd had to take over more of the chores. He didn't mind, but he wished his *bruder* wasn't so stubborn. He'd begged him, to no avail, to let Dr. Harrison examine him whenever he got the chance. He'd stayed clear of Frannie, and she'd been on her best behavior when she encountered him. Stephen must've gotten through to her to watch her tongue.

Rachael answered the door. "We're ready." She motioned for Joseph and Mamm to leave. "It's a smart idea to take separate buggies to give us more room to bring home the things we buy. We may both fill our back benches." She grinned.

"I was thinking the same thing." Joseph smiled at her.

Caleb and Rachael followed Eleanor and Joseph to the farmers' market and food stands downtown and left their buggies at the livery. They reached the boardwalk and main street, where locals were selling their handmade dry goods, desserts, handcrafted wood items, and more. The crowd was thick.

He kept his hand on Rachael's elbow as they wormed their way through the men, women, and *kinner*. "I'm glad you and Magdelena didn't keep the bakery open past regular hours during this event."

"Liza said we should enjoy the market and not worry about it. She's the best boss and friend." Rachael looked at the salted nuts at the stand ahead of them.

The short, bald man yelled and waved them over. "Salted nuts! *Kumme* and get them before they're gone!"

Joseph leaned close to her ear. "Let's go to the peddler's cart. I'll buy us each a small bag."

"I like salted nuts." Rachael nodded, and they made their way to the cart.

Joseph handed them each a bag.

She plopped one in her mouth. "*Danki.*"

Caleb liked Joseph. He wasn't bold or loud. He had an average build and kind eyes and appeared healthy and happy. Eleanor laughed more when she and Joseph were together. She and Joseph had a strong friendship and appeared in love with each other. It was obvious by the way they interacted and leaned into each other. He could relate. He was happiest when he was with Rachael.

The four of them shopped and admired the pottery, furniture, and household items for sale.

Caleb bought Rachael a bag of different colors of yarn she contemplated buying. "What will you make with it?"

"I have several ideas." Rachael grinned. "*Danki.*" She glanced around. "We've lost Mamm and Joseph."

Caleb stood on a bench and searched for them. "They're at the beef sandwich wagon." He led her to them. "Is this what you'd like to have for supper?"

Joseph held up his palm. "You don't have to choose the same thing. You can buy food from a different vendor. There's a picnic table behind the bank. Meet us there. If it's available, the spot will be a comfortable place for us to enjoy our food."

"I'd love a beef sandwich with mushrooms and onions. How about you?" Rachael peered at Caleb.

"Done. I'll buy us each one." Joseph had already purchased sandwiches for him and Eleanor, and he didn't want to hold them up. He hurried to pay the peddler and collect his food.

On their way to the picnic table, Caleb inhaled the aroma of fried apple pies, fried chicken on a stick, and doughnuts. He would satisfy his sweet tooth later. They reached the picnic table, and there was a woman alone there. She was a pretty woman, and he was surprised she'd be there by herself. Perhaps she was waiting on a friend or beau.

Rachael put her hand on the woman's shoulder. "Ava, do you mind if we join you?"

"Not at all." Ava greeted them all.

Eleanor and Joseph chose to sit on a bench under the big willow tree, giving the excuse that it would give them more room at the table. Caleb suspected they loved having time together alone.

"How are you, Ava?" Rachael unwrapped her sandwich and took a bite.

"I'm frustrated and discouraged. I've done everything to gain Nathan's attention and he won't give me the time of day. Those *kinner* need a *mamm*." Ava frowned.

Caleb bristled at the mention of Nathan's name. Maybe if he gave the two women time to talk, Rachael would work hard at getting Nathan and Ava together. "If you women don't mind, I'm going to buy us some fry pies. I'll buy some for your *mamm* and Joseph too. I'll be back."

Rachael nodded.

Rachael waited until Caleb was out of earshot. "I wish there was something I could do to help match you with Nathan. Do you have any ideas? You would be perfect for him and the *kinner*." She wouldn't worry about them if Nathan, Joy, and Thad had Ava to take her place.

Ava narrowed her eyes. "I didn't want to say anything

while Caleb was with us, but Joy said you visited them the other day. I tried again to make an effort to get invited to supper by taking over my chicken-and-noodle dish. Nathan did invite me in, but our conversation was strained. Joy couldn't stop talking about your time at their home. They'll never move on if you don't detach from them. They need time apart from you to heal and open their hearts to me or another woman."

"I have stayed away. Joy ran away from home, and a stranger picked her up and brought her to the bakery, as Joy insisted. I returned her home. I'll admit I miss them, but I understand the point you're making, and I agree with it." Rachael wasn't happy she had to explain herself to Ava, but she understood her friend's frustration. And she didn't want this to damage their friendship.

"I'm relieved it wasn't a casual visit. Since you're courting Caleb, I was confused as to why you'd be there alone, without him. I should've known better. I'm sorry I misjudged you." Ava seemed chagrined.

Caleb returned with fried apple pies for each of them and handed one to Rachael and another to Ava. He went to give Eleanor and Joseph theirs and then returned to Rachael. "They are scrumptious. Half of mine is gone already."

"They are tasty." Ava took another bite.

Rachael was appreciative of Caleb's timing. She'd change the subject. She gestured to her bag of yarn. "I bought a bag of yarn from the vendor over there." She pointed to the couple. "They have the best price going, if you need some."

Ava finished her dessert. "I'll visit them and then head home. I'm glad we had a chance to chat. Enjoy the market. *Danki*, again, Caleb, for the fried apple pie." Ava stood and weaved through the townsfolk to the vendor.

Rachael watched her leave. She hadn't divulged what Nathan told her. Should she have? She didn't want Ava to get her heart broken, and she also didn't want Ava to think she was boasting because Nathan said he would wait on her. She wanted Ava to keep trying with Nathan. He might change his mind and consider Ava.

She didn't want to think about Ava and Nathan anymore. She should concentrate on her time here with Caleb, Mamm, and Joseph. She glanced at Joseph and Mamm. Joseph whispered something in her *mamm*'s ear. Mamm giggled like a love-struck schoolgirl. Her *mamm* beamed when she and Joseph were together. Joseph hadn't gone overboard to win Rachael over. He'd been himself. "Kind," a "gentleman," and "considerate" were the words she used when she thought of him. She had expected to have to force herself to like him, but she'd found him effortless to be around and talk to.

Caleb tilted his head. "I wanted to give you some private time with Ava, so I used the fried apple pies as an excuse. How did your conversation go?"

"She's disappointed Nathan isn't considering her. I don't know what I can do. She had the wrong impression about my visit to their *haus* Wednesday, when I took Joy home. Joy insinuated I stopped in on my own. Ava didn't understand why I would go there without you. I'm thankful she confronted me so I could explain." Rachael didn't tell Caleb that Nathan insisted on waiting on her to marry Caleb before he'd consider another woman. She didn't want to upset him, and she shouldn't have gotten out of the buggy and stayed to speak with Nathan. "I worry about the *kinner*."

"We should keep our distance from Nathan. It would be awkward for us to visit them. Give the *kinner* time to adapt to you no longer *kumming* to their place to take care of them. They'll adjust."

"You're right." Rachael took another bite of her fried apple pie, juice trickling down her chin. She dabbed her lips and chin with her napkin. "They put more cinnamon in their pies. I'm going to add more to the ones I make. It makes all the difference."

Joseph and Mamm left the bench under the willow tree and approached them.

Joseph glanced at their empty wrappings. "Do you want more food or sugary desserts?"

"I couldn't fit another morsel of anything in my stomach." Caleb patted his midsection.

"Are you ready to head home, or do you want to shop more? There's a piglet race in ten minutes. It might be fun." Joseph gestured to the race area.

"Let's stay for the race," Mamm said.

"Sounds like fun." Rachael would find any reason to extend her time with Caleb, and she was having an enjoyable time with Mamm and Joseph. She threw her wrappings in the trash can.

They reached the makeshift racecourse and laughed at the little piglets running in their narrow pathway to the dangling carrots at the finish line.

A tall and attractive man dressed in a button-down yellow shirt and brown pleated pants waved his sharp straw hat and yelled, "I won! I won!"

Rachael whispered to Caleb, "What did he win?"

"Twenty dollars. The man in charge has a list of prizes posted on the tree over by his cart. I read it as we passed by."

Joseph moved to Caleb. "Most of the townsfolk are leaving the market and heading to the livery. It's about time for the market to close. Are you ready to leave?"

"Yes. Let's head to our buggies." Caleb kept his hand on

Rachael's elbow to keep them from getting separated. Joseph did the same with Eleanor. They retrieved their buggies and drove to Eleanor and Rachael's *haus*.

The two men walked the women to the door. Joseph held up his forefinger. "Before we men depart, I'd like to invite all of you to my home tomorrow at six. I'll ask Toby and Magdelena to join us too."

Eleanor beamed. "You don't have to cook. Everyone can *kumme* here."

Joseph shook his head. "This time, let me take care of everything."

Eleanor clasped her hands behind her back. "I won't argue. I like a man who cooks."

Caleb winced. "I'm sorry. I promised Frannie I'd watch Lily so she and Stephen can go to a restaurant. But Rachael will go, right, sweetheart?"

She nodded. Did Joseph ask them to supper for a special reason? She shouldn't make too much of it. His offer might have been to continue to get to know their family better. "Yes. I'll bring dessert. Mamm, I'll *kumme* home and we'll go to Joseph's together. Caleb, I wish you could *kumme*."

"Me too." Caleb frowned.

They said their goodbyes, and the men went their separate ways home.

Rachael had had a wonderful time with Caleb, as always. She was sad each time they parted. Caleb seemed to like Joseph, and he had influenced her to accept him as a suitor for Mamm. Caleb's insight was important to her. She wanted a husband who would bring out the best in her. She felt a pang of guilt. She wished her courtship with Caleb could be as easygoing as Mamm's with Joseph, but she couldn't blame anyone but herself. She had to reveal the truth about herself sooner or later. She preferred later.

Chapter 5

Rachael met Magdelena at the livery Saturday morning, and they strolled over to the bakery together. She unlocked the door, with Joseph and Mamm heavy on her mind. "I understand we'll be going to Joseph's *haus* this evening. I understand he's invited you and Toby."

Magdelena removed her apron from the wooden peg, pulled it over her head, and tied the waist strings behind her back. "He knocked on our door last night. A knock later in the evening is always concerning. He told Toby he'd been with you, Caleb, and Eleanor at the market in town. We were relieved nothing was wrong and happy his reason for the visit was an invitation."

"Don't you find it odd he's invited all our family to his *haus*? He also invited Caleb, but he had committed to watching Lily for Frannie. Until now, Mamm has cooked, or he takes her out for dinner or supper." Now Rachael wondered why.

Magdelena stood across from her at the large butcher-block table they had in the center of the kitchen to create breads and desserts. She dropped spices into her bowl. "Maybe he'll ask us to his home more often. He may have waited to cook for us to gauge how things were going between him and Eleanor before taking this step."

"Toby has been busy, and we don't talk often. What does he think of Joseph and Mamm courting?"

"He isn't thrilled. His attitude is selfish. He doesn't want another *daed*. I have a different perspective on this than Toby. At Sunday services, or when I've run into them in town, Eleanor is glowing, and he's beaming. She should let herself fall in love again and marry if she chooses."

"Caleb has influenced me to accept Joseph and Mamm's courtship. Joseph's done nothing wrong. I was being selfish about them when I first found out. I have changed my attitude about them, and I agree with you. I'm surprised you didn't win Toby over to your way of thinking. He listens to you most of the time." Rachael hoped Toby wouldn't stand in their way.

Mamm often hummed hymns, and her cheerfulness was better than her sadness and grief after Daed's passing. She should encourage Toby to trust Mamm to make the right decision for herself.

"Toby asked me to keep what he told me about Joseph in confidence. We're best friends, and his concern has put me in a difficult position. I've been dying to tell you what has him in a tizzy, but he won't budge on letting me tell you. He promised to bring his problem with Joseph out in the open tonight."

Rachael's mouth hung open. "So something's not right about Joseph?" She didn't want Mamm's heart to break. What did Toby know? It couldn't be too bad if Magdelena was still rooting for them.

"Let's change the subject before I say too much. Did you have fun at the market? We considered going, but Toby and Andrew chose to finish a table to sell. I didn't mind. I visited with Maryann and little Betsy while they worked. She's adorable. I told her we miss her working with us, but we're glad she's enjoying her marriage to Andrew and raising Betsy. She loves being home, and Betsy keeps her busy."

"Will you leave the bakery when you have a *boppli*?" Rachael would miss her, and she didn't know any of their friends who would want to work at the bakery.

"Betsy is almost two and a half and she's into everything. She's also talking more. Maryann said she's hoping they have more *kinner*. All of this has made me think about what I will do when I have a *boppli*. I will quit to be with my family like Maryann. I won't want to miss his or her first words, first steps, daily growth, and so much more. I hope we have four or more *kinner*. Don't worry. We'll hire someone to take my place before I leave." She grinned. "If you and Caleb marry, you might have a *boppli* before me, and then you'll want to stay home."

Rachael wished what Magdelena said was true. "I pray you and Toby will have a *boppli* soon. I want to be an aunt." She smiled. "You'll both be wonderful parents." She'd spoil their *kinner* rotten. But this wasn't a subject she wanted to dwell on. She hadn't told her friends the whole story about the accident that took her fiancé John's life.

"Our dog Patches will have to do for now. He loves to snuggle with me in the evenings. Tell me about the vendors and what was on sale last night." Magdelena stirred her blueberry filling.

Rachael laughed. "Caleb and I had a good time together, and Mamm and Joseph did too. We stuffed ourselves with beef sandwiches, nuts, and fried apple pies." She told Magdelena about the picnic tables they found and her conversation with Ava. "I'm fortunate I ran into Ava, and we had a chance to clear up any misunderstanding she had about my visit to Nathan's to take Joy home. She had the impression from Joy that I'd made an effort to visit them."

Magdelena laughed. "Joy is wiser than you'd expect at

her age. She's learning a bad habit, using her words to her advantage. I hope Nathan settles on Ava or another woman who will squelch that kind of behavior in Joy. I'm glad you and Ava talked too. She's a nice girl. Did you do anything else?"

"Yes. An Englischer raced little piglets and awarded money to the winner. It was the funniest thing to watch. We had a lot of fun. I'm glad we went." Rachael looked forward to attending more events with Caleb, Mamm, and Joseph.

Rachael baked some of her favorite things all day to line the bakery shelves. She baked five loaves of white bread, four blueberry and raisin pies, three peach pies, and peanut butter fudge. She set aside a peach pie to take to Joseph's *haus*. "Magdelena, Mamm and I will meet you at Joseph's place at six."

"Are you bringing the peach pie or is it for you?" Magdelena opened the front door.

"It's for all of us." Rachael smiled.

"I was hoping you'd say for all of us. *Danki* for not pushing me to tell you more about what Toby told me about Joseph."

"I wanted to coax you into telling me, but I don't want to do anything to compromise your and Toby's relationship." Rachael kissed Magdelena's cheek. "I couldn't ask for a better *schweschder*-in-law and best friend." She departed from Magdelena and drove home. Her friend hadn't divulged a clue as to Toby's concern about Joseph. Hopefully she'd find out soon enough.

Mamm came out of her bedroom when she got there. "I'll be in the buggy."

"We've got time to spare. Are you in a hurry?" Rachael raised her brows.

"I'd like to arrive early to help Joseph. You don't mind, do you?" Mamm tucked a stray hair back in Rachael's *kapp*.

"I'll change my dress and we'll leave." She passed Mamm the peach pie.

"My favorite." Mamm grinned.

Rachael dressed in a clean dress and joined her *mamm* at the buggy.

Mamm sat beside her and held on to the pie. "I'm curious as to what Joseph has prepared for us. I didn't know he could cook."

How serious were Mamm and Joseph? Had they discussed marriage? Mamm seemed anxious.

"Are you in love with him?" Rachael held her breath.

Mamm blushed. "Yes. We haven't been courting long, but I fell in love with him early on. I wanted to marry again if the right man came along, and he did. My marriage to your *daed* was blissful, and no one can take his place. Joseph caught me by surprise with his interest in me, and I couldn't ask for a better beau."

"I'm glad you're happy." She hoped Joseph would have a reasonable explanation to Toby's inquiry. Should she warn Mamm? Her pulse quickened. She didn't want Mamm to question Joseph. Then Magdelena would know she had hinted to Mamm there might be a problem with Toby about Joseph. She'd have to keep quiet and let Toby ask Joseph about his issue. What could it be?

Mamm patted Rachael's leg. "I appreciate your support. I understand accepting another man in my life will be an adjustment. I'm certain you'll find Joseph a *wilkom* addition to our family, when and if he proposes."

"Have you spoken to Toby about Joseph?" Rachael gripped the reins tighter. She prayed Toby would be satisfied with Joseph's answer to his question and wouldn't disapprove of Joseph and cause a division between him and Mamm. They'd always been a close family.

"No. He and Toby have visited at after-Sunday services and chatted when they've run into each other a couple of times in town. I don't expect Toby to oppose if Joseph asks me to marry him." Mamm stared at the road.

Rachael's heart pounded. Mamm would be hurt and frustrated if Toby showed his opposition. Toby had taken on the role of the leader in their family after Daed died. He'd need to step aside and let Joseph take care of Mamm. She didn't want strife in their family. Did he have a valid concern, or was he being unreasonable? She dreaded Toby bringing the matter to Joseph's attention. What if Toby had a valid point? This evening could turn upside down for all of them. She didn't want any trouble. "If he proposes, you have my blessing."

Mamm beamed. "*Danki*."

Rachael nodded. They arrived and joined the others inside.

"May I help you, Joseph?" Mamm held the peach pie.

"I'd appreciate you setting the table. The beef and vegetables are almost ready to serve. The rest of you can relax and enjoy one another's company. We'll call for you soon." Joseph followed Mamm to the kitchen.

Rachael couldn't deny the connection between Mamm and Joseph had been consistent each time she'd been with them.

"This is a nice place. You could almost eat off the floor, and nothing is out of place. I'm impressed Joseph can keep it this clean and neat. I'd at least have a pile of laundry hiding somewhere if it were me," Toby said.

"He may have dirty clothes hidden," Rachael teased.

"You both stop. Joseph always has a neat appearance, and the same goes for his home. Husband of mine, you could take lessons." Magdelena sat next to Toby on the settee and nudged him.

Mamm entered the room. "Supper is on the table."

Rachael was impressed. Joseph had cooked a marvelous supper. The beef slices with broth overtop and his selection of vegetables gave the table color. His beef, buttered broccoli, carrots, and diced onions painted a beautiful meal. She loved applesauce, and he had it instead of salad. "This is amazing. I wish Caleb could've joined us. He would love the food you've prepared."

"I'm sorry he couldn't be here. I enjoy his company. I admire his devotion to his *bruder* and his family. It was considerate of him to watch Lily for them this evening," Joseph said.

Mamm clasped Rachael's hand. "I miss Caleb being here with us too."

Everyone took their seats, and Joseph prayed and thanked God for the food. "Rachael, *danki* for providing the pie."

"My pleasure. How did you become such a good cook?" The beef melted in her mouth and the vegetables were delicious. He'd used the right amount of butter, and they weren't mushy. She always overcooked or undercooked her vegetables.

"*Danki*, Rachael. Mamm died when I was twelve. She'd been sick for a couple of years before she passed away. She sat at the table and instructed me how to cook and bake many dishes. I've always liked to cook," Joseph said.

Toby cut his meat in bite-size pieces. "I prepare simple dishes, but my beef doesn't turn out this tender and juicy. What's your secret?"

"Having enough broth or light gravy to keep it moist, and I don't buy it from anyone but Magdelena's *daed*. He has the best beef around." Joseph held up his forked bite of beef and grinned.

"I will tell Daed what you said. He loves being a cattle rancher. Compliments on the quality of his beef always make his day," Magdelena said.

Toby cleaned his plate and pushed it away. "I'm full. What a scrumptious meal. *Danki*, Joseph." He crossed his arms. "Do you travel to New Philadelphia, Ohio, often?"

Rachael detected a change in Toby's demeanor. He sat ramrod straight and his tone was serious. This question was odd. New Philadelphia? Where was Toby going with this?

"Why are you asking this question as if you're challenging Joseph, Toby?" Mamm gave him a stern look.

Joseph patted her arm. "It's all right, Eleanor. I'll answer the question. I have on occasion."

"Andrew and I like their larger hardware store. Last week, you were there in front of the saloon, speaking with a scantily dressed young woman. I watched you with her, and you handed her money. You spoke for at least five minutes, and she hugged you when you left," Toby said.

Mamm's jaw dropped. "Toby, Joseph's visit to New Philadelphia or who he talks to is none of your business. Furthermore, you should have brought your concern to Joseph and me in private. Even then, I would tell you to drop it. You're being disrespectful."

"It's my business when he's courting you." Toby's tight lips brooked no argument.

"I am aware of who this woman is and why Joseph met her. Drop this conversation right now. You were raised to have better manners than this," Mamm said.

Rachael's heart pounded. Why had Joseph met this woman? Mamm said she knew all about this. There must be a reasonable explanation.

Joseph raised his hands, palms out. "Since I'm in love with your *mamm*, I'll explain."

Mamm blushed. "Joseph, I'm embarrassed. Toby shouldn't have confronted you about this. You don't need to explain anything to him."

He patted her hand. "Toby has made my visit known to your family, Eleanor. I will explain to avoid any suspicion." He addressed Toby, Rachael, and Magdelena. "The young woman I was with is my niece, Adelaide, my *schweschder's dochder*. My *schweschder*, Lois, ran away to live in the outside world at seventeen. Soon after, she was with child. The *daed* was an Englischer she was not married to, and he left her before Adelaide was born. We exchanged letters to keep in touch. She worked in the saloon in New Philadelphia, like Adelaide, and she loved her sinful life. My parents shunned her and made no effort to keep in touch with her. They passed her correspondence to me and never asked about her. After my parents died, I visited Lois and her child in New Philadelphia. Lois died last year of unknown causes. Now Adelaide and I correspond, and I visit her when I can. She refuses, like Lois, to leave her saloon life. Her earnings are never consistent. I give her money for food and to supplement what she earns. It's my way of showing her I'm concerned for her welfare and care for her."

Rachael wasn't sure Joseph should offer her money, although it was kind of him. "We have to do something. Have you withheld money to encourage her to embrace Amish life? You may be making it too easy for her to stay in the outside world. This is a suggestion and not a criticism of your generosity toward her."

Joseph nodded. "Her *mamm's* bad influence and dislike for the Amish life has had a negative influence on Adelaide. She won't consider Amish life or change from saloon work to a different and safer job. I had the general store manager ready to hire Adelaide and a family ready to rent her a room. She refused."

"Mamm's right. We shouldn't have jumped to conclusions until we gave you the chance to explain. I apologize. I commend you for helping Adelaide." Rachael admired Joseph. He'd done what he thought was right, in spite of his parents or Amish practice, to take care of his *schweschder* before she died and, now, his niece. She was in agreement with Joseph. Amish shouldn't shun family who leave their community.

Toby's expression softened. "I hope you'll forgive me, Joseph. I shouldn't have assumed the worst."

Joseph shook his head. "I accept your apology, and I understand why you confronted me out of concern for your *mamm*. *Danki* for your support. I can't, in good conscience, stay away from my niece. I worry about her. I visit her to make sure she's not sick, injured, or worse. I pray she'll choose to live a safer and healthier life someday, but I can't drag her here. If I did, she'd run away. She's an adult, but she's simpleminded, and she needs me. She doesn't believe her lifestyle is wrong. If the situation had been the reverse, I may have arrived at the same conclusion. I'm glad my visits to New Philadelphia and why I go there are out in the open with all of you. I don't like to share I'm visiting Adelaide with other Amish friends. I don't want any trouble for any of you, knowing the Amish way is to cut those who leave out of our lives. Most Amish wouldn't agree with what I'm doing."

Eleanor glared at her *kinner*. "Joseph told me about Adelaide when he asked me to court him. I love him for not abandoning Lois or Adelaide. If one of you had left home, I wouldn't have shunned you. I don't agree with this Amish practice. She won't visit Charm, but we can go to her. I'm ashamed of you, Toby, for not bringing this to my attention in private."

"I'm sorry, Mamm. My intention was to protect you." Toby's cheeks reddened.

"I accept your apology." Mamm gave him a curt nod.

"How may we help Adelaide?" Rachael was relieved Toby was remorseful.

Joseph's frown turned to a smile. "If I think of anything, I'll let you know. *Danki*. I put myself at risk by ignoring the Amish practice to shun Adelaide. I don't want to compromise any of you by asking for your help. I'm relieved all of you have chosen to be understanding."

Magdelena hadn't spoken until now. She quirked a brow. "How old is Adelaide?"

"She's twenty-two, but she's immature for her age. She craves attention, and I suppose that's why she likes to serve food and drinks and sing in the saloon. Adelaide has nothing but praise for her manager, Madge Pickerton. I've spoken to Madge about Adelaide. She's fond of my niece, and she promised to keep an eye on her," Joseph said.

"Would it help if I went to talk with her?" Rachael was curious to meet her. She couldn't imagine Adelaide being safe and happy working in a saloon.

"I'm afraid I've done everything possible to entice her to leave with me, but she's stubborn. She doesn't consider her way of life a sin or unhealthy. But *danki* for your offer. It's not a place you should go, even if I were to accompany you."

"I hope someday I can change your mind. You could take Mamm and me, and we could meet her somewhere outside the saloon. I beg you to reconsider."

Joseph raised his brows. "I will, Rachael. You might have a point."

Mamm stood. "Joseph and I keep her in our prayers, and we ask you to do the same. We will also keep in touch with her. Joseph has prepared this delicious meal, and it's time for dessert and a change in conversation." She stacked the dirty plates and carried them over to the tin wash pan already filled with water for soaking.

Rachael gathered the utensils and dropped them in the pan, along with the dishes. "Everyone remain seated. I'll serve the peach pie." She couldn't shake off her curiosity about Adelaide.

"Plates are stacked beside the pie, and forks are in the drawer below." Joseph pointed. "*Danki.*"

Rachael cut and served the pie to them. She cut Joseph's a little larger than the rest. It was silly, but it made her feel a little better for what they'd put him through this evening. The more she learned about him, the more she liked him.

"Peach pie is one of my favorite desserts, and this one is exceptional. *Danki*, Rachael, for providing it." Joseph set his fork on the side of his plate. He took Eleanor's hand in his.

Mamm didn't move her hand, but she blushed and raised her brows.

"Eleanor, I love you. We've courted a short time, but we're not getting any younger. I don't need to court you any longer to know you are the *fraa* for me. You occupy my thoughts day and night. You are kind and beautiful, and you shine with God's love in all you do." He turned to Rachael, Toby, and Magdelena. "Will you give me permission to marry your *mamm*? I promise to provide for her, love her, and be loyal to her for the rest of our lives."

Tears trickled down Mamm's cheeks. She covered his hand with her other hand. "I'd be honored to marry you."

"We didn't say yes." Toby chuckled.

"I overrule you both. I'm marrying this wonderful man." Eleanor beamed.

Rachael dabbed her damp eyes with a napkin. "Congratulations to both of you. Looks like we have a wedding to plan."

Magdelena lifted her shoulders and smiled. "This is great news."

Toby raised both his hands high and clapped them together. "Joseph, *wilkom* to the family. I approve. Have you thought about a wedding date?"

"I put the cart before the horse by doing this, but I already scheduled a date with Bishop Fisher. I figured he'd cancel the date he gave me if Eleanor said no. I chose June 29. He has marked the date on his calendar. Is this all right with all of you?"

"Absolutely." Eleanor hugged his neck.

Rachael's eyes brimmed with joyful tears. Mamm oozed joy. Their marriage would bring changes to their lives, and she'd be ready for them. "Whatever day you choose is perfect."

Rachael, Mamm, and Magdelena washed the dishes, while the men retreated to the living room.

Mamm accepted a clean, wet plate from Rachael. "Where would you prefer to live?"

Rachael froze. Wouldn't she live in the *haus* they had now? Could she manage it? If she worked at the bakery, she wouldn't have time to plant and take care of the garden or hayfield. Toby helped out, but he was busy on the ranch. "I hadn't considered it." She couldn't count on a future with Caleb until she had a serious talk with him. And she didn't know when or if he'd propose.

"Joseph told me about the small *haus* he also owns in back of this property. He hopes Adelaide one day will live there, but it doesn't seem realistic. Would you like to live there? He said it has a kitchen, a living room, two bedrooms, and a mudroom. Maybe we can look at it before we leave. He asked me to mention it to you."

Magdelena dried the utensils. "The small *haus* would be perfect for you, Rachael. You'd have your privacy, and they'd have theirs."

This might be the best solution. She wouldn't have to maintain the grounds, and the sale of their *haus* would relieve Toby of taking care of their farm, and she could help Mamm in her garden at Joseph's when necessary. "What a generous offer. Yes. I would like to take a peek at it."

Magdelena hugged Rachael's shoulders. "You'll be safe, and you'll still live a short distance from the bakery."

"I like the idea." She'd miss the *haus* where she and her family had many memories. She pressed a hand to her heart. She could take her memories with her wherever she went.

Rachael finished wiping the table and countertop. She followed Mamm and Magdelena to the living room to join the men.

"Joseph, I mentioned the small *haus* you have in back to Rachael as you requested. She's interested. Do you mind giving her a quick tour?" Mamm motioned to the back door.

"Splendid. I'm glad you will consider it." Joseph led them to the *haus* about six yards from the main *haus*. Everyone stood back and let Joseph and Rachael go in first.

She opened the cabinets. A scallop-edged white set of china, with small and large plates and bowls, plain glasses, and brown coffee mugs were in them. "I expected the cabinets would be empty. What a nice surprise."

"Katherine prepared this *haus* for Lois and Adelaide when we moved here. She wanted to make it as easy a move for them as possible. She bought the furniture and outfitted it with anything my *schweschder* and niece would've needed. You are *wilkom* to change or add things to your liking."

Her heart warmed. "Joseph, this is generous of you. I love this place." She liked the layout of the kitchen, with plenty of cabinets, a maple table, and four chairs. A desk and spindle chair sat in the corner of the living room, and the bedrooms had end tables, chairs, and clothes presses in each for hanging clothes. There were small front and back porches for enjoying a glass of tea with friends.

"It's settled, then. It's yours after your Mamm and I marry, and I can bring or change anything you'd like in the meantime. You'd give us peace of mind if you'd live here, instead of in your present *haus*. You could walk to us in lieu of having to take a buggy." Joseph grinned.

He had included her in their plans, like a *daed* taking care of his *dochder*. He was thoughtful. She was beginning to understand why he had caught and held Mamm's attention.

Toby and Magdelena followed them and took a quick peek at the inside of the place, and then they all went back to the main *haus* and sat down in the living room.

"Rachael, the *haus* Joseph offers is perfect for you. Do you have any reservations about it?" Toby gave her a questioning smile.

"No. I love the *haus*. It's a generous offer, and one I accept. *Danki*, Joseph. Mamm, will you sell our *haus*?" She couldn't have asked for a better living arrangement.

"Yes. We have no reason to keep it. Toby, will you take care of advertising the *haus*?" Mamm sat next to him and put her hand on his arm.

"What if it sells before you're ready to move? Maybe

we should wait to publicize it until after you're wed." Toby glanced from Joseph to Mamm.

Joseph batted the air. "If your *haus* sells, Rachael and Eleanor can move into the *haus* behind mine until we wed. It's not improper. We're not living together, and Rachael would be there with her *mamm*."

Toby's eyes widened. "True. I'll put it on the market June 1. I suspect it will go fast. I've made repairs, and it is in good condition."

Magdelena covered her yawn.

"I'd better take you home." Toby rose. "*Danki*, Joseph, for this exciting evening."

"*Danki* for your blessing, all of you." Joseph beamed at Mamm.

Rachael bid Joseph, Toby, and Magdelena farewell, and she and Mamm headed home. "This night turned out to be a memory you'll never forget, Mamm."

"Yes. I'm ecstatic. I couldn't ask for a better man than Joseph. I'd asked God to introduce me to my next husband, and He did. Joseph has compassion for others, he's patient, and he's fun. I'll count the days until I'm his *fraa*."

"I don't understand, Mamm. We share most everything. Why didn't you tell us about Adelaide?" Rachael wrinkled her forehead.

"It wasn't my story to tell, and you didn't need to know about her. I hadn't considered someone might recognize Joseph and question why he was in new Philadelphia."

"What if the bishop should get wind of this?" Rachael winced.

They should be prepared to suffer the consequences of being shunned in case they were found out. She would support Joseph no matter.

"We'll speak with the bishop and hope he'll consider our reasons for helping Adelaide become honorable if this should happen. If he doesn't, we'll accept being shunned for whatever time period he and the elders set forth." Mamm squeezed Rachael's hand. "*Danki* for your understanding."

"I'll stand by you both on this matter." Rachael didn't agree with no communication between family and friends who chose the outside world. Joseph was doing the right thing.

"You'll have a lot to tell Caleb about our wedding and your move when you're together again." Mamm chuckled.

"He'll be surprised and happy for you." Rachael grinned. She wondered when he'd propose. She'd marry him tomorrow if she could, but she knew he had responsibilities concerning his *bruder*. And she had to share something she'd been withholding from him. She wasn't ready to disclose it, and Caleb helping his *bruder* gave her a good excuse to hold off on revealing her secret to him. She realized it could ruin everything for them, and it was a risk she wasn't willing to take. Not yet. She'd savor every minute with him until then.

Chapter 6

Caleb sat next to Rachael at the after-service meal. "Tell me about your visit to Joseph's *haus*. Did you have a good time?" He hoped she'd gotten better acquainted with him and was reassured about Eleanor and Joseph's relationship.

"I have big news." Rachael held her butter cookie. "Joseph asked Mamm to marry him while we were there, and she said yes. He's already scheduled June 29 with Bishop Fisher for the ceremony. I'm thrilled for them."

He cocked his head and furrowed his brows. "I'm glad. He's a nice man, and your *mamm* smiles all the time she's around him. I'm relieved you and Toby don't oppose." Caleb was a little jealous it wasn't him and Rachael planning their wedding. He didn't need more time to convince himself she was the *fraa* for him, but he had obligations to fulfill with his *bruder*. He couldn't leave Stephen while he was ill. He hoped his *bruder*'s health would improve.

"And after they're married, I'll move into the vacant *haus* Joseph has at the back of his property. Toby is putting our *haus* up for sale the first week of June." Rachael held out her cookie. "Want a bite?"

He took a bite and finished it. "*Danki*. What a convenient place for you. That is perfect. I'd worry about you living alone where you are now." Did she wonder why he didn't mention them getting married?

"The *haus* is the right size for me, and it's furnished. We can sell our *haus* furnished or with whatever Mamm would like to give away. I'm fortunate Joseph has made this provision for me. I learned more about Joseph. His *schweschder*, Lois, ran away from home when she was young. She worked in a saloon as a waitress. He kept in touch with her, against the Amish way of life and his parents' wishes. She died and left a teenage *dochder*, Adelaide, behind."

"Has he stayed in touch with Adelaide?"

"Yes. He's tried to convince her to leave the same life, but she loves it. She looks up to a woman who manages the saloon in New Philadelphia. Joseph visits and gives her money for food and her room in a boardinghouse there. Please don't mention this to anyone. I don't want any trouble for him should the bishop or gossips find out. He had intended the small *haus* on his property for his *schweschder* and niece."

"I won't mention Adelaide to anyone. What a sad story. Do you agree with Joseph going against his parents and Amish practices?" Caleb could understand why Joseph made this decision. He would do anything for his *bruder*.

"We're taught it's wrong not to adhere to Amish practices, but I don't agree with shunning. I don't think we should bring into homes for extended stays people who don't believe as we do. They may try to change our ways. But we can love them where they are and pray they may want to change their lifestyle. Adelaide has no intention of leaving the saloon, but we can pray for her and make sure she has enough food and other things she needs."

"I could never turn my back on Stephen, no matter what his situation. I admire Joseph for caring for Adelaide. Is there anything we can provide for Adelaide?" Caleb hoped to marry Rachael at the end of their courtship, and Joseph would become a part of their family. He wanted to show support for Joseph.

"No. Not right now. How was your evening with Lily?"

"She's a content *boppli*. She played with her toys. I changed her nappy, dressed her in her nightgown, and read her stories. I rocked her until she fell asleep and then carried her to bed. She was no trouble, and she makes me want lots of *kinner*. Frannie insisted they go to supper, and Stephen looked exhausted. He doesn't have much stamina these days."

"You'll have to keep on him about going to Dr. Harrison."

"I did take him to Dr. Harrison earlier in the day, and the doctor said his shortness of breath and irregular heartbeat disturbed him. He offered him aspirin powder for his aches and pains and said there isn't much he can do for Stephen. He told him not to overexert himself. I explained all this to Frannie, but she thinks the visit was a waste of time and refuses to admit Stephen isn't a healthy man." Caleb was disappointed the doctor couldn't offer Stephen more help. Caleb suspected Stephen wouldn't get better. He'd have to live with his limitations.

"Frannie needs to have more compassion for Stephen. She can't keep making demands of him." Rachael worried her brows.

"She won't change. It's maddening. He'll do anything to make her happy. I wish she would do the same for him. He was exhausted. Instead of staying home and letting him rest, she drove the buggy to the restaurant in town."

"Were they gone long?" Rachael pinched her lips.

"No. Stephen stumbled to bed as soon as they returned home. Frannie ignored him. She went on and on about the beef stroganoff she ordered at the restaurant. I couldn't sit and listen to her for more than a couple of minutes. I retreated to my room about ten minutes after Stephen went to bed. I had to simmer down. She frustrates me."

Joy and Thad skipped to them. Joy hugged Rachael and ignored Caleb. "I miss you."

"Me too." Thad nodded.

"I love you both." Rachael hugged them.

Caleb squatted to Joy. "Want to play horseshoes? Thad, you can play with us." He didn't want Joy and Thad to dislike him. He could understand their loss of Rachael was difficult. He wouldn't give up trying to befriend them. He loved *kinner*.

"Yes," Joy and Thad said in unison, and followed him to the horseshoe pits.

Rachael grinned, watching the three of them walk away. She loved Caleb for showing Nathan's *kinner* he wasn't the enemy. He could've been polite but not cared enough to gain their friendship. He was more caring than many Amish men she knew.

Annie tapped her on the shoulder. "You're deep in thought watching Caleb play with Joy and Thad."

Rachael patted Annie's protruding stomach. "How are you feeling?" Rachael had hoped Annie might consider working at the bakery, but then she learned her friend was with child. She was thrilled for her. Annie stuck close to home, and she didn't get to talk to her friend often. Annie had been sick since she'd been with child.

"Excited, nauseous, and I ache all the time. I'm guessing I'm due around November 1. Abram's already hoping we have another one after this *boppli* is born." Annie chuckled.

"Any names picked out?" Rachael was happy the Hooks had moved to Charm last year.

Abram had *kumme* across gruff, and he'd confessed to Toby he'd been selling moonshine. But he turned his life around, and now he and Annie were happier in their marriage. He didn't have to hide this anymore. Annie had forgiven him, and they were a cheery couple to be around. She wished Annie's experience carrying her little one could've been a more pleasant one.

"We can't decide. We change the names we like weekly." She grinned. "How are things with Caleb?"

"He's my soul mate. I love him." Rachael blushed, but she was proud to tell Annie where she stood with him.

"I heard about your *mamm* and Joseph setting a wedding date. Maybe you could make it a double wedding." Annie gave her an impish grin. "Or do you want to keep the weddings separate?"

"Caleb hasn't proposed. But we have plenty of time. I wouldn't be opposed to a double wedding."

His responsibility to his family might keep him from proposing to her. She had to divulge to him what she'd kept to herself for so long soon, and then he may not want to marry her.

Abram came alongside Annie. "Rachael, always a pleasure. Annie, are you ready to go home?"

"Yes. Take care, Rachael."

Annie and Abram departed.

Nathan approached her. "It's nice of Caleb to play with the *kinner*. They are really enjoying themselves." He faced her. "Rachael, I've been wondering about something, and I have to ask. Please give me an honest answer."

Rachael stiffened. What on earth was left for them to discuss? She liked Nathan and she loved his *kinner*. She didn't want anything to damage their friendship or make courting Caleb any more difficult. "What is it?"

"Before you met Caleb, would you have considered a marriage proposal from me?" Nathan stared into her eyes.

She rolled a rock under her shoe. "Yes. I probably would

have married you." She would've accepted an arranged marriage with him before she met Caleb, with the hope they'd fall in love. She would've been thrilled to raise Joy and Thad with him. With Caleb, she'd been smitten from the moment they met, and her love for him had grown each time they'd spoken. Falling in love with him had been effortless.

"Do you think you would've fallen in love with me, given time?" Nathan searched her face.

"I'm not sure. I would like to think so." She didn't want Caleb to overhear this conversation. She wouldn't be dishonest with Nathan. He deserved the truth, even if it didn't matter now.

"*Danki* for your frankness. It wouldn't make a difference to you, but it does to me. I had to know. I didn't realize until you left us that I had fallen in love with you. The time you've been with Caleb has made it more apparent to me. I chide myself often for taking you for granted." He gave her a lopsided grin. "You'll be pleased to know, I won't ask you any more awkward questions."

She managed a grin. "Thank goodness."

"Congratulations. The happy topic for the day is your *mamm* and Joseph's upcoming wedding. Do you and Toby approve?"

"Yes. It took me time to get used to the idea, but they're in love and want to be together. Toby and I won't stand in their way. The more Joseph and I talk, the more I like him." Rachael glanced over at Mamm and Joseph, laughing about something, not too far away from them.

Ava approached them. "Rachael, how are you?"

"Doing well. *Danki*."

"Nathan, take a stroll with me." Ava flashed a big smile at him.

"Sure." He nodded to Rachael and left with Ava.

Rachael was surprised Ava hadn't given up on Nathan. He hadn't made it easy for her to win him over. He'd be an excellent catch for any available woman. He was smart, kind, and loving and provided a good living for his family. He was also an active *daed* in his *kinner*'s lives.

Caleb approached her. "The *kinner* wore me out, but they're a lot of fun. They've been upset with me since I took you away from them, but I may have won them over and shown them I can be their friend." He chuckled.

"You were kind to entertain them. Where did they go?" Rachael searched the yard for the *kinner* over the sea of black bonnets and straw hats.

"Some of the other *kinner* invited them to play hide-and-seek." Caleb removed the handkerchief he had tucked in his waistband and wiped his forehead. "It's a beautiful day."

"The sunshine is cheery and the temperature just right. All the running the *kinner* had you doing must've made you warm. They are a handful and full of energy." Rachael caught sight of Joy running as fast as her short legs could carry her across the yard to a big oak tree.

"What did Nathan have to say?" Caleb cocked his head.

"Nothing much." What was the point of upsetting Caleb? She'd keep their conversation to herself.

"Joseph and your *mamm* are getting a lot of attention today. Their big announcement has been met with a lot of support." He guided her to a spot away from the crowd. "Rachael, I love you. I don't want to wait another second without telling you."

Her heart soared. "I love you too."

Frannie rushed to them before Rachael could say anything else. "Caleb, *kumme* quick! Stephen has collapsed. I can't rouse him."

She and Caleb hurried to where Frannie and Stephen had been sitting at a picnic table near them. She gasped.

Stephen was on his back on the ground. A crowd stood over him. She stepped back as Caleb pushed his way through the crowd and dropped to his *bruder*'s side. "Someone fetch Dr. Harrison."

"Toby went to get him." Magdelena held her hands to her cheeks.

Rachael knelt beside Caleb. "Do you hear a heartbeat?"

He had his ear to his *bruder*'s chest. "No."

She checked for a pulse. "He doesn't have a pulse." This man was young, and he had a *dochder*, a *fraa*, and a *bruder* who needed him.

Frannie screamed. "Do something!" She got on the other side of Stephen and patted his cheeks. "Honey, please wake up. Wake up now!"

Rachael pressed a hand to her throat. Frannie's desperation was sad. She wanted to help her and there was nothing she could do.

The crowd of their friends stood around them.

Dr. Harrison pushed his way through to them and addressed Caleb. "I was near here when Toby found me. I hope I've made it in time to help." He crouched down beside Stephen. "All of you, please give me some room." He threw open his bag and removed his stethoscope. He listened to Stephen's chest and checked for a pulse. He sat back and shook his head. "I'm sorry. He's gone. There's nothing any of us can do."

Rachael's eyes pooled with tears. Her heart hurt for Caleb.

Frannie stepped between them and collapsed in Caleb's arms. "What am I going to do?"

Rachael dabbed her eyes with the pads of her thumbs. She wished she could wash away their pain.

Frannie separated from Caleb. She headed for Hannah and Lily.

Hannah held Lily, who had fallen asleep in her arms. "Frannie, would you like me to take Lily home and keep her overnight for you? I'll bring her home tomorrow. You'll need time to yourself and to prepare for the services."

"Yes. *Danki*." Frannie nodded as she sobbed and accepted Rachael's handkerchief and dabbed her eyes.

Rachael loved Hannah. She had worked at the bakery with her until she married. She was such a thoughtful friend to her and others. Always there to lend a hand when needed. She had a sweet spirit and was always the one to give the best advice. Lily would be in good hands.

Rachael looked at Caleb. "My heart breaks for you. What can I do?"

"You being here is all I need." Tears trickled down his cheeks.

Toby put his hand on Caleb's shoulder. "Andrew and I will take Stephen's body to the undertaker for burial preparation."

"*Danki*." Caleb swiped a tear from his cheek.

Toby and Andrew carried Stephen's lifeless body to Toby's wagon and left.

"I'm sorry this has happened, Frannie and Caleb. When would you like the visitation and funeral services? I'll be glad to clear my schedule and help with whatever you need." Bishop Fisher held his Bible to his side.

Caleb rubbed his temple. "The undertaker will return his body tomorrow. Let's have the visitation at three in the afternoon on Tuesday, and the funeral and burial right after." He turned to Frannie. "Are you in agreement?"

"Yes. I don't want to drag the services out. It's too much for me to contend with guests. I may choose to stay in my room to grieve alone and have you tend to the visitors." Frannie wiped her damp cheeks.

"As you wish." Bishop Fisher asked their Amish friends

to gather closer to him. "Stephen's visitation will be held at his home at three on Tuesday. The funeral and burial services will follow. Ladies, please provide a dish of food for the family and attendees. *Danki*."

Rachael's friends gathered around her, offering their assistance. She answered their questions and then managed to get away and speak to Mamm. "I'm going to Caleb's. He and Frannie may need me. Frannie's emotional state is fragile. She may want another woman to talk to."

"She's in shock. She and Caleb will need you. I'll provide chicken and noodles and a ham casserole for us to take on Tuesday. Give Caleb our love." Mamm hugged her.

She nodded. "I will."

Mamm had said "our" love. She'd glanced at Joseph when she said it. She'd get used to them being a couple, but it was the little references, such as this, that caught her off guard. Daed would've wanted Mamm to marry again. He wasn't a selfish or jealous man. Rachael would be more supportive of them. She didn't want Frannie and Caleb to suffer like she had when her fiancé and Daed passed away, but there was nothing she could do but be there for them. She parked her buggy in front of the *haus* and tied her horse to the hitching post.

Caleb opened the front door, a genuine look of love and relief on his dear face. "I heard your horse. I'm glad you're here."

"Where's Frannie?" Rachael glanced around the room.

"She's in her bedroom. I hope asleep. She's not what I would call a strong person in any situation. I worry about her." Caleb motioned for her to sit as he plopped on the settee.

"I'll *kumme* and clean the *haus* after work tomorrow, and I'll be here early Tuesday to greet guests and organize the food dishes. Toby will arrange for the men to bring benches and tables. You must be in shock."

Caleb sighed and shook his head. "I am. He was my best friend. I expected to have a lot more time with him. We've always been close. There were things I wish I would've said to him."

"He knew you loved him, and he had no doubt he could depend on you for anything. You and he shared a close companionship. Not all *kinner* have a special bond. It's a gift. You were there for each other."

She could relate to this. Toby was her rock. She could depend on him and discuss anything with him. She couldn't imagine not having him in her life.

Tears stained Caleb's face. He ran his fingers through his sandy-blond hair. "*Danki* for your help and encouraging words."

"There's nowhere I'd rather be. Are you hungry? Would you like some tea?" Rachael wasn't sure what to do. Her heart was breaking for him. She'd *wilkomed* her friends around her to distract her from the agony of her fiancé's, and then her *daed*'s, deaths. But not everyone would feel the same. Should she leave and let him grieve? He seemed lost.

"No. I had enough at dinner after the church service."

Rachael covered his hand. "You've had a difficult day. I'm sure you could use some time alone."

"Please don't take offense, but I could use some time to myself. There's much to consider, and I'm numb." Caleb brushed his fingers against her cheek. "I meant what I said earlier. I love you, Rachael."

"I love you more, Caleb." She grinned and hoped to bring a smile to his face. She headed for the door.

He walked her to the back of the buggy, where no one would notice them, cupped her cheeks with his hands, and kissed her gently. "I would have to argue your point."

She was giddy with happy butterflies in her stomach.

He'd kissed her, and she'd often imagined what it might be like. It had been a sweet kiss and better than she'd anticipated. She hoped the kiss had brought him a minute of happiness on this sad day.

Caleb peeked in on Frannie. She'd fallen asleep. He wasn't used to the quiet, and he didn't like it. He grabbed a sweater and sat in the weathered rocker on the porch. He'd have to put a little oil on it to make the noise disappear. He pictured his *bruder* sitting next to him in the other rocker as they had done so many times. They'd been there for each other as they grew up, when their parents passed away, and at Stephen's wedding. God had taken Stephen home at a young age. He knew God had Stephen's best interests at heart, but it didn't take the agony he felt inside away. He wondered if the ache from his *bruder*'s loss would ever end.

Caleb made scrambled eggs and bacon for Frannie and himself Monday morning. He hadn't spoken with her since they'd returned home from Sunday services. He rapped on her door. "Frannie, breakfast is ready."

She opened the door and followed him to the kitchen. Her light brown hair was matted against her face and she wore her robe over her nightdress. She had dark circles under her eyes. "I'm not hungry, Caleb."

"Drink some warm coffee. It will help you wake up." Caleb poured her a mug and set it in front of her.

She had always been impeccable. She'd never left her room unless she was dressed in her Amish skirt and blouse or dress. Her hair had always been in a neat bun under her *kapp*. Her long hair fell over her shoulders and down her back. She was a mess.

She put her elbows on the table and dropped her face into her hands. "I can't believe Stephen isn't here with us.

What am I going to do without him, Caleb? I don't want to live without him," she blubbered.

He knelt before her and pushed a strand of light brown hair from her cheek. "I'm here for you and Lily. We'll get through this together."

She wrapped her arms around his neck and sobbed.

He waited a minute and then gently pulled her arms away from him. "Drink some coffee and eat your eggs. You need your strength. We have much to do today and to-morrow."

She relented and did as he asked. She stayed quiet and stared out the window. "Where's Lily?" She gripped his shoulders and pleaded. "Where is she?"

He took her hands in his. "Hannah has her. Remember? She'll bring her to you today. She wanted to give you time to yourself." Caleb wasn't sure anything he said registered with her.

He set his plate of eggs and bacon on the table and drank his coffee. She'd finished half her eggs and left most of the coffee. He didn't leave a morsel of anything on his plate. They kept silent. He rose and carried his plate to the sink. He had filled the washtub for dirty dishes earlier. "I'll be in the barn if you need me."

Frannie didn't answer.

He walked outside and met Hannah by the barn. "Greetings."

Hannah parked her buggy. "Good morning. Lily was an angel. I loved keeping her last night. How are you and Frannie holding up?"

"Unkie." Lily held out her arms to Caleb, and he accepted her from Hannah.

"We're both in shock. Frannie's in a bad way. She's grief-stricken. I'm not sure she's gotten dressed, and I'm not used to her being so despondent. She's not said much."

Frannie wasn't at a loss for words most of the time, and this was new to him.

"I can stay and help her dress. Don't worry. I'll tend to her and Lily." Hannah headed to the *haus*.

"*Danki*." Caleb understood why Rachael loved Hannah. She'd told him Hannah had befriended her and what a loyal, loving, and patient friend she'd been to her. Hannah hadn't stopped trying to befriend Frannie, and his *schweschder*-in-law didn't make it easy. She was negative on most subjects, and she didn't have the same caring attitude as Rachael and Hannah.

Rachael left the bakery after work on Monday. She stopped at home. "Mamm, I'm going to help Frannie. I may stay the night if she needs help with Lily. I'm not sure how she is faring."

"You should stay the night. This has been traumatic for their family. I'll *kumme* to their home and help you tomorrow." Mamm rubbed her back. "Give them my best. I still can't believe Stephen has died. He was young."

"It's such a tragedy for Frannie and Caleb. Stephen was a loving *bruder*, husband, and *daed*. My heart aches for them. I'll pack a bag to take and be on my way." Rachael kissed Mamm's cheek.

She went to her room, folded a clean dress, and grabbed a bonnet. She packed them in her clean flower sack and went to the Yutzys' home.

Caleb met her buggy. "I'm glad you're here. Hannah's inside. She brought Lily home, but Frannie's in no condition to take care of her. She has stayed in bed all day. I'm hoping she'll get dressed and attend the services tomorrow."

"Don't worry. I'll stay tonight and care for Lily. Liza gave Magdelena and me permission to close the bakery tomorrow to free us to help with whatever you need. Mamm said she'll *kumme* early. Our friends will organize the benches for the service, bring food, and lend a hand for anything we need." She squeezed his hand. "How are you?"

"I'm numb. The undertaker returned Stephen's body. He had a plain pinewood casket on hand. I moved the furniture around, and we put it on the long dining room table for viewing. I've already washed and dressed his body. We wouldn't have had to embalm the body, but I needed Stephen out of the *haus* for Frannie's sake, and maybe mine, for a day."

"Most of the Amish in our community prefer to have the body embalmed, since they sometimes wait a longer period of time to have the services. It's every family's decision. I understand why you needed time to digest Stephen's passing."

Caleb took her bag. "*Danki* for being here for all of us."

She clasped his arm. "Anything for you, Caleb."

He walked with her, and they went inside the *haus*.

Hannah was on the living room floor, playing with Lily. "Lily, Rachael's here."

Lily clapped her little palms. "Rachie." She toddled over to Rachael and held her arms high. "Unkie." She grinned at Caleb.

Rachael lifted her into her arms and balanced her on her hip. "Are you having fun making pretend food with Hannah?"

Caleb set Rachael's bag in the corner of the living room and rubbed Lily's back.

Lily rested her head on Rachael's shoulder.

Hannah chuckled. "Do you think we have enough bowls and wooden spoons? I found them in the kitchen. She loves them. I peeked in on Frannie. She's asleep. Should I stay? She's not up to caring for Lily."

Rachael shook her head. "I brought an overnight bag. I'll take over. *Danki* for all you've done."

"Yes, *danki*, Hannah." Caleb stood next to Rachael.

"I'll *kumme* early to greet guests, organize the food dishes, and assist in any way I can."

Rachael and Caleb nodded.

Hannah bid them farewell and headed out to her buggy.

Caleb followed Hannah to the buggy.

Rachael carried Lily to the kitchen. She removed the cover from a platter sitting on the oven. Hannah must've made meat loaf and potatoes. She set Lily in her high chair, tied a bib on her, and set a small bowl of applesauce and a spoon on her tray.

Lily banged the spoon on her tray and then dipped it into her applesauce.

Caleb returned and chuckled. "Lily's having a good time with the applesauce."

"She has more on her than in her mouth, but it keeps her occupied. Hannah cooked meat loaf and mashed potatoes while she was here. It's warm and ready."

"I'm not sure Frannie has had any food today. She should have something." Caleb combed his fingers through his hair.

"I'll try to wake her." Rachael went to Frannie's bedroom, sat on the edge of the bed, and pushed Frannie's hair off her face. She'd left her hair loose. "I have meat loaf and mashed potatoes on the stove. Can I bring you a tray?"

Frannie opened her eyes and nodded.

"I'll bring your food and water in as soon as it's ready. Or would you like to *kumme* to the table? I can help you put on a dress and pin up your hair."

Frannie shook her head and buried her face in the pillow, weeping.

"You rest. I'll return soon." Rachael's throat dried.

Frannie scared her. She was too bereft to take care of

herself, let alone Lily. The food would give her energy. Maybe she'd bathe, dress, and face the day tomorrow.

"How is she?" Caleb winced.

"Not good. I'm not sure she'll be in any shape to greet friends or attend the services. She's grief-stricken like no one I've ever been around. My heart aches for her. But she has a *boppli* who needs her." She took the food off the stove, pulled a tray from the cabinet, spooned potatoes and a small serving of beef on a plate, added utensils, and filled a glass of water for her. "I'm taking this to Frannie."

"I'll fix our plates." Caleb stood at the stove.

Rachael nodded, carried the tray to Frannie's room, and set it on the nightstand. "Frannie, would you like me to help raise you into a sitting position?"

Frannie raised herself to sit up in bed.

Rachael tucked a pillow behind Frannie's back. She positioned the tray over the widow's lap. She was glad the tray had built-in short legs to support it.

Frannie stayed silent and lifted a forkful of potatoes to her mouth. Her eyes had a blank stare. "*Danki.*"

"I'll *kumme* back to take the tray." Rachael left the room but didn't close the door.

Would Frannie snap out of this? Rachael had her doubts. She might have to ask Hannah to care for Lily for a while until Frannie became responsible again. The woman hadn't even asked about her *boppli*.

She returned to the kitchen and joined Caleb and Lily. "*Danki* for fixing my plate."

"Did Frannie accept the tray?" Caleb offered her sliced wheat bread.

"Yes, but she didn't utter a word other than '*danki*.' She has a blank stare. She managed to get into a sitting position, and she had a forkful of potatoes when I left her. I hope she empties her plate. The way she is now, she couldn't care for Lily. She may not be fit to attend the services tomorrow."

Caleb traced the rim of his glass. "When will she snap out of this? What am I going to do?"

She reached for his hand. "I don't know when she'll be ready to face life again. But you have me and our friends to help you. Hannah would love to take care of Lily. She loves *kinner*. Her *mamm* will also help. Our friends, Maryann, Liza, and Ellie, will take turns checking on Frannie until she's feeling better. I will take care of the laundry and *haus*-cleaning after work. I'm hoping Frannie's energy will return with the food she's having, and then she'll be in better shape tomorrow."

Rachael and Caleb finished their supper. Rachael carried their plates to the sink. "I'll fetch Frannie's tray."

She stepped into the room, and the woman ignored her. "I'm glad you finished most of your food. Is there anything I can get for you?"

Frannie shook her head, curled into a fetal position, and pulled the covers over her head.

Rachael returned to the kitchen. "I'm encouraged. She finished most of her food."

"I'm glad." He washed and dried the dishes.

"Do you want help with the dishes?" Rachael grabbed a dish towel.

"No. *Danki*. I'd appreciate it if you could put Lily to bed."

"I'd love to." She lifted Lily from the high chair. "Time for bed, little one."

Lily patted Rachael's cheeks. "Read?"

"Yes. We'll read a story before you go to bed." Rachael poured water from the white porcelain pitcher into the matching bowl on a small table in the corner of Lily's room. She lowered Lily onto the changing table next to it,

undressed her, and washed and dried her cute little body.
"You're a beautiful *boppli*."

Lily grabbed a pink plastic rattle on the changing table
and shook it.

Rachael dressed her and rocked her in the white rocking
chair. She picked the small book that told about Noah's ark
and read to Lily.

Lily snuggled in her arms, and her eyes shut halfway
through the story.

She lowered Lily into bed, covered her, and gazed at her
sweet and innocent face. She would give anything to have
a *boppli*. To experience being a *mamm*. She'd been at her
happiest caring for Joy and Thad. She missed them and
thought of them every day.

Caleb needed her. She should check on him. She went
to the living room and Caleb sat in front of the fireplace.

"*Kumme* sit. The kitchen is clean."

She glanced at Stephen's casket on the long dining room
table through the open doorway. Her eyes watered. She was
sad he would no longer be with them. She liked his calm
and kind demeanor. She would've liked to have gotten
better acquainted with him. She couldn't imagine how difficult it would be for her if Toby passed away. Her heart
went out to Caleb.

She chose the chair next to him and *wilkomed* the beautiful orange hue of the small flames in the fireplace. "How
are you feeling?"

"I can't believe he's gone, even though the pine box in
the living room on the dining room table tells me otherwise. My best friend, my confidante, my *bruder* and ad-
viser is gone. I'm going through the motions of what needs
to be done, but I'm not myself. It's as if I'm in a fog, and
it's difficult to think of anything but Stephen's death." He

gazed into her eyes. "I love you, Rachael, with all my heart." He raised her hand and kissed it.

She beheld him. "I love you, and we'll get through this together." She hadn't loved another man since John died. Caleb, like John, was patient and God-fearing. They both were hardworking. Caleb was more opinionated and outspoken than John. He'd shown her this when he'd voiced his frustration with Frannie. Although she didn't blame him. Frannie wasn't like any of her Amish friends. She was a challenge, with her unfair expectations of Caleb and Stephen. The woman was also unreasonable about how much she depended on both Stephen and Caleb. What changes would Stephen's death make in their lives?

Chapter 7

Rachael rose from the couch early Tuesday morning at Caleb's *haus*. She fixed omelets for herself, Caleb, and Frannie. She scrambled eggs for Lily. She carried a tray into Frannie's bedroom, and Caleb was there. "Frannie, I have breakfast for you. Caleb, yours is on the table."

"*Danki*, Rachael." Hands on hips, he gave Frannie a stern eye. "After you've finished your food, I expect you to dress and greet visitors. This day will be difficult for both of us. Lily needs you, and God will get us through this."

Frannie accepted the tray from Rachael and lifted the coffee mug with a trembling hand. "*Danki*."

"Do you want to attend the services today? Visit Stephen's body before he's buried? I'm sorry, Frannie. I realize this is all difficult for you." Rachael covered Frannie's hand with hers.

"I can't face any of it. I'll be in my room for the day. I don't want to face anyone." Frannie fixed her eyes on the tray.

Rachael followed Caleb out of the bedroom. "She chooses to hide away in her room. Maybe we should honor her wishes." She worried Frannie couldn't cope with being at the services. The widow hadn't even asked about Lily. She didn't want to push her to face the services today if she wasn't ready.

"I understand she's upset. But she has to accept this, and she can't shut off the world around her. It's not healthy. The more she withdraws and refuses to care for Lily or herself, I'm afraid she'll grow worse." Caleb answered a knock at the door. "Toby, *danki* for being here. *Kumme* inside."

Toby shook his head. "I've got twelve men outside ready to unload benches from their wagons. Do you want some inside and out? It is sweater weather, and I'm hoping we have another sunny April day."

"Yes. And the food tables can be outside." Caleb stepped onto the porch. He held the door open. "Rachael, I'll be outside if you need me."

Rachael nodded. She was relieved Toby had distracted Caleb. She hoped Caleb wouldn't insist Frannie dress and greet people. She could understand Frannie wanting this day to pass fast. She remembered the day of John's services. Her true love was no longer the vibrant man she'd known. She'd wished she hadn't viewed him in the casket and instead kept the last time she'd been with him alive burned in her mind. She'd leave Frannie alone and take care of Lily. She went to Lily's room. "Good morning, sunshine."

Lily held the railing and bounced up and down on her bed. "Rachie, up." She stopped and held out her arms to Rachael.

She changed Lily's nappy and carried her to Frannie's room.

Lily held out her arms to Frannie. "Mum."

Frannie had left her tray on the dresser. She was in bed and rolled to her other side with her back to them. "I'm sorry, Rachael. Please take care of her for me. I don't have the energy to get out of this bed."

"Very well." Rachael left the room, and Lily buried her face in Rachael's shoulder and whimpered.

She patted Lily's back. "It's all right, sweetheart." She put her in the high chair and slid her omelet from the skillet onto a plate. She poured the scrambled eggs she'd put to the side to cool earlier in a bowl for Lily. She covered the skillet with the remaining omelet for Caleb. She and Lily emptied their plates, and then Rachael changed Lily into a fresh dress and set her in the playpen in the corner of the living room to play with her toys. Lily had a pleasant disposition and didn't mind playing alone. Frannie had been blessed her *boppli* was easygoing.

Thirty minutes later, Mamm, Magdelena, Hannah, Ellie, Maryann, and other friends arrived. They cleaned the kitchen and greeted guests as they arrived. Hannah picked up Lily.

Rachael checked on Frannie. "Guests are here. What should I tell them?"

Frannie rolled to her side and met Rachael's gaze. "Tell them I'm not up to greeting them or being a part of the services." She closed her eyes.

Rachael left the room and organized the food outside.

Mamm came alongside her. "Where's Frannie?"

"She prefers to stay in her room. She doesn't want to face the guests or the services." Rachael heaved a big sigh. "I'm worried. She's shut herself off from us and Lily. I'll stay here with her and Lily, instead of going to the burial. She shouldn't be alone."

"It's been a shock for her, and staying with her is a good idea."

Mamm's friend pulled her away.

Magdelena pulled her aside. "How are you doing, dear friend? I can't believe this has happened. Where's Frannie?"

"She's not up to greeting friends. This is a sad day for her, and I don't mind taking care of Lily. My heart goes out to her. Her world has turned upside down with Stephen's death."

"I've not experienced a friend who has acted out this way, where they refuse to attend the services of a loved one or care for their *boppli*. Is there anything I can do?" Magdelena reached for Rachael's hand.

Rachael clasped her friend's fingers. "You're already doing it by talking with me. I stayed here on the couch last night. This is a lot for Caleb to handle. He's stepped into Stephen's role with taking care of the land, *haus* chores, and Frannie and Lily. It's a big adjustment."

"Do you need time off from the bakery? We can ask Hannah to fill in." Magdelena put her hands on Rachael's shoulders.

"I don't need to. Hannah can watch Lily. Caleb will be working. I'll *kumme* after work to tidy the *haus* and cook meals if Frannie doesn't resume life." She loved Magdelena for her willingness to do whatever she could to help. She knew her friend would run the bakery by herself if she'd asked.

"Caleb is blessed to have you in his life." Magdelena pointed to Hannah outside. "Hannah wants *kinner*, and she's upset she's not with child. I'm sure she'd love taking care of Lily until Frannie is up to watching her."

"Yes. Lily loves her." Rachael followed Magdelena outside.

Friends had worked like busy bees to prepare for the services now as they had for so many others. Caleb was surrounded by the husbands of her friends. Satisfied he was being taken care of, she headed inside and bumped into Bishop Fisher. "Excuse me. I should watch where I'm going." She blushed. "May I offer you coffee or tea?"

"It's my fault. I've been clumsy all my life." He shook his head. "No coffee or tea for me. I've had more than my share this morning. *Danki* for asking. It's time to begin the service. Please gather the ladies and have them meet outside and take their seats. I'll let the men know." Bishop Fisher stepped outside.

"Ladies, Bishop Fisher is ready to begin the service." Rachael opened the door for them and followed them outside. She took Lily from Hannah. "*Danki*."

She sat with her friends and held Lily. She had avoided the dining room all morning and she was relieved to be outside. Her heart sank knowing Lily wouldn't grow up with her *daed*, and Frannie would be without her husband.

Caleb had shed tears in private last night in his room. He'd buried his face in the pillow and let his emotions erupt. Today, he'd prepared for the visitation and funeral, and now he had friends to talk to. He wished his friends could've had more time to get to know his *bruder* better.

Bishop Fisher opened the service with a prayer. He raised his head and opened his Bible. "We look forward to our forever home, but we don't know when God will take us to Heaven." He gazed out over the crowd. "Those of us who have had loved ones die miss them. I pray, Caleb, that you and your family will find comfort in knowing Stephen is happy and healthy with God. I understand Stephen had health problems, and now he's no longer suffering. Please lean on me and your friends as you go through this difficult time."

Caleb nodded. "*Danki*."

He would miss their conversations the most. Stephen made him laugh, told corny jokes, and had more patience than any other man he'd ever known. Frannie had no reason to change her behavior, because Stephen allowed it. He didn't understand how Stephen could've loved Frannie so much, in spite of her selfish attitude. Stephen had asked him to take care of Frannie and Lily should anything happen to him. Had he suspected he might not survive much longer?

Bishop Fisher spoke for two hours, led them in hymns, prayed, and dismissed them to the cemetery. He was grateful the Amish of Charm had purchased land for this purpose years ago. It was ten minutes away, and Caleb was thankful for the short distance.

Rachael bounced Lily on her hip. "I'm not comfortable leaving Frannie alone and I don't want you to coax her to go with you to the service. She should mourn in her own way. I'll stay here with her."

"You're a lifesaver. *Danki*."

Toby pointed to his buggy. "Caleb, ride with Magdelena and me."

"I appreciate the invitation." He smiled at Rachael and walked with Toby to the buggy.

Magdelena was already seated inside.

They arrived at the site, and Bishop Fisher stood by the large hole, waiting for the casket. "Let us pray. Please bow your heads." He offered a prayer to God and then spoke another message.

Caleb closed his eyes. He'd always disliked this part of funerals the most. His stomach churned. It was the finality of it.

Toby leaned close and whispered, "Remember, he's not here. He's gone to his home in Heaven."

Caleb opened his eyes and nodded. Memories flashed through his mind. They'd fished, swam, played games, and been there for each other through sad and difficult times. His parents' deaths had been hard to accept, but they had grieved and supported each other. He'd expected to make many more memories with Stephen.

Bishop Fisher motioned for two of the men to lower the

pine box holding Stephen's body into the grave. He offered another prayer to God. "Please return to Caleb's *haus* and partake of the food the women have prepared."

Caleb wanted to run to the buggy and leave the burial site as fast as he could. He'd washed and dressed Stephen's body, and it had been the most difficult task of his life. He'd let tears flood his eyes. From that moment on, he hadn't visited the casket until now, and he was relieved the casket was closed. He hurried to the buggy, and Toby and Magdelena kept up with him. They got inside the buggy.

He said, "*Danki*, you both, for your friendship and support. You've made this day bearable for me."

Toby held the reins and glanced over his shoulder at Caleb in the back. "Don't hesitate to reach out to me for anything. It's what friends are for, and you're courting my *schweschder*. We might be family someday."

Caleb smiled. Any man would be blessed to have Toby for a *bruder*-in-law. He'd connected with Toby right away. And Toby had introduced him to his friends at after-church meals and included him in conversations often. He was thankful Toby and Rachael had made it easy to make friends in Charm. Toby had a resemblance to Rachael in appearance, but not much. He had brown eyes instead of green and a square jaw, where Rachael's was rounded. They both had big hearts and were willing to help most anyone. Magdelena was also a sweetheart, and he could understand why Rachael was close to her. The two of them acted like *schweschders* as well as best friends. Toby was a blessed man to have found Magdelena.

"I would like nothing better, and that is my plan."

Magdelena grinned. "Rachael has been beaming since she's been courting you."

"Me too." Caleb stared at the road. He had promised Stephen he would take care of Frannie and Lily, but with the way Frannie was acting, he didn't know what it might mean. They were his responsibility now. He didn't want to think about that today. He pushed the thought from his mind.

Rachael opened Frannie's bedroom door. "Are you awake? Is there anything I can bring you?"

"Is everyone gone?" Frannie stayed covered in bed.

"They're returning from the burial to partake of the food the women have prepared. Would you like me to fix you a plate?"

"Please." Frannie raised her head.

Rachael closed the door, but only part way. At least Frannie would accept food. She checked on Lily in her playpen.

Lily hugged her Amish doll and picked up a wooden horse with her other hand. "Horsie."

"Yes." She tousled the *boppli*'s hair and went outside to where the crowd had gathered to fill their plates. Magdelena was next in line. "Do you mind if I get in front of you? I'm fixing a plate for Frannie."

"Of course not. And fill one for you also. We'll use the kitchen table and share some of our food with Lily," Magdelena said.

"Perfect." Rachael filled the plates and followed Magdelena inside. She set her plate on the table and the other one on a tray for Frannie. "I'll take this to her. Will you put Lily in her high chair? She'll love the noodles, cooked carrots, and peas."

"Be happy to." Magdelena grabbed a tin plate and scooped food onto Lily's plate.

Rachael pushed Frannie's bedroom door open to carry the food in. She was surprised Frannie sat up in bed. "Here you go." She positioned the tray over her lap.

Frannie dipped her spoon in the mashed potatoes.

"Would you like anything else?" Rachael gripped the knob and glanced back at her.

Frannie shook her head. "I don't know how I'll live without him. Thank goodness Caleb will take care of us. I'm sorry this will end your courtship."

"What do you mean?" Rachael gulped.

"I'm sure Caleb understood Stephen to mean he should marry me if something happened to him. It will be for the best. I need a husband, and Lily needs a *daed*. I need a man who will be here each day to help me take care of Lily. He will also need to take care of the *haus* and the farm chores."

Rachael's cheeks warmed. "Caleb has a say in this. He can take care of you and Lily without marrying you."

Would Caleb marry Frannie to fulfill a promise he made to Stephen? It wasn't uncommon for a widow to marry her dead husband's *bruder*. Caleb would be miserable having Frannie for a *fraa*.

She'd help anyway she could not to have that happen. "I can also lend you a hand."

"You don't have a *boppli* and you've not been married. I'm young. Caleb owes it to me and his *bruder* to marry me. I can give him a good life and more *kinner*. After what's happened, it's wrong of you to stand in our way."

Rachael was dumbfounded. She gripped the doorknob until her knuckles hurt. Was Frannie right? Frannie had showed no sign of being capable of living with her *dochder* on her own. What would Caleb have to say about all this?

She exited and closed the door just shy of it being shut all the way. She trembled. Frannie had said she could give Caleb more *kinner*. She walked to the living room window and watched Ellie and Liza with their precious little *dochders* playing together. *Kinner* of all ages caught her attention.

Joy and Thad waved to her and grinned.

She waved back. She had gotten close to the two *kinner*, and she'd begun to feel like their *mamm*. Something she had wanted for a long time. She hadn't told Caleb everything. Frannie might have a point.

Caleb came inside after the last buggy had left. "We loaded the benches and tables we borrowed, and Toby and his friends will return them to the shed on the Yoders' property. Do you need help in the kitchen? I can't believe the time is seven already." He faced her in the living room.

"I fed and put Lily to bed. She was exhausted. She was passed around to many of our friends and loved the attention. She's such a friendly *boppli*. Magdelena cleaned the kitchen before she left. Are you hungry?"

He patted his stomach. "I'm full from the food all the ladies brought. I've had enough. How about you?"

"I'm stuffed also."

"Let's relax and enjoy time for the two of us." Caleb patted the cushion on the settee beside him.

"I should look in on Frannie first." She left and returned. "She's asleep. She did finish half her breakfast and dinner. I'm hoping she'll dress and take care of Lily tomorrow."

"She'd better. It's ridiculous how she acted today. It's not easy for any of us, but we do what we have to." He wished she was more like Rachael. A strong, caring, and selfless woman.

"Don't judge her. I can understand why she wanted to avoid the guests, the casket, the bishop's message, and the burial. She's made acquaintances but not close relationships with any women. Hannah has made the most progress winning her over, but she's had to work hard at it. We need to encourage her to participate in future socials and to stay longer after Sunday services. She always seemed in a hurry to go home."

"Frannie built her life around Stephen and Lily and me. Her parents had her late in life and didn't expect much from her. Stephen was a born caregiver. He doted on her as much as her parents. Her *mamm* died in her sleep and her *daed* passed away a year later, working in the garden on a hot summer day. Stephen said he thinks the man died of a broken heart. He wasn't the same talkative and jolly man once his *fraa* died."

"Frannie must have traits Stephen found attractive. It's understandable why he found her pretty. She has silky brown hair and beautiful round eyes. She has a slender frame and dainty features."

Caleb rolled his eyes. "She's attractive and she can be a doting *mamm* to Lily when she chooses to. Stephen said she made him feel needed and they were best friends. He didn't mind she expected him to help her clean, cook, and take care of Lily. He's responsible for giving in to her demands."

"What will you do? She'll need you." Rachael fiddled with a stray thread on her sleeve.

He watched her. She wouldn't look at him. He didn't want her to question his love for her under any circumstances.

He placed his finger under her chin and turned her face to him. "I love you. I've put off buying a farm for us, but no longer. I'm meeting with Bart Byler on Monday to buy his place. He's leaving the furniture and equipment. He's moving to Lancaster, Pennsylvania, to live with his *dochder*'s family. He'll be eighty-five this month."

"I know the place. Good choice." Rachael grinned. "I'm happy for you."

"You can be happy for you too. Once I have the place and figure out how to take care of Frannie and Lily and this farm, I'll propose to you." Caleb would marry her tomorrow, but he wanted to have a home to offer her and give himself and Frannie a week to figure out what would work best for both of them.

"You may want to speak with Frannie before you buy another farm. You can't manage both properties." She fumbled her hands and dropped her gaze.

"I'll hire a man to take care of Stephen's place." He reached for her hand. "Nothing Frannie can say will change my mind."

She rose. "It's getting late. I should head home. I've got work tomorrow. Are you all right to care for Lily in the morning? If Frannie isn't fit to care for her, Hannah would *wilkom* her for the day."

Caleb faced her and held both her hands in his. "What's wrong? Do you have doubts about us? You're not your usual cheerful self."

He couldn't remember saying anything to her she might have found offensive or worrisome. She'd said she loved him. Why was she acting odd?

"You've been wonderful. I'm tired and have to work tomorrow. I need to get some rest and so do you. If you need me tomorrow after work, *kumme* by the bakery and let me know. I'd like to give Frannie some privacy and a chance for you to discuss the future with her."

"All right. I'll walk with you to your buggy; I hitched it earlier."

They went outside and walked in silence, holding hands.

He kissed her soft lips. "I'm buying the Byler *haus* for us. I promise."

She nodded and got in the buggy and accepted the reins from him. "I love you, Caleb, with all my heart. I pray you sleep sound tonight."

"I'm comforted knowing Stephen is no longer in pain. He tried to hide it, but he winced and held his side and bent over fighting to catch his breath often. I'll miss him every day." His lips quivered. He swallowed. "Be careful going home, my sweet Rachael."

"I will."

He didn't move until she disappeared around the bend. He loved her and he wanted to spend the rest of his life with her. He had no doubt Frannie would be a challenge. What did she expect of him now Stephen was gone? Stephen had asked him to take care of her. His stomach churned. He was afraid to dwell on the answer.

Chapter 8

Rachael pulled two warm sugar milk pies out of the oven Monday morning. It had been almost a week since Stephen's funeral and burial. Caleb had been busy finalizing the purchase of his farm, and he'd stopped in the bakery only twice since they'd parted the night of Stephen's services. She'd stolen about ten minutes each time to talk to him. The bakery had been too busy with customers when he'd chosen to visit to have any more time. Had he and Frannie had a serious conversation about what each of them expected? He hadn't mentioned it.

Magdelena interrupted her thoughts. "Sheriff Williams and Dr. Harrison are here asking if we have warm pie. They want something different for breakfast." She eyed the pie. "I'll take the sugar milk pie to them."

"What news are they reading in the newspaper? Anything of interest?" Rachael wasn't supposed to inquire about outside world news, but Dr. Harrison and the sheriff split their paper each morning and discussed interesting topics. She needed something to take her mind off what she needed to tell Caleb.

"Nothing good. The war with countries fighting each other scares me. The sheriff and Dr. Harrison insist it's only a matter of time before the United States will have to become a part of the war to protect our freedom. The news about the war going on in other countries always makes me sad because of soldiers losing their lives. I like it better when they talk about new inventions." Magdelena tilted her head. "You've been quieter than usual this morning. Anything wrong?"

She didn't want to tell Magdelena before she told Caleb her secret. He deserved to know first. "I'm all right. *Danki*."

Caleb entered the bakery kitchen and grinned. He waved papers. "The farm is mine. I'd like to take you to supper tonight. I'll meet you here after work and we'll go across the street to the Inn's restaurant."

She'd waited long enough. It was time to tell him everything. She couldn't let their courtship continue any longer. "I'll be ready."

Magdelena hurried to them. "I'm sorry to interrupt the two of you, but I need help to fill the display cabinet with the cookies and the second pie you made. I've got three customers in line."

"I'll leave and let you get back to work. Both of you, have a good rest of your day." Caleb smiled and left.

Rachael carried the pie and maple cookies on a large tray to the display case. "I'll arrange these for you."

"*Danki*." Magdelena accepted the customer's change. "Enjoy your goodies. Next, please. Eunice, *wilkom*. Always good to see you. What would you like?"

"Magdelena, I'll take a maple sugar pie. And, Rachael, I noticed your pretty face through the glass as you were filling the case."

Rachael stood. "*Danki* for the compliment." She blushed. "The pie you're purchasing is still warm from the oven."

"Mine aren't as good as yours. You are quite the baker."

She paid Magdelena. "*Danki*, dear." Eunice came around the counter and hooked her arm through Rachael's. "I need a couple of minutes of your time. Let's go to the kitchen."

Rachael loved Eunice. She had brought the most food to Stephen's services. She was generous and caring. What did she want to speak to her about?

"I delivered a casserole last night to Frannie and I asked if she needed anything. She said Caleb and she were managing fine. She told me she has no doubt he will take good care of her and Lily, as he'd never go back on the promise he made to his *bruder*. It's no secret you and Caleb are courting. Please be cautious of her. She asked me if I stitched wedding dresses. I told her yes, and I didn't ask any questions. I couldn't rest until I told you about this."

Eunice wasn't a busybody, and Rachael loved her for caring about her enough to share what was in her heart. She was also Mamm's closest friend. Her motives were pure.

Rachael's heart pounded and she twisted her hands. "*Danki*. Caleb and I are meeting tonight. I'm unsure of what the future holds for us."

"Seek God's guidance through prayer and Scriptures. He has a plan for you and for Caleb. My prayer is for you to marry Caleb or whoever you choose is right for you, and to be happy." She furrowed her brow. "Your limp is more noticeable today. I can stay and help you bake. You wouldn't need to pay me."

Rachael kissed her friend's cheek. Lack of sleep always made her leg ache. "I appreciate your concern. I'll be fine. Some days my leg feels heavier than others, but I don't have much pain. I'm used to it."

She had another reason she wasn't herself. She was ashamed. If Caleb was the one with the secret and he'd waited as long as she had to reveal it, she'd be upset. It was time to consider Caleb and what he wanted. She'd also let

Joy and Thad down. God wouldn't approve of her putting herself before others. She had some difficult decisions to make.

"I won't keep you from baking any longer. Always a treat anytime I talk to you. Your *mamm* and I have become fast friends over the last couple of months. I'm thrilled she and Joseph are courting." Eunice grinned.

"He makes her happy and he seems perfect for her." Rachael had warmed to the idea of Mamm and Joseph getting married.

Mamm had a lilt in her step, sang hymns as she did her chores, and had a sparkle Rachael loved. She wished her and Caleb's courtship was less complicated.

Caleb couldn't believe the change in Frannie. She'd cooked more meals, cleaned the *haus*, and taken care of Lily more this last week than she had when Stephen was alive. Why now? He mucked the barn stalls, fixed the loose latch on the corral, and stopped at the water pump for a drink.

Frannie strolled over to him. "Do you have plans for this evening?"

He stepped back and wiped water from his chin on his shirtsleeve. "Yes. I'm taking Rachael to the restaurant in town."

"We need to talk before you go. Will you spare the time now?"

He should tell her he bought a farm. "Yes. Is Lily taking a nap?"

She nodded. "Let's go inside. I've made warm cinnamon bread and tea."

He loved cinnamon bread. She was up to something. He didn't trust her. Perhaps she realized he wouldn't stand for her laziness like Stephen. This conversation should be interesting. They went inside the *haus* to the kitchen and sat at the table. She served him a cup of hot tea and a warm slice of cinnamon bread slathered with butter.

"*Danki*." She'd taken care to add extra butter, the way he liked it. "What would you like to discuss?" He'd tell her about the farm last.

"I'm aware Stephen asked you to take care of Lily and me in the event of his death. The proper way to honor his wishes is for you to marry me. You'll need to inform Rachael you're no longer available, and then we can schedule our wedding with the bishop. The sooner the better."

He sat upright and narrowed his eyes. "I don't need to marry you to make sure you and Lily have what you need. I've bought a farm. I plan to marry Rachael. I'll hire a farmhand to take my place here. We'll check on you and Lily, and you're *wilkom* to visit as long as you respect Rachael."

Stephen might've been relieved if Caleb had consented to marry his widow, but it wasn't necessary. He could keep the promise to his *bruder* without marrying Frannie.

Spoiled Frannie smacked the table with her hand. "You owe it to us to do the right thing. If you abandon us, you've lied to your *bruder*."

He stared into her eyes. "Calm down. Your idea and mine about what type of care you and Lily need is different. My way will work out fine. There are available men in our community. You might have some of them approach you, now you're a widow. With your permission, Rachael and I can make known you're interested in remarrying. She and Magdelena might be open to playing matchmaker for you."

Frannie's cheeks reddened and she scrunched her face. "You are a liar. You know Stephen meant for you to marry me if something happened to him. How can you abandon us and not fulfill your promise to him?"

Caleb struggled not to walk out. She was selfish to

expect him to wed her and end his courtship with Rachael. He wouldn't let her make him feel guilty about this. "Stephen wouldn't expect me to become your husband, knowing we don't get along. He would expect me to make sure you and Lily have what you need. You need to accept my courtship with Rachael, and be assured I will take care of you and Lily my way."

Her face softened. "Rachael is stronger than I am. I depend on you, Caleb. I can't bear to be alone in this *haus*. Please consider what I'm asking of you. We can build a life together and have more *kinner*. Lily needs siblings." Frannie's eyes pooled with tears.

He was hurting since Stephen's death, and she was too. He wanted her worries about money and the farm to disappear. She needed to open her heart and consider another man. "Listen. It will take time for you to mourn and accept Stephen's death. My heart aches over his passing too. I believe you have it in you to be stronger than you think."

She glared. "Stephen would be disappointed if he knew you didn't fulfill your promise to him. You knew what he meant when he asked you to take care of us. You choose to ignore it so you can fulfill your own selfish desire to marry Rachael. She probably would've married Nathan if you hadn't *kumme* along. Let her marry him." The woman had no scruples. She could turn her emotions on and off within minutes to attempt to get her way.

He shook his head. "She chose me. Stephen would've understood why I'm marrying Rachael. He'd be happy for me. He would also trust me to still take care of you and Lily. You should too. This conversation is over. I'll be moving to the farm I purchased and I'll hire a farmhand to take care of yours. Would you like to have a say about who I hire?"

Frannie narrowed her eyes. "No." She stood, turned on her heel, and flounced from the room.

Caleb turned his back to her and went outside. He fed the animals, weeded the garden, and brushed the mare. At five, he washed his face and changed his clothes. He went to meet Rachael at the bakery. He wouldn't let Frannie spoil his evening. He parked his buggy and smiled at her. She was standing outside the bakery.

"Are you hungry?"

"Yes. I'm hoping they have chicken pot pie tonight," she said.

He returned her smile and nodded. "I might order the same. Sounds delicious." He kept his hand on her elbow as they crossed the road to the restaurant in the Inn.

"Rachael, *wilkom*. Who is this handsome fellow?" The hostess wore a high-necked, ruffled blouse and a black fitted skirt.

"Greta, this is Caleb Yutzy." Rachael blushed.

"Pleased to meet you." Caleb grinned.

"What a sweet couple you make. I'll seat you at our best table, away from the rest of our guests. We're not busy tonight, so you'll have plenty of privacy." She led them to a table in the corner, which was the farthest from the other two couples dining at the restaurant.

"*Danki*, Greta. This is perfect."

Caleb helped scoot in Rachael's chair before he sat.

"The special this evening is fried fish, boiled redskin potatoes, and slaw. We sell Rachael's creations from the bakery, so you'll want to leave room for spice cake. Tilly will be your waitress. Enjoy."

Caleb unfolded his red-and-white-checkered napkin and set it on his lap. "I don't remember meeting Greta before.

Last time I stopped in and had supper here, Juanita was the hostess."

Rachael nodded. "Juanita moved away. Greta is her *schweschder*. She took Juanita's place here."

Tilly poured them each a glass of water from a pitcher. "Rachael, always happy to wait on you. Now, in addition to the special Greta told you about, we have chicken pot pie, chicken and noodles, beef vegetable casserole, and pork chops. The vegetable blend of the day is carrots and peas. Would you like anything to drink besides water?"

"Not for me. *Danki*. Tilly, I'd like you to meet Caleb Yutzy." Rachael gestured to him.

"My pleasure." Tilly glanced at Caleb.

"Water is fine for me. *Danki*. We're ready to order."

Tilly set the pitcher of water on the table. "What would you like?"

"We'll both have chicken pot pie." Caleb raised his brows. "Rachael, would you like anything more?"

"A basket of bread and honey butter, please."

"You've got it, and you know it's delicious because you baked it!" Tilly chuckled.

"*Danki*. We appreciate you buying our breads and desserts for the restaurant." Rachael gazed back at Caleb as Tilly left them to help another customer.

"Rachael, I planned to wait until after supper, but I didn't expect we'd have privacy here. I love you and I want to spend the rest of my life with you. I pray God gives us a houseful of *kinner* to raise. You and I have a lot of love to give them. What do you say? Will you marry me?"

She wrenched her gaze from his and her smile faded. "I would love to, but I can't answer you until I tell you something I've kept to myself that may change your mind."

"Nothing you say will change my mind." Caleb didn't understand. He expected an overwhelming "yes" to his proposal.

"You remember when I told you about the accident causing my limp?" Rachael folded her hands on the table, her knuckles white.

Why was she nervous? She'd already told him about the accident. "Yes. If this is about your limp, I think you're beautiful in every way."

"You have made it clear you want as many *kinner* as God allows us. I should've told you when our courtship became official, but I was afraid of losing you. I can't have *kinner*." She swiped a tear from her cheek.

Caleb's eyes widened and his mouth opened. He'd looked forward to being a *daed*, and he hadn't considered that he or Rachael might not have them. "Are you sure?"

She nodded and leaned her head closer across the table. She whispered, "I'm embarrassed to share such personal information, but you must understand. I stopped having my monthly courses after the accident. The doctor said there was nothing they could do. He's sure I'll not bear *kinner*. I love you, and I want the best for you. Frannie told me she expects you to marry her to fulfill a promise you made to Stephen in the case of his death. She can give you *kinner*."

Caleb shook his head and took a deep breath. "I'm not marrying Frannie. We had a discussion today about it, and I made it clear to her I'm marrying you. I assured her I can provide and take care of her and Lily without having to wed her. Your inability to bear *kinner* doesn't change my wish to marry you, Rachael." He was sad about her news, although it wouldn't hold him back from spending the rest of his life with her. Not having *bopplis* was a sacrifice he was willing to make. "Rachael, please marry me."

"I'm standing in the way of the promise you made to

Stephen and of you having *kinner*. I've been selfish and dishonest by not telling you I couldn't have *kinner*. What I did was wrong." Rachael wrung her hands.

Caleb reached for her hands across the table. "None of what you're saying changes my mind." He was shocked, but it was true. He would miss not having *kinner*, but having Rachael for his *fraa* was more important.

"How can it be God's will for us to wed? I deceived you. I hurt Thad and Joy when I left them and I've been ridden with guilt over both of those things. God has pricked my conscience during my prayer and Scripture time each day, to be honest with you. I'm so sorry." She stood and rushed outside.

Caleb hurried to find Tilly. He asked her to box the food and promised to return to pay her in a couple of minutes. He ran outside to the livery close by. She was in her buggy, ready to leave. He stepped inside the buggy and sat beside her. "Please stop, Rachael. I don't understand. We love each other. I believe our meeting wasn't by chance. What if God's plan is for us to marry? It doesn't matter to me that you waited to tell me you're barren."

"If I truly love you, I'll let you go. You've mentioned how important *kinner* are to you many times since we've met. I've noticed how happy you are playing with the *kinner* after the services on Sundays. Your eyes sparkle when you're holding Lily. I live with the sadness and disappointment of never becoming a *mamm*. It's painful, and it never goes away. I don't want you to regret not having *kinner* when you see our friends enjoying theirs. Again, I'm so sorry. Please, Caleb, let me go. Please."

Caleb relented and left her buggy. He waited.

Rachael glanced at him with tears streaming down her face and back at the road ahead. "*Kumme* on, girl, let's go."

Caleb removed his hat and raked a hand through his hair.

Why didn't she believe him? He meant what he said. He would never regret choosing a future with her. He'd been drawn to her the first time they met. He had no doubt God had picked her for him. He had no doubt she loved him. He wouldn't give up on her.

He set his hat on his head, returned to the restaurant, paid for the food, and took the leftovers Tilly had packaged for him. The meal he had hoped to share and wanted to remember as part of his proposal to Rachael for years to *kumme*. The evening had been a disaster.

He drove home. He couldn't move into the farm*haus* until tomorrow. The last person he wanted to run into was Frannie. He hoped she'd gone to bed. He entered the *haus*. All was quiet, and he sighed. *What a relief.* Frannie must've gone to bed. Tomorrow, he'd advertise for a farmhand. He had a plan and he wouldn't veer from it. God had made it clear to him from the day he met Rachael that she was the one for him. He just had to convince her.

Rachael unharnessed her mare. She couldn't stop weeping. Why had the accident taken away her ability to have *kinner*? As if losing her fiancé, John, wasn't enough. Caleb made her heart sing. He had a strong work ethic. He loved God. She'd not be the same without him. She crossed the threshold. Mamm sat in her favorite chair, knitting a blanket. She plopped on the chair next to her.

Mamm dropped her knitting in the basket on the other side of her chair. "Before I forget, Joseph has asked us to *kumme* to his place tomorrow evening. *Kumme* to his place after work." She wiped a tear with the pad of her thumb from Rachael's cheek. "Oh, my dear *dochder*, you've been crying. What happened?" She reached for Rachael's hand.

"I've made a mess of things with Caleb. I haven't told

anyone in Charm about being barren. I didn't tell Caleb until he proposed tonight."

Mamm's eyes widened. "Proposed. Why didn't you say yes, and why are you upset? You love him."

"Because I love him, I couldn't say yes. Caleb wants and loves *kinner*, and he would make a wonderful *daed*. I should've told him from the start of our courtship. I wanted one more day with him, and then one more week. I found excuses to keep my secret. It was an awful mistake." Rachael swiped a tear from her cheek.

"What does Caleb have to say about all this?" Mamm rubbed her hand.

"He said it doesn't matter to him. He still wants to marry me. But he's mentioned often how much he wants *kinner*. I kept silent. Deep in my heart, I knew this day would *kumme*." She'd put her happiness above his.

"Take Caleb at his word. Don't rob yourself of the joy of having him as your husband and building a future with him. He's forgiven you. Believe him." Mamm caressed her cheek.

Rachael shook her head. "*Kinner* are an important part of what he wants for the future. I would always wonder if he'd grow to resent me in the years to *kumme*. What kind of marriage would we have if I carry the guilt of not giving Caleb the one thing he wants most? I don't believe marrying him would be God's will. I've learned an important lesson. I caused myself this pain by pretending it could work."

"You're being too hard on yourself." Mamm sighed.

Rachael swiped a tear from her cheek. "Our marriage would always have a dark cloud over it. Even if he never mentioned it, I would always wonder if he had regrets every time we were with our friends and their *kinner*. God doesn't approve of deceit. I was living a fairy tale."

"Pray and seek God's guidance through prayer and the

Scriptures. Ask God for forgiveness, and then forgive your-self, whether you marry Caleb or not." Mamm kissed the back of her hand.

Rachael scooted out of the chair and sat on the floor with her head in Mamm's lap. "I long to have a *boppli*, and my heart aches when I allow myself to dwell on it."

"I'm not sure I agree Caleb isn't God's will for your husband. Please seek God's guidance. Joy and Thad love you. You didn't do anything wrong when you fell in love with Caleb. They'll understand when they grow older."

"I've missed Joy and Thad a lot. My experience with them is part of the reason I have to let Caleb go. They are an example of the joy Caleb will have someday when he's a *daed*. He deserves it, and he'll be a devoted *daed*. As dif-ficult as it is to end our courtship, I'll cherish the time we spent together. He's a wonderful listener, interesting to talk to, and easy to love. I may never get over him."

Rachael kneaded the bread dough Tuesday morning. She'd skipped breakfast and left home earlier than usual, having tossed and turned most of the night, unable to take her mind off Caleb. She had to focus on work and anything besides him to bring herself out of this heartbreaking slump.

Magdelena entered and slid her apron over her head and tied the apron strings behind her back. "What brings you in this early?" She grinned bright and cheery. "How was supper with Caleb?"

Rachael's cheeks heated. "He asked me to marry him."

"Congratulations. Did you discuss a wedding date?" Magdelena clapped her hands. "I'm thrilled for you."

"I declined." Rachael's stomach churned.

"Why? You love him. He loves you. I don't understand." Magdelena tilted her head.

"The accident I told you about that caused my limp also rendered me barren. Caleb said it doesn't matter to him, but having *kinner* is all he's talked about since we met. I'm guilty of withholding this information from him until he proposed. It wasn't fair to him. As time passed, I thought *kumming* to grips with my condition would get easier, or I'd accept it. It grows worse. I won't have Caleb experience the same."

"Why haven't you told me? We're best friends. I could be helping you through this. You could've talked to me about it." Magdelena placed her hands on Rachael's shoulders.

"You are my best friend, and I tell you most things. This is the most difficult topic for me to discuss. I love *kinner*. I, like Caleb, wanted as many *boppli* as the Lord would allow me. For some reason, it's not in God's plan for me. I've accepted it, but it still hurts."

"Why won't you believe Caleb when he says it doesn't matter and he wants to marry you anyway?" Magdelena gently shook Rachael.

"I would never forgive myself for taking away something so important to him. When I realized how much having *kinner* meant to him, I should've ended our courtship. I kept putting it off because I wanted more time with him. Each time he played with our friends' *kinner* or Lily, I'd wonder if he had regrets. It's no way to begin a future together. I believe, knowing this about myself, God wouldn't approve of me becoming Caleb's *fraa*. I can picture him with his *kinner*. He'll teach them how to do farm chores, catch fish, row a boat, and so much more."

Hannah rapped on the open doorframe. "Good morning. I hope I didn't *kumme* at a bad time. The door was open. I wanted to visit you before you opened the bakery to customers."

Rachael sprinkled more flour onto her bread dough. "You are always *wilkom*."

Magdelena dragged a stool to the working table centered in the kitchen. The kitchen allowed them plenty of room to create their breads and desserts. "Would you like a cup of coffee?"

"I would. *Danki*."

Rachael dropped her dough into a loaf pan. "I brewed some when I arrived."

Magdelena left and returned. She passed Hannah a cup of coffee.

"I couldn't help overhearing something about Caleb and *kinner*. Rachael, you look as if you're carrying a load of wood on those shoulders. What can I do to help? Your sad eyes tell me something is wrong." Hannah's eyes were filled with compassion.

Rachael loved her for it. She expelled a heart-wrenching sigh. "I'm barren. The accident that caused my limp also damaged me. I stopped having my courses each month. I left out this detail when I told you about the buggy tipping over on me. I won't marry Caleb because I shouldn't prevent him from being a *daed*. He's talked about it a lot." Rachael was tired of repeating her story, but Hannah was a close friend and she always gave good advice.

"Isn't this his decision too?" Hannah stood and set the coffee on the table. She circled her arm around Rachael's waist.

"I stayed with him long enough for him to fall in love with me. Then I broke his heart. I wasn't thinking of anyone but myself and my happiness. I must think of his. It's the right thing to do." Rachael sighed.

"God is all about forgiveness, and those we love are too.

I also understand how you're righting your wrong by allowing him the opportunity to fulfill his dream with another woman. I'm not convinced you wouldn't be happy together without *kinner*, given he has said you're enough for him." She returned to her stool. "I don't understand why Timothy and I haven't been blessed with a *boppli*. We want *kinner*, but we would've still married if I knew I couldn't have them. I can understand why you made this decision, on one hand. On the other, you should take Caleb at his word." Hannah's lips trembled.

"I'm praying about my decision. As for you and Timothy, there's still time. You're young," Rachael said.

Magdelena nodded. "She's right, Hannah."

"Timothy and I will accept whatever God decides. He knows what's best. We're hopeful." Hannah traced the rim of her cup. "We're here for you, Rachael. My door is always open, anytime you need to talk."

"*Danki*, sweet friend. I must accept my circumstances and remain strong in my decision, for Caleb's sake."

Hannah stayed and chatted with them another few minutes, then left.

Rachael splayed her hands on the table. "I forgot to tell you, Frannie expects Caleb to marry her. He refused. He bought a farm, and he plans to move into it soon. He did promise to check in on her and Lily, and to hire a farmhand to manage her place."

Magdelena measured a teaspoon of brown sugar and added it to her butterscotch pie filling. "She's not the easiest woman to know. We'll have to work harder at befriending her. She'll need friends. I can't imagine how sad she must be, losing her husband."

"Yes. She's young and alone. I pray she will find love again. She's not used to working hard. Stephen and Caleb did all the inside and outside chores. They did more than their fair share of caring for Lily also. She might be more open to befriending you than me," Rachael said.

"She'll have to be kind to you if she wants to befriend me. I'll be praying you will be at peace with Caleb's forfeiting having *kinner* to marry you. It is his decision too. Not just yours. He's made clear to you his choice. I wish you'd accept it." Magdelena gave her a hard stare.

"I believe I'm doing what's in our best interest. It's a hard decision to stand by." Rachael assumed her days ahead with Caleb would be sad, but she had to remain strong.

At five, Rachael drove to Joseph's and found him and Mamm seated at the kitchen table. Her gaze flitted to the stove and back at them. "I hope you don't mind, I didn't knock. Am I late for supper?"

"I don't mind, and not at all." Joseph grinned.

"I have a plate for you on the stove." Mamm stood and grabbed the plate. She unwrapped it and set it in front of Rachael.

Joseph patted his stomach. "Your *mamm* cooked beef sliced thin covered with a mushroom gravy, mixed vegetables, and applesauce. It was delicious."

"I'm sure I'd agree with you if I had a better appetite. Today hasn't been the best." She took a bite of beef.

She didn't want to go into what had transpired between her and Caleb with Joseph. She hoped Mamm had shared what happened with him. She didn't mind him knowing. He seemed like family already.

Joseph's smile faded. "Your *mamm* told me you ended your courtship with Caleb and why. I'm sorry, Rachael."

"*Danki*, Joseph." She didn't want to talk about it.

Joseph snapped his fingers. "I have an idea. I'm leaving early in the morning to visit Adelaide in New Philadelphia. You want to meet her, and I've decided I'd like you to. I'll stay overnight at the boarding*haus* in town, and then I'll be home day after tomorrow. Why don't you join me? I'll secure a room for the both of you. I'll show you around town, and maybe it will take your mind off your sadness for a couple of days." He gave her a compassionate smile. "I'm praying Caleb will be relentless in his pursuit of you and you'll accept he'll be happy without *kinner* as long as he has you."

Mamm grinned. "I'd love to go. Rachael, you can ask Hannah to fill in for you at the bakery. I realize this is short notice, but you can ask her this evening. It might do you good to get away."

Rachael loved the thought of getting away. She was curious about Adelaide and why the woman liked living in the outside world. When Toby had confronted Joseph outside the saloon about seeing him talking to her when he was in New Philadelphia, she was relieved when Joseph told them Adelaide was his niece. She admired him for keeping in touch with her, in spite of not approving of her lifestyle. He should shun her, according to Amish tradition, but she didn't agree with this practice either. He couldn't make Adelaide change her ways. She was alone. He loved her as her uncle.

"*Danki*, Joseph, for your kind words and for asking me to go with you. I'll help wash and dry the dishes, and then I'll go to Hannah's place." She couldn't help but smile. She was grateful to Joseph for thinking of her.

Mamm waved a dismissive hand. "You hurry to Hannah's. I'll take care of the dishes."

"*Danki*."

Joseph grabbed a dish towel. "I'll dry."

Rachael chuckled as she headed out of the kitchen. "You two make a good team."

She drove down the road about a mile from her *haus* and

turned into Hannah and Timothy's lane and parked the buggy. She knocked on the door.

Timothy answered the door. His smile faded and his eyes widened. "Is everything all right?"

She waved a dismissive hand. "Yes. I'm sorry to startle you. This is a little late to visit. I came to ask Hannah a favor."

"You're *wilkom* here anytime." Timothy opened the door wider for her to step inside the living room.

Hannah came from the kitchen. "Did you have supper? I have leftover stew."

"*Danki*. I had supper before I came. Joseph invited me to go with him and Mamm to New Philadelphia tomorrow to meet his niece, Adelaide. We'll be gone for two days. Would you take my place at the bakery? I understand I'm not giving you much notice. Don't feel pressured to say yes if it's not convenient."

"I'd love to." She smiled at her husband. "Timothy, do you mind?"

Timothy smiled at both of them. "No. You go have fun. You'll enjoy baking again, and you can catch up on gossip with Magdelena." He frowned. "I'm sorry about your courtship ending with Caleb. Magdelena told me."

"*Danki*. I'll *wilkom* this trip. The diversion won't heal my heart or erase him from my mind, but it will give me other things to focus on. I'm looking forward to meeting Adelaide. She intrigues me. If I can help her in any way, I will. Joseph's devotion to her warms my heart, and the more I'm around him, the more I like him."

She stayed for a couple of more minutes and then left. Magdelena would be surprised to find Hannah at the bakery tomorrow, but she'd be happy and understanding. Caleb might visit the bakery and she needed to keep away from him. She didn't trust herself. She loved him so much. She knew in her heart she was doing the right thing.

She returned to Joseph's *haus* and went inside. "*Danki* again, Joseph, for supper and the invitation to meet Adelaide. I can go. Hannah has agreed to fill in for me at the bakery. She'll tell Magdelena why I'm not there, and she won't mind."

She was thankful for her close friends. They all looked out for one another.

"I'm glad. I'll pick you both up at six in the morning. It will take us six to seven and a half hours to arrive at New Philadelphia, if we make quick stops along the way. We should be there by two thirty or three."

"We'll be ready. I'll pack sandwiches and snacks, and I'll bring water." Mamm motioned to Joseph. "I'm heading home, husband-to-be. You need your sleep. We have a long day ahead of us."

Chapter 9

Rachael rode with Joseph and Mamm to New Philadelphia early Wednesday morning and enjoyed Joseph's childhood stories. He'd kept her and Mamm entertained, and they had made good time, keeping their stops short and eating the sandwiches Mamm packed for them. She had *wilkomed* the trip's distraction, although her mind had drifted off several times to Caleb. Would he visit the bakery? She longed for the sound of his voice, to gaze into those brown eyes, and to plan a future with him. She clutched her fists in her lap. She wouldn't budge on her decision. Anytime she wavered, she forced herself to remember the many times he'd said he wanted *kinner*.

The little-over-six-hour drive had gone quickly, and they were in New Philadelphia before she knew it. Shoppers bustled from one store to the next, and peddlers stood on the corners selling food, fruits, and gadgets. She loved the hustle and bustle of the town, which was larger than Charm.

Joseph left the buggy at the livery and escorted them to the boardwalk in the middle of New Philadelphia. "I'm thankful we have sunshine and a warmer day than usual for this time of year."

Mamm pointed to a shop. "Yes, it makes this trip more fun. I'd love to stop in at the quilt shop."

"We have time. Go browse. I'll wait outside." Joseph held the wrapped package she and Mamm had brought to give to his niece.

Rachael followed Mamm into the quilt shop, carrying their luggage with them. She scanned colorful quilts filling the walls. Some of the patterns had too many colors. She eyed a row of quilts in softer blues, yellows, whites, and greens. They were simple wedding, patchwork, and star patterns she liked to stitch. The shop was the largest one she'd visited. She wished she could tell Caleb about it. Better yet, she wished she could buy a quilt to save to use on their bed after their wedding. No more wedding. No more Caleb. No use for a wedding quilt.

Mamm yanked a bolt of navy fabric from the stack. "Do you like this color and thickness?"

She rubbed the material between her thumb and forefinger. "It's the right texture for the quilt you're making."

Joseph entered and joined them. "The smile on your face tells me this navy fabric has caught your eye. How many yards? I'd like to buy it for you." He reached for the bolt.

Mamm blushed. "*Danki*. Three yards should be enough."

Rachael was sure Caleb would've done the same had he found her admiring the fabric. Her trip away from Charm hadn't taken her thoughts from Caleb. Mamm's and Joseph's exchanges of endearments and obvious admiration for each other mirrored the courtship she had shared with Caleb. She had to let go of her reservations and selfish reasons about Joseph courting her *mamm*. She'd be disheartened if anything happened to separate them now.

Joseph paid for Mamm's selection, and they headed outside. "Let's go to the boarding*haus* and secure our rooms." He carried his bag, Adelaide's gift, and Mamm's package.

Rachael and Mamm carried their bags.

Rachael nodded. "That's a grand idea. We can leave our baggage and purchase in the room."

A peddler stepped in front of Rachael and dangled a necklace inches from her face. "Pretty lady, I have a locket you'll cherish for a lifetime. The perfect place for your and your beau's photographs."

"No. *Danki*." Rachael dodged the pushy Englischer.

The railroad train whistle blew. She'd never been on a train. It would've been fun to experience it with Caleb. Where would they go? She wouldn't care where they went if they were together. She shook her head. She had to quit thinking that way. It was useless.

They entered the boarding*haus*.

She scanned the entry. Red curtains at the windows were tied back with ornate gold-tasseled rope. The plush rug was gorgeous, with swirls of red, blue, and gold. Soft to stand on. This place was much fancier than she'd anticipated.

A woman in a ruffled white blouse and a long blue skirt greeted them. She wore fancy, cream-colored leather shoes. Rachael didn't know how she could walk in the chunky high heels. They looked too small for her feet.

"How many rooms would you like?"

Joseph opened his leather satchel to remove his wallet. "Two, please."

"Breakfast for the three of you is included with your rooms. Both rooms are upstairs and to your right. Here are your keys." She passed one to Joseph and one to Mamm. "There's fresh water in pitchers for you to pour into the large bowl provided on a stand opposite your beds. We empty and refill them twice a day. Towels and washcloths are in the drawer of the stand. Each room has a clock on one of the nightstands. The rules of our establishment and our restaurant's hours of operation are on a paper posted on the door in your room. I ask that you please honor them."

"*Danki*, madam." Joseph gestured to the stairs. "This way, ladies."

Rachael wondered if the woman had to recite this same speech to each customer. It must get tiring.

"*Danki*, Joseph, for our room." Mamm went ahead of her up the stairs.

"I'm glad you both could join me on this trip." They reached the top of the stairs, and Joseph passed a key to Mamm. "You're in room five and I'm in room six. Each room has two beds. I always stay here when I visit Adelaide. It's three thirty. Let's meet downstairs in the lobby at three forty-five. We'll find Adelaide and ask her to join us for supper."

Rachael and Mamm nodded, and Mamm unlocked their door.

Rachael entered and walked around the room. She stroked the beautiful gold satin bedspread. "How pretty." She hugged the pillow. "It's fluffy and the pillowcase is smooth." She buried her nose in it. "They must spray rosewater on them." She felt a pang of guilt, admiring the room and the things in it.

Mamm washed her face and hands. "We've not been on a trip like this. In the candy shop window, they were making taffy. I noticed shelves lined with an assortment of candy. It's a much larger store than the one we have in Charm. We'll have to take an assortment of hard candy home with us to share with Toby and Magdelena."

Rachael was surprised at the detail of the yellow roses etched on the ornate pitcher and the scalloped edges on the matching bowl. The stand had scrolled legs and a glass knob with a rose etched on it. She didn't understand the need to have such nice things. It all seemed unnecessary for everyday living. She went to the window. The shore deck along the river was busy. Men loaded crates, barrels, and boxes onto a barge. Passengers stood in line to board an impressive stern-wheeler with two levels. A small band played music on the bottom floor. This town had more to offer than Charm. She couldn't wait to meet Adelaide and to explore New Philadelphia. "I'm ready when you are."

Mamm opened the door, and they met Joseph waiting for them at the bottom of the stairs in the lobby. The chandelier had rows of crystal teardrops and must've been very expensive. The Englischers sure had lavish things compared to their simple life. She would've used the money to help the Amish widows and those in need.

Joseph worried his brows. "Are you comfortable walking to the restaurant next door to the saloon? It's about two blocks, and you can window-shop on the way. I want you to have fun on this trip."

Rachael and Mamm nodded.

They passed a shoe store, and Mamm paused. "There are rows and rows of all kinds of shoes. Those leather shoes have a gold buckle and two-inch heels. I'd trip if I wore them." She pointed to another pair of shoes. "There's the same pair of shoes the hostess had on."

Rachael imagined her feet in a pair of shoes like the hostess wore, and the thought of it made her feet hurt. She'd never have an occasion to wear such silly shoes, and she was glad Amish women didn't wear them.

Rachael pointed. "What about the fitted leather boots with all those buttons? They cost a dollar and eighty-six cents. I've never seen so many showy shoes and boots."

Joseph chuckled. "Wait until we pass the dry goods shop. You'll be amazed at how many fancy towels, blankets, and dry goods they have for sale."

A peddler stood alongside his wagon. "Grab your Cracker Jack box before they're all gone. You don't want to miss the prize inside."

Joseph stopped, tucked the package he carried under his arm, and paid the peddler fifteen cents for three boxes of Cracker Jack. "I love this caramel popcorn and peanut candy." He opened a box and pulled out a baseball card. "Eddie Plank. He's a professional baseball pitcher."

A young boy stopped. "You're lucky. I'd like to have Eddie Plank's card." He held a small metal baseball.

"Would you like to trade?" Joseph passed the boy the card.

"Yes, sir. Thank you so much." The boy pressed the small baseball into Joseph's hand and took the card. "I can't wait to show this to my buddies. Thanks again, mister."

Rachael smiled at the act of kindness. She was sure Caleb would've done the same thing. Joseph reminded her of Caleb, with his giving heart and caring attitude. But she couldn't dwell on him. She was here to meet Adelaide. She opened her box of Cracker Jack and found a tiny metal doll. She examined it. "The details in this tiny metal doll and in the other trinkets this company makes and puts in these boxes amaze me."

Mamm laughed. "I have a tiny sewing machine charm." She held it out to them.

Rachael hooked her arm through Mamm's as they strolled along the boardwalk and enjoyed the window displays in the dry goods store, bridal shop, dress shop, and candy store. She'd never understand how women wore those pencil skirts and fancy dresses. She was sure they were uncomfortable. "What are the large buildings in the distance?"

"They're iron and steel factories." Joseph led them to an

ice cream parlor. "Would you like a drink? They have the best lemonade."

"Sounds very refreshing," Rachael said.

"I'd like one." Mamm blushed.

Joseph handed Mamm the package and went inside the crowded shop.

Two older women sat on a bench in front of the ice cream shop. The heavier-set one waggled her finger. "Woodrow Wilson wasn't my choice for president. I'm not happy with the man. He's not the kind of leader we should have for this war we are for sure about to enter into. My grandsons are signing up to join the army, and they're ready to serve if the United States becomes a part of it. I'm sick about it."

The elegant older woman grabbed her friend's forefinger. "Rowena, I wish there was something I could say to comfort you, but I'm as worried as you. My grandson told me yesterday he's signing up." She clutched her friend's hand in both hers and pressed it to her chest.

Rachael had listened to Dr. Harrison and the sheriff discuss the war as they read the paper on their daily visits to the bakery. She grimaced each time they mentioned it was just a matter of time before the United States would be involved. She couldn't imagine having sons and sending them off to war. Once, Dr. Harrison had explained how they would be fighting for freedom. Rachael better understood and vowed to pray for the soldiers and their families each day.

Mamm glanced at the ladies but kept silent. Rachael was sure she didn't want to discuss their conversation because politics was part of the outside world.

Joseph returned with three lemonades. He passed them each one. "We're close to the saloon."

They finished their Cracker Jack and lemonade and proceeded to the restaurant next to the saloon.

Joseph showed them to a bench in front of the restaurant. "I'll bring Adelaide to you."

Rachael closed her eyes to concentrate on the piano music coming from inside the saloon. She wished Amish would allow violins and piano music. It lifted her mood and replaced the worry in her mind. She'd enjoyed two Englischers who had played violins on the street corner in Charm last year. They were passing through and stopped to make a little money. The way their hands glided the bow across the fiddle's strings to create such beautiful music had mesmerized her. The dancing hall in Charm had a piano, and she walked past it slowly to listen to the chipper and fun songs. She didn't dare tell a soul. Amish shouldn't subject themselves to such things.

Mamm fidgeted her hands. "Maybe we shouldn't have *kumme*. The bishop and many of our friends wouldn't approve. I came to support Joseph and to help Adelaide, but we should've sent her gifts instead of *kumming* in person. The hotels and stores are much too lavish for us. We shouldn't be here, using fancy things. And now we're close to a saloon. It's all too much. God wouldn't approve." She gave Rachael a stern stare. "And you're enjoying the music way too much."

"You're right. I'm sorry. I wouldn't give up Amish life for it, but I wish we could play our hymns on the piano." She clasped her Mamm's hand. "We don't agree with shunning our loved ones who leave the Amish life. We also don't shun those who need help, whether they are Amish or Englischer. We're here with the best intentions. I'm glad you chose to accompany Joseph, and I appreciate being included as a part of this visit to help Adelaide in whatever way she'll allow us to."

Mamm's face softened. "When did you become so wise?" She kissed Rachael's hand.

Joseph walked up with a young woman with long blond curls pinned at the sides, who appeared to be with child. "Adelaide, I'd like you to meet my fiancée, Eleanor Schlabach, and her *dochder*, Rachael."

Rachael struggled to keep surprise from showing on her face. Adelaide wore a tight, low-cut green dress, which stopped just below her knees, and matching worn heeled shoes.

"I'm pleased to meet you."

Adelaide's stomach protruded a lot, and Rachael didn't know how she could sit in the dress without it splitting. She wondered if Adelaide had enough money for clothes. She couldn't be comfortable.

Adelaide gave her a sly grin. "I'm guessin' you weren't expectin' me to be dressed like this." She shrugged. "I like dressin' this way much better than wearin' the dresses you have on. I was never cut out to be Amish. No offense. Uncle, congratulations. I'm glad you're gettin' married."

"No offense taken, Adelaide. I'm glad we have your blessing on our upcoming marriage." Mamm smiled. "We brought you bedsheets and hand towels." She offered the package to Adelaide. "I hope they're something you can use."

"Thanks. I can always use more sheets and towels. I use them until they're threadbare. I don't have enough money to replace them most times." Adelaide clutched the package against her chest.

"Adelaide, let's have dinner inside the restaurant, where we can chat and you can all get better acquainted." Joseph opened the door of the restaurant. "I'd like the table for four in the corner."

The hostess frowned at Adelaide.

Rachael glanced at the Englischers seated at the tables. Some of the men and women stared at them. Would the hostess refuse to serve them? Adelaide didn't fit in with the prim and proper women dressed in prettier dresses than the tight, faded, and garish dress on Joseph's niece. They were dressed in Amish clothing, unlike the rest of the guests. The hostess didn't seem to mind they were Amish. She hoped the hostess wouldn't cause a fuss. Adelaide might be a little rough, but Rachael liked her honesty. She didn't have to agree with her choices, but it didn't mean they couldn't express concern and offer help.

Joseph cocked his head. "I'd appreciate your help."

The hostess's face softened. "Right this way." She seated them at the table.

The waitress carried a pitcher of water and filled their glasses. "Welcome. I'm Verda and I'll be your waitress. We have spaghetti with meat sauce, beef stroganoff, and chicken pot pie today."

They all ordered the spaghetti.

"Adelaide, how are you doing? Do you need anything?" Joseph slipped her an envelope.

"This should help. Thank you." She folded it and stuffed it into her soiled red velvet reticule and snapped it shut. "Uncle, I have news."

"What is it?" Joseph cleared his throat.

"I kept my short marriage to Albert a secret from you. He was part-owner of the saloon, only because his father was the prior owner. Albert inherited it after his father died two years ago. We weren't married a year, and he was gone most of the time. You wouldn't have approved of him. He had a temper, and he wasn't faithful or dependable. But he made me laugh, called me pretty, and encouraged me to sing when he was here. Before, I'd been too shy. Now I'm earning extra money by doing what I love. I didn't care about his faults. I loved him."

Rachael leaned forward. Adelaide had referred to the man in the past tense. "Is he all right?"

"He's fine. He left town. He sold Madge the business, and he wasn't happy I'm with child. I'm not thrilled about the baby, but we'll get by." She frowned. "A week after he left, an attorney in town visited me here and asked me to sign divorce papers my husband had left." She patted her stomach. "Like I said, my baby and me, we'll survive without him."

Joseph gasped. "What is Albert's last name, and I suppose your last name too?"

"Lakes. I have no desire to have anything more to do with him." She cast her gaze to her lap.

Joseph closed his eyes for a moment. "Under the circumstances, please return to the Amish life. Your *boppli* will need a home. You live in a room above a saloon. How do you get any sleep? Who will help you care for the *boppli* while you work?" He shook his head.

Rachael gripped her hands until her knuckles turned white. Didn't Adelaide realize the gift she'd been given? She would give anything to be a *mamm* and she wouldn't have refused to give her *boppli* the best life possible. She shouldn't judge Adelaide. Joseph mentioned her *mamm* lived this way and enjoyed it. It was what Adelaide was used to. Rachael did worry, though. Adelaide was young to be divorced. Rachael wished Adelaide would *kumme* home with them.

"Some of the girls here will help me. The money you give me will supply what the baby needs. I have enough room to set a crib beside me. I'll make it work." Adelaide rolled her eyes. "I seem to get myself in one mess after another."

Mamm managed a weak grin. "We'll bring or send with

Joseph *boppli* blankets, nappies, and some other things for your *boppli* to help you get ready."

"You're sweet. I'd appreciate anything you can spare," Adelaide said.

"What draws you to the outside world?" Rachael set her elbow on the table and rested her chin in her hand. She couldn't understand how living above a noisy saloon, and serving gamblers and rough men who could be dangerous, was a better life than living in a home where she would be surrounded by family and not worry about food or safety for her *boppli*.

Adelaide's frown turned to a smile. "I love to sing along with the piano. I have a strong voice, and the patrons leave me and the piano player tips. The other girls who live above the saloon each have a room like mine. I've become close friends with some of them. I like to dance, and I enjoy wearing the colorful and different clothes and shoes. We go to the secondhand store to buy them."

Joseph sat ramrod straight and met Adelaide's gaze. "I'm worried you'll be overwhelmed with raising a *boppli* on your own. Please reconsider moving in with me for the sake of your child."

The waitress delivered their food and a basket of bread with a dish of butter. "Would you like anything else?"

They shook their heads, and Rachael thanked her. The hostess walked away.

"Nothing you can say will change my mind. I don't mean to be rude. I love you, Uncle." She tapped her reticule. "I'm very grateful for the money you've given me. I hope this won't mean the end of our friendship." She darted her gaze to Rachael and Mamm and then stared at her water glass. "You're always welcome to join my uncle when he comes to visit. I was worried you'd judge me, but you've been right nice. I like you girls."

Rachael slathered strawberry jam on her soft white bread. "*Danki*. I'd like to visit you again."

Adelaide blushed. "Are you married?"

"No." She didn't want to mention Caleb. She came here to escape the pain of letting him go.

"I noticed your limp. What happened? Do you mind me asking?" Adelaide set her fork on the plate.

"No. I don't mind." Rachael recounted the story of the accident.

Mamm patted her arm. "Rachael's been through some tough times. I'm blessed to have such a strong and compassionate *dochder*. She's an excellent baker, and she works in the bakery in town."

"With your limp and all?" Adelaide worried her eyes.

"I'm used to it, and it doesn't hurt most of the time. When I'm tired, my leg seems heavier and more of a nuisance. I have a stool in the kitchen. I sit if it bothers me."

"I love cake, fried apple pies, and fudge. If I worked in the bakery with you, I'd gain four hundred pounds." She chuckled.

Nodding, Joseph finished his last bite. "I have to limit my dessert portions. I could devour a whole fruit pie if I'm not careful."

Mamm laughed. "He had three pieces of cherry pie the second time I had him over at our place."

Adelaide blushed. "I've had a good time with all of you. I appreciate the gifts. I can understand why Joseph is fond of you both." She scooted her chair back and stood. "I'd visit more with you all, but I've gotta go back to work."

Joseph held a hand to his cheek and shook his head. "I'll walk you back to the saloon." He glanced over his shoulder. "Do you ladies mind if I leave you here? Please order dessert."

"We'll be fine." Mamm went to his niece and hugged her. "Take care."

Rachael rose and squeezed Adelaide's arms. "I hope we meet again." She meant it.

This girl needed them, and her *boppli* would too. God wouldn't want them to turn their backs on her.

"I've enjoyed getting to know you. I hope to visit you again."

Adelaide held her package in one hand and clasped Rachael's with the other. "You almost make me consider Amish life to have a friend like you." She gave Rachael a warm smile. "Travel safe and thanks again." She stepped to head toward Joseph, who was paying the bill.

Rachael smiled. "I am your friend, and I pray you will consider living in Charm, where we could spend more time together."

"Thanks. I might surprise you." Adelaide held her gaze, then left the restaurant with Joseph.

Mamm shuddered. "I had no idea what to expect. Adelaide is like a child. I don't know how she survives with the life she's living. She's putting herself and her *boppli* at risk."

"I'm glad this town is in Ohio and not out of reach for Joseph to visit her. He can make sure she's all right while encouraging her to *kumme* home with us."

Joseph returned to join them after taking his niece to the saloon. "*Danki* for your acceptance of Adelaide. I'm grateful you'll allow me to share about her and ask your advice. She was happy to meet you, and she responded to both of you much better than I anticipated. I wasn't sure if she'd shy away from you due to her line of work and you being Amish."

Mamm clasped his hand for a quick moment. "She's family."

Joseph nodded. "Enough about Adelaide. Let's tour the city more."

Rachael loved the train whistle, the peddlers' calls to the public to buy their products, and the newspaper boy waving a paper over his head and shouting about the latest news of the world war. She shuddered. It must be hard on the families who had sons and husbands fighting in this war. She sighed with sadness. A couple strolled past her holding hands and giggling. She wished Caleb was with them to tour the city. She'd never stop thinking about him.

Caleb hadn't slept or had much of an appetite since Rachael ended their courtship on Monday. He wouldn't have jabbered on about how much he looked forward to being a *daed* if he'd known she was barren. Giving up *bobblis* would be a sacrifice he would make to have a future with her. He missed her sweet face. Here it was, Thursday evening, and he sat alone on the porch swing at the *haus* he'd bought for them. He would stop in the bakery tomorrow. He had to convince her they were right for each other.

He studied the buggy approaching the *haus*. He rolled his eyes. *Frannie.* He wasn't in the mood to talk to her. Maybe she'd noticed the advertisements he'd posted in the general store and post office for a farmhand for her place. She could be here to tell him she was pleased he'd done this. He hoped the men he hired wouldn't quit if she proved to be too bossy.

Frannie parked the buggy. "Thought you might like some company." She untied Lily from the makeshift *boppli* chair Caleb had put in her buggy to transport his niece.

She was the last person he wanted to visit him. He

accepted Lily from her. "How's my little ray of sunshine?" He held her in the air.

"Unkie." Lily giggled.

Frannie tied her reins to the hitching post. "You haven't invited us over since you moved."

"All the furniture wasn't arranged in the rooms until last night." He carried Lily on his hip, and she rested her head on his shoulder.

"I thought I'd find Rachael here."

"She ended our courtship." Caleb looked past her at the ducks in the pond.

"Why?" Frannie put a hand to her hip.

"She's barren. I'd said too often how I'd love to have *kinner*. She's convinced I should marry a woman who can provide *kinner*. She's wrong. She's still the woman I want to marry."

"She's doing you a favor. You'll realize it soon enough." Frannie batted her eyelashes and raised her chin.

Caleb considered her arrogant and loathed her. He shouldn't have told her why he and Rachael were no longer courting. He was upset with himself for doing so. She'd caught him off guard. But he wouldn't have any further conversation with her about it.

They strolled to the porch, and he chose the swing. Frannie sat next to him and Lily. Too close for his liking. Why didn't she sit in the rocker? He resisted the urge to scoot away or get up and sit in the chair. He wouldn't move because she might make a smart remark about it in front of the bishop. Her mere presence had his stomach in knots.

"Caleb, with Rachael out of the way, you should reconsider marrying me. I need you, and Stephen wouldn't be pleased with you leaving Lily and me alone. Don't you feel bad about letting your *bruder* and us down?"

"Frannie, I've made myself clear, and I'm firm in my decision."

"I'm hurt you don't want to marry me and appalled you're not fulfilling Stephen's wishes." She had been manipulative with Stephen. Why was he surprised she would try to manipulate him?

A buggy approached the *haus*. He stood, holding a sleeping Lily. Who was this stranger? He was glad for the interruption. He was done with this conversation with Frannie.

The average-height man he guessed was a little older than himself tied his reins to the hitching post and approached them. He tipped his hat. "I'm sorry to intrude. My name's Luke Kilmer. I'm here about the advertisement you posted in the general store for a farmhand. I'm from Winesburg, Ohio. I'm twenty-five and in good health. I have no family, and I previously worked for an Englischer who had a farm. I lived in the outside world for two years, but I'd like to return to the life. The farmer died not long ago. I've visited Charm before and liked it. Would you consider hiring me?"

Caleb rocked Lily in the swing. "Have a seat. This is Frannie Yutzy. She's my late *bruder*'s *fraa*, and this is her *dochder*, Lily. The job is to care for her farm."

He nodded to Frannie. "I'm pleased to make your acquaintance, ma'am."

She blushed. "There's no need for you to be formal. Call me Frannie. Have you cared for a *boppli* before?"

Caleb gritted his teeth. The man would run out of here any moment with that kind of question. But it was better he'd find out now what he was getting himself into.

"Yes. I adore *kinner*. The man I worked for, Harold Sanders, had six *grosskinner* who lived close and visited often. We played hide-and-seek and board games and tossed a ball. I'll miss them. I'd have no objection to caring for Lily when you need me to."

"Didn't his *kinner* want the place and need you to still manage the property?" Caleb quirked his brows.

"They sold it to a family with older *kinner* who supplied plenty of help to run the place," Luke said.

Caleb raised his brows. This was good news. The opposite of what he'd expected the man to say.

Frannie grinned. "How wonderful. Do you cook, clean, and wash and hang clothes to dry?"

"Sure. I used to help out with all those chores when Patricia, Harold's *fraa*, needed an extra hand. I had more time in the winter for such tasks."

Caleb stifled his chuckle. Frannie and Luke couldn't stop smiling at each other, and they acted as if he wasn't there. He wouldn't get his hopes up. The man might quit after one day with his demanding *schweschder*-in-law.

"Have you been married before? Do you have *kinner*?" Frannie balanced her elbow on the chair arm and rested her chin in the palm of her hand.

"I was married for six months to Beverly, until she died four years ago. I don't have *kinner*." Luke stared at his finger-laced hands.

"I'm sorry that happened to you." Fannie gave him a sympathetic smile.

"*Danki* for your understanding." He raised his gaze to meet hers.

Caleb stayed quiet and enjoyed the conversation between the two. He was sure Frannie would scare the man off before the interview was over. Maybe not, considering the way Luke seemed smitten with her.

"Caleb, do you have any questions for Luke?" She gestured to the man.

"Do you consider yourself a handyman?" Caleb needed

a farmhand who could mend fences and stalls, among other things.

"Yes. There isn't anything I can't do when it *kummes* to managing a farm. I'm good with animals, the garden, and crops." Luke seemed confident, but he didn't *kumme* across as arrogant.

"Do you have any questions?" Caleb rubbed Lily's back.

"Does room and board *kumme* with the job?" Luke sucked in his upper lip.

"There's an empty shed with a hardwood floor and stove you can move into. It came with the *haus*, but we haven't used it. It has a bed, a nightstand, a small table and a chair inside it. I had planned on moving into it, but my *bruder* insisted I live inside the *haus*, and it was easier for me." Caleb discussed his wages.

Frannie grinned. "Luke, will you accept the job?"

"Yes. *Danki*. When may I start?" Luke stood.

Frannie rose. "Now?"

Luke relaxed. "I'd love to. May I stay in the shed you've prepared?"

"Of course. I'll bring you a clean set of sheets and towels soon after we get home. I'll provide your meals." Frannie gave him a shy grin.

He smiled and tipped his hat. "How kind of you."

Caleb blinked a couple of times. He was sure this was a dream. Frannie flirting with Luke? He would be happy if they fell in love if this man turned out to be genuine and a suitable *daed* for Lily.

Caleb held out his hand. "If you have questions, you know where to find me. I'll stop over now and then to check in with you. Frannie will inform you when our next Sunday service is, and where."

Frannie grinned. "Yes. Luke can accompany Lily and me. Caleb, I'll take Lily, and Luke can follow me home."

She'd just met the man and she trusted him already. She should be more cautious. Caleb wasn't sure it was a good idea to be so trusting without taking the time to observe him and his work ethic. Talk was cheap. Results were important.

Luke straightened his hat. "You don't know me, and you must be wary, leaving me alone with Frannie and Lily. I assure you, they are safe with me."

So he said. Caleb wanted to believe the man was genuine, and he hoped he was right. "We haven't had but this single meeting together. I may be Amish and taught to avoid conflict, but if anything should happen to them, I will find you."

Frannie batted the air. "Don't be silly, Caleb. We'll be fine."

Luke looked him in the eye. "I understand. I'm a God-fearing man who has never had any trouble with the law, nor will I disobey Amish rules. I promise you."

Caleb believed him. Frannie was comfortable with Luke, so he'd take a chance on the man. "Take good care of them."

Luke nodded, and Caleb had peace about Luke.

Frannie waited at her buggy with Lily.

Caleb walked halfway to them and stopped.

Luke met her and held Lily while she got in the buggy and passed her back to her.

Lily rubbed her eyes and waved to Luke. "Bye-bye."

They left, and Caleb prayed Luke would be the perfect match for Frannie, as a farmhand and a husband. He laughed at himself. It hadn't even been a day since he'd met Luke. These expectations were unrealistic. He would be surprised if the man lasted a week.

Chapter 10

Friday midmorning, Rachael baked a double-layer white cake, frosted it, and squeezed red frosting from her make-shift cone to create red roses on top. This cake would be perfect for a couple celebrating their anniversary. Her eyes pooled with tears. She blinked them away. Caleb and she should be planning their wedding, but she'd been dishonest and ruined any chance of marrying him or celebrating milestones with him. She didn't deserve him. Her punishment would be loving him at a distance for the rest of her life.

She gasped. "Caleb, how long have you been in the doorway?"

"A minute or two. You look lost in thought. Care to share what's heavy on your mind? I hope it was me." He crossed the room and faced her. "I stopped in here yesterday. I understand you went on a trip with your *mamm* and Joseph. How was it?"

"I met Adelaide, his niece. I'm baffled she's happy working there, serving food and drinks to strange men. We were all shocked when she said she'd married a man who was unfaithful to her. Their marriage was short, and she kept it from Joseph. Her husband divorced her and left when she told him she was with child. She still wants to maintain her lifestyle. I pray Joseph will get through to her someday and she'll return with him to Charm."

"I'll pray for her. Did you like New Philadelphia?"

"Yes. I wish you'd been there with us. The canal was busy with boats *kumming* and going, and the whoosh of the train and its whistle were loud. The hustle and bustle of the city, and the shops along the boardwalk were fun to tour, but I wouldn't want to live there. It's a little too much activity for me. They have five school buildings, and they manufacture steel and mine coal. Joseph schooled us on the facts about the city. We had a wonderful time." She shouldn't have said she wished he'd been there. It hadn't been appropriate. She was sending him mixed messages. She'd have to be more careful.

"We could travel there together if you'd marry me. We could take a short train or boat ride. Don't rob us of these experiences." Caleb took the cone from her and set it on the baking table. He held her hands. "Please, Rachael. I don't want *kinner* if it means not having you."

Rachael closed her eyes tight. "What about Frannie? You may have to marry her to fulfill your promise to Stephen. And she can give you what I can't." It pained her to say the words. The picture of them in her mind made her stomach churn.

"Luke Kilmer may be my answer to caring for Frannie and Lily." He recounted the story of Luke's visit to his *haus*, Frannie's questions to Luke, and ultimately hiring him. "He's worked with Frannie for less than a day, but, so far, he hasn't quit. I wouldn't have been surprised if he'd lasted but two hours."

"I'm shocked." Rachael didn't take her hands from his. "Tell me more about him."

"He's of average build and I'd guess around the same age as us, twenty-five. He has a likable personality, and he seems genuine, sincere, and humble. I can understand why Frannie may find him attractive, with his wide shoulders and muscular arms tight beneath his shirt. He didn't take his gaze off her for long. I'm confident they had a connection when they met, like us. I'm curious if anything will *kumme* of it."

"I'm sure she meant to make you jealous. Does he have family or a *fraa*?" Rachael had reservations about Luke. How could Frannie and Caleb be comfortable with him staying on her property knowing so little about him?

"Her plan didn't work if her flirting with Luke was to make me jealous. No. His *fraa* died, and he doesn't have *kinner*. I had my doubts about letting him stay with Frannie and Lily so soon after meeting him, but Frannie was for it. The man was to start work at her place sometime. May as well be now." Caleb shrugged. "I'll stop over there this week to make sure all is well."

"I hope it works out for both of them and you." She hadn't wanted Frannie to make him feel guilty for marrying her. He should have a woman who would treat him better than his *schweschder*-in-law. The thought of any woman being Caleb's *fraa* other than herself triggered waves of nausea.

"I need to ask a favor." He gave her an impish grin.

"What?" She would help him any way she could. She couldn't tell him no. She loved him too much.

"I have two shirts with small rips in them. Would you fix them for me?"

"Yes. Bring them over tonight and I'll fix them on the spot."

"*Danki*." He kissed her hand, winked, and bid her farewell.

Two different couples visited the bakery, and they each bought one of the cakes she'd made earlier. She was thrilled they liked the red roses she'd made on each one. She baked pies, breads, and cookies the rest of the afternoon until quitting time and drove home. Half of her baked goods would go to the restaurant at the Inn. She was glad the restaurant owner paid them well for their desserts.

Nathan met her. He helped her out of the buggy. "I hope you don't mind me calling on you."

"Not at all. Where are Joy and Thad? I've missed them." She would always cherish her time with them. They'd given her a glimpse of what being a *mamm* would've been like.

He motioned for her to sit under the old willow tree by the pond on a bench there. "Let's stay outside where we can have a discussion in private. It's why I didn't bring the *kinner*."

"Is something wrong? You're making me nervous." She didn't understand why Nathan was here.

"I'll be frank. Frannie stopped by my *haus* today and told me your courtship has ended with Caleb. Is that the truth? May I ask why?"

She bristled at his question. Caleb must've told her why they ended their courtship. Frannie should've kept her mouth shut. There was no need to alert the community about where she stood with Caleb. Frannie was clever and knew who the gossips were, and no doubt went straight to them with her story. She might as well tell Nathan why. He had been a good friend, and she should've told him when he asked her to marry him. "Yes. I'm barren." It hurt to say the words. Frannie was despicable for running to tell Nathan.

"I'm sorry, Rachael. I don't know Frannie, and I wasn't sure I could trust what she said was true. I'll get right to the point. You should know I would've wanted to have more *kinner* with you if we'd married, but I'm content with raising Joy and Thad. Now you're free, please consider my proposal again. I need a *fraa* and a *mamm* for my *kinner*. Given time, we may fall in love."

She raised her brows. Her stomach rolled with nerves.

"I'm proposing we consider arranged marriage again. This way you can be a *mamm*."

She sat silent. Thoughts raced in her mind. Caleb was persistent. He'd never consider another woman as long as she remained alone. The only way he'd be forced to accept their parting was if she wed another man. Nathan offered her what she thought she could never have, and that was *kinner*. Joy and Thad had filled the void in this dream in her life before. But Caleb would always be the man she loved.

Nathan caressed her cheek. "Please, Rachael. There's no reason not to marry me. I've healed from losing Katherine. I'll always remember her, but I want to begin life anew with you. After this, if you decline, I'll leave you alone. I had to try one more time, knowing the change in your circumstances. I feel in my heart it is God's will for us."

"I'm in love with Caleb. I don't know if I'll ever stop loving him. I can't accept your proposal under these circumstances. You deserve to fall in love again, Nathan, and have your *fraa* feel the same."

He kissed her palm. "Please, Rachael. I'm confident we'll fall in love over time. I promise we'll have a good life together."

She trembled. This was a big decision. Would she regret declining Nathan's proposal? It was her chance to be a *mamm*. Most Amish men passed her by since she had a limp, and there were plenty of available and prettier Amish women in their community. She knew in her heart marrying Nathan was wrong. She would rather remain a spinster than agree to an arranged marriage. "Nathan, we should remain friends. Jumping from one man to another wouldn't be right, and I can't upset the *kinner* again. I hope you understand."

He helped her stand. "You can't blame me for trying. You would be such a wonderful *mamm* for Joy and Thad."

She squeezed his hands. "You're a good man, Nathan, but I must decline."

"I should go home. I asked Mrs. Yoder to watch the *kinner* for me. I told her I wouldn't be gone long. I'm disappointed, Rachael, but I'm glad we can part friends."

"Of course. Give Joy and Thad a hug for me."

"Give your *mamm* and Joseph my best."

Rachael bid him farewell and waited until his buggy was out of sight before going inside the *haus*.

Mamm and Joseph were washing and drying dishes at the kitchen sink.

"I noticed Nathan was out front. Is everything all right with Joy and Thad? We didn't want to interrupt and thought you'd invite him to *kumme* in." Mamm picked up a plate and set it on the table. "We have pot roast and potatoes left over. Here's a plate for you." She set the plate on the table and removed the cover. "Why the sad eyes?"

"*Danki*." Rachael breathed in the aroma. "This beef looks delicious." She sighed. "Frannie told Nathan my courtship with Caleb has ended. He proposed again."

"Rachael, I wouldn't have given my blessing if you had agreed to marry Nathan. You need time to ponder your future and to pray and ask God what you should do about Caleb." Mamm placed her hand on Rachael's shoulder.

"Don't worry. I agree with you." She hadn't lost the knot in her stomach since she let Caleb go.

Joseph kissed her cheek. "Your *mamm* is giving you good advice. You don't want to throw away a lifetime with the one you love. You need to reconsider Caleb's proposal."

Minutes later, a knock at the door startled her. She opened

the door. "Caleb, *kumme* in." She was glad he hadn't *kumme* at the same time Nathan had been there.

He passed her two shirts and pointed out the rips in both. "*Danki* for repairing them for me."

Rachael's cheeks heated. "I'm glad you asked me."

His smile faded. "I passed Nathan leaving your lane. It isn't any of my business, but I have to ask. Did you invite him here and why?"

Her cheeks heated. She didn't want him to get the wrong idea. "He was here when I got home from work. He had something he wanted to discuss." She didn't want to cause any more animosity between the two men. He didn't need to know Nathan had proposed again.

"Will you tell me what he wanted to discuss? Let's not keep secrets from each other. They create distance, and I'm working hard to win you back." Caleb sat next to her on the settee and shifted his body toward her.

She should have known he'd insist. She would've done the same in his shoes. She had nothing to hide. "Nathan proposed again. Frannie told him we were no longer courting."

"What?" Caleb huffed.

"Don't be upset. I said no. He was thinking of Joy and Thad. He wants a *mamm* for them, and I'm the most reasonable choice since we have a history together before I met you. I'm surprised he asked me to wed him again, but it doesn't matter. I declined. I didn't want to tell you. I don't want you to be upset with Nathan. You'll run into him at socials and Sunday services."

"The nerve of him, and I'm frustrated with Frannie for telling him about us. She's such a conniver." Caleb's jaw clenched. "How could my *bruder* marry such an aggravating and cunning woman? I'll never understand it. Rachael, you have to believe me when I say I could never consider her. My obligation ends at making sure she and Lily are taken care of, which doesn't mean I have to become her husband."

"The more she shows how desperate she is to have you, the more I understand why it would be difficult for any man to consider a lifetime with her." She'd be cordial to Frannie, but she would keep her distance. The woman was trouble.

"Regardless of what Frannie or Nathan want, I believe God had us meet and showed us what we can have together by falling in love. Please, Rachael, I beg you. Marry me." He held her hands to his heart.

She blinked back tears. "My decision is difficult for me also, but I can't help but think it's the right one. You'll forgive me when you have *kinner*. I'm sure of it." She closed her eyes to block out the utter sadness and disappointment in his eyes. She wanted to hold him and never let him go. She'd never erase this moment, no matter how hard she tried.

"I'm broken, frustrated, disappointed, and the list goes on. I'll never love any woman the same as I love you."

She shook her head. "You're compromising something that means a great deal to you if we marry. I can't let that happen."

"Please don't presume to tell me what I think and feel."

She wiped tears from her eyes, then she took his shirts to the treadle sewing machine in the corner of the room. She was glad she had kept the needle threaded with dark blue thread because it was the color thread she needed for his shirts. He sat in silence as she worked. She repaired the two rips and passed him the clothing.

He clasped her hand. "I will wait for you as long as it takes to change your mind." He kissed her forehead and left.

Rachael ran to her room, curled up on her bed, and wept. Caleb's words had hurt. They'd hurt because they were true.

She'd take his advice and search her heart and pray for guidance with an open mind.

Rachael sat across from Mamm at the kitchen table drinking her coffee on Saturday morning.

"Rachael, what more can you expect of Caleb? It's not fair for you to make this decision on your own. Listen to him," Mamm said.

Rachael traced the top of her coffee mug. "You haven't seen his excitement when he talks about having a houseful of *kinner*, or the way he revels in playing with them." She'd not forget the shock and utter sadness he showed in his eyes and expression last night. She'd wanted to hug his neck, tell him she'd marry him, and make them both happy. But she was torn between what Caleb had said last night and what she'd been convinced was best for them. She finished breakfast and left for the bakery.

Magdelena sprinkled sugar on top of her butter cookies. "Good morning."

Rachael lost all her resolve and broke down in tears. She'd made a royal mess of everything by not being open and honest with Caleb from the beginning. She knew it.

Magdelena wiped her hands and hugged her. "What's wrong?"

She sobered, pulled a handkerchief from her sleeve, and blew her nose. "Nathan asked me to marry him again. Frannie told him Caleb and I were no longer courting and added that I'm barren."

"Please, Rachael. Don't do this. Marry Caleb. Trust him. You're both miserable without each other. Frannie is a poor example of a God-fearing woman. How dare she spread your personal business to Nathan and who knows who else." Magdelena rubbed Rachael's back.

She dropped her head to her chin and sighed. "I'm confused. All I want is what's best for Caleb."

Magdelena lifted Rachael's chin. "Tell me you didn't say yes to Nathan."

"I declined. I would be making a big mistake if I married him. Being a *mamm* to his *kinner* isn't enough reason to wed. We're not in love."

"Thank goodness. I would've had to talk you out of it. He's not the answer. You're putting too much emphasis on *kinner*. Marriage *kummes* first. Some Amish parents arrange marriages and the bride has no choice. You have the luxury of having a *mamm* who allows you to choose your groom. Couples love and support each other through good and hard times, including when they aren't blessed with *bopplis*."

Rachael lifted her apron from the hook and pulled it over her head. She tied the strings behind her back. "Magdelena, I understand you're coaxing me to do what you think is best for me, but please stop. You're making this more difficult for me if you do."

Magdelena held up her palms. "All right. I'll keep my mouth shut about this today, but no promises in the *kumming* days. I'm passionate about this. We've all observed how happy the two of you are together."

"Let's talk about what we'll bake this morning to sell. I'll make sugar cookies with peach jam in the center."

She and Magdelena discussed recipes and how to tweak them for the next two hours as they baked.

"Time to open the shop. I'll turn the sign and unlock the door." Rachael opened the door for customers and Ellie entered. She hugged her. "Greetings, dear friend. Where's your sweet *dochder*?"

"Emma is at Maryann's. Her aunt wanted to spend time

with her, and her little one, Betsy, adores her. I came to town to have a couple of minutes with you and Magdelena."

Magdelena joined them. "Ellie, I'm glad you're here. How are you?"

"Worn out. Emma's a handful, but I love every minute of my time with her. Joel is a saint for putting up with me. How are you both?"

"We enjoy working here, and I find more reasons to fall in love with Toby every day. He's such a romantic. For example, he leaves notes in the laundry or in the cupboard." Magdelena blushed.

"You're talking about my *bruder*?" Rachael chuckled.

Toby was a thoughtful and caring man, like her *daed*. His way of showing Magdelena he loved her didn't surprise Rachael.

Magdelena gestured to Rachael. "Enough about me. Our friend is in turmoil."

"Why?" Ellie frowned.

Rachael recounted to Ellie why she'd ended her courtship with Caleb and refused Nathan's proposal. She would be eager to get this conversation out of the way. The story didn't get any easier each time she told it.

Ellie smacked her hand on the table. Her eyes were wide. "No. No. No. You must fix this. There will be nothing you'll regret more than not choosing Caleb."

Her opinionated friend never withheld her thoughts. Of course, she would disagree and insist Rachael change her mind.

Rachael shook her head. "Ellie, please try to understand."

"No. Caleb and you are already in love. Don't make this complicated. It's not." Ellie huffed. "Magdelena, tell me you're not going along with this."

"You and I feel the same way, but she asked me to drop

the subject, so I will respect her wishes." She rested her hand on Rachael's shoulder.

Ellie shook her head. "I won't make the same promise. I love you too much." She shook her head sadly, hugged them both, and left the bakery.

Rachael held her hands to her cheeks. "I hope Ellie won't keep nagging at me to change my mind." Her friend would make it her mission to change her mind. She would have to remain firm and show Ellie nothing she could do would alter her decision.

"Ellie's protective of us. She means well." Magdelena followed her to the kitchen, grabbed a tray of white bread loaves, and took them to the front of the bakery.

Rachael measured a teaspoon of cinnamon and dropped it in a bowl of flour. Had she already added the ingredient? She couldn't concentrate. Her friends knew she was happiest when she was with Caleb. She knew it too. No wonder they didn't agree with her decision. They didn't understand the importance of *kinner* to her and Caleb. She had to stick to her conclusion and not theirs.

Caleb sat outside the barn on a weather-beaten chair he'd brought from his *bruder*'s *haus*. Stephen often sat on it in the barn. He missed their talks and working together. He wished he could talk to him about Rachael and Frannie. He wasn't sure what Stephen would've expected of him where Frannie was concerned. Sometimes she was downright mean. He'd been absentminded all morning. Rachael had lost hope where they were concerned. He was annoyed she thought she knew what was better for him than he did. What more could he say to convince her?

Caleb stood and squinted against the sun. This should be an interesting visit.

Joel, Ellie's husband, pulled his wagon near Caleb. He and Nathan jumped out. Joel tied the reins to a nearby tree.

Why would Joel bring Nathan here? Didn't he know Nathan was the last person he wanted to visit him? "Greetings."

Joel pointed to the porch. "Let's sit. I've brought Nathan along with me to sort things out between you. Ellie visited Rachael today, and she came home upset over her ending your courtship, Caleb. I want to make sure you two men aren't going to be in discord since you're both interested in Rachael."

Caleb crossed the yard with them, and his visitors sat in the two rocking chairs, while he chose the porch swing. He'd wait for Joel to strike up the conversation. He avoided looking at Nathan.

"Rachael told Ellie Nathan proposed and she declined. Ellie insists Rachael is still in love with you, Caleb. Do you both agree with this statement?"

"Yes." Caleb stared at Nathan. "The minute Rachael broke off our courtship, you proposed to her. You didn't even let the dust settle." He had a difficult time liking Nathan, and this frustrated him even more.

"Yes. I didn't want to take a chance some other man would capture her attention. We have a history. I could give her what you can't. She was mine first." Nathan didn't avert looking straight at Caleb.

"You don't own Rachael." Caleb glowered at him.

"I didn't mean it the way it sounded." He gave Caleb a disgruntled look. "It doesn't matter since she said no."

"Of course, she did." He didn't like himself for arguing with Nathan. He should rise above this.

Rachael had turned Nathan down, and there was nothing more to discuss.

Joel raised his palms. "Let's not let this conversation get

heated. I'm here to create peace between you two." He addressed Caleb. "Since Rachael is choosing neither of you, I'd like for you both to accept her decision and be cordial. Nathan, you've looked at Caleb with disdain, and Caleb, I've noticed you do the same. You don't need to be best friends, but let's get along."

"I don't want to be nasty or hold a grudge. I understand better than most of the men and women in this community why you chose her, but you asking her so soon was disrespectful to me. God has a woman planned for you. I don't believe the woman is Rachael or you'd already be in love with each other."

"I didn't propose to her to disrespect you. You and she were no longer courting. What does it matter how long I waited to approach her?"

Joel held out his palms again. "Gentlemen, I agree with my *fraa* on this. We've been around Caleb and Rachael when they courted at after-church meals, and they couldn't stop smiling. Their adoration for each other was apparent. Nathan, Rachael has made it clear she's not interested in marrying you. You can understand why Caleb is holding out hope she'll change her mind."

Nathan crossed his arms against his chest. "I understand. It doesn't mean I'm happy about it." He took off his hat, stared at it, and traced the edges. "I can agree to be cordial."

Joel narrowed his eyes. "'Cordial' means greeting each other at services and socials."

"I'll be cordial too," Caleb mumbled.

Nathan stood. "I'm ready to go."

"Wait a minute, Nathan." Joel rose. "I'd like to pray before we leave." He bowed his head and closed his eyes. "Dear Heavenly Father, you have a plan for our lives. Guide Rachael, Caleb, and Nathan through the Scriptures to discern your will for each of them. Help me and their friends to support them in the way You would have us do. Amen."

Caleb raised his head. "Joel, *danki* for your concern. Nathan, I don't know what more to say. I won't apologize for loving Rachael." He believed God would intervene. He hoped Nathan would take his focus off Rachael. Ava had shown interest in Nathan. She seemed like a kind woman who would be a good choice for Nathan. "I'm curious. Ava showed interest in you. What happened?"

"Ava is a kind and beautiful woman for any other man but me. Rachael was my choice."

Caleb shrugged. He hoped Nathan would reconsider Ava and leave him and Rachael alone. "Understood." Caleb held out his hand. God wouldn't want him to hold a grudge against Nathan. He doubted they'd be best friends, but they should be cordial, as they'd agreed.

Nathan stayed stoic as he gripped Caleb's hand and shook it.

Joel rose. "I hope we've erased at least some of the animosity between you two. I wanted to give you both a chance to state your positions and ease the tension. My door is always open if you'd like to discuss anything, including this matter. I'm a friend to you both, and I want what's best for each of you."

"*Danki*," Nathan muttered.

"You're a faithful friend, Joel. I appreciate your time." Caleb waited on the porch as the men returned to Joel's wagon and drove away. His best option was for God to work a miracle in Rachael's heart. God could move mountains. He had faith God would do this.

He went inside, sliced a biscuit, and slapped a piece of ham on it. He stood at the counter and devoured it in three bites. He should visit Frannie and Luke. He hoped she hadn't run him off. He harnessed his mare to the wagon and traveled to Frannie's.

He rapped on the door, and Frannie answered, holding Lily on her hip. "*Kumme* in."

"Unkie." She reached for him.

Caleb held her. "From the crumbs on your face, I'd say you've had a cookie."

Lily chuckled and nodded.

Frannie greeted him. "You have competition. Luke has won Lily's heart. If you came here to talk to him, he's out back sawing a tree he cut down into firewood."

"I came to speak with you first, and then him. I understand you told Nathan Rachael was barren. It's not your place to tell anyone about that." He stared at her.

"Face the truth. You're worried Nathan can give her what you can't. Why, they may have gotten married if you hadn't stolen her away from him." She snickered.

"Your plan didn't work. Nathan proposed and she said no. Stay out of Rachael's and my business. Your motives aren't pure and you need to stop interfering." Caleb had grown tired of Frannie's selfish and manipulative behavior.

She shrugged and turned her back on him.

Caleb frowned. "I'm going out to speak with Luke."

He set Lily down and went out the back door. "Luke, how are you *kumming* along on the farm chores?" He might have to intervene if Frannie was wearing him out with inside chores.

"The crops are *kumming* along well, and I'm working into a routine." Luke wiped sweat from his forehead with his shirtsleeve.

Frannie opened the back door. "I fixed sandwiches. *Kumme* inside."

They washed their hands at the outside pump and went inside the *haus*. Frannie knew he wanted to talk to

Luke. Why couldn't she leave them alone for a couple of minutes? Was she afraid Luke would tell him he'd had enough of Frannie?

Frannie put Lily in her high chair. "Caleb, what did you say to Luke? You thought I was monopolizing Luke's time, didn't you?" She rolled her eyes. "I'm not."

He ignored her comment. "Luke, do you need help with anything while I'm here?"

"No. *Danki* for asking." Luke grinned.

"Ook." Lily pointed at Luke.

Frannie added more applesauce to Lily's bowl. "Luke doesn't mind helping me with Lily and, as you can see, the outside work is getting done. Don't you agree, Luke?"

"Yes. This little one is precious. I don't mind helping with inside chores, and Lily is the highlight of my day." He hurried to finish his sandwich and carried his plate to the sink. "I'll be in back if you need me." He left the room.

Frannie lifted her chin and batted her eyes. "Don't think for one minute everything is fine. I'm still frustrated with you for making me beg you to marry me. I shouldn't have to."

"The answer is no, and it will remain so. Understood? And I'm upset with you for stirring up trouble by telling Nathan the minute Rachael and I were no longer courting."

"She can be a *mamm* if she marries him. I was doing her and Nathan a favor." Frannie scowled. "And no, I don't understand. It should be you here and not Luke, and you know it." Frannie lifted Lily from the high chair and bustled out of the room.

The woman was like a thorn in Caleb's side. He took a step to follow her and scold her more. But what was the use? She didn't listen. He headed outside. "Luke, do you have any concerns?" He was curious to talk to Luke away from Frannie. He found him by the cut tree he'd been working on earlier. "Frannie is used to being coddled. You can tell me if she's too demanding, and I'll speak with her."

"She's bossy and hardheaded, but I don't mind. She's also kind and taking care to cook meals and wash my clothes. I couldn't ask for a better job. The shed is a comfortable place to live, and I enjoy farm work."

Caleb was shocked Frannie had done these things for Luke. This was more than she'd done for his *bruder*. Maybe she liked Luke more than she was letting on. But why was she still so adamant about him marrying her? Nothing with Frannie made sense. "I'm pleased you're settled in and happy. Don't hesitate to let me know if you need anything."

"*Danki*." Luke filled the wheelbarrow with wood.

He had been busy, and Frannie seemed pleased. Caleb prayed Luke would stay with this job for years, but it was early to have these expectations.

Caleb bid him farewell and drove home. At least Luke was taking care of the place and Frannie hadn't run him off.

Caleb finished weeding his garden, freshened up, and drove to the bakery.

Magdelena was waiting on customers and pointed to the kitchen. "Rachael's in back, baking pies."

He nodded and entered the kitchen. "I love the aroma each time I find you here."

Fresh bread, cinnamon, and sugar filled the air.

She grinned. "Would you like a butter cookie? I have some with and without icing."

"One of each, please." He sat on a stool near the worktable centered in the room.

She placed the cookies on a plate and passed it to him, avoiding his gaze.

He caught her hand. "Rachael, Nathan and Joel visited me today." He told her about their conversation.

Eyes wide, she blushed. "I should've known Ellie would

have Joel speak with you and Nathan. Her motive would be for you and Nathan to know where you both stand with me. Joel's motive would be to have you both become cordial. She was here earlier. She's upset I've ended things with you."

"Even your friends agree with me." Caleb searched her face.

Her eyes were sad and her lips trembled. "Caleb, please. Let's not discuss this again."

"Rachael, we love each other. Marry me."

She hadn't dropped her hand from his. He'd hold on to any glimmer of hope she gave him.

"No."

Caleb reached for her other hand. "I'll not push you, but I'll keep praying." Defeated, he crossed the room and exited the bakery. He was glad Magdelena was engaged in conversation with two customers. He didn't want to talk to anyone right now.

Chapter 11

Rachael sat on the floor with Thad and Joy and played board games with them Monday evening. Nathan had asked her to watch them for him while he went to repair a neighbor's porch swing. He and the *kinner* understood she was there as a friend, nothing more.

Three weeks had passed, and Caleb had ignored her request for him to stay away. He'd visited her at the bakery every other day. She was too weak to tell him to stay away again. She was always looking for one more minute with him. Each time they had a conversation, she held on to each word he said. He made small talk and didn't mention marriage again. Those sky-blue eyes were one of her favorite features of his, and they made her heart melt.

Nathan returned. "Rachael, did you hear me?"

"I'm sorry. I didn't notice you'd returned. What did you say?" Her cheeks heated.

"You were miles away. What has you in deep thought?" Nathan's mouth stayed in a grim line.

"Daydreaming is all." She smiled and hoped it was convincing.

Joy clapped her hands. "I won!"

"Daed can't bake. I'm glad you brought us sugar cookies." Rachael chuckled. "You're sweet."

"I wonder who is knocking." Nathan answered the door.

A young woman with golden-blond hair smiled. "I'm Pauline Stoll. I moved here with my parents a couple of days ago. The wheel on my buggy needs tightening, and I'm afraid to travel on it any farther. I'm sorry to trouble you, but will you check it for me?"

"*Wilkom* to Charm. I'm Nathan Wagler, and it's no trouble."

Joy skipped to the door. "I'm Joy. You're pretty."

Rachael agreed. The petite woman had dark-brown eyes and flawless skin. "Please *kumme* in and make yourself comfortable. I'm Rachael Schlabach, a friend of Nathan's and the *kinner*. Would you like some lemonade?"

Nathan hadn't quit smiling since Pauline appeared, and he was flustered as he went outside.

"No. *Danki*." Pauline sat in Nathan's favorite high-backed chair with navy cushions.

Rachael sat across from her on the settee. "I noticed you entering the general store the other day with an older couple. I'm a baker at the bakery, and I was running an errand."

"Yes. I planned to stop in at the bakery. The sugary aroma *kumming* from the bakery's open window made me want to go inside and buy some goodies, but my parents were too tired and wanted to return home. I'm a widow and live with them."

"Please visit the bakery soon. We'd love to have you. I'll introduce you to my friend and coworker, Magdelena. It's difficult to make friends when you first move and don't know anyone. You'll fit right in with us and our other friends who you'll meet at Sunday service."

"You're right. I'm driving around to get used to where things are in Charm, and I'm looking forward to making friends. *Danki* for being accepting of me here today."

"I'm glad we met." Rachael smiled.

Thad sat quietly next to Rachael.

"I'm sorry, Thad. I should've introduced you to Pauline earlier. This handsome lad is Thad."

Thad's cheeks pinked. "It's a pleasure to meet you, Miss Stoll."

"Please call me Pauline." She grinned.

"Thad, you and Joy play another game while I visit with Pauline."

Joy was on the floor, playing with the tokens that were part of the game. "Yes. Let's play this game again."

He nodded and sat on the floor with his *schweschder*.

Pauline watched the *kinner*. "They're pleasant and well-behaved."

"Yes. I enjoy their company. I never have a minute's trouble from them." Rachael grinned.

Pauline scanned the room. "What a beautiful home. You said you're a friend of Nathan's?"

She couldn't help but wonder if Pauline hoped Nathan was available. A spark seemed to ignite when they met. Nathan had become nervous, and Pauline had blushed and smiled at him. Would she have been jealous if Pauline had this reaction to Caleb in front of her? She had no doubt she'd have been more defensive. Caleb wouldn't remain available forever. She couldn't stand the thought of him courting another woman. "Yes. Nathan's a friend, nothing more. I was here to care for the *kinner* while he fixed a porch swing for a neighbor."

Pauline's smile widened. "Is he married? I hope you don't mind me asking."

"No. He's a widower. His *fraa*, Katherine, died close to eight months ago."

Joy popped up. "I won again!"

Rachael cocked her head and stared at Thad.

Thad put the game away. "She really did beat me. I didn't let her win."

Rachael grinned.

Joy showed Pauline her books, doll, and quilted stuffed animals.

Pauline oohed and ahhed at them.

Thad sat and stared at her. He went to his room and returned with a small train. He handed it to Pauline. "Daed and I built the train together, but I did most of the work."

"I'm impressed. You did a great job." Pauline turned the train from side to side and admired it.

Thad beamed.

Rachael didn't blame the *kinner* for being taken with her. Pauline made a good impression. She was easy to like, gracious, and attractive. She had a pleasant voice, which added to her appeal.

Rachael pressed a hand to her heart. Pauline had captivated the *kinner*, and it was as if she wasn't there. The woman was good with them.

Nathan returned. "I tightened your wheel. You shouldn't have any trouble now." He grinned. "I'm not rushing you off. Please stay and visit."

Joy held up her palm. "Pauline can't go. I want her to play a game with Thad and me. Daed and Rachael, you can play too."

Pauline moved to the floor. "I'd be happy to play a game. Do you mind if I stay a little longer?" She glanced from Nathan to Rachael.

"I'm glad you want to stay. I'll watch." Rachael stayed seated.

"Not at all." Nathan had his gaze fixed on Pauline. "I'll watch too."

Thad got out a game and moved his token three spaces on the board. "Pauline, you're ahead and already winning."

Pauline laughed. "It's early. Anything can happen."

Rachael's heart warmed. Nathan and Pauline and the *kinner* laughed and told Pauline funny stories about things they'd experienced. The spark between Nathan and Pauline was apparent. They were giddy.

Joy clapped her hands. "I won again!"

Pauline stood. "Congratulations. *Danki* for letting me play a game with you and Thad. I should head home. This has been a fun evening. I haven't laughed and played games for a long time. You've all blessed my heart. *Danki*." She hugged Joy and Thad. "Rachael, it's been a pleasure to meet you."

"I'm glad you stopped by. Nathan, you should walk her to her buggy and show her the repair of the wheel."

"Sure." He blushed and opened the door for Pauline.

"Time for bed." Rachael followed Joy to her room, dressed her in her bedclothes, prayed, and tucked her in bed.

Joy hugged her neck. "Will you tell *daed* to ask Pauline to *kumme* over again? I like her."

"Of course." Rachael kissed Joy's forehead. "Sleep tight, little one."

She poked her head in Thad's room. He was in bed. "Did you say your prayer?"

"Yes. Pauline was real nice, wasn't she?" Thad lifted his head from the pillow.

"Yes. She's a delightful woman. I'm proud of you. You were a perfect gentleman to her. Get some rest." Rachael closed his bedroom door and waited in the living room for Nathan to return. She waited another thirty minutes and peeked outside. The two of them were laughing, and Pauline had her hand on his arm. He lifted the woman into the buggy and handed her the reins. Rachael ran to sit in the rocking chair. She'd be embarrassed for him to know she'd been gawking at them.

Nathan returned to the living room and sat on the high-backed chair next to her. "Are the *kinner* in bed?"

"Yes."

"I owe you an apology." He stared at his hands in his lap. "I was too attentive to Pauline, and I didn't mean to disrespect you. I don't know what came over me." He shifted his body toward her.

"Don't apologize. Pauline is a lovely woman. I'm glad we had the opportunity to meet her. You like her, and she was relieved when I told her we're friends and nothing more. What I observed tonight between you and Pauline showed me you're ready to fall in love."

"The truth is, I had doubts about us too when I proposed to you. But I threw caution to the wind. I convinced myself you'd forget about Caleb, but it hurts to know you love him and not me. Maybe I was trying too hard to make this work for all the wrong reasons. You were right to decline."

"I imagine Pauline will be sought-after by a lot of the available men in this community with her beauty. The *kinner* are infatuated with her, and they asked when she can visit again. The time is right for all of you. Don't let her get away."

"I'll think about it." His cheeks pinked.

She rose and opened the front door. "I want you to be happy, Nathan."

He walked her out and handed her the reins. "Caleb has his heart set on you. Maybe you should reconsider marrying him. I'm giving you the advice you gave me about Pauline."

"I'm not sure. I'm praying about Caleb and me. My condition is a big consideration."

Nathan and Pauline could have a fresh start. Get to know

each other and see what the future held for them. She
prayed Nathan would pursue Pauline.

"I won't say any more. I don't want to meddle in your
business." He held her gaze. "Rachael, I'm glad we're friends.
It would break my heart otherwise."

"Me too." She bid him farewell and drove home. She'd
had the same spark when she met Caleb as she'd witnessed
with Nathan and Pauline. She couldn't dwell on Caleb. She
remained confused. She would like to leave town for a
short getaway to clear her head. She wasn't sure it would
be possible with work. She'd discuss it with Mamm and
Magdelena.

Mamm peeked around Rachael's bedroom door on
Tuesday morning. "Are you awake?"

Rachael rubbed her eyes. She glanced at the clock. "Is
everything all right? It's really early." She sat up and her
heart beat fast. "Is it Joseph?"

Mamm plopped on the edge of her bed. "I usually wait
on you to *kumme* home before I go to bed, but I had a mild
headache. I had planned to talk to you about something
important."

"You're scaring me. What is it?" Rachael gripped the
sheet.

"You were happiest when you were in love with John
and, now, Caleb. You need to trust Caleb and tell him
you'll marry him. I was in love with your *daed*, and I've
found love again with Joseph. Being in love makes the
difficult times in a marriage easier, and there are fewer
arguments. The joy it brings is irreplaceable." Mamm
reached for her hand.

"I'm praying about Caleb and me."

"I've learned worrying about you will never end, no
matter how old you get. I'm always going to want what I

think's best for you." Mamm kissed her cheek. "Time is precious. You're wasting each day you're not with him." She rubbed Rachael's arm.

"Always tell me what's on your mind. I'm glad God chose you for my *mamm*." She kissed Mamm's cheek. "I love you."

"I love you too." Mamm padded out of the bedroom.

Rachael dressed for work, grabbed her plain cloth drawstring bag, and held the front door open. "Mamm, I'm leaving. I'll grab a muffin at the bakery for breakfast."

Mamm rounded the corner. "Drive safe."

Rachael enjoyed the quiet morning ride. She parked her buggy at the livery and walked to the bakery. "Good morning, Magdelena." She stuffed her bag in the cabinet, slipped on her apron, and approached the butcher-block worktable.

"You're chipper this morning. This past week you seemed quieter than usual, as if something heavy is on your mind." Magdelena stopped stirring her cake batter.

"Caleb occupies my thoughts most of the time. I'm baffled about what to do. I don't want to talk about it right now. On another subject, I watched the *kinner* for Nathan last night." She rummaged through the drawer for her favorite big spoon. "I have interesting news."

"What?" Magdelena stared at her.

"Pauline Stoll is a newcomer to Charm. She's a widow, and she moved here with her parents. She knocked on Nathan's door and asked for help with her faulty wagon wheel while I was there. She and Nathan had an instant spark. We invited her inside, and she was charming. She connected with the *kinner* right away too. She asked if he was a widower, and I said yes. I made it clear we were just friends. They couldn't take their eyes off each other. I'm hoping a friendship will develop between them. Maybe more."

"Do you believe God used Pauline to show him he's ready for love? It seems her wagon-wheel trouble at his farm was fateful."

"Yes. I can't help but think God had them meet since it went so well. Pauline's visit was an unexpected surprise for him."

"I'll pray Nathan and Pauline become friends too." Magdelena set her loaf pans in the oven. "Your *mamm* and Joseph's wedding isn't too far away. You could still have a double wedding and marry Caleb." Magdelena dumped two cups of flour in her bowl.

Rachael rolled her eyes and raised her hands. "Not you too. Mamm suggested the same. Please don't beg me to reconsider. I said earlier I don't want to discuss Caleb. Please. Let's talk about something else." She had been fickle, and she didn't like it. She had to remain strong, push forward with her life, and wait on God to show her through Scriptures and prayer what was ahead for her. She would still like to get out of town for a couple of days. "I'd like to escape town for a couple of days. Leave Charm and let the gossip die down. But I don't want to leave you here alone." She shouldn't have brought up the subject. Again, it was selfish. "Forget I mentioned it. I don't know what's gotten into me. I'll be fine."

"It's an excellent idea. When will Joseph visit Adelaide again? Sounded to me she liked you. Why not ask him when he's going next? Hannah or Liza will fill in for you. You're doing a good deed to befriend and help her. Maybe you're the one who will change her mind about living here," Magdelena said.

Rachael grinned. "I'll ask him and let you know what he says." She couldn't wait to visit New Philadelphia again. Most of all, she looked forward to having dinner or supper with Adelaide. Maybe they could spend time alone and

Adelaide would confide in her. She truly wanted to help her. She worried about her. At the end of the workday, Rachael went home, where she found Joseph and Mamm at the stove in the kitchen.

"Fried chicken." She sniffed the air. "Love the aroma. Mashed potatoes?"

"Of course." Joseph held out to her the bowl filled with mashed potatoes.

"I'm glad you're here, Joseph. When will you visit Adelaide again? I've been wondering about her."

"This Thursday." Joseph dropped a dollop of butter on the potatoes.

"I'd like to *kumme* with you, if you agree. I'll ask Hannah or Liza to fill in for me at the bakery. If they give me permission, I'll be all set. Mamm, you don't mind, do you?"

"No, dear. I can't go this time. I'd feel better if Joseph had someone to accompany him. I'm all for it." She forked the chicken onto a platter and set it on the table.

They carried the rest of the food to the table and talked about their last visit to New Philadelphia while they finished their supper.

She carried the dirty dishes to the dry sink. "I'll fetch the water, Mamm."

Joseph took the tub from her. "You go visit Hannah and ask if she'll work for you this Thursday and Friday. I'm certain you're anxious to find out."

"You know me too well already." She grinned. "I'd be happy to help with the dishes first."

Mamm nudged her. "You go ahead. Joseph and I can take care of these dishes."

"*Danki*." She smiled, waved, and hurried to Hannah's.

Hannah opened the door and smiled. "You've made my day *kumming* here." Her smile diminished. "Is everything all right?"

"Yes. I came to ask a favor. Where are Timothy and your sweet dog, Sunny?"

"Timothy and our mutt are fishing over at the Bylers'. He should be home in the next half hour. This is perfect time for some privacy. How are your *mamm* and Joseph's wedding plans *kumming* along?"

"Mamm is a master organizer. Their wedding plans are almost done. I had an interesting visit with Nathan and the *kinner* last night. I was there as a friend, of course, watching the *kinner*, and a newcomer knocked on his door." Rachael recounted what happened with Nathan and Pauline Stoll. "Pauline is a widow and a sweet woman. I'm sure she'll be at Sunday services. I'll introduce you if you haven't met her before then. I hope Nathan will grow a friendship with her."

"I look forward to meeting Pauline." Hannah tilted her head. "Any hope for Caleb and you?" She rocked in the white chair. "Ellie is ready to lock you in a closet until you agree to marry Caleb. She teases about it, but I wouldn't put it past her."

Rachael laughed. "She's loyal and fierce. I love her, but she can be too much at times."

"We'd be lost without her, but I agree. I have to calm her down with sweet tea and oatmeal cookies more often than not. Little Emma has been the best *boppli*. Ellie has more patience with her than she does with anyone. We're all sad about Caleb and you."

"I'm sad too. Maybe I'm wrong about all this. I can't quit thinking about him. I'm reconsidering. He, you, and all our friends are rooting for us."

"Now you're making sense." Hannah smiled.

"You may be right." Rachael chuckled. "I promise to reconsider, and getting away might help me to ponder it. I came to ask you to work for me at the bakery Thursday and

Friday. I'd like to accompany Joseph to New Philadelphia to visit Adelaide again. If it isn't convenient for you, don't hesitate to tell me. I don't have to go."

Hannah waved a dismissive hand. "Don't be silly. I'd love to work for you. I miss the bakery. I wouldn't want to return full-time, but I like filling in once in a while. I pray you get through to Adelaide. She'd be much better off here, especially raising a *boppli*."

"*Danki*, Hannah." Rachael hugged her goodbye and returned home. She went inside the *haus* and found Joseph and Mamm enjoying coffee. "Hannah agreed to work for me. I'll tell Magdelena our plan tomorrow. She'll be supportive. It's her nature and another reason we're close."

"Your help has meant a lot to me, Rachael. There's only so much I can talk to Adelaide about, and I realize she needs a woman to discuss delicate matters. Your faith in God and good influence is what I need to get through to her. I'm praying she'll change her mind and return with us. If not tomorrow, someday soon. I'm not willing to give up on her." Joseph sighed and traced the rim of his coffee cup.

"We'll make as many visits as we must to sway her to relocate to Charm. We have her *boppli* to consider. Her *mamm* chose to live in the outside world, and Adelaide didn't experience Amish life. Her *mamm* talked bad about life in Charm and convinced Adelaide living in the outside world is much better, wearing the clothes they choose, singing with instruments like the piano, and I don't know what all. I'm hoping she'll miss us and want to live in Charm."

God had placed on her heart to befriend Adelaide. She didn't know why, but she didn't need to.

Rachael bid Mamm and Joseph good night and slipped into her bedroom. Was Caleb thinking of her tonight? She missed the sound of his voice, his advice, and their plans for the future. She had to concentrate on Adelaide. The woman and her *boppli* had given her a new purpose and focus. There was a *boppli* at stake. She rubbed her temples. Her head ached. What would become of this *boppli* if she couldn't persuade Adelaide to leave the outside world? She was afraid to ponder it.

Rachael cut a leftover mixed berry pie from yesterday into slices to sell by the piece at a discount Wednesday morning. She told Magdelena her plan to visit New Philadelphia on Thursday. "Are you sure you don't mind? We'll visit with Adelaide when we arrive and then leave Friday morning. I'll be back to work on Saturday."

"Of course not. Helping Adelaide is important, and the more she gets to know you, the better chance you'll have of bringing her to Charm." Magdelena's eyes turned serious. "But don't run from Caleb. You're wrong to let him go."

"Please, Magdelena, I'm begging you. Let's not discuss Caleb. I'm in turmoil enough about him. I'm too upset to talk about him." Rachael thought of him nonstop. The last thing she needed was to rehash with her friend why or why not they should marry. The conversation would accomplish nothing. She was wavering on her decision, but she didn't want to hash this out with Magdelena until she decided what to do.

Frannie walked into the bakery's kitchen, carrying Lily on her hip. "Rachael, I ran into Nathan on the way here, and I asked him why he hadn't proposed to you again. He said you turned him down. Why on earth would you do such a thing? It's your chance to be a *mamm*."

Rachael was certain Frannie had ulterior motives for wanting her to wed Nathan. Frannie had her sights set on marrying Caleb. "I'm not interested in marrying Nathan." She didn't owe Frannie any explanation, but she had given one to the woman to avoid what she was sure would be endless badgering.

"Those poor *kinner*. They need a *mamm*." Frannie harrumphed. "You should be ashamed. Now, there's still time to fix this. Tell him you've made a mistake. Become a much-needed *mamm* to those *kinner*. Soon you'll be *kumming* to Caleb's and my wedding. I've almost gotten him talked into it. I can feel it."

Magdelena's cheeks reddened. "Frannie, keep your nose out of Rachael's business. Now, why did you *kumme* to the bakery?"

Frannie turned on her heel. "I'll be on my way since she won't listen." She stuck her nose in the air and bustled out of the kitchen.

Rachael and Magdelena walked to the front room. Magdelena twisted the towel in her hands. "Frannie raises my dander like no other woman. She's infuriating."

"She is. I wish she'd stay away from me."

Magdelena scoffed. "Caleb won't marry Frannie. No man deserves a woman as unkind as her. She's such a manipulator and conniver. Those kinds of women are the worst. I'm glad we don't have many of her type in our Amish community."

Rachael shrugged. "Frannie is determined. I hope she doesn't make him feel guilty and forced into it." She couldn't stand to picture them together, or any other woman with him, for that matter. She hoped, in time, she could run into him without her heart aching so much.

Chapter 12

Caleb weeded the garden Thursday morning. He hadn't planned on living in his *haus* alone. He'd envisioned Rachael making the inside of the *haus* a home. He would have to depend on God to intervene.

He wouldn't stop his bakery visits. Any chance he could get to speak to her he'd take. He washed his hands and face and went to town. He entered the bakery. "Hannah, good to see you. And Magdelena, good morning."

Magdelena handed him a cup of coffee. "I suppose you came to speak to Rachael, but she's gone to New Philadelphia again with Joseph to visit his niece, Adelaide. She'll be back to work at the bakery Saturday. I'm sorry you're no longer engaged. Hannah and I have tried to reason with her. We want you back together. There's no doubt she loves you."

Hannah leaned against the wall. "We're praying for you and Rachael."

"*Danki*. I appreciate your prayers and concern." Caleb was hopeful, having their friends support him.

Magdelena threw the towel over her shoulder. "She's lost the lilt in her step and the glow and joy that shone through her when you and she were courting."

"Maybe I still have a chance with her. You've made my

day a little brighter." He bent low and scanned the display cabinet. "I'll take a cinnamon streusel cake to celebrate."

Magdelena came closer to him. "May I give you some advice?"

"Of course. I *wilkom* any advice from you. You're close with Rachael and know her best. I'll take it to heart."

"Give her a couple of weeks before you approach her again. Let her miss you. It couldn't hurt." Magdelena lifted her brows.

Hannah nodded. "I have to agree with Magdelena. Don't chase her. Maybe she'll *kumme* around to your way of thinking. We'll be praying God will intervene and work on her heart."

"I'll heed your advice. *Danki.*" He paid Hannah for his purchase, bid the women farewell, and headed home. It would be difficult to stay away from Rachael, but he'd try. They didn't have Sunday services this week. He'd wait until they did and then approach her.

Frannie had Lily on her lap. Bishop Fisher sat on Caleb's porch, across from her in a rocking chair. They waved to him.

What was Frannie up to now? Caleb parked his buggy and tied the mare under a shade tree. He yelled to them, "I'll be right with you after I offer the mare some water." He pumped water in a bucket and offered her a drink.

He approached his visitors. "How may I help you? Would you like something to drink?"

Lily wiggled off Frannie's lap and toddled to Caleb. She raised her arms. "Unkie."

He'd missed his niece since moving into his *haus*. She melted his heart with those big brown eyes. He put down the cake and picked her up. "How's my little niece?" He held her at arm's length and laughed.

She sucked her thumb, then rested her head on his shoulder.

"Nothing for me. *Danki*. We don't plan to take much of your time." Bishop Fisher smiled.

"I don't need anything." Frannie gestured to Caleb and Lily. "Aren't they adorable together? She adores him."

The hairs on the back of Caleb's neck prickled. Frannie was being too nice. And he didn't believe she was here for nothing.

"Lily does seem comfortable in your arms, Caleb. Frannie asked if I would meet with you and her together and discuss marriage. She said you promised your *bruder* you'd marry her to take care of her and Lily if he died."

His cheeks warmed. "Not true. Stephen asked me to care for his family. He didn't ask me to marry his *fraa*. Frannie, why would you tell the bishop such a thing?"

Frannie scowled. "It's customary for a *bruder* to marry his *schweschder*-in-law when her husband dies and you know it. Why are you fighting me on this? I promise I'll be a good *fraa*. Lily needs a *daed*. You love her, and you want *kinner*. I want more *kinner* too."

Bishop Fisher held out his palms. "Let's don't fuss. Caleb, why are you opposed to the idea?"

He didn't want to explain himself to the bishop. Frannie had dragged this man into their business, and he was frustrated with her. He respected the bishop, and he didn't want them to get on bad terms. He struggled to control his tone. "I love Rachael Schlabach. I'd like to wed her."

"Rachael broke off your courtship. She doesn't want you," Frannie grumbled.

"Why would you wait on her if she's turned you down?" Bishop Fisher adjusted his spectacles.

"Rachael is confused. She can't bear *kinner*, and she

believes I need to have them. I made the mistake of talking too much about my love for *kinner* before I knew she was barren. She and I love each other. God introduced us, and He has a plan for us. I'm praying God will intervene." His and Rachael's story must be confusing. He hoped the bishop would understand.

"Maybe you should take her decision to heart, Caleb. I'm sure she's aware Frannie and Lily need you." Bishop Fisher leaned forward.

"Everyone but Caleb seems to be in favor of our union. I shouldn't have to beg." Frannie pouted and crossed her arms against her chest.

"Bishop Fisher, all I can offer Frannie and Lily is my help as an uncle to Lily and *bruder*-in-law to Frannie. I've hired Luke Kilmer to manage the property. He's agreed to help with inside and outside chores. I'm fulfilling Stephen's wishes to care for them." He hadn't taken a seat and he leaned against the post with a sleeping Lily in his arms. "Frannie, are you still happy with Luke?"

She shrugged. "I am, but he's not a substitute for a husband or *daed* to Lily. Why are you being stubborn? You're a free man pining over a woman who doesn't want you."

"Bishop, I'm not going to marry Frannie. I've been honest with her. I'm sorry she involved you. I love Rachael, and as long as we're both unwed, I'll wait on her. I have faith God will find a way to bring us together."

"How ridiculous you are, Caleb. Don't you agree he's being ridiculous, Bishop Fisher?" Frannie pinched her lips and glared at Caleb.

"Frannie, Caleb has made his decision, and it's not wrong. He's meeting your and Lily's needs, and he's made sure you have paid help to manage your farm. I'd like for you to *kumme* to an understanding with Caleb so you can be on good terms. If you keep pushing, your communication with him may suffer. I don't want this to happen, do you?"

Frannie shook her head and stared at her lap.

"Please stand. Let's hold hands and pray." Bishop Fisher prayed, "Dear Heavenly Father, help Caleb and Frannie *kumme* to an understanding and support and love each other as family. Bring Frannie the husband and *daed* for Lily you have planned for them and have your will in Caleb's and Rachael's lives. Forgive us all for our sins. We praise and love you. Amen."

The bishop placed a hand on her shoulder. "Frannie, I have no doubt God has the right man for you, and the right woman for Caleb. I pray Rachael may be that woman. Please be patient. Pray and read the Scriptures. Have faith and make your requests known to God. I'm always here to listen. I care about each of you, and I want God's will for you both. Do you understand, Frannie?"

"I'm sorry, Bishop. I was desperate." Frannie kept her arms crossed.

"It's all right. Please accept Caleb's decision and be a supportive *schweschder*-in-law and appreciate what Caleb is providing for you and Lily." Bishop Fisher smiled.

Caleb rubbed Lily's back. "Frannie, I don't want to argue with you. Let's call a truce and salvage our relationship as *bruder* and *schweschder*. What do you say?"

"I can't forgive you in an instant for hurting my feelings. No one likes rejection. But I'll work on it." Frannie gave him a faint smile. She lifted Lily from Caleb, and Lily roused enough to change positions and fall asleep again. "Ready to go?"

"Yes." Bishop Fisher shook Caleb's hand. "I'll be praying for you, Caleb."

"*Danki*, Bishop." He waited until Frannie and the bishop got in the buggy and left before taking his mare into the barn. He fed the horse and then checked on all his livestock. He'd not been sure where the meeting with Frannie and the bishop was headed, but the bishop had done his best to reason with Frannie. He prayed Frannie had exhausted her endless efforts to persuade him to be her husband. He was tired of the burden she was putting on him.

He would wait to speak to Rachael as Magdelena suggested. He wondered what she was doing at that moment. He didn't know how long he could stay away from her. Maybe he'd been too pushy before, visiting her so often at the bakery. It'd be difficult to stay away from her, but he'd try anything.

Rachael inhaled the aroma of cotton candy at the peddler's stand. She was glad Adelaide had two hours to spend with her and Joseph. She was tired after their trip there, but she wouldn't waste time resting when she could be with Adelaide.

She dug in her coin purse. "Would you like some cotton candy?"

Joseph waggled his finger. "I'll buy us all some." He handed the peddler coins, and they each took a stick of cotton candy."

Adelaide chuckled. "I'll never get to be too old to enjoy good ole cotton candy." She picked off a big piece and stuffed it in her mouth. "This is yummy."

"How are you feeling?" Rachael was afraid Adelaide would have the *boppli* any minute. She had large arms and legs, and the *boppli* made her stomach protrude a lot. She loved Adelaide's humor and forthrightness. She didn't hold back on anything she thought.

"I'm uncomfortable no matter if I sit, stand, walk, or sleep. No position is comfortable. The doc thinks I will birth one baby, but I'm thinkin' there are at least three in here. I could have breakfast, dinner, and supper six times a day and I'd still be hungry." She patted her stomach. "'Course I do love my desserts, candies, and breads. Madge is an amazin' cook. She makes lots of casseroles, pies, cakes, and peanut brittle. She's watchin' how much weight I put on since I'm carryin' this baby, but I sneak food."

Rachael chuckled.

Joseph pointed to a bench out in front of the post office. "You ladies chat and I'll browse in the hardware store."

Adelaide waved her hand. "You go wherever you'd like. You've left me in good hands."

Joseph grinned and walked across the street.

Rachael pulled off a piece of her cotton candy. "Is Madge married?"

"Nope. She's been managin' the saloon girls since before I was born. She's had some beaux, but they came and went. I'd be lost without her. Since Mother died, Madge has become my best friend. Some of the girls who work with me are my friends too. I'm sad my husband divorced me, but they say I'm better off, and I suppose I am."

"I looked forward to being with you today. I consider you a new friend, and I hope you will ask me for anything you need, or if you want to talk about anything bothering you." Rachael took her empty paper cone and Adelaide's.

"You're sweet, Rachael. I consider you a friend too."

"Adelaide, if you came to Charm after the *boppli* was born, you could live with me in the *haus* behind Joseph's. He'll be marrying Mamm soon, and they'll live in the larger *haus*. We'd all be there to help you. You wouldn't have to work. Would you consider it?"

"I don't want to leave the saloon or my friends. It's my home, but you can come visit me as often as you can get free. I like havin' time with you. Don't be offended, but those bonnets covering your pretty hair and those loose dresses aren't for me. I love to dance and sing too. I play a little piano, and I enjoy it. I'd make the bishop's hair stand straight up if he met me. The Amish life sounds like being in jail. No offense."

Rachael understood she'd have to accept Adelaide's way of life if she wanted to befriend her. She prayed she'd win her trust and God would change her mind. She could never sever ties with Adelaide and the *boppli* now they'd met. She cared for her and her unborn *boppli*. She'd be Joseph's step*dochder* and she and Adelaide would be family.

A woman with a snug-fitting blouse and skirt approached them. "Adelaide, who's your friend?"

"Jewel, this is Rachael. Her mother is marrying my uncle Joseph. They're here for a short visit." She shifted on the bench. "Rachael, Jewel works with me at the saloon. Isn't she gorgeous? You should listen to her sing. She has the voice of an angel."

"Rachael, Adelaide's the most lovin' and givin' woman in the saloon. We all love her, and we're signed up to take turns helpin' her with this baby." She eyed Rachael up and down. "I've got a half hour before my break is over. Would you like us to take you shoppin'? You need some bright colors and pretty shoes. Come on, darlin'." Jewel clasped her arm.

Adelaide rolled her eyes. "Wait, Jewel, Rachael is Amish. She don't want to go shoppin' for no dresses or shoes like ours. They wear these kinds of dresses and bonnets as a part of the Amish tradition."

Jewel put a hand to her open mouth. "I'm sorry, Rachael. Please forgive me. I didn't mean to hurt your feelin's."

Rachael waved her hand. "I don't mind. It's a pleasure to meet you."

Jewel had smiled big when she approached them, and the care she had for Adelaide was apparent.

"Joseph has been a dedicated uncle to Adelaide. He says he worries about her, but we take care of one another. And Madge is no match for any man. She'll enlist the sheriff or one of his deputies to remove any unruly men from the saloon. They don't cross her. She ran that husband of Adelaide's off more than once. We're not sorry he's gone. Adelaide, you'll get over him. Just give yourself time."

Rachael prayed Adelaide wouldn't be around any troublesome men. She didn't like Madge having to worry about defending herself or others. She shivered at the thought of Adelaide being anywhere near danger. Her life was such a mystery compared to how Rachael lived in Charm.

Adelaide licked her sticky fingers and wiped them on a handkerchief she pulled out of her reticule. "Each day is better. I don't cry as much about him." She returned her handkerchief to the worn reticule. "Enough about him. Where are you off to?"

Jewel chuckled. "I'm shopping for a new reticule at the secondhand store. Betty said a woman brought in a handful yesterday. And I'll check for some baby clothes for your little one."

"Thanks." Adelaide squeezed Jewel's hand.

They bid Jewel farewell, and Rachael put away the handkerchief in the clean flour sack she'd used to wipe her fingers. "Have you picked out any names?"

"I like Marie for a girl and Joe for a boy."

"I like those names too."

Adelaide's eyes popped wide. "The baby's kickin'." She reached for Rachael's hand and flattened it on the side of her stomach. "Do you feel the baby?"

Rachael gasped. "Yes!" It was such a miracle. "The *boppli* keeps kicking. He or she is active."

Her friends had talked about their experiences carrying

their *boppli* before the *kinner* were born, but Adelaide was more open, grabbing her hand and letting her feel the kick.

"The first time it was excitin'. Now I wish this baby would stop kickin' so much." Adelaide grinned. "You need to marry and have some babies." She slapped Rachael's knee.

"I'm barren. I was in a buggy accident years ago. My fiancé was killed, and I ceased having my monthly courses." She dropped her hand from Adelaide's stomach. "Then I fell in love with Caleb Yutzy, but he's over-the-moon excited about being a *daed* someday. I had to let him go. I'm sad about not having *kinner*, and he would be too."

"I'm sorry about what happened to you. I don't understand. Did Caleb end your courtship or did you?" Adelaide frowned.

"I did. He insisted my condition didn't matter to him." Rachael sighed.

"No. No. No. It's not for you to decide. Believe him. Don't rob yourself of marryin' a good man. They're hard to come by. You need to be correctin' this when you get home."

"You have a point, and my friends and family tell me the same thing. I hope I'm not too late. I've put him through a lot." She wouldn't blame Caleb if he said he wasn't sure about her at this point.

"You're afraid he'll regret marryin' you, but he won't. Don't wait to talk to him. You do it as soon as you can. Then bring him with you when you visit me again. I want to meet him." Adelaide patted her hand. "I want this little baby to know my family. You all have to visit often." She squeezed Rachael's hand.

"*Danki*. I'd love to." She held Adelaide's hand.

"I sure hope I fall in love again. This time with a loving husband and father for my baby and me."

Joseph returned. "I hope I wasn't gone too long."

Two men bumped into Joseph, and Joseph righted himself. "Excuse me."

The thick and short young man snickered. "Watch where you're going, you simpleton. Go home where you belong, with the rest of your kind."

The tall and lanky man sneered. "Leave him alone. Let's go." He pulled his friend away.

Adelaide fumed as she shook her fist at him. "Get out of here before I tell the sheriff."

Joseph shook his head. "Adelaide, it's all right. They're gone."

"Uncle, those men are bullies. I won't have them treating you unkind." She leaned her head on Rachael's shoulder for a moment. "It's like I've known you all my life and we just met. Please visit me again soon." Adelaide stood. "I don't want to say goodbye, but I should get back to work. They'll be lookin' for me. It's about time for me to sing."

"I feel the same about you. I'll do my best to return here when I can." Rachael's heart warmed.

Rachael and Joseph escorted her back to the saloon and bid her farewell.

Joseph stopped on the way back to the hotel. "Rachael, Adelaide has been more open with you than I anticipated. *Danki* for accepting and befriending her. It means so much to me. There's only so much she will tell me. She needs a woman like you to talk to."

"I like her a lot. We became fast friends. She makes me laugh, and she doesn't hold back what's on her mind. I care about her, and I want to make these trips a habit. I plan to help any way I can with this baby, and it will be fun for me. I invited her to live with me in Charm, but she refused. Maybe one day she'll relent."

"I have a better chance of her considering moving to

Charm now that you're involved. We'll keep praying about it." Joseph opened the door for her to the boarding*haus*. "Are you hungry?"

She shook her head. "I'm still full from our meal at the restaurant. I'm tired. I'm ready to rest."

"Me too. We'll be leaving early tomorrow. I'll meet you in the lobby tomorrow at five in the morning."

"Good night." Rachael went into her room and shut the door. She hadn't achieved the results she'd hoped, but she'd had a wonderful day with her new friend. They had vast differences, but God had given them common ground with this *boppli*. She looked forward to meeting him or her soon.

Sunday, Caleb scanned the Amish sitting on the benches outside the Yoders' *haus*. He had waited a little over a week to speak to Rachael. That was all he could stand to be away from her. The hardest day to stay away was last Sunday, their day of rest, when they didn't have a service and would've been free to talk. But he wanted to listen to her friends. They probably meant more than a week, but he couldn't ignore her at the service. He spotted Rachael with her *mamm*. He was relieved she'd made it back safe to Charm from New Philadelphia. He'd kept busy on the farm so he wouldn't be tempted to visit her at the bakery. He'd speak to her as soon as the service was over.

Bishop Fisher prayed, led them in song, and opened his Bible. "Today, I'm delivering a message on marriage."

Caleb wondered if the bishop chose this subject after his conversation with him and Frannie.

Bishop Fisher seemed to focus on him. "Each partner should consider the other partner's wants and needs before their own."

Caleb's stomach churned. He didn't want the bishop's message to be misconstrued in Rachael's mind as validation that she was putting his needs before hers and confirm her decision not to marry him.

Bishop Fisher scanned the congregation. "Listen to what your partner tells you. Trust them."

He liked the bishop's last comment better. Rachael needed to do both those things for him to convince her they were meant to be together.

He wanted to discuss Nathan, Frannie and the bishop's visit, and marriage. He shouldn't want to rush the service. He'd try to be patient.

Two hours later, the bishop prayed and dismissed them for the afternoon meal. The women hurried to the food tables to remove wrap and lids from their dishes, and then they let the men and *kinner* go first in line.

Caleb rushed to Rachael. "Magdelena said you went to New Philadelphia. Let's fill our plates and sit together. Tell me about your trip, and I have some news."

Her eyes weren't as bright as usual. She must be tired. It didn't matter. She was always beautiful.

She smiled. "I'd love to."

His heart thumped fast in his chest. She hadn't turned him down. This could turn out to be a very good day. He followed her to the table and they filled their plates, grabbed glasses of water already poured by the ladies manning the tables, and sat under the willow tree on a worn bench. "Nathan seems to be enjoying his time with the woman next to him."

"Yes. Her name is Pauline Stoll. She's a widow and a newcomer. It's good to see them getting along well. I wish them the best."

"I sincerely do too."

Rachael frowned. "Caleb, I'm sorry I've put you through rejection and pain. I've been upset since we parted. Are you sure you'll not regret not marrying Frannie to fulfill your promise to Stephen?"

"I promise you, I won't regret not marrying Frannie. I have made it clear I will take care of her and Lily as a *bruder*-in-law to her and uncle to Lily, not as a husband and *daed*. Frannie has been relentless in her pursuit of me, even though I've told her more than once I won't marry her. She brought Bishop Fisher with her to plead her case."

"Bishop Fisher?" Rachael's mouth gaped open.

"Yes. I'm convinced Frannie will do anything and use anyone to get her way. I told Bishop Fisher I would care for her and Lily, but I'm in love and waiting on you. He understood and told Frannie he'd pray for God to send her the right husband and *daed* for Lily. She didn't like his response, but she'd lost the battle to win him to her side. I'm hopeful he got through to her. She likes Luke or she would've complained about him."

"How is Luke working out at her place?" Rachael quirked a brow.

"They get along fine. She hasn't chased him off, so far." Caleb chuckled.

Rachael grinned. "They're together at the table across the yard. She's smiling, and he's bouncing Lily on his lap. Maybe there will be a spark there."

"I hope so."

"Me too." She grinned.

"Enough about Frannie. How was your trip?" His heart thumped with hope at her genuine smile. It had been a while since he'd seen the smile he loved.

"Joseph and I enjoyed our visit with Adelaide. He left us alone to talk in private for a short time. She's funny, and she doesn't hold back on how she feels about anything. Much like you. I'm fond of her, even though we just met. Caleb, the *boppli* kicked while we were together. She grabbed my hand and held it to her stomach. I enjoyed the moment so much. She makes me feel a part of her time carrying the *boppli*."

He was hesitant to discuss Adelaide's *boppli*. Any talk of *kinner* seemed to shy her away from him, but he didn't want her to think him insensitive. He'd meant how Adelaide was in general. "Is there any chance she'll move here?"

"No. She's set in her ways. Too many things the Amish are against, she's for. The musical instruments, like the piano, singing Englischer songs, and wearing colorful, fancy clothes. She's content to serve food and drinks to Englischers in the saloon, and she's comfortable living in the small room she calls home there. The women who work there are her close friends. I met Jewel, one of her friends, and their concern for each other is genuine. Madge, the manager, watches out for Adelaide, and Adelaide is close to her. She trusts her."

"I'm glad she has some support there, but it's no place to raise a *boppli*." Caleb disapproved of Adelaide's choices, especially living in a saloon with her *boppli*, which was at the top of his list. She would be subjecting the *boppli* to strangers, and the women who would help her might not be the best to give her advice.

"No, it isn't, but the *boppli* is hers. We have no business telling her what to do. We must show her our love and support. I pray she'll change her mind, but so far she shows no sign of this."

"How was your week at work after you returned?" He hoped she missed him.

"The bakery kept me busy. How about you?" She gave him a warm smile.

"I missed you." He brushed her fingers with his.

"I missed you too." She gave him a shy smile.

Mamm and Joseph approached them. Joseph patted

Caleb on the back. "Sorry to interrupt. We're ready to go home. Did you want to go with us, Rachael?"

"Good to see you, Caleb." Mamm grinned.

"Yes. I'm ready. Take care, Caleb."

He exchanged an endearing look with her before they departed. She'd said she'd missed him. He wanted to do a jig, but his friends would've thought he'd lost his mind. Amish weren't allowed to dance. He chuckled thinking about it. He had pushed her hard up until now, and he didn't want to ruin their positive conversation. He would be patient this time, but he'd keep reminding her of how much he loved her. Next, he'd take her flowers at the bakery soon.

Rachael pressed a hand to her heart on the way to the buggy with Mamm and Joseph. She was tired of being without Caleb. Her family and friends supported Caleb's efforts to win her over and accept their circumstances. Even Adelaide had scolded her for ending their courtship. She couldn't wait to talk to him again.

Monday afternoon a week later, Rachael pinched the edges of her piecrust, poured in her cherry filling, and slid it in the oven. The last time they spoke was at last week's Sunday service. Why hadn't Caleb stopped in the bakery this week? They didn't have church service yesterday, and it would've been the perfect time for him to visit her at home. But she shouldn't expect anything from Caleb after the way she'd treated him.

Pauline entered the bakery's kitchen. "Rachael, can you spare a couple of minutes?"

She wiped her hands. "Yes. What can I do for you?"

"Would you say Nathan is ready for courtship? He said

Katherine was the love of his life." Pauline sat on the bench across from the big worktable centered in the room.

"Yes. He's ready. He needed time to mourn her and adjust, but now he's ready to move ahead with his life. Nathan is a genuine, kind, and honorable man. You don't need to have any reservations about him." She was glad Pauline had asked her about Nathan. She wanted to encourage her to grow her friendship with him.

"My husband was a loving man. I enjoyed being married, and I miss him every day. The doctor didn't know what caused his death. He died in his sleep. He'd complained of chest pain the day before, but we'd had a big dinner and blamed it on the meal. Nathan is a lot like him. His *kinner* are delightful. We've both had our spouses die, and we can empathize and talk about them without any jealousy. But I wanted to make sure."

"I pray you and Nathan find happiness together." Rachael wanted Pauline to leave with no doubts.

"You don't know me well, and you've been kind to talk to me about Nathan. *Danki* for giving me advice. I feel much better after our conversation. *Danki* again."

"You're *wilkom*." Rachael smiled. She liked Pauline. She might have done the same thing in her position. It was smart. She didn't want any surprises.

Pauline bid her farewell and left the kitchen.

Magdelena appeared. "What did Pauline want? She was a little mysterious."

"You're funny. No mystery involved. She wanted to ask my opinion of Nathan."

Suddenly, Mamm appeared and hurried to her. "Rachael, Caleb's hurt. *Kumme* quick to Dr. Harrison's office."

"Magdelena, I have to go." Fear ripped through her as she ran from the bakery.

"Go! I'll be praying for him." Magdelena followed them to the door.

Mamm and Rachael ran to Dr. Harrison's office, across the street and past the post office. They entered hurriedly.

Rachael bent over to catch her breath, then straightened. "Where is Caleb? Is he all right? What happened?"

Mamm clasped her arm. "Give the doctor time to answer."

Dr. Harrison washed blood from his hands in the bowl of water in his office area outside his patient room. "He's resting. Let's give him a minute to get his shirt back on. He fell from a ladder and got a jagged cut on his back near his left shoulder from broken glass on the ground. It bled a lot, but he'll be fine with the stitches I put in. He's fortunate your mother and Joseph stopped to visit him when they did."

"Mamm, you and Joseph brought him here?" Rachael quirked her brow.

Mamm nodded. "Yes. We had been meaning to stop at Caleb's and lend a hand with anything he needed as a house-warming present. I intended to offer to wash his clothes and clean *haus* for the day while Joseph and Caleb worked on something they could do together. Joseph had been meaning to lend Caleb a hand when he first moved in, but he hadn't had a chance. We found Caleb on the ground, passed out and bleeding. We shook him a little, and he woke. I put a bandage on the wound, and we brought him here."

Caleb and Joseph opened the door and joined them. "Rachael."

She wiped tears from her eyes. She was afraid he could've been hurt much worse. She hadn't even asked Mamm what was wrong on their way to Dr. Harrison's office. She ran until she could find out from Dr. Harrison. She'd been afraid to ask Mamm.

"I'm so thankful you're all right. You had me worried sick."

"Joseph and your *mamm* acted fast and brought me here. Then Dr. Harrison took excellent care of me." Caleb nodded.

Joseph blushed. "Glad we could help and relieved your injury wasn't more serious."

Frannie bolted in the doorway and brushed by Rachael. "Caleb, what happened?"

"How did you know?" Caleb frowned.

"I went to the bakery and overheard Magdelena tell Hannah why Rachael wasn't there. Where were you hurt?"

"I fell off a ladder onto my shoulder. There was broken glass on the ground, and I fell on the shards. I was going to clean it up after I repaired the roof. I'm fine. It doesn't hurt much. I didn't break anything, and I'm more embarrassed than hurt. Where's Lily?"

"Luke agreed to watch her for me for an hour while I did a little shopping in town. I came right over when I heard you might need me." She gave Rachael a sideways glance.

"No need to worry. But I will ask you to take me home. I don't want to trouble Joseph and Eleanor. Joseph, *danki* for your offer to help, but I don't need any right now. I've got everything in place and a routine. Plus, you're planning a wedding, which will be happening soon. I'm sure you're busy."

"Don't overdo and don't hesitate to call on me if you change your mind and need a hand with anything. You may find it's harder for you to do chores with your injury. I've got plenty of time to help you if need be before the wedding." Joseph headed for the door and opened it for him and the ladies.

"*Danki*, Dr. Harrison." Caleb paid him for his services.

Dr. Harrison smiled and shook his hand. "Just doing my job. Take some aspirin powder if you have any pain."

"I will."

Rachael followed all of them outside. "Caleb, if you need someone to change your bandage, I'll *kumme* by and take care of it after work."

Frannie waved a dismissive hand. "No need. I live closer. I'll take care of it. You have a bakery to manage. I'm sure Caleb doesn't want to inconvenience you. Right, Caleb?"

She bit her tongue. Frannie was like a wasp sting. She set her teeth on edge in seconds with her slyness. The bishop mustn't have gotten through to her about Caleb. She came to claim what she thought to be her territory once again. Caleb had been too gullible this time to recognize it at the moment, and he was being considerate of her, Mamm, and Joseph's time. She was sure he chose to let Frannie take him home so as not to inconvenience them.

"You're always *wilkom*, Rachael." He held her gaze for a moment.

Frannie nudged him. "Time to go. I don't want to trouble Luke any longer than necessary with watching Lily." She stuck her nose in the air.

He bid them farewell and left with her tugging him toward the livery, as if he were a reluctant puppy.

Mamm circled her arm around Rachael's waist. "I left Dr. Harrison's office and ran to the bakery to tell you. I thought you should know."

"You did the right thing. I would've wanted to know. I'm relieved the incident wasn't worse. Joseph, *danki*."

Caleb's heart sang. Rachael had rushed to his side the minute she found out he was injured. It'd been difficult, but he'd stayed away from her home and the bakery this past week. Her concern was evident, and the love they shared was still there. Magdelena and Hannah had been correct. Being patient was working.

"Caleb, are you listening to me?" Frannie glowered.

He hadn't paid any attention to her. "I'm sorry. What did you say?"

"You haven't been over to check on me or Lily for over a week. We could've been dead for all you knew," she harrumphed.

"Frannie, Luke is there with you. If you needed me for anything, I knew you'd ask. What is the problem?" He was frustrated with her each time they were together. If she were the last woman on earth, he wouldn't marry her. He was thankful Luke had made it this long working for her.

"You're a poor excuse for a *bruder*-in-law. At least care about Lily. She misses you."

"Lily's fine. I have a farm and livestock to manage. I don't have time to run over to your place to visit often. You've been to my place enough for me to know you're doing all right. How is Luke working out?"

"He's a jewel, compared to you. The man dotes on Lily and me. He can do the work of two men. He doesn't complain and he likes to cook." Frannie held her head high and batted her eyelashes.

He stifled a chuckle. Was she trying to make him jealous? She couldn't achieve that. He was ecstatic she might like Luke. He doubted Luke would have such favorable comments about her. He should ask Luke how he was faring. "Why don't you take me to your *haus* first for a couple of minutes? I'll chat with Luke and hug Lily." His wound barked with pain, but he'd go home with her to visit with Luke and Lily to silence her complaints.

Her mood changed. "Wonderful. And stay for supper. Luke's making chicken noodle casserole." She drove down the lane to the barn. "Wait. Who is Luke talking to?"

Caleb had the same question. The woman was in Englischer clothes. She was a pretty Englischer. She wore a low-cut red dress with ruffles and had a belted waist and long, coal-black ringlets. Her high-heeled shoes matched her clothes. He didn't know how she could walk in the grass in them without falling. He stayed in the buggy. "Let's give them some privacy and sit here a couple of minutes."

"I will do no such thing. This is my *haus*. I have every right to know who she is and what she wants with Luke." Frannie jumped out of the buggy. "Take care of the harness and mare."

Caleb covered his grin. Was Frannie jealous or afraid she'd lose Luke as a property manager? He couldn't tell. He tied the mare to a tree. He should check on Luke and the women. He approached them, and the two women waggled fingers and yelled at each other.

Frannie scrunched her face. "You're on private property. Leave and don't *kumme* back."

"You have no business joining our conversation. You little simple Amish woman. Look at you. No style or personality. Luke, why would you settle for her?"

Luke held up his palms. "Stop this arguing. Frannie, please go inside."

"I'll not move an inch. What are you trying to hide, Luke? Do you have plans with this woman? Have you been in contact with her?" Hands on her hips, Frannie glowered.

"I have not been in contact with Helena since she broke our engagement a year and a half ago when I lived in the outside world." He glanced at Helena and back to Frannie. "She asked the postman if he knew me. I left your address there for my mail. I have a couple of friends I thought may write."

Helena caressed Luke's arm. "Please, let's talk in private. I love you. I left Ernie. We've divorced. You don't have to worry I'll go back to him. I'm sorry. I made a terrible mistake when I broke off our engagement for him. I'll be the best wife in the world if you'll give me a chance. You still love me, don't you, Luke?"

Caleb kept his distance and stayed silent. He didn't want any part of this conversation, but he didn't want to leave until Luke said he would either stay or leave Charm.

Luke glanced over his shoulder. "Caleb, I'm sorry about all this."

"We need to talk after you've finished your discussion," Caleb said.

Luke gestured Helena to a bench by the pond, farther away from Caleb and Frannie.

Frannie stomped her foot. "Do something, Caleb. I want to know what they're saying."

"You and I should stay out of their business."

Frannie's cheeks blazed. He doubted she could've pinched her lips any tighter. He hoped she was jealous, and then maybe she'd leave Caleb alone. If Luke stayed, maybe she'd appreciate him more, or realize she might have feelings for him.

"You're no help." She glared at him. "Luke has been an excellent farmhand, and he has cooked, cleaned, and taken care of Lily. Not many men would be amenable to such chores. I don't want to start over again with a stranger." She plopped in the rocking chair on the porch beside him. "I care about him." She stared at the couple sitting on the wooden bench across the yard by the pond. "I wonder what he's saying to her. I'm going to find out." She stood.

Caleb grabbed her arm. "Check on Lily. We'll give them a few more minutes and then we'll interrupt." He didn't have all day, and he needed Luke to wrap up this squabble.

One minute Helena was shaking her forefinger at him

and the next she was hugging him. Luke had backed away from her each time.

Frannie returned. "Lily's asleep. Luke plays blocks and reads to her. He brings her outside and holds her hand as she walks. He's patient, like Stephen. Many things about Luke remind me of your *bruder*. He doesn't complain, he's kindhearted, and he's easygoing. This woman's intrusion on my property is very unsettling."

"I will always be here when you need me as 'family,' but, as I've said a number of times, I won't marry you. From what you've said, you may like Luke as more than a farmhand or friend. If so, take your focus off me and put it on Luke. Admit it: If he walked away right now, wouldn't you miss him as a man you might be falling in love with and not just for his skills as a farmhand?" He prayed this was true.

She stared at her folded hands in her lap. "I had my mind set on you."

Caleb cocked his head. "But not your heart."

"No. I was hoping we'd marry and fall in love over time. I'd be lying if I didn't admit I'm attracted to Luke, and we've had our moments where we've laughed and shared stories of our past over suppers. Until today, I hadn't allowed myself to admit it. I didn't know I could depend on him. He has nothing keeping him here." She raised her eyes, met Caleb's, and glanced over at the couple.

"Have you told him you may be interested in him, or has he hinted he may like to pursue a courtship with you?" Caleb noticed her face soften.

She shook her head. "We haven't discussed where we stand. We've built a friendship, but I suppose for me it's more. I'm surprised to hear myself say it. I was afraid Luke may be the type of man who may not grow roots in Charm. He's unmarried and has no ties here. You were a sure thing.

I'm not happy alone. I need a reliable husband." She kept her chin to her chest.

Helena yelled, "This isn't over, Luke." Then she ran to her buggy and stepped inside, then left with her mare galloping.

Luke approached them and sat across from them in the swing. "I apologize for Helena's rudeness and visit. The furthest thing from my mind is her seeking me out and begging me to rekindle our relationship."

Frannie gripped her white apron. "Are you still in love with her? Would you consider leaving with her?"

Luke reached for her hand. "Not for a second. I'm here to stay, if you still want me to work for you." He darted a look at Caleb.

"Frannie, the decision is yours." Caleb motioned to her.

"Yes. Yes. Yes. I don't want you to ever leave. I care about you. I didn't realize how much until your ex-*fraa* made every effort to coax you to go with her. I've been relentless in my pursuit of Caleb, but I would rather find a man to fall in love with to marry." She squeezed his hand. "I'm falling in love with you, Luke."

Luke kissed the back of Frannie's hand and then gazed at Caleb. "I'm falling in love with Frannie. I hope this doesn't upset you."

"No. I'm happy for you." Caleb could've jumped with glee, he was so giddy about this.

Luke was solving his problem of Frannie driving him mad. She wanted to be coddled and taken care of. But she might be sincere about her interest in Luke. He prayed they'd have a future together. Luke had been an upstanding man since they met.

"I believe we have something special. Frannie, would you consider a courtship with me?"

"Yes." She beamed. "I would love to." She tapped her

forefinger to her chin. "I have an idea." She gazed into Luke's eyes. "Why wait? Let's skip the courtship and plan a wedding."

Caleb cleared his throat. "Maybe you need to court first. You haven't known each other long."

He didn't want Frannie to have regrets and *kumme* whining to him a month from now. Or Luke to get exasperated with her and leave. She wanted to make sure Luke would stay in Charm, and this was her way of making sure of it.

"I agree with Frannie. I assumed a marriage would be out of the question or I would've proposed. I love her, and I'm ready to marry her."

"I believe I'm falling in love with you too." She hugged herself. "Caleb, please give us your blessing."

"You're grown adults. I'm a little dubious, but I'll relent. How fast should we put this wedding together?"

Rachael's soon-to-be step*daed* and her *mamm* were to wed June 29. He wasn't sure they could arrange everything any earlier.

Luke drummed his fingers on the arm of the swing. "I'll ask the bishop first thing in the morning what he has available on his calendar. We'll post an announcement in the bakery and ask our friends to spread the word. Not everyone will have enough notice to *kumme*, but we don't need much. We'll have the wedding here and use the Sunday service benches. We should have a date in mind. How about Tuesday, June 22?"

"Yes. June 22 or whatever is close to that date would be great. I can't believe it! We're getting married!" Frannie clapped her hands to her cheeks and grinned. "Caleb, you must think I'm mad, the way I've chased you. I've been such a terrible *schweschder*-in-law."

"What matters to me is you're happy, and I believe God

has a plan and Luke is the one for you." He rose and Luke did too. He shook Luke's hand. "Congratulations."

"*Danki*. And you should know I have money saved and I will take over paying for our needs and the farm's, if you aren't opposed."

"The farm is Frannie's and yours once you're married." He smiled.

"I appreciate it, Caleb. I will be an honorable and loyal husband and take care of Frannie and Lily."

"That's all I ask." Caleb couldn't wait to tell Rachael. She'd be shocked and thrilled. He was sure of it. This would erase any obligation she considered him to have as far as marrying Frannie. He hadn't gotten through to her that was never going to happen, but now she'd know for sure.

Luke put his hand on Caleb's back. "Would you *kumme* with me to ask the bishop about our wedding? I've had conversations with him, but he might be more receptive if you're there to voice your approval."

"Sure. I'll meet you here tomorrow morning and we'll go over to his *haus* together."

"*Danki*."

"I'll leave you both to plan and, again, congratulations." He tipped his hat and left.

Would this push Rachael closer to him? All he had to do now was pray she would accept he wanted to marry her. She'd been more open with him, and he kept hearing her say she missed him. He had hope.

Chapter 13

Caleb had an idea. He hoped he wouldn't be disappointed, but it was worth a try. First, he'd carry through on his promise to Luke. He mucked the stalls, redressed, and drove to Frannie's to meet Luke. June was pleasant and sunny so far, and this Tuesday was no exception. He arrived at Frannie's, and Luke met him at the wagon.

"*Danki* for accompanying me to Bishop Fisher's." Luke stepped into the wagon.

"I have another reason to visit Bishop Fisher, so this works out well for both of us. Luke, are you sure you're ready to marry Frannie?" Caleb didn't want Luke to feel pressured.

"I'm ready. It's sudden, but we've worked together since I accepted the job. I love her and I love Lily. Frannie can be demanding and difficult at times, but her kindness and the ways she shows she cares far outweigh her bossiness. It's a breath of fresh air to have a woman who loves the Amish life, loves God, and now, me. Lily is a treasure, and I hope God blesses us with siblings for her."

Caleb was thankful God had brought these two together. His life would be much easier without Frannie insisting he marry her. She could have the love she desired with Luke.

"You've got my blessing, and I wish you and Frannie much happiness."

Luke fumbled his hands. "I'm nervous about what Bishop Fisher will say when I ask to marry Frannie. I pray he doesn't refuse since we're getting married so soon after meeting."

"Bishop Fisher is a reasonable man. Relax." Caleb liked Luke. He was a humble man, and not afraid to speak his true feelings.

Caleb parked the wagon and walked with Luke to the front door.

Bishop Fisher greeted them. "Caleb and Luke, what brings you here?" He motioned for them to step inside.

Caleb and Luke sat on the settee. Caleb gestured to Luke. "Luke and Frannie would like to get married on June 22."

"Luke, you haven't lived in Charm long. Isn't this sudden?" Bishop Fisher sat on the edge of his chair and didn't smile.

"I suppose to Frannie's acquaintances, our wedding may be a surprise. I've spent all the time I've been here with her and Lily. We've both lost our spouses, and we want to wed and enjoy marriage again. I'm committed to the Amish life. I promise to love, honor, and take care of her and Lily the rest of the days I have on this earth."

"Luke, your first *fraa* died?"

"You're correct, and yes, Beverly died in her sleep. The doctor wasn't sure of the cause of her death."

The bishop focused his gaze on Caleb. "Have you given Frannie and Luke your blessing?"

"Yes. I support this union. Luke is a hard worker, and he's gone above and beyond for Frannie and Lily. After giving it some thought, I realized I should trust them. Luke and Frannie are sure this is what they want, and I won't stand in their way." Caleb glanced from Luke to Bishop Fisher.

"We won't have time for counseling." Bishop Fisher frowned.

Luke raked a hand through his thick brown hair as he held his hat in his lap. "Since we're a widow and widower, we've both had counseling before our first marriages. I have faith Frannie and I will glean what we've learned through our previous counseling, and throughout our marriages."

"You have a point, Luke. I'll trust you to do as you've said." Bishop Fisher dragged his calendar to his lap from the small table by his chair. "June 22 it is. Congratulations, Luke." He reached for Luke's hand. "I've been praying for Frannie and Lily, and I asked God to bring the right husband and *daed* for them. I'm glad you and Frannie have found each other. Let's pray together." He offered a prayer to God to bless this union.

"*Danki*, Bishop." Relief was evident in Luke's words.

"I've enjoyed our conversations at Sunday services, and friends have noticed how kind you are to Frannie and Lily. Don't hesitate to stop by any time you'd like to talk. My door is always open." Bishop Fisher grinned.

Luke stood as if to leave.

Caleb clasped his arm. "Luke, please sit for a minute longer. I have something I'd like to ask Bishop Fisher, and you can be present." It was important for Luke to understand he considered him family, even though the wedding hadn't taken place. This was one way he could show him he was accepted as more than a man who was marrying Frannie.

"Bishop, I plan to ask Rachael Schlabach to marry me again. She turned me down because she is barren. I have remained firm to her after our courtship ended that I'm still sure I want to marry her. I've been patient, and she's been more responsive to me this past week. If she says yes, I'd like to have the double wedding we planned in the first place with Joseph and her *mamm*. We have little time for our counseling."

"Most everyone in this town has nothing but high regard for you and Rachael. You've said you haven't wavered in your love for her while she's floundered to find her way. She has a loving heart, and I know she was doing what she thought was best for you, allowing you to be free to marry someone else and have *kinner*. I have prayed she'd have faith and trust God had brought you two together and let herself have the happiness she really wants in marrying you. God has answered not only my prayer, but I would guess many of your mutual friends, as well."

"We could meet any evening before June 29." Caleb held out his hands in question.

"Let's schedule Thursday, June 24, for a counseling session. I suspect you and Rachael don't need much instruction. You're both dedicated to God and the Amish life. I'll make an exception in your case. I will enjoy the double wedding. Now, don't dally. Go ask your girl. If you don't return to ask me to change it, I'll assume we're on for our session and the wedding."

Caleb rose with Luke. He hugged Bishop Fisher. "You've been so understanding and a good friend. I appreciate it." He liked the bishop's kind and compassionate heart. The man was a true follower of God.

"Let's pray again before you leave." The bishop offered a prayer to God for Caleb and Rachael.

They bid the bishop farewell and retrieved Caleb's wagon.

"I respect Bishop Fisher. He's a kind and understanding man who loves God," Luke said.

"Yes. We're fortunate to have him as our bishop. He

doesn't waver in his belief and teaching of the Scriptures, which is important for our leader. He is also reasonable, a good listener, and uses compassion in dealing with difficult circumstances. He'll speak his mind, but he's not a dictator."

"You shocked me, asking for your wedding date to be back on the schedule. Frannie says Rachael is adamant she won't marry you, and you've been stubborn to believe she will."

"Frannie wanted me to marry her for necessity and convenience, until she fell in love with you, and she considered Rachael a threat to her plan. Now, we can all have what we want if I can convince Rachael to wed me." Caleb pulled the wagon to the barn at Frannie's.

"I hope she says yes." Luke jumped out.

"*Danki*." Caleb tipped his hat. "Congratulations again."

Luke grinned and headed for the *haus*.

Caleb went home to pick some flowers before he went to the bakery.

Rachael pushed the heart cookie cutter into the dough. She loved Caleb, and no other man would measure up to him. She had prayed enough to know God was telling her to trust Caleb. God had pricked her conscience and shown her through the Scriptures in the Bible that she had been wrong.

Magdelena gave her a mischievous grin. "You have a visitor. I'll leave you two alone to talk."

"*Danki*, Magdelena." Caleb came to her side and passed her the flowers. "These are for you."

She was impressed he'd put them in a Mason jar with water. "I'll set them on the counter, where I can look at them while I work. They're beautiful. *Danki*. I should wait until I'm not up to my elbows in flour and dough, but I have waited long enough. Caleb, I'm sorry for all I've put you through. Will you forgive me?"

"Yes. Rachael, I've never stopped loving you, and I mean what I said. You are the bride for me. I have a *haus* for us. Frannie and Luke are getting married. You don't have to worry about her and Lily and what you thought was my obligation to marry her. Nathan and Pauline are courting. God has taken care of all your worries and objections. *Kinner* for me without you was never a problem, no matter what you thought."

Rachael pressed her forefinger to his lips. "I should've believed you the minute you said having *kinner* didn't matter. I love you, and I'll never love anyone like I do you." She reached for his hand. "Caleb Yutzy, will you do me the honor of becoming my husband?"

He picked her up and twirled her around. He set her on her feet. "I must confess I asked the bishop to schedule us for the same wedding date we had before, making it a double ceremony with Joseph and Eleanor."

"You did! Wonderful! I couldn't be more thrilled. Mamm and Joseph will be ecstatic. They've been rooting for you all along."

Magdelena joined them. "And me and all your friends. Yes, I eavesdropped, and no, I won't apologize for it." She chuckled.

Caleb pointed at Magdelena. "She and Hannah gave me the best advice. They told me to be patient, and they were right. *Danki*, Magdelena."

"What?" Rachael clapped a hand to her open mouth. "You won the hearts of everyone, it appears, Mr. Yutzy."

"Yes. He did. You both are meant for each other." Magdelena clapped her hands. "We must plan two wedding cakes!"

"Make it three. Frannie and Luke need one too. Their wedding is June 22. Two weeks away."

"They aren't wasting any time. He hasn't been here long. Are you all right with this?" Rachael had heard nothing but positive comments about Luke. From what she had observed of him at Sunday services, he reminded her of Stephen, Caleb's *bruder*, who was mild-mannered, with nothing seeming to ruffle his feathers, even Frannie's barking orders. Luke might be perfect for her.

"Yes. Luke could be my *bruder*'s twin as far as his personality goes. They'll be fine."

"I'll leave you two. Congratulations again." Magdelena skipped out of the room.

Caleb snapped his fingers. "One more thing. I asked the bishop for one counseling session instead of several. We'll be going to Frannie and Luke's wedding, and we don't have much time before ours."

"When?" Rachael had attended counseling sessions with her fiancé, John, before he was killed years ago, and she had no doubt Caleb and she would have little difficulty agreeing on finances, putting each other before themselves, and always making God first in their lives and marriage.

"Thursday, June 24, after you finish work. Is that date all right with you?"

"Of course. I'm grateful the bishop has confidence in us to allow us to meet one time. Although he doesn't need to worry about us. We have our priorities in order."

"Yes. I look forward to talking over concerns, problems, finances, and more with you as true partners in marriage. I want you to do the same, and I have no doubt you will." He kissed the back of her hand.

"I will, and I do feel the same. Oh, Caleb. I can't wait until we're together forever." She never thought this day would *kumme*. She'd been her own worst enemy. No more. God had been trying to tell her all along that Caleb was the one, and she just needed to be still and listen. She had never felt lighter in her step or happier. "*Kumme* to supper. We'll have a night of planning with Joseph and Mamm."

"I'll be there at six. Goodbye, my love." He tipped his hat and walked out of the kitchen.

She took a deep breath and hugged herself.

Rachael hurried home from work, went inside the *haus* to the kitchen, and breathed in the aroma of beef stew. "Mamm, I invited Caleb to supper tonight."

Mamm stopping stirring the stew. "Should I get my hopes up?"

"I sure hope so." Joseph smiled.

"Yes. Caleb came to the bakery this afternoon, and I asked him to marry me. I've been foolish to assume I know what's best for him. I'm taking him at his word. We're getting married in a double ceremony, like we planned before." She had been thrilled and happier than she'd been in a while. God had worked in their lives, Frannie's, Luke's, Nathan's, and Pauline's. She never should've doubted Caleb or taken things into her own hands. She hadn't really given her concern over marrying Caleb to God. She'd held on to her doubts, grown impatient, and made wrong decisions. She was grateful to have this second chance with Caleb.

Mamm set her spoon on the counter and engulfed her in a hug. "This is wonderful news."

Joseph beamed. "Your *mamm* and I have been praying and waiting for this day. I'm looking forward to congratulating Caleb this evening."

"Did Caleb already check with the bishop on adding you and Caleb to the ceremony?" Mamm returned to the stove.

"Yes. The bishop was pleased about our wedding, and he's making an exception in our case to have one counseling session rather than several. Caleb accompanied Luke there to lend him support when Luke asked the bishop to marry him and Frannie, and he used the same meeting with the bishop to ask about our wedding."

"What?" Mamm's eyes widened. "I'm shocked."

"Caleb said Luke reminds him of his *bruder*, Stephen. He doesn't mind Frannie's bossiness or laziness, and he adores her and Lily. Frannie liked Luke but didn't know whether to trust him to stay in her life. Caleb was here in Charm to stay, and he was a man she could count on. She wasn't in love with him. She wanted to marry him for convenience. She admitted she has feelings for Luke, so he suggested they get married."

Joseph set the table. "I noticed Nathan and Pauline sitting together at the meal after the Sunday services after the bishop's message, and I ran into them in town too. They seem like a couple courting."

"They are courting. God has taken care of all of us." Rachael pulled back the white curtain. "Caleb's here." She ran to greet him and opened the front door. "I told them our news. I couldn't wait."

"I want to tell the world!" He kissed her cheek.

They went to the kitchen and took their seats. Mamm and Joseph congratulated them as they sat down to supper.

"Mamm, are your dress and Joseph's suit all finished?" Rachael spread a generous amount of apple butter on her biscuit.

"Yes. And I've been stitching your dress since the first time Caleb proposed. I was sure you'd wear it one day. Now, we need Caleb's measurements, and I'll have his suit complete before the wedding." Mamm covered Rachael's hand.

"Mamm, *danki*. I wasn't sure how I was going to find time to stitch a dress, and it's not my best talent. I'm relieved I don't have to fret about it." Rachael squeezed Mamm's fingers.

"Joseph has friends assigned to bringing over the benches

and tables. I pray the weather will cooperate. If need be, we can move everyone inside and push the furniture aside."

"What more do we need to do?" Rachael wished she was as organized and talented as Mamm for having everything in place for a social or other event.

"We're all set. I've spoken with our friends, and they're bringing plenty of food dishes. You just need to make our cakes. Liza insisted on making the centerpieces for the tables, which are daisies in Mason jars. Our friends are letting us use their tablecloths, along with ours, so we'll have enough. We're ready." Mamm grinned.

"I wish Adelaide could attend our wedding. Caleb, you'd like her. I want you to go with Joseph and me to New Philadelphia soon so I can introduce you." She had a fondness for Adelaide, and she missed her. She couldn't explain the fast connection of friendship they'd had, but she was grateful for it. She'd never abandon her, and she'd help her all she could with her *boppli*.

Joseph frowned. "She wouldn't be accepted here in the kind of clothes she wears. She's a sweet woman, but I'm sure you've noticed, she's simpleminded. She's not as sharp as most women, like yourself, at twenty-five. I love her innocence, but it is also to her detriment. She's determined to live the life her *mamm* showed her as she grew up in the saloon. She's not even tried the Amish life. To her, our lifestyle is too stifling."

"Does she believe in God? Did her *mamm*?" Rachael bit her lip. Maybe this was too personal a question to ask. She didn't want to upset Joseph.

"Yes, she believes in God. Her *mamm* did too. I'm not sure if they had a personal relationship with God. They didn't attend church. She said they had enough prejudice from the ladies in town when they shopped. They didn't want to open themselves up to it from the church ladies at Sunday services."

"I'm sad they didn't stay Amish. Then we would've had Adelaide with us already. She would've gone to Sunday services with us."

"God knows their hearts. It's not for us to judge. He wouldn't have approved of their lifestyle. But they don't see their life in the outside world as wrong. None of us are perfect. We all find ways to justify things in our life from time to time that God may not approve of. Then we recognize it and ask for forgiveness. All we can do is pray for Adelaide and her unborn *boppli*."

They finished supper, and Rachael and Joseph did the dishes while Mamm measured Caleb for his suit.

Joseph accepted a wet plate from her to dry. "Adelaide wouldn't be *wilkom* here, but we could squeeze in a quick visit since your *mamm* has everything in order for the wedding."

Rachael beamed. "Maybe Caleb can go with us. I want to introduce them, and then she'll understand she has another member to add to her family besides you, me, and Mamm."

Rachael washed and Joseph dried the dishes, and they put them away in the maple cabinets.

Caleb and Mamm returned to the kitchen. "We're all done. How's it going in here?" Mamm scanned the kitchen.

"We're done too." Rachael hung the dish towel on the iron hook beside the sink. "Caleb, could you take two days off to visit New Philadelphia with me?"

"When?"

"Before our wedding?" Rachael folded her hands under her chin.

Mamm gasped. "We don't have time for you to make a visit before the wedding, do we?"

Joseph shrugged. "You've organized everything we need for the wedding. Caleb's suit is all you have left to do, and Adelaide would love knowing about the wedding before it happens."

"For you, I'll do anything," Mamm said.

"Mamm, will you join us?" Rachael went to her.

"I'm sorry. I can't. I'll stay and finish Caleb's suit and make sure everything is in order for our day. You, Joseph, and Caleb go. Adelaide will appreciate a visit from you, and she'll be delighted to meet Caleb. Also, you can check and find out how she's feeling."

"I don't know, are we out of our minds going to New Philadelphia now?" Rachael winced. "There's also Frannie and Luke's wedding a week before ours."

"Yes, but let's go anyway." Caleb chuckled.

Rachael gestured for them to join her in the living room. She opened the desk drawer and pulled out a calendar. "We have a church service this Sunday. Is it possible for all of us to go Thursday and return on Saturday?"

"I can." Joseph removed a small pad of paper and marked it with a pencil from the inside hidden pocket of his shirt.

"I didn't think we were allowed to have pockets," Caleb teased.

"We aren't, but this one is hidden." Joseph gave him an impish grin. "I don't wear this shirt often."

"We all have our secrets. I have a loose board in the bedroom where I've kept pictures of Mamm, Daed, and Stephen. A photographer in town took our pictures without us knowing it and then offered to sell them to us. Daed was furious at first, and then Mamm coaxed him into buying them. He'd do anything for her. She promised to hide them in the *haus* and not mention them. She showed me where they were in case anything happened to them. I treasure those forbidden photographs."

"I won't tell." Joseph clapped a hand to his shoulder.

"I will make arrangements so I can go those days," Caleb said.

Rachael couldn't wait to show Caleb New Philadelphia, and to introduce him to Adelaide.

Wednesday, Rachael asked Liza if she'd fill in for her at the bakery while she was gone. She told Liza that Caleb was able to go to New Philadelphia this time to meet Adelaide, and Liza supported her decision. She was happy to take her place at the bakery.

Rachael left Charm early Thursday morning with Joseph and Caleb. Mamm had packed jars of water to drink and sandwiches to eat along the way. They made short stops and arrived in New Philadelphia seven hours later.

"Caleb, they have a peddler who sells cotton candy, and another who sells Cracker Jack. The town is full of vendors and the shops are larger than ours in Charm. They have large factories where they manufacture steel and rubber products, farm equipment, and more. They have big clothing and shoe stores. It's fun to go to the Erie Canal, where there are passenger and cargo boats using the locks to transit."

"You've learned a lot about New Philadelphia on your visits here. I'm impressed." Caleb watched the crowd.

"Joseph has schooled me on most of it. New Philadelphia is a fun place to visit, but I wouldn't want to live here. The streets are too full of townsfolk, and the shops have little to offer to the Amish. We don't need much of what New Philadelphia offers. I feel out of place here." She liked her simple Amish life, the order of things, the camaraderie she had with her friends, and being sheltered from the news about the war going on in other countries. She heard enough of it from Dr. Harrison and the sheriff to make her want to cry for the families who had *kinner* enlisted to serve in case the United States decided to join the war. She remembered some of the young men's names they mentioned on their visits to the bakery and prayed for them often.

Joseph dropped his buggy at the livery, and they walked over to the boarding*haus*, where he secured two rooms. He handed Rachael her key, and Caleb would room with him. "Let's meet in the lobby in twenty minutes. I'd like to wash my face and rest for a couple of minutes."

Rachael and Caleb agreed, and they went to their rooms.

Caleb washed his face and told Joseph he'd be in the lobby. He hadn't been to New Philadelphia before and he was curious to tour the town. The more he was with Joseph, the more he liked him, and it was easy to consider him family. Rachael and Joseph seemed to share a close bond, and he admired Joseph for sharing his niece's whereabouts and lifestyle with them. Not all Amish would've accepted his close relationship with his niece.

Rachael came downstairs and met him. "What do you think?"

"The lobby is fancy, with heavy curtains and chandeliers. The carpet is red to match, and the clothes worn by the Englischers are quite the assortment. Men wear an array of casual pants and shirts with pockets in both and different style hats than the Englischers who live in Charm or visit. I suppose it's because this town is much larger than Charm. This town is busy with buggies, wagons, and automobiles. We don't have many automobiles in Charm." The train whistle blew, and he covered his ears. "I don't like it so far."

Rachael chuckled. "It's definitely a big dose of the

outside world. But it will be worth the trip for you to meet Adelaide. She's family. She should know you."

Joseph meandered down the stairs. "Ready?"

They nodded and ventured out onto the boardwalk. Peddlers approached them to sell their candy, watches, hats, and more.

Caleb kept Rachael between himself and Joseph. He didn't like all the Englischer men around Rachael. They were inconsiderate and loud.

They arrived at the saloon. Joseph motioned to the restaurant beside it. "Rachael, you wait here. Caleb, you should wait with her."

Caleb sat on the bench out front. Rachael sat next to him.

Two men argued on the bench next to them. The stout man waggled his finger. "President Wilson is the worst, in my opinion. I'm not pleased with the decisions he's made."

"He's doing the best he can with the war going on around us. We'll become a part of it soon, mark my words. Let's talk about something else. I don't want to argue with you all day. Remember, I told you I met Sir Sandford Fleming on my trip to Canada to visit my cousin? He's the man who invented standard time. Smart scientist and engineer. Sad, though, he's miserable and won't leave his house. After all the man has accomplished with the railroad and time zones."

Rachael and Caleb exchanged a surprised look. They listened to the two men and pretended to stare out into the crowd. Caleb didn't want the men to become aware they were eavesdropping.

"I remember you telling me about that man, Fleming. Interesting, and unfortunate he isn't living a happy life. I hope your friend gets better."

Caleb had grabbed a newspaper now and then to read what was going on in the outside world. He didn't talk about it. The Amish were against learning outside news. He remembered Sir Sandford's name. The man had been a brilliant inventor and scientist, in addition to being an engineer. It seemed like an insurmountable task to create universal time. He was thankful the man accomplished this because it benefited everyone. "Are you amazed at what some of the men of the world accomplish?"

"Yes. Do you sometimes wonder what it would be like if you'd gone all the way through school and on to higher learning?"

"No. I'm content living Amish and working on a farm. We'll have a comfortable life, and we don't need most of the things the world has to offer. I have no desire to be an inventor or scientist. I'm looking forward to being your husband. That's enough for me."

Rachael wouldn't have wanted him to be curious about the things the outside world had to offer. She wanted a husband who was dedicated to the Amish life without reservations, and she was grateful Caleb was the man for her.

Joseph rushed back to them. "Madge told me Adelaide is in her room and the *boppli* is *kumming*. Rachael, she said you can be with Adelaide. I don't know how you feel about being in the saloon."

Rachael wanted to go to her. She'd be in Adelaide's room and not part of the saloon business. "Caleb, what's your opinion?" She didn't want to go if he thought it unacceptable. She would probably have to walk through the part of the saloon where they were serving patrons. She was uncertain if she should be with Adelaide, given the circumstances.

"You should go to her. She's family. Joseph and I will be here if you need us."

Rachael loved him for understanding. She headed to the saloon.

"Wait." Joseph grabbed her arm. "I'll take you to her room."

"*Danki.*"

He escorted her through the saloon and to Adelaide's room. "I'll be outside with Caleb, or we'll be in the restaurant next door."

"I'll let you know in an hour or so how she's doing."

"I'm worried about her. Please do, and be careful if you leave her room. Have Madge or one of the girls walk you out."

"Don't worry. I can manage." She waited until Joseph went back down the stairs. She tapped on the door, opened it, and found Madge wiping Adelaide's forehead with a wet cloth. The doctor was at the end of the bed.

Adelaide groaned and then reached for her. Her face was pale and her voice was weak. In almost a whisper, she said, "Rachael, you're here. Please stay beside me and hold my hand."

Rachael's eyes pooled with tears. She hurried to her, dragged a chair close to her bedside, and clasped her hand. "I love you, Adelaide. I'll be here as long as you need me."

Madge's worried eyes stared into Rachael's. "She's been in labor since yesterday afternoon. She's exhausted. Since Dr. Kelly and you are with her, I'll go grab a sandwich and some tea and change my clothes. I'll return soon."

"Yes. You must be tired. Take your time." Rachael accepted the cloth and bowl of water from Madge. She set the bowl on the nightstand beside the bed. She dipped the cloth in the water and dabbed Adelaide's cheeks.

Adelaide screamed and writhed.

The doctor's eyes widened. "Push!"

Adelaide's eyes were closed, and it was as if she were asleep.

Dr. Kelly worked to deliver the *boppli*. Rachael shook Adelaide's shoulder. "Adelaide, please wake up."

The doctor held the *boppli*, and tears stained Rachael's cheeks. She was tiny and beautiful. He cut the cord and tied it. There was another table in the room with a bigger bowl of water to wash the newborn, and a blanket to wrap her in.

Dr. Kelly handed her the *boppli*. "Please wash and wrap the baby. I need to check Adelaide."

Rachael accepted the *boppli*, who was kicking her little legs and moving her arms. She wished Adelaide would wake up. She needed to hold her *boppli* after all her hard work in birthing her. The doctor seemed to want to keep her busy and away from the bed. Something wasn't right. She glanced over her shoulder over and over again as she washed and wrapped the *boppli*.

He had hurried to grab his stethoscope and hold it to Adelaide's chest. His shirt was damp with sweat. He then checked her pulse and breathing. "I'm sorry. She's gone." He slumped in the chair and held his head in his hands.

Rachael held the tiny *boppli*. "What! She's going to be fine. She's tired. She's asleep. She talked to us a minute ago." Her lips quivered as she carried the precious bundle to Adelaide's side. She shook her arm. "Please, Adelaide, your *boppli* needs you. Please. Doctor, do something."

"I'm sorry. There's nothing I can do. I suspect Adelaide had a bad heart, but I never know for certain what takes the life of a mother giving birth." He washed his hands in a third bowl on the other nightstand, lifted the *boppli* from her, unwrapped the blanket, and examined her. "She's a healthy little girl. Again, I'm sorry for your loss." He handed the *boppli* back to Rachael, then gathered the soiled cloths, dropped them in a clean flour sack bag, and washed and dried the rest of what he'd used from his bag and put them back in it. "I'll find Madge and have her *kumme* to Adelaide's room."

Rachael was numb. She wept as she held the newborn, who was sucking on her little finger. She stared at Adelaide with her bloodstained gown and sheets. Her blond, damp hair from sweat against the pillowcase. Her eyes closed, as if she would wake any moment. It wasn't supposed to happen this way. Adelaide would've been overjoyed they'd been here together to *wilkom* this little one into the world. They would've marveled at her *dochder*'s tiny hands and feet.

Madge and Jewel, crying, entered the room and shut the door behind them. Madge shook her head. "I can't believe she's gone."

Jewel wiped her eyes and opened the clothes press. She pulled out a clean sheet and covered Adelaide. She lifted the *boppli* from Rachael. "She's beautiful. She has Adelaide's deep blue eyes and her blond hair." She swiped a tear from her cheek. "Rachael, Adelaide talked about you a lot. She said she couldn't explain it, but she loved you from the time you had your first conversation. She said she couldn't wait for your visits, and she wanted you in her *boppli*'s life."

Rachael pulled a handkerchief from her sleeve and wiped her damp eyes. "She was easy to love. I felt the same about her." She couldn't imagine not talking to her again. None of this seemed real.

Madge circled her arm around Rachael. "The doctor said he'll notify the undertaker. He should be here any minute."

"Should we wash the body?" Rachael wanted to take care of Adelaide.

"The undertaker will wrap her and take care of washing her for us. I'll notify the funeral director and make the necessary arrangements. He also owns the cemetery. Would you like to attend? We could have the service tomorrow if you choose to stay."

Rachael nodded. "*Danki*. Yes. I'd like to attend. I'm sure Joseph and Caleb will too." She didn't want to leave until she had put Adelaide's body to rest. "I'd like to wash and dress her in a fresh gown."

Jewel rocked the *boppli* in her arms. "I'll hold the baby."

Madge opened the clothes press and removed under-clothes and a blue dress with a ruffled, low-necked collar and covered buttons to the waist and a full skirt. "Here's her dress." She lifted sheets and a clean flower sack. "You can put the soiled linens in the flour sack. I'll bring you a fresh pitcher of clean water and towels."

Jewel followed Madge. "One of the girls likes goats' milk and keeps it in the ice chest. I'll feed the baby."

"Her name's Marie. Adelaide had her name picked out," Rachael said.

"Marie it is." Jewel glanced at Adelaide and then hurried out of the room.

Rachael cut the gown off Adelaide, and Madge returned with the linens and water.

Madge wrung her hands. "I'll go to the funeral home. It's within walking distance. I'll be back soon. Will you be all right doing this by yourself? The other girls are working and filling in for Adelaide and Jewel. The undertaker may be here before I return. Teresa Bell works for the funeral home, and she assists Mr. Young. She schedules the service and burial."

Tears pooled in Rachael's eyes. "I'll be fine. I've had to do this before. I want to prepare Adelaide's body." She didn't want to leave her.

"I'll leave you, but I'll hurry. We'll hold the visitation, funeral, and burial all in one day since you're from out of town. I'll tell you the time when I return. I noticed Joseph outside, and I'll tell him."

"*Danki*." Rachael was short on time and didn't want to leave for fear the undertaker would arrive and she wouldn't have finished preparing Adelaide's body. She rolled her body from one side to the other as she changed the bedsheets. She washed, dried, and changed Adelaide into clean underclothing and a dress not as revealing as her other clothes. She brushed her curly hair as best she could. She then covered her with another clean sheet. She knelt and prayed, "Dear Heavenly Father, I'm brokenhearted. Please give me the courage and strength to say and do the things you would have me say to Adelaide's friends. Adelaide said she believed and trusted in you. I pray she's with you. I don't want Marie to grow up here. Please intervene on Marie's half. Guide and direct me. Please, Heavenly Father. Amen."

Rachael rose and answered the knock at the door. A short, stout, and bald man with empathetic eyes removed his hat. "I'm George Young, the undertaker, and this is my son, Benny. I brought a clean blanket to drape over the body as we remove her and take her to the funeral parlor. Madge is at our office now, making the arrangements with Teresa. You must be Miss Schlabach."

She nodded and stepped aside. "Yes. Adelaide is family." She watched them take her out of the room on a stretcher, then followed them outside. She figured she'd be safe with them rather than leaving on her own to meet Joseph and Caleb. She scanned the saloon for Jewel, but she wasn't there. She shook with grief as she followed the men. She stepped outside, and Caleb opened his arms. She didn't care that they were in public. She fell against him and wept.

Joseph stood next to them, holding a handkerchief to his eyes.

She pulled away. "She was exhausted, but she spoke to

me. Her voice was weak and she looked bad, but never did I expect she was near death. I miss her so much already. Marie, the *boppli*, resembles her. She's precious."

"I want to hold her." Joseph dabbed his eyes. "Where is she?"

"Jewel, Adelaide's friend, has her. She knows where to get goat's milk to feed her. I don't know where she is at the moment. We'll ask Madge when she returns from the funeral home. Let's wait on the bench in front of the restaurant."

Joseph wrung his hands and paced. "I can't believe Adelaide's gone. My *schweschder*'s death was sudden, like this. It's difficult to take in. Who will care for Marie? I want to take her home with us. We're her family."

Rachael blew her nose and gathered her thoughts. "After I prepared Adelaide for the undertaker, I prayed to God to guide us on what to do about Marie. I'm hoping Madge will offer us Marie without any opposition. Everything has happened so fast. I'm in shock, and I'm sure you are too, Joseph. My mind was muddled. There wasn't a right moment to address it with Madge."

Caleb shook his head. "One thing at a time. Let's wait and see what Madge has to say about Marie, if anything. We'll ask her for Marie if she doesn't offer her before we leave. Here *kummes* Madge."

They stood.

Madge swiped a tear with the back of her hand. "I'm closing the saloon then to allow the staff to attend Adelaide's service. The visitation will be held at one, the service at two, and the burial at three. Mr. Young has agreed to say a few words. I gave him a note about Adelaide and to guide him on what to say. You can add anything to the note you'd like tomorrow. Mr. Young will have everything ready at noon, in case you'd like private time with Adelaide before the mourners arrive. I hope I haven't offended you by taking over the arrangements."

Joseph cleared his throat. "No. You're gracious to set everything in place. We're in unfamiliar territory, and we're grateful you're willing to help us. It's to our advantage that you know Mr. Young and Miss Bell. Is there anything I can do? I'll pay for the undertaker's services and cemetery plot. Did you have to make a partial or full payment?" He removed paper bills and passed them to her.

Madge pushed his hand away. "I insist on paying the undertaker and for the cemetery plot. He and I are old friends. He won't charge me much. Adelaide was like a daughter to me. This is something I want to do for her. Adelaide was special. She had a childlike innocence. She blessed our hearts with her voice. No one else has a voice like hers at the saloon." She put a finger to her trembling lips. "I'm sorry. I had to take a moment. It's hard not to cry."

Joseph let tears drip from his face and didn't wipe them. "Don't apologize. I'll miss her too. I appreciate your generosity and kind words. I'm thankful she had you to watch over her."

Rachael could understand why Adelaide loved Madge. She didn't understand Englischer ways or what their lives were like in the outside world, but she was glad Madge had been close to Adelaide. "*Danki* for all you've done for us."

"Some of the ladies will make sandwiches, and I'll have the bakery deliver a cake to the social room of the funeral home. I hope you'll stay after the burial and enjoy the food before you leave for Charm."

Joseph wiped his face. "We'll be there. *Danki*."

Madge removed a handkerchief from her skirt pocket. "May I have a word?" Madge waved them closer to her.

"Rachael, would you take and raise Marie? The saloon isn't the proper home for her. Without Adelaide, the girls and I don't want the responsibility. We work long hours as waitresses, singers, dishwashers, cleaners, and whatever else needs done to keep this place in good shape. We were willing to make it work while Adelaide was alive, but we would rather not now. Please don't judge us as coldhearted. You're a much better fit to raise Marie."

Rachael thanked God for His intervention. He'd answered her prayer. "I'd love to take Marie. Oh, Madge. I will miss Adelaide every day. This way, I'll have a part of her with me whenever I look at Marie."

Joseph held a trembling fist to his mouth. "Bless you, Madge."

Caleb nodded. "We'll be happy to take her. You can rest assured she'll be protected and raised in a loving home."

Madge wrapped her arms around Rachael, and they cried together.

Jewel joined them, holding Marie. "Did you tell them?"

"Yes. Rachael's agreed to take Marie." Madge gestured for Jewel to give her to Rachael.

Rachael accepted the precious bundle. She'd be a *mamm*. Adelaide had made her a *mamm*. She had a *dochder*. It didn't seem real or possible. She was grief-stricken to have lost Adelaide, but she'd make sure Marie knew how much Adelaide meant to her. She held the miracle in her arms. She was happy and sad. "*Danki*."

Jewel left and returned quickly with a large bag of bottles, nappies, blankets, *boppli* clothes, goat's milk, and more *boppli* things. "This should be enough while you're in New Philadelphia and on your ride home."

Caleb peered in the bag. "This is amazing. There's plenty of everything."

Madge shrugged. "We had a baby shower for Adelaide last week. The girls and ladies from the church, plus some of the townsfolk, were generous. She was loved."

Rachael thanked them again. She held Marie as they walked to the boarding*haus*. "I'm ready to take my shoes off and rest. I'll put this little one in one of the dresser drawers in the bureau in the room. I hope she'll sleep."

Caleb caressed her cheek. "Joseph and I will have supper in the dining room, and we'll bring you a dish of food before we retire to our rooms."

Joseph kissed Marie's forehead. "She's such a contented *boppli*. I'm thankful we're taking her with us. It would've ripped my heart out to have her stay here. Thanks be to God." He folded his hands and raised them to Heaven.

Caleb set the big bag inside Rachael's room and left with Joseph.

Rachael opened the last drawer in the dresser, set two thick blankets inside, and lowered Marie onto them. The *boppli* slept. Rachael stared at her tiny face. Madge was right. This day was like a whirlwind. It didn't seem possible she'd *kumme* to visit Adelaide, thinking she'd be delighting with her over Marie's birth, and ended with taking Marie with her as her new *mamm*. Adelaide had given her the most precious gift in the world. She removed her shoes and fell back on the bed.

An hour later, she woke to a knock. She opened the door.

Caleb had a beef sandwich and noodle soup. "How's our *dochder*?"

She started. Marie was their *dochder*. She and Caleb were parents. It seemed strange, sad, and wonderful at the same time. "She's sleeping. I can't believe we are her parents."

"I have to say it to myself over and over again. It doesn't seem real. We've been blessed beyond measure. I'm happy, but I'm full of sorrow over Adelaide. It's such a jumbled bunch of emotions." He glanced at the plastic box in his hand. "I almost forgot. This is ice to put the goat's milk in to keep it fresh. I bought it to take with us. We can stop for ice on the way. Until then, the general store has some. I'll let you rest. I'm across the hall if you need me."

"*Danki*. I love you, Caleb. This is all a bit easier with you here. You're my rock to lean on. I'm sure Joseph is grateful too."

"You can always depend on me, Rachael." He kissed her cheek. "Try to rest. Good night." Caleb went to his room.

Rachael closed her door. She took two bites of the sandwich and managed to keep down the soup. Her stomach churned and her body ached with sorrow. She prayed to God for comfort for all of them, and she thanked Him for precious Marie.

Rachael woke twice to Marie's cries, and she changed her nappy and fed her. She was weary, but she didn't care. Each time she held Marie, she reveled in holding her. Then she'd remember Adelaide, and she'd talk to Marie about what a sweet soul her *mamm* had been. She didn't care if Marie was too young to understand. She'd keep telling her for years to *kumme*.

She didn't know what to expect at an Englischer funeral, though she wouldn't let anyone stand in her way of going. Adelaide had meant too much to her. Joseph, Caleb, and she would stand out in their Amish clothing. She was afraid they might have second thoughts about attending the services because they wouldn't be conducted in the Amish way. She also hoped they'd be accepted without prejudice.

Chapter 14

Rachael dressed and washed her face Friday morning. She readied Marie, then emptied a smaller flour sack she'd brought some jars of water in and filled it with what she needed for her. Joseph and Caleb came out of their room at the same time she left hers.

They had a late breakfast in the dining room. Rachael had little appetite.

The waitress oohed and ahhed over Marie. "I'm Evelyn, Jewel's sister. I'm sorry for your loss. Jewel stopped by last night and told me what happened to Adelaide, and how relieved she is you and her uncle are here to take Marie. Jewel said you were someone she admired. I'm glad you'll be raising her daughter."

"It's a pleasure to meet you," Rachael said.

Caleb paid the bill, and the waitress left to wait on another customer.

They left, took their time, and walked to the funeral home, arriving at noon.

"Welcome. I'm Teresa Bell. I'll leave you alone to have some private time."

They nodded and went to the casket.

Joseph offered a prayer to God.

Rachael stared at her friend she'd *kumme* to care about

in a short time. She looked peaceful, as if she was sleeping. Joseph said Adelaide believed in God. It wasn't for her to judge. God knew Adelaide's heart. She'd miss not having Adelaide in her life. She'd always remember Adelaide's hand covering hers when Marie had kicked before she was born, her laughter, and her hugs. Her body shook as she struggled to keep from sobbing.

Caleb gestured to Madge and Jewel and a group of women with them entering the room. The casket was made of cherrywood and had scrolled corners. Vases full of pretty roses, carnations, and other flowers were displayed on wooden pedestals on either side of the casket.

There were rows of wooden benches, much like theirs, in rows on either side of the room, leaving an aisle between them. An ornate podium was off to the side. A piano was in the corner of the room. There was a stained-glass window with the outline of a cross in the middle.

Madge, Jewel, and the girls greeted them and then went to view Adelaide. Madge gestured to the women to take their seats, and she went to the piano. She began to play a hymn.

Mourners filled the room, each offering their condolences to her, Caleb, and Joseph. She knew Bishop Fisher wouldn't approve of all this, but Rachael had to be there.

Mr. Young stood behind the podium at one, and the room was full. "Please take your seats." He offered a prayer to God. "Madge has provided me with notes about Adelaide. I'll share them with you. Adelaide was kind, thoughtful, and loyal. She was genuine, and she helped her friends any way she could. The word 'no' wasn't often said by Adelaide when she was asked to waitress extra hours or to clean the floors. She had a wonderful sense of humor, and she could lift your mood in no time with her silly jokes or made-up songs." He finished his speech. "Please join me and the family as we walk to the burial site to the left of the funeral home."

Rachael carried Marie. She was thankful the newborn was sleeping. She was such a good *boppli*. She whispered to Caleb, "I dread the burial. Even though I know she's not in the casket, I don't like the lowering of it. It's all so final. I long to hug her one more time." She sniffled.

"I wish I could've met her." He looked lovingly at Marie. "She's so tiny. I can't believe she's ours. This has all happened so fast. I'm sad about Adelaide. She left us such a precious gift."

"Yes. I have a difficult time putting her down. I want to hold her forever and never let her go." Rachael had memorized every inch of Marie. She had the roundest eyes, and the fullest cheeks and lips. She had dainty hands and feet.

Joseph kept silent.

The three of them stood in front of the mourners, and Rachael shivered with nerves.

Mr. Young prayed, led them in a hymn, and said kind words about Adelaide again. "Please return to the social room in the funeral home to partake of the food prepared by Adelaide's friends."

Two men stayed and filled the hole where the casket was lowered earlier. Rachael watched them shovel dirt for a moment, and then she followed Joseph and Caleb to the funeral home. She, Joseph, and Caleb took their seats. The ladies told happy stories about Adelaide. She'd made them laugh, sang their favorite songs, and had been a loyal friend to them.

An hour later, they stood to leave.

Mr. Young shook Joseph's hand. "I pray you have a safe journey home."

"*Danki* for all you've done today." Joseph sucked in his wavering lip.

They bid Adelaide's friends farewell and returned to the boarding*haus*.

The next morning, they traveled home, making a couple of short stops along the way.

"What will we tell the bishop and our friends who don't know we've been going to New Philadelphia to visit Adelaide?" Rachael worried many of the Amish might not understand.

Joseph inhaled and exhaled slowly. "We went to check on Adelaide. She was with child. She died during childbirth, and we brought Marie home to raise. I doubt we'll encounter any judgment since she died. They won't object to us bringing Marie home to raise as Amish. If we should encounter disapproval, I'll take the blame. I'll tell the bishop or Amish who confront me that I asked you both to join me for help."

Caleb put his hand on Joseph's shoulder. "No. I'll stand with you. I don't expect to have any Amish do anything but express their condolences and shower Marie with love."

Joseph glanced at Rachael. "Your *mamm* will be shocked. So will many of our friends. One look at Marie, though, and they'll drop any judgment."

"It's going to take a long time not to grieve Adelaide's death. I had looked forward to many conversations and sharing our stories about our childhoods, our friendships with others, and more." She never thought she'd be as close to an Englischer like Adelaide. She'd connected with her the first time they met. She'd truly been family. She'd cherish the conversations she'd had with Adelaide.

They arrived home late Saturday afternoon, and Caleb got his buggy and headed to his *haus*. He had asked Luke to take care of his place and livestock, and he was eager to check on him and the animals.

Rachael and Joseph entered the *haus*.

Mamm gasped. "You have a *boppli* in your arms. Did Adelaide have her *boppli*? Did she ask you to care for her for a couple of days?" She rambled and then stopped.

Rachael sat on the settee with Marie and cried. She could let her emotions out with Mamm, and being home brought Adelaide's death to the forefront again. "Joseph, you tell her."

"Tell me what? You're scaring me."

"Please sit, Eleanor." Joseph gestured to the settee. He sat in the chair across from her. "When we arrived, Adelaide was giving birth. Rachael went to be by her side. She wasn't there long before Marie was born, and Adelaide died. Madge relayed to Caleb and me what happened while Rachael was still with Adelaide and Marie. The doctor's not sure if it was her heart or what was the cause. Adelaide's friends were gracious enough to arrange the service the next day. They closed the saloon, and the funeral director conducted the funeral and burial. Her friends also provided food after the burial for us."

Mamm's eyes filled with tears. "I'm speechless. I should've been with you. I'm sorry." She stared at Marie. "I take it Adelaide's friends asked you to take Marie? She has Adelaide's blond hair and turned-up nose. I can't believe she's gone."

"Madge, the manager and a close friend of Adelaide's, asked Rachael to take her. Adelaide had praised Rachael to her, and Madge had no problem handing Marie to her. She said Adelaide loved Rachael and considered her a *schweschder* after their first meeting." Joseph gazed into Rachael's eyes. "I'm overwhelmed with gratitude to you for offering to meet Adelaide, wanting to grow a friendship with her, and accepting her without hesitation."

"I'm the one who should say *danki*. She taught me lessons about how far and wide God's love stretches, and we're not the only believers. She also gave me this little miracle. I'm a *mamm*. I've desired to be a *mamm* for a long time. I wouldn't have wanted Adelaide to have to sacrifice her life for me to have Marie, but I'll always be grateful to her."

Mamm circled her arm around Rachael's shoulders. "You will make a loving and wonderful *mamm*. Marie is a miracle."

Joseph recounted more of the details of their stay in New Philadelphia.

Caleb arrived and walked inside the *haus*. He set the cradle he'd made on the floor. "I forgot to take this with us. I never imagined we'd be using it."

Mamm hugged him. "You're a *daed*."

Rachael admired the cradle. "Caleb, this is amazing. I'm sure Marie will enjoy the rock of the cradle, and we'll be thankful for it when it soothes her."

"Eleanor, I consider Rachael my *dochder*. Our double wedding ceremony is but two weeks away. You'll be a *grossmudder*, and I'll be a *grossdaed*," Joseph said.

Caleb beamed. "I'm a *daed*. I repeated this several times to myself on the way home. Until I brought over this cradle, it didn't seem real. But now it does."

Rachael passed Marie to him. "She's light."

He beamed as he gazed at Marie's tiny face. "Yes. She did well on the trip. I was worried it might be too much for a newborn." Caleb tightened the blanket around her. "I'm never going to let her court when she's of age."

Rachael chuckled for the first time since Adelaide's passing. "I'm with you. I want to keep her all to ourselves."

She had much to look forward to, being a *mamm*. She'd knit booties and a blanket and stitch little dresses.

Rachael was excited and apprehensive to go to church. She wasn't sure how their story about Adelaide would be received. She carried the bag she'd packed for Marie. She was tired from the trip, but she couldn't wait to show her friends the *boppli*. "Are you ready to leave, Mamm?"

"The mare is harnessed to the buggy."

They walked to the buggy together and got in.

"I'm proud of you. You're prepared with a bag for Marie and you're on time." Mamm headed to the Yoders for the church service. "Will you work at the bakery? If so, I'll watch Marie."

Rachael tensed. She didn't want to leave Marie even for a day. "I don't want to work at the bakery anymore, but I'll not leave Magdelena without anyone. I'll ask Magdelena what to do. Maybe I can coax Liza or Hannah to take my place until they hire a new baker."

"I'm sure they'll be accommodating."

They arrived at the Yoders', and Mamm parked the buggy with the others. Mrs. Yoder loved having the services at their place, and she often hosted social events. The Yoders had a perfect spot for entertaining. They had a large farm, and they were a gracious couple. Mrs. Yoder said she didn't care if her *haus* was a mess with dirty dishes in the sink and laundry piled in a chair, she'd rather be entertaining visitors. "The more the merrier" was her motto.

Joseph and Caleb met them. They complimented the *boppli*'s sweet face and tiny hands and feet. Joseph escorted them to the church benches outside.

Mrs. Yoder placed a hand on Rachael's back. "Why do you have a *boppli*?"

Mr. Yoder pulled her away. "Tell the women where you

want the desserts. You change where you want things every time. I don't know what to tell them."

"Excuse me." She waddled away with him.

Caleb chuckled. "And the questions begin."

The men went to their side of the benches and Rachael sat with Mamm on the other side, in the back. "Let's stay here. If Marie fusses, I can move farther away from everyone and not be disruptive."

"Thinking like a *mamm* already." Mamm winked.

She stifled a laugh, thinking this would be a long service for her friends, wondering why she was holding a *boppli*. Magdelena and her other friends kept giving her questioning glances. They'd be anxious to find out why she had a *boppli* with her and what happened in New Philadelphia. She worried Joseph would be admonished by the bishop or some of the Amish. She didn't want him to shoulder the responsibility. She was to blame too. She wouldn't let him stand alone. She knew Caleb would feel the same. He hadn't gone on the first trip with her. He didn't have as much to answer for as they did, but she suspected he'd stand with them no matter.

Bishop Fisher stood before them. The comfortable, warm day with a slight breeze was perfect for having the service outside. The grass was lush and green. The Yoders' barn stood tall and freshly painted white. The horses grazed in the corral far off. They had perfect rows of vegetables in their large garden. The pond traveled through their property off to the side, providing a picturesque addition to the *haus*. It would make a beautiful painting the Englischers might buy.

The bishop offered a prayer to God, led them to sing hymns, and spoke on teaching *kinner* to obey God and their parents, work hard, and be respectful to their elders. He led them in more songs, prayed to God to bless the food, and dismissed them.

Her friends hurried to Rachael.

Ellie bounced Emma on her hip. "Where on earth did this *boppli kumme* from?"

Magdelena peeled back the blanket. "She's precious."

Hannah lifted Marie from her arms. "She's adorable."

Maryann and Liza oohed and ahhed over Marie.

Ellie pulled back the blanket. "Who is this?"

Rachael recounted what happened in New Philadelphia. "I love everything about Marie and being her *mamm*. Nothing with her is a chore." Rachael's stomach danced with happy butterflies.

Hannah rocked Marie in her arms. "I don't suppose you want to work at the bakery any longer. I've missed the shop. I'll take your place and work until I tire of it, and then we'll hire a new baker. Are you all right with that, Magdelena?"

"I love working with you, Hannah. Rachael, I'll miss you, but this is your dream *kumme* true. You should enjoy every moment with this adorable little blessing from God." She reached for Rachael's hand.

"*Danki* for understanding." Rachael had no doubt her friends would be happy for her.

Liza waved a dismissive hand. "Don't think twice about it. I'll fill in if Hannah or Magdelena need a day off, and we can always hire another baker. Enjoy your little one."

"*Danki*, Liza." Rachael was glad they were receptive and nonchalant about it. She didn't feel like she'd put them in a predicament at all.

Maryann had Betsy in her arms. "I have *boppli* clothes for you. I saved Betsy's."

"I can sure use them. I appreciate it." Rachael grinned.

Magdelena accepted Marie from Hannah and stayed

close. The girls expressed their best wishes to her and bid them farewell and went to join their husbands. Magdelena wrinkled her forehead. "Are you worried about what the bishop or some Amish may say about your trip to New Philadelphia, considering Adelaide was an Englischer?"

"Yes. I don't want any of us to be judged for checking on Adelaide. No one will criticize us accepting Marie to raise. She'll be Amish." Rachael was afraid Joseph would take the brunt of the scolding if the bishop or other Amish had a problem with their going to New Philadelphia to visit his niece. They didn't need to know how many times they'd been there.

Magdelena passed Marie to Rachael with tears in her eyes. "You can count on me and the girls to support you. Having a *boppli* means the world to you. You don't have to be sad about this anymore. Thanks to Adelaide. A miracle for sure." She hugged Rachael. "I'll miss you at the bakery. Don't be a stranger and visit Hannah and me often."

"I promise." Her smile faded.

Joseph and Caleb were with Bishop Fisher.

She didn't want them to protect her if there was any admonishment. "Excuse me." She left the girls and joined Joseph and Caleb talking with the bishop. She hoped the bishop wasn't admonishing them.

"Rachael, I'm sorry for your loss. Joseph and Caleb explained what happened. I'm sure you'll be the kind of *mamm* little Marie needs. If you ask me, God had a plan for you and Caleb. Little Marie is in good hands."

"*Danki*. Yes. I'll take good care of her." She didn't know how much Joseph and Caleb had told the bishop. She didn't want to say too much.

Mrs. Yoder pulled the bishop's arm. "I've filled your plate, and you can have a seat with our family right under the willow tree."

More friends approached them and exclaimed over the *boppli*. She let Joseph and Caleb tell the story again.

Frannie strolled to them. "Who does this *boppli* belong to?"

Caleb told her the story. "Adelaide's *mamm*, Joseph's *schweschder*, left Amish life. She raised her *dochder* in the outside world. Joseph checked on Adelaide a couple of times. We offered to go with him to meet her." He told her the rest of the story of how they came to bring Marie home.

"You should be shunned for trotting off to New Philadelphia to visit a family member who should be living the Amish life. After her *mamm* died, there was no reason for Adelaide to remain there. Why is the bishop letting you off the hook?" Frannie sneered.

Caleb's cheeks reddened. "We may have faced judgment for our visit if Adelaide hadn't died, but we were given Marie to raise. I'd appreciate you keeping your voice down, and please don't stir up any trouble."

Luke came alongside her. "What a pretty little girl."

Frannie repeated the story to him.

Luke's face filled with compassion. "I'm sorry Adelaide didn't survive the birth. It must be difficult to be here today, so soon after her death. What a blessing Marie will have two wonderful parents."

Rachael was baffled as to why Luke would be attracted to Frannie. He was handsome, a hard worker, and one of the nicest men in their community.

"*Danki*, Luke. We appreciate your compassion and understanding."

Caleb repeated to Luke that he'd rather not have anything negative said concerning their trip to New Philadelphia.

Luke shook his head. "Why would you think we wouldn't support you?"

"Frannie doesn't share your sentiment." Caleb frowned.

Frannie's cheeks blazed. "I'm hungry. Let's go, Luke."

He narrowed his eyes. "Frannie, don't be rude. And let me be clear. I expect you won't say anything unpleasant or raise concerns about their trip to New Philadelphia, Adelaide, or Marie."

"Don't be silly. Of course not. Caleb doesn't know what he's talking about. Ignore him." Frannie dragged Luke to the food table.

Rachael blew out a breath. "Before she came over to us, I had been relieved and thought everything had gone well with the bishop. She has me worried. I don't trust her."

Rachael knitted the last two stitches she needed in the second pink-and-white bootee Monday afternoon. She held them. They would fit Marie's tiny little feet. She'd not missed working at the shop since she'd returned from New Philadelphia. She couldn't believe it had been a little over a week since they'd attended Adelaide's funeral. She loved Marie so much. She'd relished having her days with the newborn, who was easy and contented.

Mamm sat next to her, knitting a *boppli* blanket. "Frannie and Luke's wedding is tomorrow. She'll be your *schweschder*-in-law, and Lily is near and dear to Caleb's heart. Have you considered trying to talk with her to ease the tension between you?"

Rachael shrugged. "No. We'll be family, and I don't want any awkwardness between us when we're together. I'm not sure if we're better off keeping our distance from them or not. I love Lily too. Once Frannie and Luke are married, we should plan to have family suppers, but I'm not interested in being around her if she's going to be nasty."

"I'll watch Marie and you take her the other mixed berry

pie on the counter. You won't know if you don't try. Sunshine, the clear sky, and a pie might improve her disposition."

Rachael didn't want to take Mamm's advice, but, for Caleb's sake, she would. "What do I have to lose? I'll go. Should I take Marie?"

"Not this time. Give Frannie your full attention."

Rachael set the pie in her tin metal carrier and headed to Frannie's. She arrived and tied the mare's reins to the hitching post. She sucked in a deep breath and stepped onto the porch.

Frannie swung open the door. "Noticed you *kumming* toward the *haus*. What do you want?"

"I'd like to talk about you and me." She held out the pie. "This is for you. A mixed berry pie."

Frannie opened the door wider. "*Danki. Kumme* in. Lily's in bed, napping. Where's Marie?"

"Mamm has her." She set the pie on the coffee table. "Are you ready for your wedding tomorrow? Is there anything I can help you with while I'm here?"

"No. We're ready." Her reply was cold and terse.

"Frannie, we'll be family and I'd like us to socialize and enjoy being together."

"I still think Caleb should've agreed to marry me. Love had nothing to do with it. It was his responsibility to take care of us. He's lucky Luke came along and we fell in love. You should've stayed out of our way. Even though things changed for me and I no longer wanted to marry Caleb, I resent you for standing in the way."

Rachael struggled to stifle her exasperation. This woman wanted to hold on to a grudge when there was no need. "You and Luke will build a future together. Lily will have a *daed*. Luke adores her. Why would you want to hold on to your frustration over the past? We have *dochders*, which gives us something in common. I'm here to mend fences with you, but I need you to meet me halfway."

Frannie fidgeted her hands. "Luke mentioned he's interested in socializing with you and Caleb. He asked me to visit you and discuss it. I've been putting it off and you *kumming* here has saved me the trip."

"I'm not sure if you do or do not want to socialize with Caleb and me." Rachael's stomach clenched. She didn't want to have tension each time they were together at church services or community socials, even if they didn't have family suppers.

"I suppose I can work on letting go of my frustration with you. I can't promise we'll be friends. But I'll agree to be cordial. Luke expects us to make plans to get together now and then. He likes Caleb, and he doesn't understand why I'm rude to you. He asked me to work on my attitude." She rolled her eyes.

Rachael winced. "Why are you frustrated with me? I'm no threat to you. You and Luke will marry and have a future together. You no longer need Caleb for a husband." She didn't want a strained relationship with Frannie. She'd dread family events with Frannie if this woman made snide remarks to her.

Frannie's face softened. "You were in my way after Stephen died, and I wanted Caleb to commit to me. I was afraid of being alone. Luke has asked me to befriend you. I'm not sure we'll ever be friends, but I'll work on it now I don't need Caleb to marry me any longer."

"*Danki*. I appreciate your effort. I'd like for us to become friends. We'll be family." Over time, Rachael hoped Frannie would allow herself to get to know her. She prayed her visit today was the first step in a more positive direction for her and Frannie. "Do you mind if I pray before I leave?" Rachael reached for Frannie's hand.

Frannie allowed her to clasp her hand, but she didn't grip her fingers.

Rachael bowed her head. "Dear Heavenly Father, bless Frannie and Luke's marriage. Give them warm weather, good health, and an enjoyable day. Help me to be the *schweschder*-in-law you would have me be to Frannie. Intervene on our behalf and help us grow closer together. We love you, Heavenly Father. Amen."

Frannie jerked her hand back into her lap. "*Danki* for the pie. Mixed berry is one of my favorites."

"You're *wilkom*. Best wishes for your wedding tomorrow. Give Lily a hug for me."

Frannie gave her a curt nod. "And one from me to Marie." She shut the door behind Rachael.

Rachael stepped off the porch, carrying her empty pie carrier. A small step was better than nothing. Her visit today would make attending the wedding tomorrow more comfortable. They might never be close, but she would pray Frannie would let go of her bitterness and be less confrontational.

Tuesday, Caleb had a lilt in his step. He wished it was his wedding day instead of Luke and Frannie's, but he had but one more week until he and Rachael and Marie would be living together in his *haus*. Marie had been such a blessing to them, and they had a lifetime with her to look forward to. He went to Rachael's *haus* and walked inside. "Is everyone ready?"

Rachael had a bag slung over her arm, and she carried Marie. "Mamm and Joseph left a couple of minutes ago. Mamm wanted to set our food dishes on the table in plenty of time before the service and ceremony."

He removed the bag from her shoulder, kissed Marie's

tiny hand, and strolled across the yard with them to the buggy.

She recounted to him her visit with Frannie.

"It was gracious of you to visit her. I'm sorry she wasn't more receptive. I appreciate your efforts. Luke and I haven't had a hint of any conflict, and I enjoy his company. Of course, Lily is near and dear to me. *Danki* for doing that." He drove to Luke and Frannie's. "Many of our friends are here already."

They stepped down from the buggy.

Ellie hooked her arm through Rachael's. "Greetings. We'll be attending your wedding soon. I can't wait. I had to make myself attend this one, since I'm not fond of Frannie." She scrunched her face.

"I'm counting the days." Caleb held his head up high.

Rachael grinned at Caleb and cradled Marie. "Where's Emma?"

Ellie gestured to Joel across the yard. "Her *daed* has her. What did you and Caleb bring for a wedding present?"

Caleb gestured to the buggy. "The presents are tied to the small cart we have behind the buggy. A potato box and a new bread holder. I asked Luke what they needed, and he mentioned those two things. We bought them from Andrew's store."

"I brought a set of kitchen towels. She doesn't deserve anything. She's such a troublemaker. I don't like the way she's treated you." Ellie pinched her lips.

"Frannie's a challenge." Caleb didn't want to elaborate on his *schweschder*-in-law's wedding day.

"I had a frank talk with her yesterday. She said she'd work on letting go of her grudge against me. I'm encouraged she'll make more of an effort to be nicer. I'll take anything positive from her that I can get."

"She'll have to do better to win me over." Ellie rolled her

eyes. "The woman is wearing a hard shell. She makes you work for a friendship with her. She mutters a greeting when we pass each other at Sunday service, and I always have to greet her first."

"I'm determined to ignore her rudeness and work at befriending her. It may take a long time, though, but we're family. I don't want to be tense around her when we're together, and I have been since we met."

Caleb admired Rachael for not feeding into Ellie's negativity.

Ellie was a loyal and protective friend of Rachael's. He understood her animosity, but she could be harsh herself sometimes.

"You're a better woman than me. I wouldn't waste another minute on her." Ellie put her finger under Marie's. "She's a contented *boppli*. You're blessed. Emma is too. She takes after her *daed*." Ellie laughed.

"I always wanted to be a *mamm*, but being one is different than I expected. It's even more of a special bond than I'd imagined." Rachael smiled. "Marie has no regard for the clock. She's kept me from sleeping through the night, but I expect she'll soon get on the same schedule as me."

Caleb had been awed by how natural *mamm*hood had been for Rachael. She hadn't been rattled by how many times Marie got her up at night or the constant caring for the newborn.

Ellie grinned. "How well I remember. There are no words to explain what a *boppli* brings to your heart. We're all thrilled for you, Caleb, and Marie. I'd better take Emma from Joel and check her nappy before the ceremony starts." She went to find Joel.

"Greetings, Caleb." Magdelena hugged Rachael. "I miss working with you at the bakery."

"I miss you too. Stop over and visit Mamm and me after

work sometime. After Caleb and I marry, you're *wilkom* to visit us there too." Rachael nudged her.

"Yes. Bring Toby. We'll enjoy supper together." Caleb was fond of Magdelena and Toby. They were one of his favorite couples.

"I wanted to leave you alone to enjoy your little one." Magdelena ran her finger over little Marie's soft cheek.

The bishop waved the guests over to the benches outside. "Please be seated. I'd like to begin."

They took their seats. Caleb sat with Joseph on the men's side, and Rachael sat with her *mamm*.

Bishop Fisher offered a prayer, had them sing hymns, and spoke on the importance of communication in a marriage. Two hours later, he motioned to Luke and Frannie. "Please join me."

Luke passed Lily to Caleb.

Lily reached for Luke. "Dada."

Caleb rubbed her back. "He'll be back."

Lily sucked her thumb and rested her head on his chest while he held her.

The bishop directed Luke to say his vows.

Luke opened his mouth to speak.

An attractive woman in a ruffled white blouse and fitted ankle skirt rose and interrupted him. "I object to this marriage."

Luke's mouth hung open.

Frannie glowered.

Caleb passed Lily to Joseph, then rose and went to the woman.

Their friends murmured and whispered to one another.

Bishop Fisher raised his hand. "Everyone, please be quiet. Luke and Frannie, please be seated. We'll resume this ceremony in a couple of minutes. Please stay seated."

He reached Caleb and the woman. "Let's step away, where we can have more privacy, please."

Caleb, the woman, and Luke followed the bishop a good distance away from the family and friends in attendance.

The bishop glanced over his shoulder. "Luke, I didn't know you were behind me."

Luke didn't answer. "Helena, what are you doing here?"

Frannie stomped over and faced Helena. "Who are you?"

"She's a woman I was engaged to in the outside world a year and a half ago. She found a man she liked better, and she broke our engagement. I don't know why she's *kumme* here."

Bishop Fisher stepped between the women. "Frannie, calm yourself. Take a seat on the front bench. We'll handle this."

Frannie scowled at Helena and then went back to her seat.

Helena wiped a tear. "Bishop Fisher, we were engaged once. I made a mistake and left him. I love him. I'll do anything if you'll take me back, Luke. Please. You said no when I came to where you're living, but I had to make my plea one more time before I leave town."

Luke faced her. "You ended our engagement. I regret leaving the Amish life. I've grown roots here, and I've moved on, Helena. Frannie and I love each other. I'm looking forward to a future with her and her *dochder*, Lily. It's wrong for you to interfere and ruin our wedding day. Please leave and don't *kumme* here again."

Bishop Fisher pointed to the buggies. "Madam, you need to leave. There's no reason for you to stay here."

"You're all a bunch of simpletons. Luke, you'll regret staying here. I could have showed you a much better life if you'd tried the outside world. It's your loss." Helena scowled and swiped angry tears from her face and then hurried to her buggy.

Bishop Fisher ushered them back to where everyone was waiting for them. "Let's resume the ceremony."

Caleb sat next to Joseph, who held Lily, fast asleep in his arms.

Bishop Fisher faced the attendees. "Luke and Frannie, please *kumme* to the front and face each other."

Bishop Fisher offered a prayer to God and then helped direct them to say their vows to each other. He didn't acknowledge Helena's outburst earlier. Caleb admired how the bishop handled the situation.

"I now pronounce Luke and Frannie Kilmer married." The bishop offered another prayer to God for the food they were about to eat. "You're dismissed."

Luke clasped Frannie's hand, and they walked down the aisle between the men and women.

Their friends and family gathered around and offered their congratulations.

Caleb went to Rachael. "In spite of Helena's un*wilkom* visit, it was a nice ceremony."

She nodded.

They watched as the couple beamed. He was happy for them.

Frannie approached them. "May I hold Marie for a moment?"

"Sure." Rachael placed the *boppli* in her arms.

"Congratulations, Frannie." Caleb was baffled at Frannie approaching them. She'd never made the first effort to be pleasant. Maybe Rachael's visit to make peace with her had helped.

Joseph joined them. "Your *dochder* is precious."

Lily held her arms out to Frannie. "Mum."

"Wait a minute, honey. Isn't Marie pretty?" Frannie held Marie close for Lily to view.

"Bebe." Lily touched the blanket.

"Marie didn't wake throughout the ceremony. She mustn't be a fussy *boppli*." Frannie admired her.

"She's not. She doesn't cry unless she's hungry or needs to be changed," Rachael said.

Caleb liked how this conversation was going. Rachael must've made more progress with Frannie than he'd expected. "I hope you won't let Helena ruin your day. She's gone, and this day is about you and Luke."

"*Danki* for asking her to leave. I shouldn't have let my temper flare. Yes. Nothing can ruin my wedding day. Luke becoming my husband is all I'll concentrate on." Frannie handed Marie back to Rachael. She took Lily and balanced her on her hip. "Let's feed you. Enjoy the day. *Danki* for *kumming*."

Caleb waited until Frannie was out of earshot. "I'm impressed. She must've pondered what you said after your meeting and took your words to heart."

"She recovered from Helena showing herself here much faster than I would've anticipated. I'm relieved for her and Luke. This day will be a special memory, and it's best if she doesn't allow Helena to destroy it. I'm proud of her." Rachael headed to the food table. "I'm hungry."

"Me too." Caleb went with her.

He wanted Lily and Marie to grow close as they grew up. Lily was two years older and like a big *schweschder*. He wasn't confident Frannie would allow this, but Rachael had made an impact on her the day before, and the future for their families to blend well had changed. Another reason he loved Rachael.

Caleb enjoyed his time with Rachael and their friends at the wedding, and then Joseph, Mamm, and Rachael headed home, and he went to his *haus*. He secured his mare and then got ready for bed. He was ready for their counseling session on Thursday and then their wedding.

Thursday evening, Bishop Fisher waved Caleb and Rachael inside his *haus*. "Make yourselves comfortable. I have warm tea or coffee. Which would you prefer?"

They both declined.

Bishop Fisher offered a prayer before their counseling session. "Have you discussed finances?"

"Yes. I'll make the money and Rachael will spend it," he teased.

"What? I'm not a spendthrift." She chuckled. She loved their fun banter.

Bishop Fisher laughed. "This session will be enjoyable with you two. Will you discuss all your purchases with her, Caleb?"

"Yes. We communicate well most of the time."

"I agree. I enjoy our discussions on everything. I trust Caleb to manage our money and to be the head of the *haus*." She didn't have any doubts about Caleb, and she was sure they'd agree on most things. Anything they disagreed on, she was sure they could compromise.

Bishop Fisher emphasized God being first in their daily lives and putting each other's needs before their own and being good parents to Marie. "You've answered my questions. I'm eager to marry you in five days. Are you ready?"

They both nodded.

"*Danki*, Bishop Fisher," Caleb said.

They bid him farewell and retrieved their buggy.

"We've had one major hiccup in our courtship. You being stubborn and thinking you knew what was best for me."

"I was convinced I was being selfless and I was being selfish. But I came to my senses, and soon my name will change to Rachael Yutzy. I'm anxious for us to marry and live in the same *haus*. I'm jealous Frannie and Luke got married before us. It's difficult waiting for our wedding day. Marie needs her *daed*." Rachael grinned and cradled her close.

"I couldn't agree more." He squeezed her arm.

Rachael woke on June 29, her wedding day. One week after Luke and Frannie's wedding. She didn't mind their weddings were close. She chuckled. She doubted Frannie would want to celebrate their close anniversary dates in the future together. She wouldn't be opposed. What a whirlwind these last couple of weeks had been. She couldn't be happier. She loved Marie, but she also missed Adelaide. She had planned to grow the bond she and Adelaide had created into a close friendship. She would've taken the risk to visit her as often as she could. She admired Marie in her cradle. "I wish your *mamm* could be with us."

Mamm rapped on the door and came in already dressed for the ceremony. She wore an apron over her dress. "I'm wearing this apron to avoid any stains before the ceremony. I'll take my precious little *grossdochder* so you can get dressed. Most of the women will arrive early with their food dishes. The benches and tables are all arranged. The weather is cooperating. The clouds are puffy white, and the sun is shining bright. Let's take a minute and pray together." She held hands with Rachael and offered a prayer for God to bless their unions, the day, and their future lives.

"*Danki*, Mamm." Rachael passed her a wrapped package. "I made this for you."

Mamm opened it. "This tablecloth with embroidered daisies along the edges is beautiful. You know how I love daisies."

"I planned for you to open it after the wedding, but I couldn't wait." She blushed.

Mamm held up her forefinger, left, and returned moments later with a gift. "Here's yours."

Rachael opened the package. "You made us a wedding quilt. I will treasure it. Caleb will too." She hugged the quilt to her chest.

"I'm not much of a quilter, but I was on a mission. I had it in my head it would be what you'd love most."

"I like it more because you don't usually make quilts. I will treasure this. *Danki.*" She hugged her. "Let's dress me."

Mamm waited for her to change out of her bedclothes, and then she dropped the wedding dress over Rachael's head. She arranged the short cape over her shoulders. "Sit. I'll brush your hair."

Rachael handed her the brush. Mamm had brushed her hair often when she was a little girl. She'd leave her home and live with Caleb. Her heart leaped with joy over this, but she had a pang of sadness at leaving her childhood home. "I'll miss you and all the things you do for me."

"I'll miss you too." Mamm's eyes filled with tears. "We'll visit each other often."

Rachael loved Joseph. They'd built a close friendship. No one would ever replace her *daed* in her heart, but she couldn't ask for a better step*daed*. He'd been instrumental in bringing Marie into their lives by introducing her to Adelaide. Her *mamm* had been happy since she'd met Joseph. They'd both found love with two incredible men. They'd always share this special day each year together.

The hours passed fast, and before she knew it, she stood with Caleb and her *mamm* and Joseph in front of their friends.

Bishop Fisher had delivered a message about God having a plan for their lives, and he'd picked some of her favorite hymns to sing and offered the most heartfelt prayers. Maybe everything flowed together as it should because it was her special day.

"I do." Caleb smiled at her.

They said their vows, and Bishop Fisher gestured to each couple. "I pronounce them married!"

Caleb clasped her hand and led her away from their friends and family, picked her up, and twirled her around. "I had to have you for a minute to myself. I love you so much, Rachael Yutzy! And I have a surprise wedding gift for you. You'll have to wait until we get home to open it." He set her feet on the ground.

Rachael gave him her best puppy-dog eyes and tilted her head. "Please tell me."

He kissed her forehead. "I'm terrible at keeping secrets anyway. It's a hope chest. I made it for you."

"What a perfect gift! *Danki*, Caleb." She grinned. "And I made you a patchwork quilt to use as you wish. I picture you using it to cover your lap in your favorite chair in the winter."

"I'll love it." Caleb smiled.

Rachael glanced at Joseph and Mamm. She pressed a hand to her heart as her friends gathered around them. She reflected on the last year. She'd had no idea she'd be where she stood today, happily married to her true love, Caleb, and with a *boppli* to raise, or that her *mamm* would find love again. She had *kumme* to love Joseph as a step*daed*. She praised and thanked God and gave God all the glory for making all her dreams *kumme* true.

GLOSSARY

PENNSYLVANIA DUTCH/GERMAN TO ENGLISH

baby	*boppli*
brother	*bruder*
children	*kinner*
come	*kumme*
covering for Amish woman's hair	*kapp*
dad, father	*daed*
daughter	*dochder*
grandchildren	*grosskinner*
granddad	*grossdaed*
granddaughter	*grossdochder*
grandmother	*grossmudder*
house	*haus*
mom, mother	*mamm*
non-Amish male or female	Englischer
sister	*schweschder*
thank you	*danki*
welcome	*wilkom*
wife	*fraa*

RECIPES

RACHAEL'S BUTTER COOKIES
WITH MAPLE FROSTING
Serving 6 dozen

Ingredients

- 1¼ cups softened butter
- 1 cup white sugar
- 1 egg
- 2¼ teaspoons cold milk (whole milk is best)
- 1¼ teaspoons vanilla extract
- 3 cups all-purpose flour
- ½ teaspoon baking powder
- ½ teaspoon salt

Directions

In a medium mixing bowl, cream together softened butter with white sugar. In the same bowl, add the egg, cold milk, and vanilla extract into the butter mixture. Mix until smooth. In a separate large bowl, add and whisk flour, baking powder, and salt. Combine dry ingredients into your other mixture and beat the dough with your mixer until smooth. Cover your mixing bowl of dough and chill for two and a half hours in the refrigerator.

Preheat the oven to 400°. Remove your chilled dough from the refrigerator. Take a generous tablespoon of dough, roll with your hands into about a one-and-a-half-inch ball, and place it on an ungreased cookie baking sheet. Repeat this method for each cookie and keep your dough balls about one inch apart from each other on the cookie sheet. Bake the cookies for six to eight minutes, until they're just a little brown. Remove the cookie sheet from the oven, and let your cookies cool on the cookie sheet for six minutes. Then remove them onto your desired plate or wire rack until they are no longer warm. Once cooled, eat them plain or use the following frosting recipe.

Maple syrup frosting
>   1¼ cups softened butter
>   3¼ cups confectioners' sugar
>   1¾ tablespoons maple syrup
>   10 tablespoons evaporated milk
>   6½ cups confectioners' sugar

In a large mixing bowl, combine and beat with mixer the softened butter, 3¼ cups of confectioners' sugar, maple syrup, and evaporated milk until creamy. Slowly stir in the other 6½ cups confectioners' sugar into your mixture and beat with mixer until smooth. Add additional confectioners' sugar or evaporated milk if needed for your desired outcome. Frost cooled cookies.

RACHAEL'S CHOCOLATE SHEET CAKE
Serves about 35 people if pieces are cut 2 x 2 x 2

Ingredients
>   1 cup butter, melted
>   ½ cup cocoa
>   1 cup water
>   2 cups all-purpose flour
>   1¾ cups brown sugar
>   1 teaspoon baking soda
>   1¼ teaspoons cinnamon
>   ½ teaspoon salt
>   14 oz. sweetened condensed milk
>   2 eggs
>   1 teaspoon vanilla

Directions
Preheat oven to 350°. In a medium saucepan, add melted butter, cocoa, and water and bring to a boil. Remove from heat. In a separate large mixing bowl, add the flour, brown

sugar, baking soda, cinnamon, and salt and stir. Combine this mixture with your butter, cocoa, and water mixture. Stir in one third of the sweetened condensed milk, then add the eggs and vanilla and stir or beat with a mixer until smooth. Pour the mixture into a greased 10 x 15 x 1-inch baking pan. Place in the oven. Bake at 350° for fifteen minutes or when you stick a knife in it and it comes out clean. Take cake out of the oven.

Frosting ingredients
    ¼ cup melted butter
    ¼ cup cocoa
    Remaining sweetened condensed milk
    1¼ cups confectioners' sugar

In a medium saucepan, combine the butter, cocoa, and remaining sweetened condensed milk and heat on medium until smooth. Do not let it boil. Then stir in the confectioners' sugar. Remove from the burner and pour over your warm cake and spread.

RACHAEL'S APPLESAUCE CAKE
Serves 9

Ingredients
    1 tablespoon softened butter
    ½ cup butter
    1¼ cups white sugar
    3 egg whites
    1½ cups applesauce
    1½ cups all-purpose flour
    1½ teaspoons baking powder
    ¾ teaspoon ground cloves
    1 teaspoon nutmeg
    2¼ teaspoons ground cinnamon

Directions

Preheat oven to 350°. Spread 1 tablespoon of butter on the bottom and sides of your 8 x 8 pan. In a large mixing bowl, beat with your mixer the butter and white sugar until fluffy. Add egg whites to your mixture and beat until still fluffy. Pour applesauce into the mixture and beat with a mixer. In a medium mixing bowl, sift dry ingredients together. Combine the dry ingredients with your other mixture and beat with your mixer until smooth. Pour your mixture into the prepared pan and bake for 45 minutes. Remove from the oven and let your cake cool until it's warm but not hot. You may top with your own whipping cream or cream cheese frosting recipe or serve it plain.